From the burnt-out bunkers of Nazi
  Germany—
to the tangled jungles of South America—
to the power centers of Russia and
  America—
a formidable plot is taking over.

"Throughout this skillfully constructed puzzle-within-a-puzzle runs the tale of an international conspiracy unbelievable enough to be believable! Author Stein knows about political power, those who crave it, and those who trade in it. He also knows how to tell a fascinating story."   —*Booklist*

"Dynamic, fast-moving!"
                    —*South Bend Tribune*

THE CROESUS CONSPIRACY

Benjamin Stein

BALLANTINE BOOKS • NEW YORK

Library of Congress Catalog Card Number: 78-1401

ISBN 0-345-28159-4

This edition published by arrangement with
Simon and Schuster

Manufactured in the United States of America

First Ballantine Books Edition: August 1979

FOR MY WIFE

PROLOGUE

The crowd lined up neatly on the runway waiting for the giant 747 to appear. Many of the men and women craned their necks toward the gray sky. The honor guard, of course, did not move from its parade rest position. Behind the waiting people, the chrome-and-glass expanse of the new Konrad Adenauer airport stretched for thousands of yards. The small group of diplomats from the American embassy in Bonn talked amiably in German with the diplomats of the Federal Republic's Foreign Office. Ambassador Wilson took Foreign Secretary Schrum by the sleeve of his topcoat as he told a joke.

A few yards from them two men stood and scanned the sky. Senator Travis A. Bickel and his administrative assistant, Simon Kart, spoke softly and in English. The conversation was repetitive. Kart kept saying that Bickel needed some help, and Bickel kept telling Kart that it was coming on the 747. "If Kosters doesn't have it, Si, then we'll worry," the senator said, leaning forward so that his powerful blue eyes could bore in on Kart.

There was a dull drone from overhead and everyone in the diplomatic party looked up. It was exactly 2:30 PM, and the skies were brightening rapidly. Patches of blue could already be seen. At 2:32, coming in from the northeast, the 747 of Arthur Kosters, secretary of state of the United States of America, glinted in the sun, a bird of warmth and light gliding into the cold Westphalian December. Or so Travis Bickel thought.

Slowly and lazily, but with extreme grace, like a prehistoric bird, the 747 descended toward the ground and settled smoothly, with a loud screech of the tires, on the runway.

There was a last-minute arrangement of dignitaries as the 747 taxied toward its resting place. At the end of a red Acrilan all-weather carpet from the humming mills of 3M's German division stood Secretary Schrum, at the spot where the staircase from Air Force Three would touch the ground. Next to him were a couple of deputy foreign secretaries, and then U.S. Ambassador Henry Wilson. Next to him was Senator Bickel. Simon Kart had no place in the welcoming line. That was protocol.

Behind the welcomers the honor guard of the Bundeswehr still stood at parade rest but were ready to snap to attention the moment the secretary of state poked his head outside the fuselage.

The gigantic engines of the 747 screamed as the plane reached its stopping point, then were silent. The *Oberleutnant* shouted out an incomprehensible command to the honor guard and they tensed themselves, at the ready. There was a slight clanking of gears, and the door of the 747 popped open. Because the plane usually arrived at airports where it went directly to a specially built berth and Bonn's *Flugplatz* did not yet have one, a stairway had been constructed. It was rapidly wheeled up to the door.

Just as it touched the plane, two attendants rushed up and secured it to the fuselage of the plane.

Standing on the ground next to Ambassador Wilson, Senator Bickel stared at the whole scene with a mixture of awe and humor. Arthur must really love this, Bickel thought to himself. Who wouldn't? It's like the entrance of Caesar into Cairo. Or was it Alexandria?

"*Achtung!*" The honor guard snapped to a rigid attention.

Up at the top of the stairs a plump man of medium height poked his head out the door, then the rest of him emerged, and then he smiled. He walked rapidly down to the waiting dignitaries and shook hands with Foreign Secretary Schrum.

"It is good to see you again, Carl," the secretary of state said with a smile. His English was accented but grammatically perfect.

"Always an honor to see you, Herr Secretary," the German said, and gave a short, stiff bow. His black hair descended about to the level of Kosters's nose and then snapped back up again. "This will be an important visit, a difficult visit."

A twinkle appeared in the secretary's eyes, and for a moment he lost his puffy-eyed and melancholy look. "Yes, but we'll make it work. We have to."

"I most fervently hope so," Schrum said, and bowed again.

Kosters passed down the line with a smile, a handshake, and a greeting for all until he came to Bickel. Then he looked genuinely happy. "How are you, my boy?" Kosters asked the youthful senator, who stood nearly six inches taller than Kosters, as they warmly shook hands.

"I'm fine, Arthur. How are you?" said the senator with a grin.

"Oh, tired," Kosters said with a martyred look. "I'm tired. I'll tell you more later. First I have to give this speech. By the way, I am hearing wonderful things about your performance at the meetings." He smiled in a proud, fatherly way. "But we'll talk more about that later."

Kosters winked one brown eye at Bickel and then returned to the foreign secretary, who led him on a tour of the honor guard, while the military band played "The Star-Spangled Banner" with a slowness that gave it even more majesty than it usually had. As Kosters passed the last row of the guard, with its automatic rifles gleaming in the sun and each clean-shaven face set staring straight ahead, the band began the Federal Republic's anthem—"Einigkeit and Recht und Freiheit."

It sounds just like "Deutschland Über Alles," Kosters thought, and for a moment he thought of other days and other formations of men. He thought of autumn and chestnut trees and children crowding around, listening to loudspeakers in the streets and men with strained faces chasing his friends. But he only thought about it for a second.

Kosters completed the inspection and went back to the line of welcoming dignitaries. He stepped up to a microphone, and a group of newsmen just to the left of the dignitaries pressed toward a line beyond which they were not allowed to cross. Television and movie cameras rolled briefly when Schrum spoke a few words of welcome, but everyone was taking pictures when Kosters began to talk. Motor-driven Nikons set up a background hum, the standard aural backdrop to fame.

The secretary of state stood with his gray topcoat buttoned and coughed politely after Schrum's words.

"Thank you, Herr Schrum, for that welcome. Ambassador Wilson, Senator Bickel, ladies and gentlemen, I want to say to all the world today what our astronauts said to the world when they first set foot on the moon more than thirteen years ago. 'We come in peace for all mankind.' "

There was a substantial round of applause from the crowd.

"The question of German rearmament is not a question of preparing for war, but of preparing to avoid war. We and our German friends threaten no one, covet no territory, and, indeed, envy no one."

There was a plaintive note in Kosters's voice, and the slight German accent that went with it made his words sound even more academic than they might have. Kosters looked like a professor, too. He had a sad and weary look but also an air of kindness. And, since the Cairo Pact, an aura of getting things done had surrounded him. An aura of power.

Kosters coughed again and resumed speaking. "To

those in the United States who question the wisdom of this policy, we say that we welcome debate and questioning, but we also demand that the debate be based in the present and not in the past. Who knows, if not I, that the realities of 1982 in Germany are far different from the realities of decades past?" He did not wait for an answer. More polite, but sincere, applause came from the crowd.

"The Federal Republic is a stable and firm ally, in whose continuing democratic institutions we have the highest trust. If there are different points of view, we want to hear them—but let them be differences of fact and not of imagination and, if I may use the word, paranoia."

If possible, the cameras went even faster at the uncharacteristically sharp blast at the opponents of the Rearmament Treaty. Again, the people in the audience clapped politely.

"When the meetings begin tomorrow, we will look at the issues in the clear and cold light of reason. In that light, we can see that we must not fail." He bowed and nodded at Secretary Schrum.

Kosters had spoken without notes, and now, as the notables and spectators clapped politely and the newsmen ran off to the terminal, Kosters walked over to the senator from California and said, "I'd like you to ride with me into the city. We'll go in the ambassador's car."

Five minutes later, Ambassador Wilson, Secretary Kosters, and Senator Bickel sat in the spacious passenger compartment of Wilson's huge Cadillac limousine as it raced along the highway into Bonn. It was a slight break with protocol for Kosters and Schrum to ride in separate cars, but Kosters knew that his talk with Bickel was important. He also knew that he could talk in front of Wilson, who literally would not know what he was talking about. Wilson was a bluff, loyal party man, but no more.

As the landscape flew by, Kosters leaned forward and put his hand on Bickel's knee. Bickel looked down at the pudgy hand on his grayish-black trousers.

"I am proud, really proud, of the job you're doing

here." He beamed. "I think that no one else could have done such good work as you have. Everyone on the delegation agrees that you're doing great work. A great delegation head, that's what everyone says."

Bickel looked at him coolly. "It'll take more than that, Arthur," Bickel said. There was an edge of sarcasm in his voice. "You know I'm taking all the heat on this whole goddamn thing, and it's not doing me any good. I should've just laid low. That's what everybody else is doing, and it's not doing them any harm." He looked annoyed. "I'm taking the point on this one, Arthur." He waited for Kosters to answer.

Kosters returned Bickel's stare. "You don't like the publicity?" he asked. "You don't like your face on the cover of *Newsweek?*"

"Oh, for Christ's sake," Bickel said, "that's not the problem. The problem is that a lot of people are scared about giving the bomb to the Germans and they're taking out their insomnia on me, and I don't need it. I was doing fine before you and the President picked me to head this delegation." He sounded angry. His unaccented California speech beamed straight at Kosters. Wilson was looking out the window and humming to himself. He was humming "The Way We Were."

Kosters put on a disappointed look, like a professor who was unhappy with a student. "I really don't understand this, Travis," Kosters said. "Did you think that your path would be strewn with roses? Just what did you expect when you went to work on a major international project?" Kosters shook his head in wonderment. "There is a certain netting out process, Travis. The question always is, what is the net of it? That's what you should be thinking, and that's what I can tell you about."

That was what Bickel had wanted to hear. He leaned forward. "Have you been polling?" Bickel asked.

"Of course," Kosters said. Now he was the benevolent parent about to make a gift. "The polls show a very serious concern about the Soviets in Europe. That's first. A majority are very concerned. A majority favor the treaty. And a clear upward trend in public thinking about you as a result of your work here has developed. It's absolutely clear. It's about a five-percentage-point jump in three months, and that is not bad." Now he was the confident political analyst, and he looked out the window, awaiting Bickel's response. Not that there was much to see out the window. Kosters thought that whole world was getting to look like northern New Jersey, including the approach to Bonn.

"I appreciate your putting in the questions about me. I know you could get into some trouble about that, and I appreciate it. Sometimes it's hard to tell by the mail," Bickel said.

"Look," Kosters said, with a brotherly air, "you're doing a national service, and anything we can do for you, we are glad to do. Your ambitions are no secret, and we want to help."

"Some of the letters make me wonder," Bickel said. "I hope we aren't making a mistake. Not politically, of course, but still . . . giving the bomb to the Nazis . . ."

"You don't have to tell me about Auschwitz," Kosters said with a hurt tone in his voice. "I'm the last person you have to tell."

"Of course," Bickel said quickly. "I'm sorry."

"It's a new day," Kosters said. "A new day. These Germans are not Nazis. That's what people have to realize. Today's Germans are our friends, and people in America had better get used to that. They had better get used to it right away, because that's the way it's going to be." His voice was hard.

No one in the car said anything until the embassy was only a mile away. "What the President and I need to know," Kosters said as the limousine slowed down in the densely built streets around the embassy complex, "is how the treaty will do in the Senate. What do you think?"

"It'll pass," Bickel said. "Not because of me, but because of you. It'll definitely pass. The enemies will do everything they can do to stop it, and the Russians will gin up a lot of publicity, but they can't stop it." He smiled generously. "Since Cairo, you can do no wrong, Arthur. That's the way it is."

Kosters grinned so that his heavy cheeks glistened. "I just am happy to serve," he said, mocking himself. His tone changed. "The Russians do not have votes on the Senate floor, do they?" he asked.

"No, not in the Senate. But they can do a lot. And they're scared. They'll try anything. The new Germans are not their friends," Bickel said.

"Yes," Kosters said as the limousine pulled through the embassy gates, "they'll be on the move. They'll try anything."

"And I don't blame them," Bickel said.

"I don't either," Kosters said. "I would, if I were the Russians." He paused. "But don't you worry. The President is talking you up all over the country. He's already spoken to McMurray over at the AFL–CIO, and that's where he can do you a lot of good. McMurray can do more for you than the ADA any goddamn day of the week." Kosters patted Bickel's shoulder. "We know where you need help, and we're going to help."

"Maybe you could put in a word with some of those oil people in Texas, like Hanford at Texaco. It doesn't help to have them mad at me over the depletion bill," Bickel said.

"Of course," Kosters said. "I'll take care of it right away." The limousine came to a stop and a Marine guard opened the door. Kosters looked over at Bickel. "We have to help each other," he said.

"Right," Bickel said. He was genuinely grateful for what Kosters was doing.

"That's only natural," Kosters said as he hopped out.

"I agree," Bickel said, and they both smiled.

As he got out of the car, Ambassador Wilson hummed "Isn't It Romantic?"

CHAPTER

1

"Hitler built this road, you know," Simon Kart said without taking his eyes off the smooth, unwinding A–14 southeast of Bonn.

Bickel looked over to the slight, balding Kart. There was a trace of humor in his blue eyes. "Right now," he said without anger, "I'm more concerned with how the L.A. *Times* is going to write up the latest rounds of negotiations than I am with who built this road." Still, he thought as he looked ahead of him, it was a fine road, even if Hitler *had* built it.

"We'll get the papers when we get back to Bonn," Kart said. "We could have waited there for them. It would have been all right with me. You were the one who wanted us to see Bad Kreuznach." He, too, spoke cheerfully, with the accents of familiarity bred by a working partnership of almost ten years.

"I think," Bickel said, "that we're going to have to count on the *Chronicle*'s being against us. There's nothing we can do about that. On the other hand, it's not that big a problem. The *Chronicle* always comes out on

9

the losing side. But the L.A. *Times* swings some weight."

"They've been all right so far," Kart said.

"Yeah, but now we're getting down to specifics," Bickel said. "It's all right to talk about it in the abstract, but when we get to the point of actually telling the folks back home that Germany's going to have a hundred and twenty Trident II missiles, then it sounds scary. That's when the experts at the newspapers can pick nits until we're dead."

"But you've spoken to Chandler about it; I know that," Kart said.

"The truth is that these guys who own the big newspapers can't control what the reporters write in every article. They're all afraid that if they start controlling, they'll appear in a story somewhere as a dictator of the press. You know that," Bickel added.

"Frankly, Travis, I don't think you need to worry about L.A. or San Francisco at all. You're doing fine in all the Field polls, and I just wouldn't worry about it." Kart paused. "I'd start worrying about McMurray at the AFL–CIO. He gets mad and then he stays mad. And he's mad because you didn't go to the mat about the open shop," Kart said.

"That's not the only problem," Bickel said. "I am strictly out in left field as far as the black groups go. They just don't know me. I sent César Cortez to talk to some of the black leaders, and they just didn't commit themselves at all. They're waiting for someone like Carter, who'll promise them the moon," Bickel said. "But that can backfire. I'm just not going to do that."

The rented Mercedes 500 SLC glidded effortlessly down the Autobahn. For a moment a huge truck tried to catch up with Bickel and Kart, but a slight pressure by Kart's foot on the accelerator sent the Mercedes flying far ahead of the straining rig. Outside, the skies were leaden with occasional glimpses of blue in the southwest. Fenced pastureland interspersed with solid-looking farmhouses made for monotonous scenery.

"You're right," Kart said. "There's no sense promising what we can't deliver. That's absolutely right. But if we're not going for the blacks, we've got to start making a big effort with the ethnics, and a lot of them are worried about this treaty."

"You think I don't know that?" Bickel asked. "I wanted Kosters to do some 'national security' polling about how I'm doing with the ethnics, and he said he would. But they won't be starting again for a few weeks."

"What about Kitlowski, over at the Steelworkers?" Kart asked. "Maybe you'd better talk to him."

"Couldn't hurt," Bickel said. "I just want to be damn sure we've got our ducks in a row on the treaty before we start asking people for commitments, though. I don't want the treaty blowing up in my face."

"I don't see how it could," Kart said. "It has a certain compelling logic."

"Well, you know that, and I know that, but I don't know who else knows that," Bickel said.

"I think most people do," Kart said. "Kosters has told them enough. It was all those 'agreements' and 'letters of understanding' with the Russians. We just kept disarming and they kept arming, and by now, they're in the catbird seat. Nobody much thinks we're going to go to war over Europe when they've got strategic superiority. But we don't want to lose Europe," Kart continued.

"Jesus, we let things get away from us awfully goddamned fast," Bickel said.

"Tell it to Carter and Nixon. Tell it to Vance and Kissinger," Kart said. "They believed every line of garbage they said, about détente and linkage and all that crap."

"So now I'm over here handing over the keys to the Tridents to the Germans," Bickel said. He looked down at the guidebook for Bad Kreuznach in his lap. He wore a Burberry lined raincoat of a grayish eggshell color.

"Somebody's got to do it," Kart said, "and if you do it and it works, it makes you look like a hero. And if it doesn't work, well, you can wait six more years."

"It has to work," Bickel said. "Kosters has told everyone that the only way to keep the Russians out of Western Europe is to give the Germans the bomb, and I think the message has gotten across."

"The people trust Dr. Kosters," Kart said. "He's always right."

"Always," Bickel agreed.

Both men sat in silence as the car sped down through the farming valley. Occasionally a cow glanced up at them and then returned to chewing grass, as if to say that the cow had seen a lot of cars and there was nothing special about that one.

"I'm still worried about Lydia," Bickel said quietly. "I don't know how I can get through a campaign with her. I really don't."

Bickel thought that at that moment his wife was probably lying in bed reading a mystery story. It was almost the only thing that gave her any surcease from the anxiety and neurosis that had dogged her for the last five years—at least. Lydia had been to psychiatrists of all kinds, hypnotists, chemotherapists, and nothing gave her peace. She had an anger that simply could not be bridled, except when she lay in bed and read detective stories. She drank a great deal, but until she actually lost consciousness, she had no peace. She walked from room to room in the Wesley Heights house, screaming and shrieking.

Kart did not say anything. What could he say about it when a man's wife stood between that man and the presidency?

"I could get divorced, of course," Bickel said. "But that wouldn't smell right just before an election. And anyway, I don't know what the hell she would do. She's got to go to a hospital or somewhere eventually." Bickel stared out the window glumly. The sky was lightening considerably.

Suddenly he snapped his fingers. "I know what I remember about Bad Kreuznach," he said, coming out of his somber mood. "It's where Doctor Faustus sold his soul to the devil."

Kart grinned. "He got a beautiful teenage girl in return, didn't he?" Kart asked.

"I wonder if he's making the same deal now," Bickel said. "I'd definitely have to consider it."

"Me too," Kart said.

Both men felt more cheerful. Brooding about Lydia would have to wait for another time. Meanwhile, the car was coming into Bad Kreuznach.

On both sides of the Autobahn houses were more frequent. There were a few small shops, and then in a few seconds they were back in the fifteenth century. They turned off the highway and were winding down narrow streets with dark, stone-faced buildings and wooden gingerbread houses hanging far out over the top of the car. They drove silently around the town for a moment until, by a process of trial and error, they found the main square.

It was a park across the street from the Court of Justice and, on the other side, from the sprawling Schneider optical works. Bickel remembered that he had seen the name "Schneider-Kreuznach" on the lens of his ancient Rolleiflex.

"I am a hungry sonofabitch," Kart said. "What kind of places do they have here where you can get something besides all that boiled garbage?"

"I don't know," Bickel said. "This guidebook tells where all the museums are, but it doesn't say a word about where you get a good meal."

Kart parked the car on Jungstrasse, under an ancient house that looked as if only luck held it upright. As the two men got out of the car, Bickel snapped his fingers.

"You know, it just hit me that the reason this place is called *Bad* Kreuznach is that it has mineral baths. So if we find the main bathhouse, it probably has a restaurant."

"I think we passed it when we drove over the river," Kart said. "It looked like a very classy place, especially for a town like this."

They backtracked along Jungstrasse, and then on Salinenstrasse, named for the mineral salts, until they came to what looked to Bickel like the main drag, Mannheimerstrasse. After a few minutes they could see the muddy waters of the Nahe river, and off to the left, the complex of buildings over the town's main mineral spring.

The largest building, the "classy" one, was the Kreuznacher Kurhaus, according to Kart's guidebook. It sat like a gigantic New England boarding house in the middle of the island in the Nahe. Around the entire first floor of the house ran an airy veranda on which there were columns and latticework forming a slight screen.

To the left of the main door, there were tables where a number of plump women in aprons were serving a number of plump men.

Kart and Bickel walked over to the Kurhaus and soon they could smell broiled chicken. In halting German, Bickel said to the plumpest waitress, who looked like the boss, *"Ein tisch für beide, bitte."*

The waitress smiled at Bickel and said, with a slight English accent, "On any particular part of the veranda?"

"Anywhere will do," Bickel said, laughing to himself.

They found themselves sitting in a rather deserted section of the restaurant, facing a large, plain building which Bickel assumed was the actual spot where the baths were.

"It's really incredible," Kart said as he drank a stein of Göttingen. "The war ended thirty-seven years ago. Did you know that? Thirty-seven years ago, that's all. And the place looks as if it were the most innocent, childish place in the world."

"Germans are a crazy group," Bickel said, looking into his glass. "They have a genuinely frightening split personality. In some way I haven't been able to figure out, the land of Hansel and Gretel and Bach is intimately connected with the land of Bergen-Belsen and Treblinka. I really don't know what the connections are. I really don't. But they're there, and it just makes the Germans a fascinating group."

Another plump waitress appeared with two plates of broiled chicken and corn. She smiled and put the dishes down on the table and then asked, *"Sonst noch etwas?"*

"Nein, danke," Bickel said.

"I think all of these waitresses have been cloned from the same person," Kart said.

"I think you've been reading too many books," Bickel said. "Let's eat."

"That's you," Kart said. "No imagination."

About fifteen minutes later Bickel, who prided himself on his quick eating, looked over at Kart and asked, "What are you going to do while I'm in the library?"

"I'll walk over and look at the Fausthaus," Kart said, "and then maybe I'll just walk around the town and look at architecture. Even though it's German, it has a certain appeal."

"That's the way these people are. They do the most incredibly evil things, but then they still have some appeal. Maybe they even have more appeal because they do such evil things. I don't know. It's damn odd."

"You're the one who's so damn odd," Kart said. "You have one day off from these meetings and everybody else is at the ambassador's reception, and you're down here in a place no one ever heard of looking in a little musty library for any little curiosity you can find about the Nazis. And I'm crazy to be here with you."

Bickel made a slight grimace and then smiled. "You're wrong about one thing, Si. The devil heard of this place when he came to get Doctor Faustus' soul."

Bickel's face had a look which always troubled Kart. Normally, Bickel's clean features and wolflike eyes gave him a powerful, almost frightening appearance. Some hidden current of anger, almost violence, might have surged beneath that face. But Kart had known Bickel for five years, and he knew that if the impulse was there, it was extremely well-controlled. But as Bickel took in the gray skies and the city, a dreamy look came over the hard features. Kart could not have said why, but it was the combination of the frightening and the dreamy that worried him. Bickel looked as if he were preparing his soul for a confrontation with the creature that had come for Doctor Faustus.

Bickel turned slowly around, coming out of his thoughts, and said, "Have a good walk. I'll go back to the car and try to find the town library."

He picked up the bill, which he could barely read because of the ornate numbers that the plump waitress used. Bickel always picked up the bill. It was the right thing for a man who had inherited ten thousand shares of Amsted when he turned twenty-one.

"Let me see that map a minute," the senator said as they stepped onto the bridge over the Nahe. With his finger, Bickel traced his route to the Landrats-Amt, where he hoped to find the library. There was no visible heading of *Bibliothek* next to the buildings on the map, so Bickel figured that the City Hall would either have the library or know about it.

"I'll meet you where we parked the car in three hours," Bickel said, showing Kart his watch.

"Okay, I don't want to come back to find that you've suddenly been granted all your wishes," Kart said with a smile.

"No problem," Bickel laughed. "Lydia has half my soul and the people of the great state of California have the other half."

He turned and walked down the street as Kart walked the other way. In a moment he passed a solid-looking structure identified as the police station by an oval metal sign that said *"Polizei."* The building looked at least a hundred years old, and Bickel thought, as he passed by, that horrible scenes must have been played out there during the Third Reich. He could see the terrified looks of prisoners as they realized that they were facing not their friendly local beer-bellied constable, but the sleek, thin new men of the Gestapo.

In a few more minutes, Bickel stood in front of a glass-and-steel building, utterly out of place amid the older buildings, with a chromium-lettered sign that read *"Bibliothek."*

To Bickel, the building proclaimed that it was part of the most current phase of West Germany's ongoing economic miracle. He preferred the older, more traditional buildings. They fit better with his idea of what Germany was supposed to be. The new buildings always looked too much like imitations of American architecture at its most uninspired.

He walked up the few broad steps to double glass doors and passed through. The place was even newer than he had thought. It was also completely empty. That emptiness, plus the smell of building materials, hinted to Bickel that the place, the Bad Kreuznach *Bibliothek*, might not yet be officially open. Nevertheless, there were stacks of books arranged around a glass-enclosed central reading room with modern blond wood tables. And no one had told him that he should not be there. Yet . . .

"Kann ich Ihnen behilflich sein?"

The man's voice was guttural and rasping, even though he was asking if he could help. Bickel turned around to see a bulky elderly man with an utterly bald head staring at him through wire-rimmed glasses.

Bickel smiled and asked, *"Ja, bitte, können Sie mir sagen?"* and then trailed off. His German was not as fluent as he wished. What the hell was the word for "historical documents?" He stammered and just got out, *"dokumente aus dem Dritten Reich?"*

The man's face, which was hardly friendly to start with, clouded over. "Do you want to speak English?" he asked in a flawless, American-accented English.

Bickel laughed with relief. "Yes, thank you. I'm Travis Bickel. I'm a senator from California." He always told that to Germans right away. They were even more status-conscious than other Europeans. "I am at those meetings in Bonn. I'm down here looking for any documents you might have from the early days of the National Socialist period." He also knew that there were still a lot of Germans who did not like the word "Nazi," even in 1982, and the man who faced Bickel looked far from amiable. "It's a hobby of mine. *Liebhaberei.*" Then Bickel smiled.

"I am sorry," the man said, as if he could not have been less sorry. He stared hard at Bickel with deep brown eyes. "We have absolutely no such documents. Absolutely none. *Niemand,* you understand. The Americans took them all." He looked angry about it. "I suggest you go back to California and look there."

With that last phrase spat out, the elderly man turned on his heel, walked rapidly down the hall and disappeared into an office that said "Klaus Gunter."

Bickel was in a slight daze from the unexpected blast of hostility from Herr Gunter and stood rooted to a spot near the entrance of the reading room. What the hell was going on? Had he pronounced something wrong? Had he called Herr Gunter a four-letter word? What a mess. All this driving through an ugly countryside for a one-minute turndown.

Perhaps, Bickel thought, perhaps I am a fool for being here at all. Perhaps I ought to damn well forget about nosing around for artifacts of the Nazis when I'm about to start running for president. Doesn't look good. Looks slightly cracked. But those bastards were just so fascinating, so goddamned fascinating. There was something in them that unleashed an energy that had never been seen before in the whole world. One small country against the whole world, and winning too. What if America could be motivated like that? Without the evil and the murder, of course. But that was the fascination. Those Nazi bastards reached right into the human mind and grabbed onto it like a hydraulic vise. And it was the details of how they did it that attracted Bickel. There was something to be learned, although perhaps this was not the time or the place.

"Sir? May I speak to you?" It was a heavily German-accented female voice coming from behind him. Christ, these Germans loved to sneak up on people.

Bickel wheeled and found himself facing a twentyish, mousey young woman, who smiled uncertainly at him. Her teeth were crooked, but she looked friendly.

"I heard you talking to Herr Gunter, the chief librarian," she said. "I am sorry for you that he was cross. He is really a fine man. But sensitive about the Nazis. A lot of the *alten* are like that." She smiled again.

"Do you work here?" Bickel asked as slowly and clearly as he could.

"*Ja, ja.* I am Herr Gunter's assistant. I heard what you were asking for. I do not think that Herr Gunter knows that when the old *Bibliothek* was demolished, the workmen came upon several folders of old papers from 1933 and 1934 and a few from 1935. I think they were party records, but I have only glanced at them. They're so old the paper is yellow," she said with a giggle.

"That is exactly what I am looking for," Bickel said. This was going to be a lucky day after all.

"I'll get them for you. Please have a seat in the reading room. *Bitte.*" She smiled and disappeared down a corridor.

Bickel walked into the reading room through another glass door. There was no one else in the room, and Bickel sat in the middle of the empty modern chamber. In a moment, the door opened, and the young woman entered the room carrying a brown cardboard box about one foot in each dimension. It was the same brownish color as her hair and her eyes and her wool suit.

She set the box next to Bickel and said, "Of course, they are in German. Do you want me to help you with it?"

This is a helpful librarian, Bickel thought. "No, thanks. I read it much better than I speak it," he said with a grin.

"All right. Fine. I am Fräulein Beck. I will be there," she said, pointing at a room near Gunter's office. "If you need any help, please call."

"Thank you very much," Bickel said sincerely. "By the way, you speak excellent English."

"*Danke,*" Fräulein Beck said. "I was an exchange student at the University of Iowa." She laughed. "Eye-oh-way," she said, and walked away.

After Fräulein Beck's footsteps faded, there was absolutely no sound in the *Bibliothek*. Bickel looked around the glass-walled room and did not see any movement or sign of life. For an instant, he thought he saw a flicker of light coming from Herr Gunter's office, but it might have been his imagination. He opened the box and was immediately struck with the musty odor of old paper. He stood up to look at the top pages.

The very first thing was an envelope marked "ACHTUNG—VERTRAULICH!" Bickel's pulse speeded up. Confidential documents from 1933? It could definitely be a find.

He opened the envelope extremely carefully and took from within a sheaf of old papers. Again, the scent of mold hit him.

On top of the first page was the Nazi eagle holding a circle with a swastika. Under it, in gothic script, was the legend NATIONALSOZIALISTISCHE DEUTSCHE ARBEITER-PARTEI. Then disappointment for Bickel. The first line of typescript was, *"Hitlerjugend—Kosten aus 1932."* He had gotten himself excited over the records of the expenses of the local Hitler Youth for 1932.

As Bickel thumbed through the pages of boring references to items for printing, for uniforms, for making of insignia, and on and on, he noticed that the silence of the room had been broken by footsteps behind him. The noise came closer and closer. Bickel looked up to see Herr Gunter smiling through clenched teeth.

"Enjoying your research, Herr Bickel?"

"It's fairly dull stuff so far," Bickel said. Then he thought he should put in a plug for Miss Beck. "But Fräulein Beck was extremely kind. When I get back to Bonn, I shall certainly remember to write to whatever minister is responsible for libraries to mention her helpfulness."

Gunter's smile was even more tightly stretched across his facial bones. "That is kind of you, to be sure, Herr Bickel. But libraries are a local matter. Nevertheless, I shall bear your compliment in mind." Gunter stared down at the papers in front of Bickel. "Did Fräulein Beck tell you if there were any other papers like these?"

"No. I think this was all," he said.

"Very well. Forgive me for disturbing you, Herr Bickel." Gunter bowed slightly and walked back where he had come from.

That is a strange sonofabitch, Bickel thought. I hope I didn't just get Fräulein Beck fired. He turned to the next envelope, which also said ACHTUNG—VERTRAULICH!

This time he spared himself the excitement. The first of the mildewed pages in the envelope again bore the National Socialist German Workers Party legend and then, underneath, *Hitlerjugend—Mitglieder—1933."*

He was glad he had not gotten excited. It was simply a list of members of the Hitler Youth from 1933. It occurred to Bickel that probably a lot of them were still alive.

The next list was apparently misplaced. It was not headed by the Nazi insignia, and it was a list of high school graduates, as far as Bickel could tell. It simply said, *"Realgymnasium—1936."* Bickel glanced downward. Typical German names, many of which were like the names in the Los Angeles telephone book. There was even a "Bickel, Hans."

More interesting, there was a "Kosters, Sigmund," with an asterisk next to it. Bickel tried to remember where in Germany Arthur was from. He knew it was someplace insignificant. Maybe it was even Bad Kreuznach. Perhaps this was a cousin, even a brother. Bickel made a mental note to ask Kosters about it.

The beer from lunch had made him sleepy. It had also made him want to urinate. He couldn't seem to remember what the word for "Men's Room" was. "Toilette." Was that it? He slowly pushed back his seat and walked around inside the reading room, stretching and hoping to wake himself up. He also tried to see if there was anything that said *"Toilette"* or *"Männen"* or something similar.

But neither thing happened. He still felt drowsy, and he saw no sign of a bathroom. Reluctantly, he walked out of the reading room and looked around the empty, new hallways for a bathroom. It was several minutes before he found a room with a door that said *"Männen."*

He walked in and made use of the facilities with great relief. It was a clean and neat rest room, especially by European standards, and it reassured him about the similarity of Germans and Americans.

As he walked back into the reading room, the thought struck him that something strange was going on, although he could not exactly say what. The room did not look the same. It took him a minute before he realized why it looked different. The papers were gone. No papers, no envelopes, no box—nothing.

Bickel looked carefully around the room, and then he walked purposefully out toward Fräulein Beck's office. If she was going to retrieve the goddamn things every time he took a leak, that was ridiculous. That's how the Germans are, he thought. Meticulous. Everything in its place.

Fräulein Beck sat at her desk, talking into the telephone. When she saw him, she talked briefly, then said *"Auf wiedersehen"* and put the receiver on its cradle.

Bickel smiled and said, "Excuse me, Fräulein Beck. I had not finished looking at those papers. May I get them back?"

"Bitte?" Fräulein Beck said. "What are you talking about?"

"The papers I was looking at. Did you put them back? I wonder if I might see them again?"

"I am sorry. I do not know what papers you are talking about. I think you must be mistaken." She smiled thinly.

What the hell was going on?

"Look, I'm talking about those Hitler Youth papers, from 1932 and 1933. You brought them out for me. Remember?" Bickel was starting to sweat.

"I don't know what you are referring to," Fräulein Beck said. "We have no papers like that. Didn't Herr Gunter, the Director, tell you that?"

Bickel was angry. "Look," he said, "I am a United States senator. I am not supposed to be treated like a goddamn spy. I want to know what's going on here."

"I am sorry," Fräulein Beck said sincerely. *"Verzeihen Sie."*

"That's not enough," Bickel said.

"When Herr Gunter returns from lunch, you can ask him. Perhaps you imagined it. You were asleep in the reading room for a few minutes."

"What the hell are you talking about?" Bickel flared. "I was reading some papers. I wasn't asleep."

"Perhaps you could come back later and talk to Herr Gunter," Fräulein Beck explained gently.

And Bickel knew that he was never going to see those papers again.

"Very well, Fräulein Beck," Bickel said. "I'll leave. But someday someone will find out about this."

"I do not understand, Herr Senator," Fräulein Beck said with a slight smile. "Please come back later if you want to talk to Herr Gunter."

Bickel walked out and down the broad steps to the gray, December day. This was an amazing place, he thought. But I'm damned if I'm going to waste my time on their local skeletons. Let the dead bury the dead. Still, it was annoying to be lied to.

CHAPTER

2

"Travis," Kart said, "you cannot figure these people out. You ought to know that." Kart and Bickel sat on a bench in a shop in the Bosenheimerstrasse. No sooner had Bickel gotten back to his car then he discovered that it would not start. It had to be towed to the local dealer for repair. German craftsmanship.

"But, goddammit, what happened to those papers? And what made that librarian change her tune?" Bickel was annoyed, in about equal parts by the broken car, for which he had paid $100 a day of his own money, and by the incident at the *Bibliothek*. "And what the hell is wrong with this car?"

"Battery," Kart said. "At least that's what the mechanic said."

"It's all a hell of a waste of time," Bickel said, picking up a greasy copy of *Stern* and staring at a picture of himself on the cover, smiling and walking with Kosters and Foreign Secretary Schrum. The headline read, diagonally across the page, *"Bickel und Kosters—Atom Bomben Aus Der Taschen."*

Loosely translated it read, "Bickel and Kosters—Atom Bombs in Their Pockets."

While Bickel began to read the article, a bald man with an aquiline nose and wire-rimmed glasses, a man who looked like a brain surgeon, but who was in fact in charge of maintenance at the shop, approached Bickel. He asked, in slow but correct English, who would be driving the car.

Bickel pointed at Kart.

The mechanic frowned and launched into a lengthy discussion of how the battery must not be allowed to become dry. It was "imperative" to stop regularly and have the water level in the battery checked. "Imperative." Both men, impressed at the mechanic's severity, gave their promise.

Kart took the wheel and the car pulled out of Bad Kreuznach. Darkness gathered around them as the car sped silently north, away from the city of Doctor Faustus. The sun went down early in December, and it was just as well, because there was nothing to see.

Bickel looked over at Kart, who grinned back at him. "This is some car, battery or not," Kart said.

Bickel did not want to talk about the car. "Si," he asked, "is Kosters always a Jewish name?"

"I really don't know," Kart answered. "I only know one other Kosters besides Arthur, and she's certainly Jewish." He stroked his chin, bathed in a dim green from the speedometer lights. "Why?"

"Well," Bickel said, "one of the names of high school graduates for 1936 was Hans Kosters, and I thought they weren't letting Jews in the high schools then. So I just wondered. There was a lot of lack of enforcement of the Nuremberg Laws, and it could have been that."

"I just don't know, Trav," Kart said. "It wasn't Arthur, because he was called Sigmund before he came to America."

Bickel sat up in his glove-leather seat. "Just a minute," Bickel said. "I made a mistake. I think that was the name on the list of graduates."

"It couldn't have been Arthur," Kart said, "because

he came from a town outside Dresden, which is now in the Eastern Zone, the People's Republic."

A police car with klaxon screaming came up behind them and zoomed by before Kart could even slow down. It's blue whirling hoodlight lit up the night, casting strange reflections on passing cars, freezing them in a cold glow.

"I guess that's right," Bickel said. "I remember that now myself. It's Bad something, but I can't remember what."

"Were you thinking that the good people of Bad Kreuznach were trying to protect their secret—that they didn't kill the young Kosters?"

"I don't know," Bickel said. "These days I'm suspicious about everything. I'm just looking for the first newspaper editorial calling me a Nazi sympathizer for this treaty."

Kart clucked sympathetically. Bickel smiled to himself. In public, he would never have admitted such a fear. He would have called it preposterous and said that no serious-minded diplomat could take charges like that without laughing. But to Kart, who knew him from years of working together, Bickel could unburden himself as he could with almost no one else. Certainly not with Lydia. Maybe with Alexandra, but then Alexandra never traveled with him anymore. He was glad he had Kart to talk to.

"Si," Bickel said, "are we sure that Alexandra is picking up the Northeast issues? Pennsylvania is tricky ground and so is New York. I don't want to entrust everything to McMurray. He may want to deliver and he may not, and he may not be able to deliver even if he wants to."

"I think so, Trav. She's spent a lot of time on the differential income tax provision, and I think she'll get you in as a cosponsor on the fuel oil redistribution bill," Kart said. "You still haven't told her which way you want to go on nuclear power."

"I don't know myself," Bickel said. The moon came from behind a cloud and illuminated the landscape, but there was nothing to see. At night, on the highway of an industrial country, everything looked the same. "If I'm for it, it looks like I'm balls out for putting atomic material everywhere, and if I'm against it, then what am I doing here? I'd really like to duck that one if we can."

"We'll try," Kart said. "I'll think of something equivocal."

"Cousin Jimmy got a long way saying he would study everything carefully," Bickel said. "Maybe that's the way we should go."

"I don't think we can do that on right to life, and that's really a hot potato in New York," Kart said.

"And the Jews there are already mad at me," Bickel agreed. "Well, we don't have to do anything at all for a while. It's not a big issue in California, thank God." He paused. "Si, I'd like to begin focusing on a media strategy. I think when I get back to Washington, I'm going to be a very hot ticket to get on the talk shows. I know the convention is eighteen months away, but you can't start too early."

"Free publicity," Kart said. "Absolutely, totally free, and most of the questions are marshmallows."

"I can knock them out of the park," Bickel said, mixing metaphors. "Let's get someone working with the TV people on that."

"I'll do it," Kart said.

"We definitely have to figure out something to do with Lydia," Bickel said. "She needs a lot of help."

"Problem area," Kart said. "We just can't lock her in a closet or put her in Chestnut Lodge without someone wondering what's going on." Kart rubbed his neck and grimaced. "Pretty soon now, I'd like to pull over somewhere and change seats. My neck's kicking up."

"Fine. Any time," Bickel answered. "I just wonder if I put everything to her squarely and got her really busy on the campaign, whether that would snap her out of it." Outside the car, a few flakes of snow were visible. Bickel wondered if there was snow in Washington. He loved the capital city after a fresh snowfall. Almost no other place looked as lovely. Of course, within hours the snow turned to a blackish slush and for days afterward it was hideous. But it was lovely at first.

Neither man spoke for a while as the miles flew by. Each knew that if Lydia Bickel wanted to make big trouble, few could make bigger trouble. Bickel thought about all the times she had accused him of having affairs when he worked late. It had once been true, only once, but after a short while Bickel began to wish it were true. He and Lydia slept far apart on their king-sized bed, and Bickel, at forty, was too young to give up sex.

Somehow, by a psychic connection, the question of age reached Simon Kart.

"I wonder if we're working on this whole project too early, Travis," Kart said. "I mean, you'll be forty-two by the time of the election. That's not that old. It might be better for you to wait until '88. The air would be cleared over German rearmament, and you'd have even more exposure."

Bickel's jaw was set. "No, Si. We've discussed that. We don't need to wait. All the heavy hitters are off the scene, and now has got to be the time. The country's ready for someone who's young. After this conference, even if people wonder about rearmament, they'll know my name. That's important. High recognition."

"I agree. You have a damn fine shot. There are a lot of slips, though, and sometimes if you try and don't make it, it can make you crazy. Sometimes it can make you crazy even if you do make it," Kart said.

"It's kind of you to say so," Bickel said. "I don't know what I'd do without you. You keep your eye out for me. And you don't even know whether you'll be in charge of Defense or State."

Both men laughed. "I don't think it'll be State," Kart said, "because Kosters wants to stay there forever. And maybe he should. He's damn good at doing what he does."

"That is for sure," Bickel agreed. "But you're damn good at doing what you do. Don't forget that." There were only a few people in the world whom Bickel genuinely liked, beyond what they could do for him. Simon Kart was at the top of the list, even above Alexandra.

A wide shoulder appeared on the road about a

quarter of a mile ahead of them. "I think I'll pull over there," Kart said. "It's not far to Bonn."

Kart guided the car to a smooth stop on the shoulder and the men changed places. Both men were surprised at how cold the wind had become.

"You know, this has been a good day despite all that business at the library," Bickel said. "We've had a ride, gotten away from the conference, and discussed a lot of issues. It's worthwhile." The road ahead was more crowded with cars and trucks than it had been in the rural areas. Despite the light snow and its clouds, Bickel could see the new office buildings and apartments of the Federal Republic's capital.

"The crucial thing," Bickel said, "is to make the rearmament thing our own issue. We have to campaign on our issues, not on what somebody else pitches at us." Bickel peered forward through the night. His face was clean and angular, like the star of a television cop show. Someone used to tell Bickel that he looked a lot like Efrem Zimbalist, Jr., and Bickel secretly thought that whoever said that was right. He still had a fine head of sandy brown hair, which he brushed straight back, and he looked competent and trustworthy. That's what everyone said. Bickel hoped it was true. For a politician, looking like that was pure gold.

Bickel drove around the city until he came to the Koblenzer Allee, which ran parallel to the Rhine one block from it. Three blocks down from the residence of the *Bundeskanzler,* now the aging Willy Brandt, stood the enormous new American embassy. It sprawled for almost two blocks. Behind it on those two blocks was a very large parking lot.

Bickel fished in his pocket for the key to the parking lot entrance. Damn. He couldn't find it.

"Si," Bickel asked, "do you by any chance have a key for the parking lot gate?"

But there was no answer. Simon Kart was sound asleep. Bickel decided he would not wake him. Instead, he pulled around the block into the Koblenzer Allee again and pulled up in front of the guard. He stopped the car and turned off the engine. It was biting cold, so he jumped out of the car and ran out to the front door of the embassy. There was a telephone behind a cranny in the doorway, and Bickel ducked in there to ask how to get into the parking lot without a key.

For an instant, he thought that someone had turned on a blinding orange light. Then he heard the explosion and felt the building shake from its force. He heard the glass and the metal crash against the gate and the street as he was thrown against a wall.

When he looked out of his cranny to the street, he could hardly tell that the car had ever been there. From a gaping hole in the street, he could see, smoke was billowing out.

The next day, the newspapers reported that most of Simon Kart's body had been recovered.

CHAPTER

3

It was Christmas in Asunción, Paraguay, and the bedraggled city had on its finery. Colored light bulbs hung between houses on the narrow streets. Wreaths and ribbons covered cracked plaster. It was hot and sunny, but, for once, the killing humidity had subsided. Most shops were closed, but happy-looking people strolled down the streets anyway, looking in windows and greeting one another.

Over a mile from the main shopping area, on Plaza Baradero, overlooking Bahía Asunción, the inlet that gave the town its name, was a row of old Spanish-style mansions. Closed off from passersby with heavy iron gates and thick stucco walls, the houses looked unchanged from the time, two centuries before, when they were built.

But that was only if you didn't notice the television antennas. Every house had one, and some houses had more than one. But No. 19 Baradero had the most elegant antenna of all. Its antenna rose for about twenty-five feet above the tile roof and then branched out into a shape similar to a giant arrowhead.

No. 19 Baradero was remarkable in other ways as well. The gates of its neighbors were sometimes open, if only for a few hours during the morning. But the gates at No. 19 were always closed. The frequent deliveries made by small trucks from the grocery and the Tomás Farmacia arrived at a small back gate which was opened by two men who did not look Latin American. The two men carried Heckler and Koch submachine guns slung around their necks.

The walls around No. 19 were different, too. Most of its neighbors' walls were clean and flat on top. They were obviously only relics of a day when walls meant protection, not seriously intended to keep away prowlers now. The walls of No. 19, on the other hand, were strewn with broken glass. Above the wall at six-inch intervals were thin, almost invisible wires, rising three feet above the top of the wall. Occasionally a squirrel jumped onto a wire and immediately fell over, dead.

Inside No. 19, on the first floor, the rooms were large and cool, even without air conditioning. The walls were hung with tapestries and pictures of Spanish conquistadores. On the second floor, though, there was a room which was thoroughly up to date. Alone among the rooms in the house, it was air-conditioned. Its windows were almost two inches thick. In the center of the room was a large hospital bed. On that bed lay a thin, old, old man. He was unconscious, as he had been for months. Tubes ran from his body to various machines next to the bed.

There was a continual vigil of at least five people in the room. Two nurses managed the equipment that was attached to the old man. Two men sat by the door to the room with submachine guns in their laps. And yet another man sat by the bed, usually reading.

On the other side of that man was a radiotelephone receiver, which ran down to the room from the elaborate antenna twenty-five feet above the roof.

No one in the room was celebrating Christmas when the radiotelephone started to buzz softly. The young man, austere and blond, picked up the receiver and said slowly, "Hallo."

No one in the room altered his movements as the young man listened attentively for several minutes. Then, quite clearly, the young man said in German, "What do you recommend?"

Again, he listened for several minutes before saying, again slowly and again in German, "I'll ask him. Hold on please."

The young man pressed a switch next to the telephone and set down the receiver. He returned to his reading for about ten minutes. Then he turned the switch and picked up the telephone receiver again.

"Herr Bauer thinks that your plan makes good sense. He agrees that it's essential. But please keep him advised of every development."

He continued listening, and then the young man said, "He is much better and will be up and walking very soon. Just a slight hip fracture, that's all."

More listening, and then, "I will tell him you said so. Good-bye and thank you."

The young man set down the receiver and went back to reading an untranslated copy of *Thus Spake Zarathustra*.

After a few minutes of reading, the man lifted his head and turned to one of the nurses and asked in Spanish, "How is he now?"

The nurse, a flat-faced young woman with a serious demeanor, said, "He is unchanged, Señor. He will never recover from this coma. You understand."

Before answering, the young man glanced at a newspaper next to his chair. In the lower left-hand portion of the front page was a story of an explosion in Bonn the day before which had killed an American Congressional aide. His name sounded Jewish. The young man looked back at the nurse.

"Of course," the young man said, "of course."

He looked at the narrow, wizened face at the head of the bed. God, who would ever have thought it would come to this? But no one would know. The secret would be kept. The others would never know he would not recover. That was essential. Things would go forward and, from heaven, the old man would see how well they had done.

The young man looked at the crucifix above the bed—a gift from one of the nurses. He shifted his gaze slightly to an oil portrait, about one meter square, of a uniformed Adolf Hitler, smiling only slightly. There was a black sash about two inches wide coming down across the portrait at a diagonal.

CHAPTER

4

Henry Wilson, Ambassador Extraordinary and Plenipotentiary from the United States of America to the Federal Republic of Germany, thought for almost half an hour about Simon Kart's death. Then he decided that if Senator Bickel had been able to bear up well enough to finish the rearmament talks, Bickel could also live through a party honoring the talks. The talks ended two days before New Year's Eve, and Henry Wilson knew how to give a party to mark a new year and a new day for Germany. A fourteen-, no a twenty-piece orchestra would be laid on.

"Travis," Wilson said, wrapping a velvet-sleeved arm around the Californian's shoulders as they sat in the residence library, "you know this is the way Simon would have wanted it. He knew that the treaty was the important thing. He wouldn't have let terrorists stop him."

"I know you're right, Henry," Bickel said. He moved out of Wilson's grasp. "It's brave of you to have this evening under the circumstances." Bickel had little feeling one way or the other for Henry Wilson, but Wilson was one of the top dogs at the Business Round Table,

35

and it did not hurt a bit to have those guys on his side.

The next night, New Year's Eve, Travis Bickel sat among about two hundred other formally dressed men and women at the embassy dining room, as liveried waiters passed among them. Only California wines were served.

At the head table, Travis Bickel sat next to Helen Wilson, the ambassador's plump and bejeweled lady, who could not be restrained from squeezing his arm while she talked about what sacrifices he had made for his country. Christ, except for losing Kart, sitting next to Helen Wilson was the worst sacrifice so far.

"That's what I believe in, too," Helen Wilson said, as she speared a hunk of country pâté. "Sacrifice. For your country." The last word was slurred because Mrs. Wilson chewed while she spoke.

"When Henry left InterCo for this job, I knew that it was going to cost us some money. I knew that. And a lot of my friends said, 'Helen, don't do it. You'll just spend a lot of money and time, and no one'll thank you.' That's what people said. But I believe in sacrifice for country. Like your friend Cohen."

"His name was Kart, not Cohen," Bickel said evenly. "And no one gave him any choice. He was just murdered while he was asleep. Probably by a bomb that was meant for me."

Helen Wilson smiled so broadly that her face lost, for a moment, its three chins. "I'm sorry. Of course, Al Cohen is Henry's counselor." She paused to sip a California Burgundy. "Still, it's all the same thing. Sacrifice. I'm sure that if Mr. Kart had been awake, he would have chosen to sacrifice too."

God Almighty. The only thing Helen Wilson has ever sacrificed has been other people, Bickel thought. He wished that dinner were over. Still, Helen Wilson had her friends, too, so Bickel smiled and tried to act interested. He was a good actor.

But it was two more hours of Helen Wilson's inane society-girl-grown-up chatter before the ambassador rose to give a toast.

"Minister Schröder, honored German guests, U.S.

representatives and friends, every New Year's Eve is an occasion for celebrating."

Oh Christ, Bickel thought. One of these endless, platitudinous speeches in the guise of a toast. And still, his handsome strong features stayed in the shape of a humble smile.

Ambassador Wilson droned on. ". . . That's what this whole effort at German rearmament is all about, my friends. Sacrifice and trust. And I want to close this dinner—we'll get to the dancing in a few minutes in the East Lobby—with a toast to a man whom we all trust, a man who has sacrificed much indeed. Ladies and gentlemen, I suggest we all stand and sing 'For Auld Lang Syne' in honor of Senator Travis A. Bickel."

Oh, for Christ's sweet sake, Bickel thought as he obligingly stood while the entourage sang. Tears were streaming down Helen Wilson's plump cheeks. For a moment, when Travis Bickel thought about how much he missed Simon Kart and how terrible it all was, he started to cry too. But the scene was just too funny to allow him to feel like tears for long. And, besides, the public did not like for its politicians to cry. Muskie proved that a long time ago.

At last it was over. Bickel waved at the crowd, bowed, and headed for the men's room. That was always the trouble with sitting at the head table. It made taking a leak awfully hard to do.

He had to endure something he always hated—people talking to him while he was standing at a urinal. Someone even came up and, while using the urinal next to him, put his arm around Bickel. "You're doing great work, son. Great work," the man said to Bickel.

As Bickel zipped himself up, he noticed that the man who had embraced him at the urinal was a well-fed, jowly man with a bulbous nose whom he wanted to talk to. Eddie Fleischacker was the premier man in direct mail solicitation in the country. He had made himself rich, working out of Royal Oaks, Michigan, and now he was operating out of a townhouse on N Street in Georgetown. At least five senators that Bickel knew of owed him their jobs.

"How are you, Eddie?" Bickel asked as both men dried their hands.

"Say, that was a terrible shame about your pal Kart," Fleischacker said. "Terrible."

"You're telling me," Bickel said. This was Eddie's way of telling him there was mileage in it. "The man died for his country as surely as if he had been at Guadalcanal."

"Absolutely," Fleischacker said. "And don't forget," he added, poking Bickel's starched shirtfront, "you were there, too. You got hurt. It could have been you."

"Bad news," Bickel said.

"It's been on every newscast in America ten times, Senator, so it's not all bad news. It would take a pretty drunken ginney not to know who you were, and that means something."

"Something," Bickel agreed.

"It's gonna be helpful to you when you're up for re-election, trying to get some money together," Fleischacker said. "I know just how it could be done."

"Well, the time comes, I'm going to call you up," Bickel said.

"No, I'll call you," Fleischacker said. "We should get to know each other better. That publicity was national, Senator. It wasn't just in California. Let's not forget that."

"We'll get together back in Washington real soon," Bickel said as Fleischacker adjusted his bowtie and walked out the door.

That sonofabitch, Bickel thought. The first time I ran I couldn't even get him to return my calls. Now he's kissing my ass right here in the men's room. It's okay with me, Bickel thought. I won't be doing it to him. Let them kiss my ass. After this treaty's nailed down, they'll be after me like they were in heat.

As Bickel walked out of the men's room and toward the East Lobby, he felt a tentative touch on his shoulder, the touch of a delicate and lightly scented hand with pearl fingernails.

"Bitte, Herr Bickel," a girlish voice said.

Bickel wheeled around to see an angel. The angel

was a tall, thin girl with the whitest skin he had ever seen. The angel had deep blue eyes that glowed like luminous sapphires between long, dark lashes. The angel had blond hair that fell gracefully to her shoulders. The angel was thin and looked, to Bickel, just the way an angel is supposed to look. And the angel was talking fairly good English.

"Please excuse me, Herr Bickel. My name is Katherine Dorn. I work for *Der Spiegel*. May I speak to you for a few minutes, please? Just a few minutes?"

"Of course," he said in a modulated and careful tone. He had to do this right, as he had to do everything right. "Let's go down the hall a little way, where people won't disturb us. What paper did you say you worked for?"

"*Der Spiegel*," the girl said.

"Well," Bickel said as they walked down the hall, "what can I tell you?"

The girl laughed. "Oh, many things. You are one of the, how should I say it, warmest subjects in Germany today."

Bickel acted surprised. "I am?" he asked. "Why would that be?" He wondered if he could get away with it on a night like this, when everyone was watching him. He thought he could.

"Well, Herr Bickel, because nuclear rearmament is one of the most important subjects we have ever faced here in Germany. I am certain you know that."

"I thought that both the Christian Democrats and the Socialists were for it," Bickel said, acting businesslike, but taking her arm. She did not resist as they walked down the hall.

"They are, but they are hardly the only parties in West Germany. And there are many people not affiliated with parties who are very worried about it. And of course there are the terrorists, like the ones who killed your friend." The girl looked sad. "That was a terrible crime," she said.

Who was this kid? Bickel wondered. There were a lot of tricksters around who could kiss and tell and make trouble for him. But she was so lovely. Sometimes one could be too cautious.

"Yes," he said, "it was a tragedy, but there's nothing that can be done about it now. He was a wonderful fellow, and I'll miss him. I'll miss him a lot. He didn't have any family, so they won't miss him. But I'll miss him."

Katherine Dorn looked even sadder. "Do you think they meant to kill you?" she asked.

"I don't know. I had the car serviced in Bad Kreuznach, and the mechanic there acted rather strangely. But I told all that to the police, so I guess they're working on it." Bickel thought perhaps the girl was from the police. He would soon find out.

"It could have been the anarchists," she said. "They're still active. Even though Baader's dead, there are still plenty of their kind around. Plenty of people who hate the treaty."

"Yes, terrorism is a big problem," Bickel said. He gave a canned response. "But German rearmament is a must for the Western world." He looked her in the eye, as if she were a constituent, and said, "It's unpopular, of course, but we can't always take the easy way." He wanted to see just how shrewd the girl was.

Katherine Dorn looked impressed at his sincerity, a sign that her shrewdness level was not dangerously high in Bickel's eyes. "If the document reaches the United States Senate, do you think it will be ratified?"

Bickel laughed. "Is this a full-scale interview?"

Katherine Dorn blushed.

"If it is," Bickel said, "I'd like to have at least a couple of dances before we get down to the heavy questions." He smiled his best smile.

She smiled back. Bickel took her arm and led her to the dance floor. The Lord taketh away and the Lord giveth, he thought.

He held her slender arm until they reached the East Lobby, where about twenty couples were dancing to a fox-trot adaptation of "By the Time I Get to Phoenix." Katherine Dorn wore a slightly off-white gown, cut low enough for Bickel to see the tops of her small breasts.

She smiled as he pulled her gently to him and put his arm around her back.

"I don't even know if you dance the same way in Bonn as we do in Washington," Bickel said as he started a fox-trot.

"I think I can pick it up," Katherine said.

They moved around the floor slowly and Bickel pulled her gradually closer and closer to him. She did not resist at all. They danced without talking while "Send in the Clowns" began, and by now Bickel had pulled her so close that their faces were almost touching. A scent, the same one that had reached him before when she put her hand on his shoulder, swept over him. He could hear her breathing softly and could feel her breasts rise and fall with each breath.

After "Send in the Clowns," Bickel was about to suggest that they go somewhere to talk, when Ambassador Wilson mounted the stage and announced that the next number would be for Senator Bickel. It was a slowed-down version of "When You Get to San Francisco, Be Sure to Wear Some Flowers in Your Hair."

Bickel bowed to the other couples on the dance floor and waved with both hands, politician style. Then he took Katherine around the waist and started to dance with her again. This time she pressed up against him without any pressure from him.

Where the hell can I take her, Bickel wondered. I sure as hell can't go back to my room here at the embassy. That would be like putting an ad in the Washington *Post*, he thought.

He felt a hand on his shoulder. He turned around. Helen Wilson stood there, her face red, obviously more than a little tipsy from the Champagne—Napa Valley, of course—that had been flowing so freely.

"Senator, I hope the young lady will let me have at least one dance with you. You don't mind do you, honey?" the plump matron asked Katherine Dorn.

Katherine immediately released her grip on Bickel and said, "*Sicherlich.*" and then to Bickel, "*Guten abend.*"

Oh, for Christ's sake. That girl has just said good-bye, and here I am dancing with this hog of a woman, Bickel thought as he smiled and danced around the floor with Helen Wilson. Where the hell had Katherine Dorn said she worked? *Der Stern? Die Welt?* What the hell was it?

"I hope you're enjoying yourself, Senator," Helen Wilson said. "Are you going to call Lydia at midnight?"

How the hell did Helen Wilson know his wife's name?

"I really hadn't thought of that," Bickel said. "But now that you mentioned it, it's a fine idea. Of course it won't be midnight there when it's midnight here, but it's still a good idea."

"I just think it's awfully nice for husbands and wives to be as close as they can," Helen Wilson said. "I can let you use the embassy phone. It'll be free that way. That's always better, isn't it"

"Thank you very much, Helen," Bickel said. The music was just ending. "Maybe I could do that right now. Where is the closest embassy phone?"

A few minutes later, Bickel was on a telephone in an empty office near the East Lobby, being put through to his wife in Washington, D.C.

He could tell as soon as she answered that she was drunk. He could not tell if anyone else was there.

The high point of the conversation was Lydia's question: "I suppose you're sleeping with lots of blonds there while I'm sitting at home, you miserable bastard. Isn't that right?"

He wished her a Happy New Year and said goodbye. His wife's high-pitched, slurred voice stayed with him as a beaming Helen Wilson looked over at him from across the room. "Have you ever seen the residence quarters here at the embassy?" she asked him.

Oh no, he thought. She's pitching me. Oh, for God's sake.

"No, I haven't," Bickel answered with a smile. "But I think I'd better get back to the party. I've promised to answer some questions for that young lady. She's a reporter."

Helen Wilson raised her eyebrows but let Bickel out

of her psychic clutches.

When Bickel returned to the East Lobby, though, there was no sign of Katherine Dorn. Goddammit to hell. If he had missed that blond because of that idiot Helen Wilson, who had first seduced him into calling his wife and then tried to seduce him period, that would be too fucking much to bear. But there was no sign of Katherine Dorn.

He walked outside into the biting cold air to see if she might still be there, getting a breath of air. No sign of her. But then, just as he started to walk back inside, feeling as though he had two tons of bricks in his pockets, he saw her sitting behind the wheel of a battered Volkswagen that looked as if it dated from the 1950s. She was in a line of cars pulling out of the parking lot.

He ran across the flagstones of the embassy entrance to her car. She looked up at him and smiled.

"Hey, roll down the window," he laughed.

She obligingly lowered the window and smiled. "I didn't want to take you away from your hostess," she said. "We can get together for an interview when it's convenient."

"It's convenient right now," Bickel said with a smile. "Why don't we go somewhere for a drink, and I'll be glad to answer as many of your questions as I can."

"Fine, if you're sure it's no trouble," Katherine said, as she leaned over and unlocked the door.

Bickel got in, white tie and all, and then noticed that he had forgotten his topcoat. What the hell, he thought. What the hell.

"Where are we going?" Bickel asked cheerfully.

Katherine smiled and said, "Oh, a very good place, where only the best people go."

Bickel reached inside his tails jacket. Thank God, he had his wallet. He knew that Bonn places were just as expensive as the East Side of New York, if not more so.

Katherine Dorn's little beetle raced down Koblenzer Allee until it turned into Kölnerstrasse. After a few blocks more it became Friedrich-Ebert Allee. Christ, the Germans weren't forgetting anyone. Sure enough, the road then became Adenauer Allee.

Soon, the major streets ended, and he and Katherine were driving down small streets in a residential district.

The thought flashed into Bickel's mind that maybe, just maybe, by a wild stroke of luck, the equivalent of winning the triple perfecta at a racetrack, Katherine Dorn was taking him to her apartment. There were, after all, no nightclubs around. Instead there were blocks of modern-looking apartments that reminded Bickel of the modern apartments in the suburbs of Washington, D.C.

"Where are we?" Bickel asked.

"We're about a block from my apartment," Katherine Dorn said. "If my roommate is out, I can make you some coffee and we can have a quick interview. I'll have you back to the embassy within an hour. Just time enough for New Year's." She said it with a straight face.

God, she was businesslike. He liked them that way. In a way, that made the whole thing more exciting, although he could not have said why.

Katherine Dorn's apartment was small and modern, with Danish-style furniture. Everything looked just as it should, to fit his image of the way a single girl's apartment in Bonn was supposed to look. It was funny, the way things looked like what they were supposed to look like. That, he guessed, had something to do with the movies.

But, Jesus, what was he doing thinking about cultural sociology when he was with a beautiful blond in her apartment on New Year's Eve? And the blond hadn't even asked whether or not he was married. Something good was in the air.

"I'll put on some coffee," Katherine said, and disappeared into the kitchen. From the kitchen, she called out, "Have a seat." Then a moment later: "I'll be out in a moment."

Bickel sat down and looked at the room. It had a huge color TV set, a radio, assorted pieces of furniture, and, scattered on the floor, a pile of glossy magazines. Which one did Katherine work for? Was it *Der Spiegel?*

He reached down and picked through the magazines

until he came to the thickest and glossiest of them all. It was the German edition of *Town and Country*.

There was a slight rustling in the room, and then the blond goddess stood in front of him in blue jeans and a T-shirt that said, in letters like a Coca-Cola advertisement, "Cocaine."

Bickel's blue-gray eyes swept over her lean, long form and then down to the *Town and Country* on the floor. "I don't get it," he said with a smile. "Is that what *Town and Country* says you should be wearing?"

Katherine laughed and threw back her head so that her hair caught the light from a modern floor lamp. Her teeth were incredibly even and white.

"That's my roommate's magazine. I don't give a damn what it says."

She sat down on the floor in front of Bickel and pulled a tape recorder from her pocketbook. "May I use this?" she inquired gently.

"Sure. I don't mind," Bickel said.

"The coffee'll be ready in a minute," Katherine said. "Now, can you tell me this, Senator Bickel: What are the odds on ratification of the Rearmament Treaty in the Senate?" Her voice had taken on the professional inflections of a news-woman. She pointed the microphone part of the recording machine toward Bickel.

"Well, I think that it's not a foregone conclusion at this point, but I would not bet that we would lose." He paused for a moment. "You've got to remember that Secretary Kosters is behind the treaty, and his word counts for a great deal with the American people." He paused to look sincere. Christ, did he really have to go through this charade to get her into bed?

They talked, like reporter and subject, for about half an hour, going over all the points of the agreement and how American public opinion might see it. All the time, Bickel wondered what her nipples looked like.

"Will American nuclear submarine production be able to take up the loss of so many Tridents and Poseidons to the Federal Republic?" Katherine asked.

Bickel sighed. "Could you turn that thing off?" he asked, pointing at the cassette recorder.

"Certainly. Is what you're about to say confidential?" Katherine said, a note of anticipation in her voice.

"No," Bickel said. "Not what I'm about to say. What I'm about to do."

He slipped off the chair and sat on the floor facing her. He put his arms around her and kissed her lips. They parted and it turned into a long, pushing and pulling embrace. She kissed a young girl's kiss—with infinite giving.

He kissed her and put his hands inside her T-shirt up to her small hard nipples. When he rubbed them in his fingers, Katherine pressed herself against him more forcefully. He moved his hands down and pressed against denim.

"Do you have a bedroom?" he asked.

Without a word, she led him into a small darkened room. There was only a single bed in it. Clothes and newspapers covered the bed. He could see his picture on one of the newspapers. With one broad sweep, Katherine pulled off the cover and all of the clothes and newspapers fell to the floor.

She stood up straight in front of him and put her arms around his neck. After a long kiss, he lifted her arms above her head and then lifted off her T-shirt. Her breasts did not move at all. They were as firm as two small apples. He ran his hands over them and then unsnapped her blue jeans. They fell to the floor and she stepped out of them. She was not wearing anything else.

With a little jump, she got into the bed, turned her face to Bickel and smiled at him.

Bickel realized that he was in a darkened bedroom, wearing white tie and tails, with a naked twenty-year-old angel. The first thing to do was to take off his clothes. After he did that, he got into bed with Katherine. She pressed herself against him, and he kissed her violently. His fingers found her.

Before he could do anything, Katherine was kneeling over him, taking him into her small mouth. Jesus Christ. I really must have gone to heaven.

He pulled Katherine off him and laid her out next to him. With one motion, he rolled over and entered her.

She drew in her breath sharply, and mumbled something in German. It might have been "*Gott.*"

Wildly, they pushed at each other.

After a few minutes, he felt Katherine grasp his back more and more tightly, and then begin to gyrate back and forth on the bed, rocking her pelvis from side to side. Then he felt a tingling sensation.

One second later, the bells of Bonn started tolling in the New Year. "Happy New Year," Bickel said, covering her mouth with a kiss. "Happy wonderful fucking New Year."

And he relaxed. For a few minutes, he did not have to think about the Roper Poll on rearmament, or how Kitlowski of the Steelworkers saw him, or whether the Sierra Club would endorse him, or whether a *Newsweek* cover was the right thing so early or whether Lydia was going to crack up again. All he had to think about were round, conical nipples, browner than he would have expected, that was all, for a few minutes, but enough.

CHAPTER

5

New Year's Day was cold and overcast at Innisfree, some eighty miles north of New York City. The estate house was far from any road or other dwelling and the air was not disturbed by any noises except those that Elson Patterson, sole owner and resident of Innisfree, chose to make himself or to allow. The fifty-five hundred acres of timberland and lakes and gardens were as silent on that New Year's Day as a place could be where there were the occasional footfalls of deer, the scamperings of squirrels, and the conversation of two men.

One of the men was an elderly but obviously fit man with a florid complexion and straight white hair. His height, a ramrod straight six feet, still went well with his muscled one hundred and sixty-five pounds. His face had an intense, hawklike aura, even though his features were relaxed. Thin lips and light blue eyes, along with a straight nose with only a few broken capillaries, completed the picture of a gracefully aging sportsman. He wore a lambskin shearling coat which, despite the cold, was not fully buttoned up.

The man next to him was considerably younger. He looked slightly ill at ease walking in the early morning chill so far from Park Avenue. He wore a wool pinstripe suit under his tweed overcoat. God, he had been lucky to get to the cleaners before Patterson had called him yesterday afternoon. Otherwise he would have had nothing to wear except his camel's hair overcoat, and he knew that Mr. Patterson thought camel's hair was for women.

When they were about three hundred yards from the house, by the side of the lake, they saw a deer. Patterson didn't say anything. He put his left hand over his mouth and pointed at the deer with his right hand. Patterson knew that deer were easily frightened, and he wanted to keep the deer as calm as possible, so that deer would eventually come up to the doors of the house.

Frank Roberts, the man next to Patterson, did not say a word. That was something he had learned at his first meeting with Mr. Patterson. You didn't talk to Mr. Patterson until Mr. Patterson talked to you. It was a simple rule, one of many simple rules.

Even all together, the rules were by no means hard to follow. And it was well worth it. Thanks to those rules, and his following them, Frank Roberts had a co-op overlooking Central Park and a cottage—well, more than a cottage—overlooking Long Island Sound in Greenwich.

Thanks also to Elson Patterson's kindness in rewarding those who could follow simple orders, Frank Roberts's wife, Lucy, had gotten, for her thirtieth birthday, the mink coat she had always wanted.

Frank Roberts knew that this could be just the beginning. There was quite literally nothing that Mr. Patterson could not do for him, and all Frank Roberts had to do was follow a few simple rules. And one of the rules was to remain silent until spoken to.

They walked another hundred yards, and this time they headed into the woods.

"It's cold today," Patterson said. "Damn cold. Sorry to have made you get out early in the morning on New Year's Day and fly up here. I hope the helicopter was well heated."

"It was, sir. It was no trouble. I just went down to the Pan Am building and it was waiting for me up on the roof," Roberts said.

"Good. That's very good. I think we should use helicopters more often. A lot of people are afraid of them, but I think they're safer than cars. That makes sense, doesn't it?" Patterson looked at Roberts with a smile.

Roberts was still not certain what that smile meant. "It might be a good idea, sir. It might definitely be a good idea. If you approve, I could have a small study done on the relative safety of automobiles and helicopters. Shall I do that?"

Patterson laughed. "No, that's not necessary. But it's good to be thorough. I like that. You know I like that. I admire you for it. I definitely do." Then Patterson laughed again.

Roberts smiled and laughed slightly too. When Mr. Patterson laughed, it was good to laugh too.

It had taken Frank Roberts only a few weeks to get the hang of things around Elson Patterson. Ever since Roberts had been plucked out of the Arbitrage Department of the Manhattan Guaranty Trust Company to work as Elson Patterson's secretary (the Patterson Family Charitable Trusts owned 31.8 percent of the outstanding shares of the Manhattan Guaranty Trust Company), he had adapted quickly.

At Harvard, Roberts had been in all of Hasty Pudding's theatricals, no matter how ridiculous, and even in New York Roberts went to plays as often as he could. He loved acting, and he knew that it came in handy with Mr. Patterson. For a boy with parents who ran a dry-cleaning plant in Mineola, Roberts had come a long way, in pinstripe suits, into the world of Elson Patterson and the hushed corridors of the Patterson Foundations. He had even started, just started, to hear whispers about Croesus, and that meant he was really on the inside. He had to thank his acting. It wasn't just being quick that counted with Elson Patterson. It was being sincere, too. Looking sincere, anyway. And laughing at the right times.

"I remember the first time I rode in a helicopter," Patterson said, looking deep into the woods. "They were called autogyros then. I remember it was in England, back in 1934, on old Lord Portland's place in Kent. Christ, the thing looked like it was a giant eggbeater. But even then, I thought it had some value."

This was not a cue for Roberts to speak, and he didn't.

"That was when I was doing a lot of mountain climbing. I thought maybe it could help us get up to the plateaus faster so that we could save our strength for the final climb," Patterson said. He looked over at Roberts and smiled.

"I was wrong, of course. The air currents up there are much too strong." Patterson looked down at the earth. It was covered with pine needles. "It wasn't the first time I was wrong. Not the first time or the last time. Not by a long shot."

Roberts wasn't sure whether an answer was called for. Probably not. Mr. Patterson would ask him a question when he wanted an answer.

"Then I thought that autogyros, or helicopters, would be very important in warfare. I wasn't the only one, of course. A lot of people thought that. In many countries. Of course, here in America, everybody was asleep, just as they always are. But in Europe, people were damned interested."

Without saying anything more, Patterson got up and walked over to a large fallen tree. "We've got to get this tree hauled out of here," Patterson said. "Would you mention that to someone, Frank? That's how fires start. From dead trees."

"Of course, Mr. Patterson. I'll see that it's looked after as soon as we get back to the house. Or do you want me to go back to the house right away and see to it?" It wasn't part of Roberts's usual work, but the more he did, the better off he was.

Patterson smiled again. "No, Frank. When we get

back to the house will be time enough," Patterson said.

"Fine, Mr. Patterson. I'll take care of it."

"Of course, neither side really made use of helicopters. I told him about them. Of course, I told everyone about them. I mean I didn't just tell him, but I thought that he was so unconventional, so willing to try new things, that he would try it. But he didn't." Patterson looked into the woods again. A nip was in the air. Snow might come.

Patterson smiled a wry smile. "That wasn't his first mistake either. Or his last. Not by a long, long way."

Roberts knew that no comment was called for here. He waited for Patterson to get to the subject—the subject which had brought him out of his warm bed to this chilly clearing on New Year's Day. But Patterson could not be rushed.

"Of course no one, not even he, guessed how much warfare would change. I mean he wouldn't believe it if he saw how things have changed. Do you think he would?"

"No, sir. I don't. Not that I knew him, of course." Roberts always got uneasy when this line of conversation began. It was so hard to know what to say.

"No, no," Patterson said, as his eye caught a squirrel running through the woods. "Of course, you didn't know him. I mean, you weren't even alive, and people who were alive and saw him every day didn't really know him."

Frank Roberts stamped his feet on the ground. Jesus, I hope we're not going into a long routine about this, he thought.

Patterson looked down at the ground too, and then looked up. "Have you been following the newspapers, Frank?"

"Yes sir, I try too, although I don't follow the news as closely as I'd like." Where the hell was this conversation going?

"You think the Senate will ratify the German rearmament agreement, Frank? How does it look to you?" Patterson stared straight at him.

Roberts shifted his weight and stamped his feet again.

This was a problem area. How the hell should he answer? "I don't know, Mr. Patterson. I think it could go either way. My guess at this point is that Secretary Kosters will put it over. He's still got a lot of prestige from the Mideast settlements." It was a gamble to say that much, and Roberts waited for Patterson's reply. Perhaps Patterson wanted an actual vote projection, which Roberts could give him of course, but that might not be what Patterson wanted.

Patterson asked another question. "How would you vote on it, Frank?"

That was an easy one. "Oh, I would vote for it. I think it's an absolutely essential element in shoring up European defenses against the Russian threat." If it sounded memorized, it was.

"Yes, but can the Germans be trusted, Frank? That's what I'm talking about." Patterson continued to stare at Roberts.

"Of course they can. They're the most stable country in Europe. They certainly can be trusted. I think it was a mistake to wait so long." That was a little more spontaneous-sounding, which was better.

"Let's walk a little farther into the woods, Frank," Patterson said. "If you don't mind."

"Of course not, Mr. Patterson."

They walked farther into the woods, until they could not see either the lake or the estate house. The sun was climbing higher in the sky, and the day was getting warmer, although Frank Roberts still had to force himself not to shiver from the cold. In a few minutes of silent walking, they came to another dead tree, lying across their path. With a slight sigh, Elson Patterson sat down on the tree and motioned for Roberts to do the same.

"I'm worried about that treaty, Frank. I'm worried about it." Patterson looked farther into the forest. "I know that Kosters is a good man, a damn good man. But there are a lot of strong people against it."

Frank Roberts thought that this might be a good time to remain silent, which is what he did.

"Of course there are the appeasers, the leftovers from

the New Left. Don't kid yourself, there are still plenty
of them. You know that, don't you? I mean there are
still plenty of them in the Senate," Patterson said.

"I know what you mean, sir," Roberts said. He did
indeed. Part of his job was to keep track of the voting
and utterances of all the members of the United States
Congress and send highly synopsized reports to Mr.
Patterson on a daily basis. For that alone, Roberts super-
vised a staff of fifteen who worked in a townhouse on
Capitol Hill. The report went to Mr. Patterson, and to
no one else.

"They're hopeless. I mean, they are the way they are
just because they're stupid. And one thing you can
never do is make a stupid person into a smart person. It
can't be done."

"Yes sir, that's right." That was an easy one.

"Then there are some of those Jewish groups.
They're concerned. Of course, they should be. After
what Himmler and those swine at the SS did to the
Jews, they should be concerned. They should be very
concerned. I don't blame them. Do you?" He shot a
sharp look at Roberts.

This was definitely a touchy area. Roberts still didn't
know if Patterson knew that he was half-Jewish. Mr.
Patterson seemed to know everything, but he never said
anything to Roberts about it. Maybe Mr. Patterson
didn't know.

And, of course, if Mr. Patterson did know and still
hadn't said anything, especially if what Roberts guessed
about Croesus was on the beam, then maybe it was all
right. Maybe all those stories about Patterson were just
so much bullshit. Roberts hoped so. He had a certain
fondness for Patterson. He was eccentric, but that was a
privilege of power. And if Frank Roberts got to be
powerful enough, he could be eccentric too. And that
was something he wanted a great deal.

"I think you're right, Mr. Patterson," Roberts said.
That was probably a safe answer. Was Mr. Patterson
smirking?

"No, I think the Jews are right to be concerned,"
Patterson said. "That's definitely right. Some of them

are strong people, and they can make quite a fuss." And some of them, he thought, looking quickly at Roberts, are ass-kissing yes-men who will do anything I say.

Patterson picked some of the bark off the dead tree, crumbled it in his hand, and threw it to the ground. "But the Jews should not be making policy for the whole country, should they? That doesn't make sense. That's especially true when it's such a vital matter. It would be different if it were about Israel, but it's really more about Europe."

Again, there was a brief silence. Roberts thought that this might be a chance to gain a little ground with Mr. Patterson. "Well, it does concern Israel, too, Mr. Patterson, in the sense that Israel is vitally interested in what happens in Europe and in stopping the Russians. We know that the Isareli government is extremely eager to rearm the Germans."

"Yes, we do know that," Patterson said. They knew it because, for five thousand dollars a month, a code clerk at the Israeli embassy was sending copies of Israeli radio and cable traffic of international significance to an office which, through several intermediaries, was also one of Roberts's responsibilities.

"I mean it's a damned sure thing that the Israelis know a lot better what's in their national interest and the interest of Jews generally than a few Jewish clubwomen here."

"You're right, Mr. Patterson," Roberts said.

"Then, of course, there are some other groups—a few veterans here and there, who oppose the treaty, but I don't think that they're crucial." Patterson got up and dusted off the back of his shearling coat. "But ratification is by no means a sure thing. By no means."

"By no means," Roberts repeated vehemently.

"Did you read about that business with Senator Bickel and his assistant, Frank?" Patterson asked.

"Yes, I did. Very mysterious," Roberts said.

"Yes, indeed," Patterson agreed. "Extremely puzzling. I suppose it was terrorists trying to frighten Americans and make us think that Germany isn't trustworthy. You think that's it?"

"It sounds logical," Roberts said.

"Now, I think that fellow Bickel has conducted himself very well in this affair. Seems to be genuinely interested in Germany, too. How much do we know about him? Anything?"

It was almost a comic question. What the minions of Elson Patterson did not know about members of the United States Senate was definitely not worth knowing. This was where Roberts was at his best. His computer-like brain had data stored away which could be retrieved and spit out as neatly as anyone would want.

"He's forty years old. He was born in Bel-Air, California, and attended UCLA and Yale Law School. He came from middle-class parents. His father was an economist for the state of California, and his mother was a statistician, but she did not work after he was born. He was an only child. He married Lydia Domkiw when he was twenty-two years old." Roberts was an oral version of an electronic readout. Everything was flat and precise, presented with a mechanical authority.

"He first worked for Kaplan, Livingston, and Church," Roberts continued, "immediately after law school. Then he served briefly in the Judge Advocate General's Corps during the early part of Vietnam, but he was never in Vietnam. When he got out of the army, he ran for State Senate as a Democrat from a district in the San Fernando Valley. He won and within two terms was running for the U.S. Senate. He first won when he first tried, and was elected narrowly in 1976. He just won a landslide victory in this past election."

Patterson was impressed. Roberts might be obsequious, but he knew his job.

The voice continued, somehow striking Patterson as bizarre. It was as if a tape recorder were playing in the middle of the forest.

"He is known to be extremely ambitious and to have his eye very clearly on the upcoming presidential elections. He's on the Armed Forces and Foreign Affairs Committees and is well-respected. He speaks German and French and is quite interested in history, especially the history of the, uh, National Socialist period in Germany. It was always a close thing for Roberts to avoid saying "Nazi." He knew Mr. Patterson didn't like the word.

"Anything about his personal life, Frank? I mean, I don't want gossip. Hard stuff." Patterson looked piercingly at Roberts.

"His wife has serious drinking problems. She's been in therapy for years. In and out of mental hospitals. That's about it. If he's got any drug or sexual problems, or is taking money from anyone, we don't know about it," Roberts said. And you can be damn sure it's not happening, he added silently.

"Interesting," Patterson said. "It's amazing how many of these wives have mental problems. It's really amazing."

"His main problem going into the early running for the nomination is that he's not as well-known outside California as he should be. He inherited several million dollars from his mother's father, so he's well-heeled. His main problem will be recognition from the big media guns. That's going to be hard for him," Roberts said. The tape came to an end in Roberts's brain, and he stopped talking.

Patterson did not say anything for a minute, then he looked around and said, "He's an interesting fellow. I'd like to meet him. You think it could be arranged?"

"Of course, Mr. Patterson. It can be done," Roberts said. For Mr. Patterson, anything could be arranged.

"Fine. That would be fine. When he comes back from those meetings, I'd like to meet him at the Foxhall Road house. I'll come down." A pause. "Let's start back for the house. We'll have lunch, and then we'll have you back in New York in time to watch the Rose Bowl."

They walked briskly in from the woods, and Roberts was happy to be heading to where it was warm. The food was always good at Innisfree, and, as many times as he had been there, Roberts still loved to see all the photos of Mr. Patterson with the greats of the past, and some from the present too.

It was a puzzle to Roberts that he was allowed to see

even the pictures from the 1930's, but that was a sign of Mr. Patterson's trust in him.

As they walked out of the woods and along the shore of the lake toward the house, Patterson said, "It's cold as hell today. Cold as hell. Reminds me of those walks at Berchtesgaden. Christ, he didn't even wear an over-coat sometimes." Patterson stopped and looked back into the woods. Mr. Patterson looked very far away sometimes, Roberts thought. Especially when he was on this subject.

Patterson looked back ahead and started walking again, with Roberts in step. "Christ," Patterson said. "That was a hell of a time."

CHAPTER

6

T ravis Bickel sat in the upholstered chair
while the discussions about when the Tridents would be
turned over went on. Simon Kart sat next to him and
kept nudging him in the ribs. It occurred to Bickel to
wonder how Simon Kart could be in the *Konferenzhalle*
and also be blown to pieces, but he did not want to
seem impolite. After a while Bickel turned to Kart and
said, "I wish you'd stop nudging me while I'm trying to
concentrate."

When he turned to Kart, he could see that Kart was
screaming, but no sounds came out of his mouth. If
Bickel looked carefully at Kart's mouth though, he
could see that Kart said, over and over, "Run, Travis.
Run, Travis."

And the nudging continued. Bickel snapped over to
his other side and opened his eyes, and there was Katherine Dorn, sitting on the side of the bed, dressed in
blue jeans and a T-shirt, smiling at him and poking him
gently.

"I think maybe you had better get up," she said.

Bickel sat up and shook his head. "Jesus," he said, "I
think so too. What time is it?"

"It's not that late. It's about ten o'clock. But someone at the embassy may wonder where you are."

"That's a good thought," he said, still trying to pull himself out of sleep. Why had Kart been telling him to run?

"I've made some coffee and some rolls," Katherine said with a smile.

Without her makeup, dressed casually, she looked even better than she had at the embassy last night. Her hair cascaded down over her shoulders and framed her pale face and blue eyes. Why had Kart screamed at him?

Bickel was naked, and the thought of what he had to wear suddenly struck him. "I'm gong to look pretty silly walking into the embassy at 10 AM with my tails and white tie from last night." He laughed at himself.

"No problem," Katherine said, tossing back her head. "I'll bet no one will even mention it to you. If anyone notices, he'll just think you had a good time last night."

"Which I certainly did," Bickel said. "We must have stayed up almost all night."

"*Ja*," Katherine said, with a smile. "Come to the table and eat something."

He got up and walked to the bathroom to clean himself up as well as he could without his shaving kit. Luckily she had mouthwash, so he could get that cottony feeling out of his mouth.

"What were we talking about all that time?" Bickel asked, as he walked back to the bedroom.

"We weren't talking most of the time," the blond angel said with a smile.

What a night that was, Bickel thought. I have probably blown myself completely out of the water now for one night. Sin in haste; repent in leisure. Realistically, Bickel thought, the damage was probably nil.

"I know we talked for a while about the treaty," Bickel said. "I hope I didn't tell you anything secret that you're going to tell your readers." Bickel knew he had not.

"To tell you the truth, I hardly remember what you

told me," she said. "I'm not going to use any of it, anyway."

"You're not?" Bickel said.

"No, I'm not. I don't get my stories by sleeping with famous men," Katherine said, slightly indignantly. "I know some reporters who operate like that, but I don't. I absolutely don't. I do what I do because I like it. I don't do it to get ahead at *Der Spiegel*."

"I know this is looking a gift horse in the mouth," Bickel said as he put thick marmalade on a croissant roll, "but how did I get so lucky?"

"What is looking a gift horse in the mouth?" Katherine asked.

"I mean, why did you bestow that wonderful night on me?" Bickel said. "I don't want to seem suspicious, but how did I get so lucky? *Glücklich?*"

In the little eating area of the apartment, Katherine Dorn looked around at the meager amount of furniture and said, "I don't know why I should have to explain this." There was a slight edge in her voice. "If you did not want to make love with me, you didn't have to. No one forced you."

Oh, Christ, Bickel thought, what now? Another sobbing, whining bitch. Well, what the hell, he was a politician and he knew how to charm people.

He reached across the small pine table and kissed her hands, both of them, on the fingertips. "Katherine, I have never enjoyed a night like last night ever before in my life. Never. It was the single most wonderful night I ever spent. It was better than being elected to the Senate. It was better than my wedding night. It was wonderful. I'm just not used to having such a great thing happen to me, that's all. I'm just not used to it." He hoped he was not being taped. He was proud of himself and his ability with words. It was rare these days.

Katherine flushed, and she looked even better. "I lead a quiet life, Travis," she said. "I go out and interview pompous people who want to sound good, and then I come back to this miserable apartment, which I usually share with my miserable roommate. And when I see a man who is exciting and strong and has a sense of humor, I want to share some of my life with him. That's all, Travis. It doesn't happen very often, but it happens."

She stopped talking and looked down at the table. Travis Bickel thought she was going to cry. If she were an actress, she was a very good one. But he could be just as good.

"God, Katherine," Bickel said. "You are so wonderful. You must know that I'm married, and you haven't said a word about it, and I just feel as if I'm the luckiest man in the world. If I can do something to make your life more interesting, I'll do it."

She smiled at him. "You're already doing it, Travis." She looked at her wristwatch. "I'd better get you back to the embassy."

"I'm going to be here two more days. Will we be able to get together again?" Bickel asked, as he headed into the bedroom to retrieve his clothes.

"We'll try," she said. Then she laughed a wonderful, girlish laugh which tinkled through the air like a light touch on crystal and said, "Yes, I think so, Travis."

Bickel caught sight of her walking around in the little kitchen with her tight jeans and her T-shirt and he felt a pressure in his groin.

"Before I go, Katherine, could you come into the bedroom for a minute?" Bickel said.

"Only for a minute?" Katherine asked mockingly as she walked into the bedroom.

"Maybe a little longer than a minute," Bickel thought, as he pulled her toward him on the bed. She smiled and then he kissed her. As they fell back onto the bed, Bickel wondered if the girl was for real. If she was, she was wonderful. Even if she wasn't, she was wonderful. Anyway, he was in it now, and it was almost pure escape. From then on, he would have to be damned careful.

CHAPTER

7

No. 7 Dzerzhinsky Prospekt, about two blocks from the Kremlin, was not an imposing building in any sense. It had the same nondescript look as most Moscow buildings, only more so. No sign announced what was inside, but two burly men lounged outside, seemingly doing nothing. When a man or woman walked into No. 7, the men looked up idly at the visitor but did nothing. Nobody came here uninvited.

On January 2, 1983, Moscow was covered with six inches of snow. Women in babushkas, who had not yet been born at the time of the Revolution, swept the snow off the main traffic lanes of the streets with shovels and brooms. Dzerzhinsky street was one of those swept, and that made it easier for the cars that pulled up in front of it at eleven AM to get close to the curb so that their passengers would not get snow in their shoes.

As each man went into the building, the loungers looked up for only a second and then looked at the women shoveling snow.

By 11:30, in the basement of No. 7, seven men sat in a small room without windows. On one wall was a portrait of Lenin and on the facing wall, a portrait of Karl Marx. The wall between showed a map of the world.

The men sat around an old table on which there was no ornament except for a few ashtrays and several bottles of mineral water. All of the men were at least middle-aged and some were older. One man at the head of the table was particularly old, although his large size and rippling roll of chins made him look younger than he actually was. His bushy eyebrows were completely gray. Under them, his eyes were like chips of charcoal, blazing out into the room with a black heat.

Across from him sat a man who looked even older but was not. He sat straight in his chair and his eyes were sunk in the skull, which seemed to be only barely covered with tightly stretched skin like old parchment. His eyes were a light blue, and they went well with his thin, compressed lips.

One of the men in between began the meeting. He wore a heavy wedding ring on his fourth finger. His gray woolen suit looked as if it had come from somewhere better than most Russian suits of that kind. Indeed it did. It had been ordered from a tailor in Rome who had clothed a number of high Soviet officials.

"I think we all know that something has to be done," the man in the Italian suit said. "And I think we all know that we have only a few options."

"Less than a few," said a man with an ill-fitting suit across the table. "I don't see what we can do at all, without serious risk," Comrade General."

"Of course it involves serious risks," Comrade General Codlitsk snapped. "How could it not involve serious risks? When we are talking about facing the Germans, who still have former members of the SS in the Cabinet, when those Fascists will have nuclear weapons, it all involves serious risks. Get beyond that stage. I assure you it has serious risks. The question is, what do we do about it?"

At the end of the table, the fat man sighed. "At this stage, the Americans are so jittery that there cannot be a question of moving across the Oder and simply taking the Federal Republic. That's been ruled out," said Adjutant Okhmansky.

Again the comrade general seemed irritable. "Of course, it's ruled out. As long as the Americans have Kosters there telling the President what to do, we have to tread carefully. We all know we cannot make any frontal move. That's why we're here. We are supposed to be able to figure out what to do."

"Before we can do that," a man with a pencil-thin mustache said, "I think we have to know what the Rearmament Treaty really means." Deputy Minister Korchov always wanted to have everything done as neatly as possible.

The fat man, Adjutant Okhmansky, spoke again. "That's right. We have to know if this is what we've been waiting for."

Everyone at the table looked down at the old, thin man with the sunken eyes. "I suppose you think I have the answer," he said slowly, with a marked accent. "I don't know any more than I did in 1945, except for a few radio intercepts. I don't know if there's a new plan. It certainly looks a lot *like* the plan I knew about, but I cannot explain what Bickel is doing there. I don't know that. I don't know why he turned up in Bad Kreuznach. I don't know why he headed the U.S. delegation. There's a lot I don't know."

Comrade General Codlitsk looked fiercely at him. "There's also a lot you *do* know. How do we stop it?"

The thin, elderly man shrugged his shoulders. "I don't know how you stop it," he said. "The whole thing is run by a few people. Maybe they could be eliminated. You've done that before."

"Yes, we have," the fat man said. "We've done it before when you tricked us into it. We saw Stalin kill our best officers just before your master invaded us because of your tricks. Your human devil Heydrich made us think that half of the officers corps was in touch with your people. I saw my best friends go to the Lubyanka, and I was damn close to going myself."

"I have told you many times that I did not work on that project. Besides, why blame me? Our countries were enemies. Why not blame the English? They knew about it. Admiral Canaris told them. And they never told you," the German-accented man said.

"Canaris, that evil creature," the fat man said. "Is this all something he made up to keep Hitler from killing him?"

"It didn't keep Hitler from killing him," the thin man said.

"But the whole thing could be a trick. The whole thing could have been invented to make us provoke the Americans, who are crazy anyway, so much that they start a war, even though they would lose," Okhmansky said.

"If it's a trick, it's a trick that fooled me too," the thin man said heatedly. "If it's a trick and a ruse, it looks like it's a hell of a coincidence that it's all happening as the plan said it would."

Comrade General Codlitsk cut in. "It's not a trick. Something's happening. It's not up to us to fight the war again. It's up to us to stop the plan. How do we do it?"

Deputy Minister Korchov spoke. "I think taking the key people out of the picture is the best idea."

"It's a thought," Comrade General Codlitsk said. "They're old. No one would notice. It could be done."

"It could be done, but it would be wrong," Okhmansky said. "It would be wrong because it wouldn't work. Even if the top men were gone, the treaty would still go through the U.S. Senate, and the weapons would still wind up in German hands."

"I think that's right," the thin man with the tightly stretched skin said. "It has to be a little more subtle than that. In fact, it has to be a lot more subtle. Let's consider," he said, leaning back in his chair and looking around the room, "what our minimum goal should be and what our maximum goal should be."

Everyone in the room looked attentively at him. He's an animal, the fat man thought, but a smart animal.

"The minimum is to stop the treaty from going through the Senate. There is a maximum though, which is to make the treaty work for us."

"When you say 'us,' " the fat man asked, "do you

mean your SS friends in the *Kameradenwerke* or do you mean the Soviet Union?"

The thin man ignored the baiting. "I think there is a way to get it done so that our maximum is achieved as a possibility, and the minimum is achieved for almost a certainty."

"Well, don't keep it a secret," Comrade General Codlitsk said, *"Davaï!"*

"The problem is," the man with the German accent said, his eyes shifting back and forth in his skull, "that we don't know about Bickel. What was he doing in Bad Kreuznach? What do they have in mind for him? If it's what I think, he could be the key to everything. But we have to move fast," he said, his thin face starting to twitch. It had started twitching after the first month in the Lubyanka, in the fall of 1945, after he had been captured in Himmler's bunker and shipped to Moscow.

"We can move fast," the comrade general said. "You know that. But we must move in the right direction."

"The right direction, as far as I can see, is to find out as much as we can about Bickel. Not the standard stuff, but what they're doing with him now. How he is plugged in, or how he gets plugged in. That's what we need to know now."

"It can happen," the comrade general said. "I'll arrange it."

"After a few days, I think we can have a plan," the thin man with the sunken eyes and the German accent said.

"It had better not be a trick," Adjutant Okhmansky said. "It had better not be one of your goddamn tricks." There was an anger that bridged the decades in his voice.

"What more can you do?" the thin man said. "I'll die soon anyway. You all know that. I know that. What can you do that's worse than chemotherapy?"

"We might stop you from getting the chemotherapy," the fat man said. "That might be worse."

The thin man smiled wolfishly. "You think so? Only those who have not had treatment for cancer of the marrow think that the disease is worse than the cure."

"This is all beside the point," the comrade general said. "We have to organize our resources and then move them. It is a chess game once again."

"Unfortunately, in the chess that we learned, there never was a player who could buy the other players and make them work for him. That introduces a new element," the fat man said.

"We had better start with the girl," the thin man said.

"I don't think we have any choice," the comrade general said slowly. "It might take time to get someone else close to him, and now he'll be on the move for a while."

"Is she safe?" the fat man asked.

"Of course not," the comrade general said. "No one is safe. One takes risks, does one not?" He turned to the thin man across the table, as if looking for confirmation, then rose, ending the meeting. "Of course one must control the risks to the extent one can, is that no so, Herr Mueller?"

A slight flicker passed over the thin man's lips, and then disappeared. It could not exactly be called a smile, but then SS Obergruppenführer und General in der Waffen SS Heinrich Mueller, former *Befehlshaber und Chef* of the Gestapo, had little to smile about, and had never been a great one for smiling to begin with.

CHAPTER

8

As usual for Washington in January, the skies were leaden and heavy with sleet or snow. The trees around northern Virginia were bare—skeletons reaching up toward a gray nothing. The grass had turned a tan color, and only an occasional pine tree broke the dreary landscape with some greenery.

It's the same here as it is in Bonn, Travis Bickel thought as his limousine sped along the Dulles Airport Access Highway at an even eighty. His wife sat next to him without saying a word. She had had to be there at the airport to meet him, of course. There were photographers there. It would look unseemly if Lydia Bickel were not there to meet Travis Bickel, the returning hero of the German Rearmament Conference, the man who, Arthur Kosters had already told Martin Agronsky, was "as fine a negotiator as America has ever had, and that includes Arthur Kosters."

So Lydia had been there with a smile pasted on her face, and she had kissed him and she had looked pretty and alert, and she would look that way until they got home. Then she would take a drink and take the gloves off. She was angry—he could tell that. But what it was about would have to wait until they got home.

Across the passenger compartment, Alexandra Denman, Bickel's legislative assistant, sat on the gray felt jump seat. Every few seconds she handed him a neatly typed piece of paper, explaining each as she gave it to him. "Here's the L.A. *Times* take on what happened to Si. Might be worth a phone call from you to Tony Day at the edit page there," she said. Bickel scanned the page, then handed it back. She handed him another. "A fact sheet on the Sacramento River Delta water project. Might definitely generate some heat. I'd get wired as soon as possible on that one. I've got a briefing book at the office."

And so the ritual went on. Alex wore a dark mink coat, under which he could see her long, thin legs and the skirt of her sedate dress.

Alex always dressed like a banker. Bickel did not know why, but she once told him that she thought that was how a woman lawyer should dress, and that ended the discussion. Even when they were having the affair, Bickel had wondered where she got the money to get all her clothes. It certainly wasn't on her salary. She was supposed to have a sugar daddy somewhere, according to office gossip, but Alex said that was almost too funny for words. Her family had a little money, she said, and she just liked to spend it on clothes. It made sense to her and she didn't care what anyone else said.

Occasionally Bickel looked up from the briefing papers at Alex's face. She had fine, high cheekbones and a sloping nose that was slightly rounded at the bottom. Her eyes were obscured by large contact lenses, but her eyebrows were her finest feature—thin and gracefully arched, like the roof of a Saarinen building. Her lips were full, almost too full, but altogether, she looked wonderful. It made him wistful.

"Very major headache," Alex said in a businesslike way as she handed him another paper. "Gay rights again in Los Angeles. We are really getting badgered on this. I think you're going to have to do something eventually. It could become a national issue."

"I don't need to read this," Bickel said, barely glancing at the page. "I am against taking a stand for gays. Find out how Carter finessed that, and you issue a statement saying almost the same thing, but in my own words. Okay?"

Bickel still didn't know why the affair had ended two years ago. It had just stopped one day. But there never was a reason given, and Bickel needed Alexandra far too much as a friend to complain about her stopping being a lover. With Kart gone, Bickel needed her more than ever.

"Any word that Jaroslav wants a meeting down in Fresno?" Bickel asked. "I can't help thinking we should be lining up ethnics at home in California to work for me in the campaign."

Alex rummaged through her papers. "I've got something on that here," she said. "A letter for you to sign, arranging to see him in Fresno."

Lydia stared out the window. The limousine was crossing the Chain Bridge leading into Washington across the Potomac River.

Bickel read the letter to Mtislav Jaroslav, head of the Grape Growers Association, the farmers' organization for wine growers. It was perfect, as most of Alex's work was.

"And here's this one," Alex said as she handed a thick, cream-colored envelope to Bickel. "We had it fluoroscoped. It won't explode." She didn't smile when she said it.

"It looks like it's from the pope," Bickel said. "Who else would use this kind of stationery? It must cost a dollar a sheet."

Bickel ripped open the envelope. Inside was a piece of stationery about as thick as a slice of Pepperidge Farm bread. The sheet had no name at the top, simply the address, Room 4600, One Manhattan Guaranty Plaza. No city, no state.

In an impeccably neat row, typewritten characters marched across the page. "Mr. Elson Patterson earnestly requests that he be given the honor of having you to his house at 3132 Foxhall Road for dinner any time within the month of January at your convenience." It was signed Frank v. A. Roberts, "Personal Assistant to Mr. Patterson," and then there was a telephone number. Bickel read it twice and then handed it to Alex. She read it and gave a low whistle.

"Hey, hey, hey," she said. "Welcome to the world of the super rich."

Without a word, Lydia turned her head and stared at Alex. She smiled for about thirty seconds—an empty, bitter smile—and then said softly, "Could you please *try* to be quiet. I have a headache, dear." Then she turned back to face the window.

Alex was accustomed to dealing with difficult people. She was modestly famous for it. She could charm Strom Thurmond and George McGovern at the same lunch. She did exactly the right thing in this case, too. She ignored Lydia's comment.

"I don't know, Alex. Patterson. I just don't know," Bickel said. "Could it do me any good?"

"It could," Alex said. "It definitely could. He's got all these foundations studying everything under the sun. It might be good to get their studies before anyone else. It could give you an informed air." She giggled. "Not that you don't have it already."

"I agree," Bickel said. "But, there are a lot of people around who remember him sitting on the reviewing stand with Goering. And that won't do me any good."

"I know," Alex said.

Lydia turned around and said, directing her voice to a space midway between Bickel and Alexandra, "Nice people you hang around with, Travis." Then she turned again and looked out the window.

"She has a point," Bickel said. "Just how thoroughly has he cleaned up his act?"

"Pretty damn clean," Alex said. "The official version now is that he was just a youthful mountain climber who attracted the *Führer*'s attention because he was so athletic and so rich."

"That explains part of it," Bickel said. "It doesn't explain how Patterson could have been so stupid, if that's what it was."

"He's got an answer for that, too," Alex said. The limousine gathered speed as it went past a traffic blockage on Arizona Avenue. "He says it was before Hitler started killing everyone, and that a lot of people were taken in."

"But he didn't really ever come out against the Nazis, even like Lindbergh, did he?" Bickel asked.

"Not publicly," Alex answered. "I'm not sure I have all this right, but I think that he did a lot of work arranging munitions plant financing here in the U.S., and that took some of the onus off him. But he never said anything. There were even stories about mysterious disappearances during the war, presumably on secret missions."

"Jesus," Bickel said. "I think maybe he's someone I would just as soon not get close to."

"Well, but there's more," Alex said as the car drew to a stop at Nebraska Avenue. Out the window Bickel could see a large house that had a sign: KINGDOM HALL OF JEHOVAH'S WITNESSES. "After the war ended, there were a lot of stories that Patterson had been working for the Office of Naval Intelligence, that he had cozied up to the Nazis to get intelligence for us. You've heard about that."

"I guess I have," Bickel said.

"But then some Nazi bigwigs at a war crimes trial said that Patterson had been a U.S. spy, and that helped him a lot. So maybe he really is cleaner than you might think."

"Yeah, but I can get a bunch of graduate students to write articles and studies for me. I don't think I need to get the B'nai B'rith and the Jewish War Veterans mad at me for a few damn reports," Bickel said.

"He can do more than that, Travis," Alex said. "He's really wired in the banking world. He's wired with some of the more old-line journalistic people, the old hands in Washington that have gotten money from his foundations to go on first-class trips around the world."

"Dicey," Bickel said. "Definitely dicey. I'm doing pretty well right now. I don't know what good he would do. Tell him I'm too busy."

"I'd think about it," Alex remonstrated. "I'd give it a lot of thought. He can help you with press people who are down on you about the treaty. I don't know how much he can help, but he can help. I'd just think about it a little more."

Bickel stroked his chin, and his blue-gray eyes took on a dreamy look as he looked out at the elegant houses. "This is a good example of where Kart was so helpful. He could really have helped me with this. Not that you're not helpful. But you know, he had a sixth sense for this kind of thing."

Alex looked sad. "I know," she said softly. "I know. I just can't believe he's gone."

Had Alex and Simon been lovers? Was that it?

The limousine pulled into Bickel's modest home, set amid large homes, on Klingle Street. The driver carried in Bickel's luggage and then, when Travis and Lydia Bickel were inside the house, drove off with Alexandra Denman. She sat in the front seat.

As soon as the car pulled away, Lydia took off her coat and turned to face Bickel, her blue eyes blazing.

"That was very cute, Trav," she spat out. "Very cute indeed."

"What are you talking about?" Bickel asked, in genuine surprise. He had known she would be mad, but about what?

"Oh, you bastard. Going through that whole routine with Alex to show her how buddy-buddy you are, when you don't even talk to me, whom you haven't even seen for three weeks. I'm your wife, for Christ's sake," she shrieked.

"You could have talked," Bickel said. "You know you purposely stayed out of the conversation. You kept looking out the window."

"Why didn't you ask me how I'd been? Why didn't you talk about something I knew about, too? No, you can't do that. You have to show off with Alex Denman and make me think I'm stupid."

Bickel noticed that her face was beginning to sag badly. Too much drinking. He also noticed with some discomfort that she had a damn good point. He could have talked more to her. He should have talked more to her.

"I'm sorry," he said. "I'm really sorry. I should have done that. I'll be better now. I'm really sorry."

But Lydia was not appeased. "Oh, shit," she said. "That's easy for you to say now, when there aren't any other women around. But when some other girl gets around, you'll just start doing the same damn thing again. I know you will. How can you be so mean to me?"

"I'm sorry," Bickel said. "You know I didn't mean to be mean to you." It was a sign of how far apart they had grown that this conversation was happening at all. He had a fleeting and sweet remembrance of his last afternoon in Kathy Dorn's apartment, lying on the bed while snow fell outside the window.

"Well, it's not good enough to say you're sorry. I've been thinking a lot about us while you were gone and never called me," she said, pacing around the living room nervously.

"I called you on New Year's Eve," Bickel corrected her, "and at least ten other times." He noticed the newspapers piled in the corner, unopened.

"Sure, on New Year's Eve, when you were probably with some blond floozie and had a guilty conscience," Lydia Bickel said, throwing her hands up.

Well, she was partly right, Bickel thought. Still, he could not stand her shrieking. And what had she been thinking about?

"I've been thinking that you're the reason I drink too much," Lydia said. "I've been thinking that you're the reason I'm slowly going crazy. I've been thinking, Trav," and here her voice started to crack, "that we should get divorced." She looked down at the floor, then up at Bickel. Her eyes were ringed with moisture.

This was just what Bickel was afraid of. There had not been any divorced presidents, especially not any who had been divorced by such an uncontrollable woman as Lydia Bickel. On the other hand, she had a point. Maybe they should just do it and get it over with. Who was it who said that "Washington is full of successful men—and the women they married a long time ago?"

He had to stall for time. He needed someone like Kart to advise him.

"I don't know, Lydia. I know I haven't spent enough time with you. But this rearmament thing is very important."

"Goddammit, Travis, aren't I important?"

That was Lydia's last word as she walked up the stairs to her room. She would say she had a headache and close the door, and Travis would sleep in his study-bedroom.

Bickel slumped in a large green easy chair next to the fireplace. The room was a mess. Lydia probably had told the maid not to come while he was gone.

He sat by the cold and empty hearth for a long time. The sun went down slowly and the room was full of shadows and then dark. A whiff of memory of Katherine Dorn flew through his mind, and then was gone. No sense thinking about that. Now he was back with a pile of work and a furious wife. As usual.

And that was in addition to the fight upcoming on the Rearmament Treaty. He wished he had someone who could give him the right advice. He could not really depend on what the State Department told him about the reaction to the treaty back at home. If what Alex had said about Patterson was true, then maybe Bickel should see him. It could all be kept pretty quiet, even in 1983. There would be no pictures of Hitler and Patterson receiving the *"Heil"* on a balcony. Even if things were going as well as Kosters said, there was no such thing as being too careful. Every vote was important, and if Patterson could deliver more votes, that was important. Some might have called it gilding the lily, but a more sensible view was that it was making sure, getting all the ducks in a row.

He dialed the telephone next to the chair.

"Hello?" Alex Denman said.

"Hi, Alex, this is Travis. I want you to call Patterson or Robertson or whatever his name is and tell him I'll see him at the end of the week."

"Okay," Alex said. "I'll do it."

"Let's keep this closely held, okay?" Bickel said. "It won't hurt for it to be kept quiet, will it?"

"No, I think that's sensible," Alex said.

"Okay, Alex, thanks. Good night," Bickel said.

He hung up the phone and looked out the window at nothing in particular. Too much was happening. He needed time to sleep. He needed advice.

"Oh, for Christ's sake," he said to himself aloud. He had forgotten that, for a change, Arthur Kosters was back in Washington. Kosters was just the man to talk to.

If it weren't for Kosters, after all, Bickel would be just another handsome, solid-looking face in the United States Senate. Every four years, *Time* would trot out his picture and say that he was a possible dark horse candidate. He would make the rounds and give speeches every week to the Friends of the Earth or the Commonwealth Club. After a while, he would no longer be considered a dark horse contender because his youth and his flash would be gone. Then he would stay on in Washington and live it up in the prescribed Washington manner for a few more years, becoming a "powerful committee chairman," as the press liked to say. And then he would get beaten and would become the chairman of a do-good foundation and keep giving speeches and hoping that girls at junior colleges would flash their thighs at him. That would have been his destiny except for Kosters.

Kosters had picked him out at a meeting of the Quadripartite Commission when he was in his first term in the Senate. He still remembered what Kosters had first said to him. "Anyone who acts as naive as you do will make a fine presidential candidate. I will then teach you how to be president."

There was that familiar chubby smile when Kosters said that, but now, Bickel knew, that smile did not tell a thing, one way or the other.

Kosters had arranged for Bickel to be in on the *crème de la crème* of foreign policy events. Suddenly, when he had never even been asked to speak at the

Quadripartite Commission or the Council on Foreign Relations, he was giving the keynote speeches at the meetings, and they were being reprinted, word for word, in the New York *Times*.

Bickel knew that his strength had always been in putting together unlikely coalitions, and Kosters demonstrated an amazing ability to show just how far it could be taken on the national scale. In California, Bickel had united the industrialists, the environmentalists, and the San Joaquin Valley growers behind his program for massive federal aid for new water projects for "An Evergreen California." The San Francisco *Chronicle* said that it was impossible, but Bickel had seen that water was the one thing that could unite everyone in southern California and that southern California was where all the votes were. He had barely campaigned in northern California. Jerry Brown had called him an opportunist. Tom Hayden had called him a reactionary. But the votes poured in.

In the Senate, Bickel saw, far before most, that détente was dead and that defense was the key to keeping him in the Senate from southern California—home of Lockheed, Rockwell, McDonnell-Douglas, General Dynamics, and Litton, as well as the hundreds of thousands of voters who worked for them. So, when the other senators were whining about not offending Brezhnev, Bickel came out strong for every new strategic weapon. He took up Senator Jackson's mantle on defense, and Senator Jackson in return called Bickel "the best friend Israel ever had from the state of California."

With that endorsement, it was no problem for L. C. Dodge, from Mobil Oil, to start study committees that often made mass mailings of Bickel's pronouncements on how to solve the problems of oil shortage and pollution in America. Mobil, interestingly enough, often agreed. No one in the Fairfax district of Los Angeles was going to worry about Israel's best friend spending a lot of time with oilmen.

And that was where Kosters came in doubly handy. Because of Bickel's alliance with the California growers, he had never been close with the AFL–CIO. Kosters played golf with McMurray every other week. Kosters invited Bickel along. Kosters told McMurray that Bickel was the most concerned senator on the issues of the rights of the working man that he had ever known.

McMurray raised his eyebrows. "Will you be voting for repeal of 14–B then, lad?" McMurray asked.

"If it comes to the floor, you can count on my vote," Bickel said. A perfect answer. It had about as much chance of coming to the floor as a black man did of becoming head of the plumbers union.

McMurray liked the lad. So did Cardinal Spellacy, the *eminenza* of Boston. He could easily see why a man so dedicated to stopping Communism would be a force for Christianity. He could also see why opening the new Navy Yard in South Boston would give more work to the harps of that area than they had ever dreamed they would get. And it was Senator Bickel's filibuster that kept that base in the budget.

Kosters's leverage with the New York *Times* and with the media was still infuriatingly small, but he never seemed to worry about it, although Bickel did. "It will take care of itself," Kosters said sometimes. "On that score, you need not worry. It will be taken care of," he said at other times.

Kosters had other advice. "Just keep acting naive and outraged. Give 'em Jimmy Carter minus the phony smile and without the crazy look behind the eyes. We'll all keep count and there's plenty of time. But the treaty is the key."

Bickel took the advice he liked and chucked the advice he did not respect. He kept most of the advice in his head. And followed most of it. And he never missed a chance to talk to Kosters. So Kosters was his man now, after he spoke to Patterson. It could wait that long.

CHAPTER

9

A cold rain fell on Washington as Arthur Kosters looked out his window. The New Year was only five days old, but there were major problems already. Kosters could see the top of the Lincoln Memorial and out past it to Virginia across the Potomac River.

For Kosters, just exactly why Abraham Lincoln should be the greatest American hero was something of a mystery. Kosters believed in pragmatism, in real-world constraints. There was no place for idealism in his scheme of things. It was hard enough to keep the world running without people blowing it up. The intrusion of idealism was impossible.

If Kosters had been President of the United States in 1861, he would have seen things a lot more clearly. Slavery was an economically dying institution. Inventions that were already known would make the purchase of slaves and care of them economically unsuccessful. In time, perhaps only ten or fifteen years, slavery would have been dead of natural causes in the South. Lincoln should have just promised the Southerners that he would do nothing to legally endanger the "peculiar institution." There would have been no Fort Sumter, no War between the States, no six hundred thousand killed. It just didn't make sense for a President to start a bloody war without any cause but foolish idealism.

But Kosters kept thoughts like that to himself. In America, everyone professed allegiance to ideals, and he would too. That was one of the first things he had realized when he came to America as a teenager. You have to be different enough so that people think you're better, but not so different that people think that you're suspicious. For a smart fellow like Kosters, it had not been a problem.

The buzzer on his Call Director rang, and Kosters switched on the Speakerphone. "Yes, Liza," he said.

"It's 11:45, Mr. Secretary. Time for your meeting with the President. Your car is downstairs."

"Thank you, Liza," Kosters said.

As he rode down in the elevator which was for his use only, Kosters went through his points again. This was a crucial meeting for the Rearmament Treaty. Kosters knew that the President was not as strong on the issue as he should be. That was only natural. After all, the President was just a Midwestern senator, whom an untimely death had catapulted into the Oval Office. Naturally, he would not understand as sweeping and dramatic a plan, as bold a design, as the German Rearmament Treaty. That was only to be expected. That was what he had Kosters for—to explain the really big things and get him on track. If Kosters could get the President moving, then the problems, in the form of powerful Senate voices against the treaty, could be overcome. The President must be absolutely solid.

A few minutes later, Kosters tried to smooth out the rumples in his wool suit as he waited for the President to come into the First Family Dining Room on the second floor of the White House. Kosters saw that there were only two places set, and that was as it should be. No one should come between the President and his secretary of state on a major issue like this.

"Hi, Art. How's the boy?" the President said, as he

strode in.

"I am fine, Mr. President. How are you?" Kosters replied, giving a tiny bow as he shook hands with the President, who towered above him.

He looks like a grown-up surfer, Kosters thought. He has that same guileless face and smooth complexion. He's lucky he has me around.

"I couldn't be better, Arthur, couldn't be better if I were twins. Have the stewards told you what we're having today?" the President asked.

"No, Mr. President, they haven't. But, I'm sure you could get whatever you want."

"No," the President said, waving his hands deprecatingly in front of himself, "I don't want to cause anyone any trouble. I'll just have whatever they're serving."

Well, you're causing me plenty of trouble, Kosters said to himself.

Aloud, he said, "How is your wife? I hope she is feeling better."

"Sure thing," the President said, sitting down and looking around the room as if he had never been there before. "Doctor says the treatments are working and she'll be up and about in no time. She's feeling just fine."

"That is very good news, Mr. President," Kosters said.

"You notice how much rain everybody's been getting this winter, Arthur?" the President asked.

"Yes, I have, Mr. President. I certainly have. I suppose it makes the farmers happy."

"It sure does, Arthur. It sure does." The President looked up as the steward brought in two bowls of consommé. Then he looked down in front of him as the soup steamed up around his face.

Kosters looked around and took a mental inventory. Across from him, the President of the United States wore, if Kosters could believe his eyes, a doubleknit leisure suit of a light blue. Light blue, indeed, seemed to be the color of the meal. The room was painted a light blue of an unusual slickness, so that it looked almost like the hyperrealistic paintings that Kosters so detested.

A white molding with some carving ran around the floor and ceiling, and also around the room about four feet off the floor.

Antique furniture of extraordinary beauty sat in various corners of the room. Across from Kosters, behind the President, was a magnificent cherrywood breakfront cabinet. Inside it were pewter antiques, some by Paul Revere. There were plates, saucers, and pitchers. The wood gleamed like the walls, but in this case, the shine did not offend Kosters's sensibility.

To Kosters's right was another cherrywood cabinet, this one without glass. On top were more antiques, fine old china with patterns Kosters could not make out at that distance.

Above the cabinet was a large portrait of a scowling James Monroe. He looked as if he were ready at any minute to blow the hell out of anyone caught fooling around with South America.

Except for the President, Kosters thought, and that damned wall paint, the room is extraordinarily impressive.

The soup was served in a light blue bowl, which sounded as if it was china, and probably was, but to Kosters it looked like Melmac. Kosters made a note that it was absolutely appropriate that this President should have fine china that looked like Melmac. Even the White House insignia, the angry eagles with the arrows and the olive branches, looked too much like decals for comfort. Kosters knew they weren't decals, but they shouldn't even have looked like decals. While Kosters was thus making an inventory and deciding that his friends from the university could certainly give a needed lesson in elegance to the President, the Chief Magistrate stopped slurping his soup long enough to comment again on the weather.

"I understand it's mighty dry out there in California again. I hope something happens there. We don't want those people to blow away."

He's not this dumb. He's getting ready for something, Kosters thought.

The President looked up at Kosters, who was just

starting to eat his own soup. "You know, Arthur, you mentioned farmers. And that makes me want to ask you something."

"Certainly, Mr. President." Kosters met the President's gaze.

"Well, Arthur, here's the question. A lot of people are asking this question, and I just don't know how to answer it. They're asking why we sell so much food to the Russians if the Russians are so dangerous that we have to give the Germans nuclear weapons. Now, Arthur, I know you have an answer to that, but on the surface, at least, that's a pretty good question."

"Yes, it is, Mr. President," Kosters said, laying down his spoon. "May I try to answer it?"

"I wish you would, Arthur. I know we've been over this before, but I'd just like to hear it again."

"Mr. President, the short answer is that the wheat is not important and arming the West Germans is. Now let me break that down. Let me unpack what I mean by that," Kosters said.

"Sure thing," the President said. "You don't mind if I keep eating this soup, do you?"

This President was not so dumb at all, Kosters thought. Not so dumb at all.

"Of course, Mr. President. Please continue," Kosters said. "Now, we sell a lot of wheat to the Russians. That's true. They pay us cash for it. Our farmers like the money a lot. It raises prices throughout the whole agricultural sector. You bet the farmers like it."

The President smiled at him sarcastically. "I know that, Arthur. I wasn't asking if farmers liked to get good prices for their crops."

Kosters flushed. "Please forgive me, Mr. President. If I may continue, let me say that the Russians also like being able to buy the wheat. But here's something key. The Russians would not starve without the wheat. Not by a long shot. They wouldn't have the amount of meat they'd like to have, but they wouldn't starve either. They'd eat more bread and less meat. That's all."

The President looked up. His soup was finished, and he waited for the steward to bring in the next course. It was extremely quiet in the room, even though all the traffic on Pennsylvania Avenue was not far away.

"On the other hand, if we stopped selling the wheat, a lot of things would happen," Kosters continued. "First, our own farmers would be angry. Russian sales are only a small part of the market, but they make a difference. So we'd have the farmers mad at us.

"And then, the Russians would be mad at us. They wouldn't be mad enough to go to war, because, as I said, the amount of wheat we sell them just isn't that important. But still, they would be mad, and with conditions the way they are, that wouldn't help things a bit."

Another steward entered the room. He wheeled a serving cart with the main course, beef stroganoff, in a large light blue bowl with the Presidential seal, and the other parts of the meal—noodles, zucchini, and salad—in smaller bowls. Silently, he served the President and the secretary of state. When the steward left, the President picked up a forkful of stroganoff and said, while chewing, "Well, go on, Arthur. Let's have the big picture, about the Germans and so forth."

Kosters was hungry, but he wanted to explain it all at once. While the President chewed, he spoke.

"The world situation has changed a lot since the mid-seventies, Mr. President. At that time, the Soviets were making a major effort in Africa and the Middle East. It looked as if things were running their way, in Africa especially. But when he came out with our new policy of supporting the white regime in South Africa, things changed."

The President continued to chew. Kosters wondered if he should take a bite of the stroganoff. He decided not to. It was more important to talk now. He could eat later.

"The black African countries realized that the Soviets weren't going to be able to do a goddamn thing against South Africa as long as we helped the whites. People thought that would hurt us, but it hurt the Russians. They lost face all over. The blacks aren't different from anyone else. They respect strength."

"Umm," the President said. "That was a lucky gamble, Art. Damned lucky."

"It wasn't luck, if I may say so, Mr. President. We had thought about it a lot."

"Of course, you did, Arthur. Of course." The President looked at Kosters. "Say, you haven't eaten a thing. You better eat or it'll get cold." The President smiled a big smile.

He's trying to humiliate me, Kosters thought. He's eating while I have to perform. He's doing it on purpose. But I will not get mad. He's not an educated man, not a statesman. What can I expect?

"I'll eat in a minute, Mr. President. Anyway, so pretty soon, the Angolans kicked the Cubans the hell out, and Guinea did the same thing, and there it was. One day the Russians were all gone."

"That was a great achievement, Arthur. No one doubts it. But you'd better eat something or you'll starve, and then you won't be much good," the President said.

Kosters obligingly took a forkful of stroganoff off his light blue plate. At least the silver was good and heavy. I will eat the rest later, he said to himself. This is more important.

"You know, Arthur, a lot of people think I'm dumb," the President said, "and maybe I am. But I'm not so dumb that I don't know that if there's any trouble about this German rearmament I'm up shit's creek without a paddle. So before we go balls out to get it ratified, I've got to know it's right. So let's get on to that. I know about the other stuff. Nobody gives a shit about Angola anymore. They care like hell about Germany."

Kosters swallowed. He was not going to be rushed by this person in a doubleknit suit. Foreign policy was not like bowling. You could not just consider it line by line. The whole structure had to be examined. If this President could not see that, it was even more important for Kosters to see it. It was lucky that there were young men like Travis Bickel coming up to take over.

"Mr. President, you cannot look at one piece without also looking at the others. It is all connected. Let me move on to the Middle East. There, we basically had two problems—the Palestinians and the Syrians. The Palestinians were trying to upset every possible move toward peace, and the Syrians were trying to become the leading Arab militants."

"I know all that, Arthur," the President said, folding a large piece of lettuce into his mouth and chewing loudly.

"But it is all related, Mr. President. All related. You cannot understand one part of it without the other." Kosters sucked in air. That might have been too strong. Perhaps he should not have said "understand." It implied that the President had trouble comprehending difficult things. But the President ignored it.

Kosters continued. "The Lebanese civil war was going on. Big things were afoot, if we could only see our way to do the right thing, the intelligent thing. That was the beginning of Operation Elimination."

"Hmmm," the President said. "Hmmm."

How much of that does he know? Kosters wondered. I do not want to get him excited. On the other hand, I do not want to tell him less than he knows. Then he'll think I'm lying. Kosters pondered. The President surely did not know about the trades which led to the assassination of Muammar el-Qaddafi of Libya. He would keep that buttoned down.

"You know all about that plan, Mr. President. The Syrians became paranoid about the intentions of the Palestinians toward their own country. They saw plots to kill Assad everywhere." Small wonder, Kosters thought, since we planted them everywhere.

"So," Kosters continued, "we got to a point where we could recommend to the Syrians, as a third, or perhaps a fourth, party, that they join with the Israelis to eliminate all of the Palestinian terrorist and political infrastructure. The Israelis and the Syrians pulled it off together. After about a month, there was no more Palestinian movement."

"And that led to the Cairo Pact?" the President asked. His tone was friendlier. That had happened in his term.

Kosters beamed. He was getting somewhere now. He was definitely getting somewhere. He could tell that the President was more interested.

"Exactly, Mr. President," Kosters said. "Once the Palestinians were exposed as troublemakers and off the scene, the problems with the Arab countries and Israel got to be manageable. The Saudis were tired of spending their money for arms that got ruined because no one knew how to take care of them. And the Egyptians were eager to get off the ground industrially. So, we were able to have the Treaty of Cairo, ending the state of war between Israel and the Arabs, except for Iraq, and they're crazy anyway."

"It was a nice stroke, Arthur, a damn nice stroke. It really took the wind out of the Russians' sails."

That was better. That was much better. Kosters didn't need the food that much. Frankly, he preferred an intelligent understanding of how difficult his tasks had been, and how well he had succeeded at them.

Apparently the President had gotten over the indisposition which had blocked that insight, because now he smiled broadly at Kosters, pointed his fork at him, and said, "Now what about the Red Chinese, Arthur? Why aren't we supposed to be worried about them?"

Kosters in turn smiled broadly at the President and folded his arms in front of him, as he used to do when he was a professor at Stanford.

"Two events came together to help us there, Mr. President. First," he said, raising his index finger, "Mao Tse-tung died. It was no surprise, but still it happened and the Chinese were not prepared for it. There has been turmoil in that country ever since. You get most of it in your CIA briefings. We don't want to bore you with all the details."

The President nodded. As he did so, he knocked a noodle onto his lap. He carefully picked it up, then put it on his plate. Then he dipped his napkin into a glass of water and rubbed at the spot on his leisure jacket.

"They say that cold water gets out spots better than hot water. Did you know that, Art?"

Kosters could hardly believe his eyes. Americans

were incredible. The President of the United States was giving a little homily on spot removing? Best to ignore that, too.

"Second," Kosters said, holding up the index and middle fingers of his right hand, "the Chinese acquired the capacity to deliver nuclear weapons into the Soviet Union. They had small rockets, but they weren't able to build small enough warheads. Once again, if you don't mind, I won't bore you with the details of that breakthrough."

The President continued to munch on his salad. That was a relief. Kosters was not sure how much the President knew about the help Kosters had arranged for them to be given in miniaturizing nuclear warheads. That act, which had unquestionably preserved the entire world balance of power, might have been construed by some as requiring some kind of presidential or Congressional action. Ridiculous. Kosters knew that if a brilliant mind is not free to do what is best without shackles, then of what use is a brilliant mind?

In the middle of a mouthful of cucumbers, the President looked up. "That was how the Chinese were able to keep the Soviets from attacking while they were divided, huh, Art?"

Kosters knew that this was the President's dumb act. What was he doing? Was he telling Kosters that he knew something? Was he trying to hold something over Koster's head? What had all that chewing and that innocent look meant?

Best to press on. If the President knew something, let him come out and say it. Even the President would have a damn hard time finding Koster's trail on that Chinese thing. A damn hard time.

"Exactly, Mr. President. Exactly. It was the sudden deployment of about twenty of the missiles with the new warheads that actually tipped the balance while the Soviets were massing troops in Siberia."

"A by-God lucky thing," the President said. "Just the most amazing, lucky thing ever, huh, Art?"

That settled it. The President did know something. But if he knew, why hadn't he done anything about it?

Of course. This was just the President's way of telling him that everything is in the family. Foolish to worry about it.

"Quite right, Mr. President. So now the Soviet Union is checkmated in Africa, in the Middle East, and in Asia."

"Damn nice work, Arthur. Historic, I'd say," the President pronounced, as he probed at a piece of chocolate cream pie.

"Well, you and your predecessor were invaluable in helping, uhh, in guiding the nation on its course," Kosters said genially.

"Well, that's nice of you," the President said, putting the piece of pie in his mouth.

Was he being sarcastic? How should Kosters take that? Once again, best not to give any provocation.

"Meanwhile, the Soviets had, for a variety of reasons, assembled an enormous army and navy, and a strategic armory that, frankly, was bigger, and better than ours. They had always thought that they should have control over Western Europe, and NATO was getting weaker all the time."

The President looked up. "Not my fault," he said, his mouth full of chocolate. "I always voted for a strong defense. I hope people know that."

"Of course. They do, and I do," Kosters said soothingly.

"So the thought came to them, that if they were sufficiently daring, they could just reach out and have all of Western Europe in one big swoop. They thought that if they moved, they would have a conventional war on their hands, but that we would not use nuclear weapons against them. Maybe tactical nuclear weapons, but probably not even those."

"Goddammit if they weren't right," the President said. "At least, I think they were right. This goddamn Congress doesn't have two balls between both Houses."

"You may well be right, Mr. President. At any rate, we got wind of their discussions while they were still preliminary. We knew that for an operation of that size, they would have to prepare for about nine months, maybe more. But also, maybe less."

Now Kosters folded his arms in front of him again, like a professor. "So our problem was how to make sure the Russians didn't make a move in Western Europe. They weren't scared of the Europeans. And they were pretty sure that the French and the British wouldn't use nuclear weapons. So were we. But the Germans scared hell out of the Russians."

"Christ, they scare me, too," the President said. "Although I guess they've calmed down."

Was this a new problem? Was the President going back on his support for the treaty? What had that meant? Kosters felt an alarm.

Kosters put on his most serious look. "Mr. President, if they scare anyone, or if they should scare anyone, it should be me, a Jewish refugee from the Nazis. But they are no more Nazis today than Jimmy Carter was a slaveholder. The Germans are our most valuable asset at this point. The government is strong and stable. The people are comfortable with a free society, and they are damned hardworking, impressive people."

The President took a sip of the Coca-Cola that sat in front of him. He always drank Coke instead of coffee. Another American habit that amazed Kosters.

"Just one second," the President said. "Let's back up for just a moment." The President stared hard at Kosters. "How did we get absolutely certain information that the Russians were planning an invasion of Western Europe?"

Kosters frowned. Now what? Was this the beginning of a new gambit?

"Some very fine work by the CIA in intercepting radio transmissions, plus the work of people we have inside the Kremlin. Probably our greatest intelligence coup ever," Kosters said.

"Okay. Now go ahead," the President said.

"At that point, when we knew the Russians were gearing up, we decided that rearming the West Germans with nuclear weapons was our best hope. It would deter the Russians, and it would put the final cap on the bottle."

The President didn't say anything for a minute, then he glanced at Koster's plate, which was virtually untouched. "You know, you haven't eaten a thing. Do you want me to get the stewards to get you something else?"

"No, thank you. It's more important to go over this carefully," Kosters said. "I'm watching my weight anyway."

"Well, suit yourself," the President said.

"Now that we have begun the process of rearming the West Germans, it is of paramount importance that we go ahead quickly. The Russians are scared, and if we give them a chance, like a year's delay, they'll be able to move. We have them where we want them now, and we must not let them pick up the initiative. That's why we have to get the treaty through Congress and get the weapons to them as soon as we can." Kosters paused for emphasis. "That's why your personal leadership on this is crucial. We cannot let it drag on forever in the Congress. And it would be catastrophic if we lost. The Russians would take it as an invitation to invade Western Europe."

The President wiped his mouth with a napkin on which was the Presidential seal. "I can see what you mean, Arthur. There'll be some opposition, but I think we can make it happen."

"We have to," Kosters said.

"There's already ten, maybe twenty, no not that many, maybe twelve votes against it that we won't be able to change. But I think we can work on it, and get it done within a month. Now, I want you and your people at State to start having briefing sessions with every single senator. Even the ones who're opposed. Get Bickel to help you. Meanwhile, I'll get my liaison staff to bring me in on the wavering cases. And then I'm going to make a nationally televised speech about it. I'm going to write it myself."

Oh, God. I'd better get involved in that, Kosters thought. His own speeches were not great, but the President's were deadly boring.

"Fine, Mr. President. I would be delighted to have my people help you with it, but, of course, the final words should be yours."

"Art, this has been very helpful. It may not seem to you that I was paying attention, but I was. I definitely was. And I think that this whole thing will sail through the Congress. There'll be opposition, but we'll win. And, Arthur, I am, as always, deeply grateful to have a Secretary of State who understands the world as well as you do."

Kosters made a short bow from the waist at his seat. He had worried for nothing. The President was hugely powerful in that Congress, and he could get the treaty through. There was nothing to worry about now. His, Kosters's, greatest mission was about to be realized. It was difficult to have such awesome responsibility, but Kosters accepted it as his duty. Duty, after all, was above everything else.

The President took a sip of his Coca-Cola and looked at Kosters's face carefully. It's just a mask. Everything about him is a mask the President thought. Jesus Christ, it's lucky that Arthur Kosters is on our side. Lucky that this particular Jew made it out and wound up here. Damn lucky. It wouldn't be good to have Kosters on the other side. But the President had him by the balls on that Chinese warhead deal. It was a good thing, because in two years, it would be no surprise to see Kosters playing up to the Republicans if the German rearmament didn't work and blaming it all on the President.

The President was damn glad he had friends besides Kosters. To depend on Kosters was a little too risky for him. Kosters was already maneuvering to get his boy, Bickel, into the white House when the President left. The President was a fatalist. If the EMI scanner was right, he would be dead by then anyway. At least then he wouldn't have to worry about any of this crap.

CHAPTER

10

Elson Patterson's house on Foxhall Road in Washington, D.C., had once been the residence of the Belgian ambassador. It resembled a Belgian country estate, with its stone face and mansard roof. Delicately shuttered windows and an enormous wooden door marked the front of the residence, which could barely be seen, at the end of a long gravel driveway, from Foxhall Road.

At the back of the house, the appearance was quite different. The walls of the first floor had been replaced by thick glass windows, which overlooked a small park. It was fairly easy to tell that the windows were thick, but only an expert could tell that they were laminated Plexiglas, strong enough to deflect a .50-caliber shell.

Inside the residence, the thick windows ran from the living room to the gallery to the dining room. In that room, paneled with walnut, hung portraits of Elson Patterson's forebears, including Horace D. Patterson, the one who had made all the money.

At a long teak table sat three men. At the head of the table, the lean figure of Elson Patterson, elegant in a

custom-tailored dinner jacket, his blue eyes sparkling
from the subdued light of the room. Across the table
was the younger Travis Bickel, in a far-from-elegant
dinner jacket; his wife had promised to have it pressed
but had neglected to do so, because, so she said, "What
the hell have you done for me lately?"

In the center of the table, his back to the windows
facing the park, was Frank van Allen Roberts, who
looked ill at ease. His dinner jacket was from J. Press,
and while it certainly looked better than Bickel's, it was
clearly not as fine as Patterson's. It was a lot better than
what anyone else from his high school class in Mineola
would have, though, that was for sure.

"Now, you must understand this, Travis," Patterson
said, as a maid entered the room to take away the remnants of veal in cream sauce. "Young, hot-shot senators
come and go. In this town, they come and go. I've seen
a lot of them. Like new Redskin halfbacks. They're hot;
then they're nothing." He shot a look over at Roberts.
"But Frank thinks I'm wrong. Am I wrong, Frank?"

Roberts, who said nothing until spoken to, answered,
"No, you're completely right, Mr. Patterson," and
smiled.

Patterson looked back over at Bickel and asked, "Do
you think I'm wrong, Senator?"

Bickel nodded at Patterson. "No, Mr. Patterson, I
think that's about right."

Patterson beamed. "Now, you're different, Senator.
You're definitely different. That's why you're so important. Because you're different."

Patterson paused and beckoned to the maid, who
stood in the corner. When the young black woman approached the table, Patterson turned to Bickel and
asked, "Now what does a young man like you like for
dessert? I know Frank here always likes to have something with chocolate in it. That's his sweet tooth," Patterson said. In his Jewish head, he added mentally. "But
what would you like?"

Bickel started to speak, and Patterson cut him off.
"We have everything here. I don't believe in being a

sybarite, but I think good food is important. A lot of people who were extremely ascetic in every other way appreciated good food. It's like appreciating good wine or fine art." Why had he been a vegetarian? He always meant to ask him why he would wear leather shoes but not eat meat. It was certainly too late to ask now.

Bickel said, "Do you have any fresh fruit?"

"We do, Senator, but I'll tell you what. I'd like for you to try my canned pears. That's right, I said canned. But they're from my own farm in Washington state, and they're canned just for me, and if you don't like them, you can have strawberries or grapes or anything else you want. But the pears are damned good. That makes sense, doesn't it?"

"Yes, that would be fine," Bickel said.

"How about you, Frank? You still want something with chocolate?"

"No, Mr. Patterson, I'll try the pears too, if that's all right."

"Fine. Linda, that'll mean all three of us will have pears," Patterson said to the maid. She nodded and walked from the room.

"I was just saying," Patterson picked up, "that fresh, young senators are a dime a dozen. Exactly. A dime a dozen. They come, they go. Someone says they're hot stuff and then they sink into obscurity."

Bickel glanced at the grandfather—Horace—in the portrait. He did not look like he would put up with any nonsense.

"But, I just have the feeling that you're different. And I'll tell you why," Patterson continued. "I have a lot of people working for me on foreign-policy issues. I believe that's my debt to this country, to use some of the money I have to help the people of America understand the vital issues of the day. I think I owe that to America. Or is that wrong? I might be all wrong. Maybe I should use it for wild parties. Senator Bickel thinks I'm wrong. Why am I wrong, Senator?"

What the hell was he talking about? Was it about being different or giving money away? Bickel was becoming confused.

"No, I think you're right, Mr. Patterson," Bickel said.

"You do? Why?" Patterson asked.

"I think you're right in thinking that a man of great wealth owes something to his country," Bickel said. He hoped that was what they were talking about.

Apparently it was, because Patterson said, "I'm glad you agree. Now I have a lot of people studying the foreign policy of this country, and they pretty much all tell me the same thing. They say that the way you handled yourself during the Rearmament Treaty negotiations was superb. To a man, they all said that." He shot a look over at Roberts. "Am I making a mistake, Frank?"

"No, Mr. Patterson, you're right. That's what they all say." Roberts put on his best Hasty Pudding earnest look.

Patterson snapped back to Bickel. "You see, what we have now in this country is a lot of publicity hounds. The Senate is full of them. That is not what this country needs right now. What we need right now is men of serious purpose, to try to size up what America should be doing and then work on getting it done. Not talk about it, do it. You understand the difference?"

He didn't wait for Bickel to answer. "Of course, you understand. I wouldn't have you here if you didn't understand. You know what work is. That's rare. And that's why you're not just another one of those flash-in-the-pan senators, in my opinion. That's why you'll go somewhere."

What I would give to be able to tell this young man the story of another young man who really knew what it was like to work and sacrifice for his country. But he isn't ready for that. Not yet, Patterson thought.

Linda came in with a tray of desserts. There were three silver bowls; in each were four half-pears. Patterson watched expectantly while Bickel and Roberts tried theirs.

Bickel knew he was being watched. "They're very good," he said. "Very good."

"Frank doesn't agree with you. You'd rather have chocolate, wouldn't you, Frank?" Patterson asked.

"No, Mr. Patterson," Roberts said. "This is excellent."

"Good," Patterson said, and started eating his pears. He remembered when he had had these same pears packed in dry ice and shipped all the way to Rastenburg. He had gotten a handwritten note. Of course, he still had the note.

As he ate, Bickel thought that, except for certain eccentric speech patterns, Elson Patterson was not unusual at all. He was concerned about the future of America, and he was wealthy and lived well.

If he were a Nazi, there was certainly no sign of it. That must have been a long time in the past. It was incredible, though, what Roberts let him get away with. Undoubtedly, Roberts was very well paid for allowing it to happen.

"Do you like the pears, Senator?" Patterson asked.

Jesus Christ, he just asked me if I liked the pears a minute ago.

"Yes, they're very good, Mr. Patterson," Bickel said.

"But Frank doesn't like them. He'd rather have a Hershey bar or something."

"No, Mr. Patterson, I like them very much." Look of good-natured butt of joke.

Patterson looked pleased.

"Now, let me ask you this, Senator. How many votes are there against the Rearmament Treaty right now? Do you have that in your head?"

Bickel thought for a moment. He had it in his head, but it was supposed to be confidential. Well, Patterson wouldn't tell anyone.

"I would say eleven, right now. No more than that. Not rock solid," Bickel looked at Patterson.

"What do you say, Frank? What does our institute say?" Patterson asked Roberts.

Roberts looked more composed then he had been all evening. Now he was coming into his own. "We show twelve, Mr. Patterson. I know where Senator Bickel's count comes from, but I think we've got to add Bartley, from Iowa."

Bickel turned to him. "Why do you add Bartley?"

"Because our records of his statements show that at a high school commencement address last June, when he was asked about the possibility, he said he was opposed, and we find no record of his having changed his mind," Roberts said with dry precision.

Jesus H. Christ! How the hell do they know that? The goddamn White House Congressional liaison doesn't have that kind of material. Bickel was amazed.

"How do you know about that graduation speech?" Bickel asked.

"Just our standard record-keeping procedure," Roberts said flatly.

"Which institute is that, Frank?" Patterson asked.

"The Institute for Contemporary Political Research," Roberts said. "Over on P Street."

"I think it's my duty to collect this kind of information so that people can be better informed," Patterson said. He flicked a look at Bickel. "But you don't agree, Senator?"

"I don't know," Bickel said. "Who gets informed? Is the information on display?"

"Oh, no," Patterson said with a slight chuckle. "This isn't the kind of information we think that the general public would be interested in. Not at all. It's for me, and the people I think need to have it." Patterson smiled at him. "Is that wrong? For a private citizen to know what the elected officials of his government are like? What kind of men they are?"

Is he trying to tell me something? What does he know about Katherine Dorn? About Alex? Is that what's going on here?

Bickel said carefully, "No, it's not wrong. But a lot of people might wonder why one person needs that much information."

Roberts shot a glance at his watch, cleared his throat and said, barely above a mumble, "I'm sorry, Mr. Patterson. Senator Bickel. I have something I must work on. I'm sorry." He got up and walked rapidly out the door.

Bickel was surprised he didn't kiss Patterson's ring.

"He's a fine fellow, a hard worker, good family man.

An invaluable assistant to me. Unfortunately, he works too hard," Patterson said, as Roberts walked out.

"He seems to be very dedicated to you, Mr. Patterson," Bickel said. Maybe it was time for him to leave too.

"I'd like it very much if you called me Elson," Patterson said. "I'd like that very much."

"Of course," Bickel replied. "And you call me Travis." It sounded like a joke.

"You know, I'd like to go back to what you were saying, about that information being for me alone. Not true," he said, wagging his finger and shaking his head. "I said it was for me and people who needed to see it. Do you understand the difference?"

"I'm not sure," Bickel said. His blue-gray eyes stared at the basilisk eyes of Patterson. What the hell was going on?

"Well, let me give you an example. I'm very committed to the Rearmament Treaty. Of course, I'm not claiming that I'm doing any more than my duty as an American. That's all. Just my duty as an American. It's our government's policy, and I'm committed to it. I know you are, too. But you don't agree with me? Tell me where I'm wrong."

"I *do* agree with you," Bickel insisted. "I do agree. Just take it as a fact—I agree with you wholeheartedly." What was he doing? He had negotiated the treaty and he was explaining that he was for it.

"That's good, Travis," Patterson said. "Now, since you and I share that viewpoint, I think you are a person who needs to be able to use the files of the Institute for Contemporary Political Research." He smiled at Bickel. "Or am I wrong?"

It was rapidly becoming clear. Bickel looked out the window at the quiet winter woods. As he did, Patterson looked out the window too. Then they both looked back across the table at each other.

"No, Elson," Bickel said, "you're not wrong."

"And not only that, Travis," Patterson said. "Not only that. I think we've got to make sure that not only do you know other men's views, but also that they know your views. I think that's vital." He paused and looked around the room, as if appealing to a ghostly presence of an ancestor for confirmation. "Maybe I'm wrong though. Maybe it's not vital at all."

"No, no," Bickel said, knowingly picking up the bait. "I agree that it's vital."

Patterson started off on a monologue. "I know a few people. University men. Men from some of the few newspapers that deserve to be called newspapers. Some of those people on TV. You know, Travis," he said, in a confidential tone, "they need to hear about you."

"That would be kind, Elson," Bickel said.

"I don't know what ambitions you have beyond the Senate, if any," Patterson said. "I really don't know. But I know that whatever you have in mind, people should know where you stand. Or is that wrong?"

"No," Bickel said. "You're absolutely right."

Patterson kept talking about power and responsibility going hand in hand, but Bickel was not listening. He had heard what he had come to hear. Patterson was going to reach out to give him the extra visibility, the extra exposure to key people. Maybe it was gilding the lily, but it was right. Media—there was his key weakness—and Patterson said he could take care of it. It was a godsend. Yet he tried to show no emotion. It was never good to be too eager.

Kart used to say that whatever worries they had on this or that issue, if the treaty went over, Bickel basically had it sewed up. That was Kosters's message, too. Then why did Bickel feel a new thrill? He felt it because he knew that having an influential man like Patterson pulling strings with an unseen hand would be more than enough. It would be locked up. He could taste it. Getting into bed with Patterson was a small price to pay for making the 1984 convention a locked-up affair.

He felt a thrill like the thrill he felt when he knew he was going to have a woman. It was the thrill of success, of conquest, of certainty.

Suddenly Bickel felt an urge for Katherine Dorn that was almost painful.

An hour later, Bickel and Patterson sipped brandy in Patterson's gallery, a medium-sized room, thickly carpeted and lined on two sides with books and on one side with a solid wall of bookshelves that held innumerable framed photographs. The other wall was a sheet of sliding glass.

Unlike the dining room, the gallery was furnished with modern and extremely tasteful furniture. Even Bickel, who knew next to nothing about furniture, guessed that the furniture in the gallery must have been custom made. In the middle of the room was a fireplace without any walls. For a moment it was a shock to see a fire blazing in the center of the room, then after a short while, the fire made the room almost preternaturally peaceful and warm.

Bickel and Patterson sat in two modern high-back chairs facing the fire and the window. The room was quite dark. Only a few lights in the park and the light of the fire lit the room. Between Bickel and Patterson was a table on which there was a variety of brandies and liqueurs. Each man held a snifter in his hand. Each had filled and drained the snifter many times.

"Take my word for it, Travis, the Rearmament Treaty marks the comeback of the West. Nothing less than that. Or am I wrong?" Patterson asked.

Bickel did not even answer, except to say, "Uh-huh."

Patterson stared out at the fire and the woods and thought where he had heard the words he had just uttered once before. It was at Berchtesgaden, of course. That was, when? Back in '34. That early, he was planning for the conflict between East and West. And people had been so blind. How could they have been so blind? Stalin was killing people by the millions and no one said a word, and a few people, not even Jews, got shot in Germany, and everyone was raising hell. He expected it. He told Patterson that he expected it. Patterson felt tired and sleepy.

"I wonder," Bickel said, "I wonder if the Germans really can be trusted with the bomb. I wonder."

"That's a good question, Travis. A good question. I think they can," Patterson said. This was a new turn to the conversation, but Bickel was a good man. He was not tricking him. Besides, what was there to be tricked out of at this point?

"I think they can, too," Bickel said. "But frankly, you know them better than I do."

"That's true," Patterson said, without missing a beat. "That's absolutely true. I *do* know them. I make no apologies for it."

Bickel did not say anything.

"You want to know about them?"

"Yes," Bickel said.

"A remarkable people. With the right leadership, they can do anything. Absolutely anything." He paused. "Unfortunately, that includes bad things as well as good things. What they did to the Jews was unpardonable. Absolutely horrible. You agree?"

Do I agree? Is he crazy? Bickel thought who on earth would not agree?

"Of course, I agree," Bickel said. "Who the hell wouldn't agree?" Good to show some outrage. Naivete and outrage. That would do it.

"Some people wouldn't. Some of the swine who did it are still alive, and they wouldn't agree. No, no. They wouldn't agree."

That was a relief. Bickel felt as if he were still among the sane. He paused for a moment and then asked, "What's to keep some people like that from popping up again?"

"That's a problem, of course. But on the other hand, what's to keep them from popping up anywhere? What's to keep them from popping up here?" Patterson's voice was slurred from fatigue.

"A free people," Bickel said.

"Yes," Patterson said, "and good leaders."

"Do the Germans have good leaders now?" Bickel asked. "They seemed very solid to me."

Solid. Poor boy. You should have known him. That was *solid*. Patterson smiled to himself.

"They have good leaders, and they are strong," Patterson said, "but they lack a vision. They're too busy making money and not busy enough thinking in global terms."

"Well, Christ," Bickel said. "We don't want them thinking in global terms like the Nazis."

Keep everything under control. You've had too much to drink. You're tired. Don't blow anything with Bickel.

"No, of course not. Not like the Nazis," Patterson said slowly. Not like *some* of the Nazis. Like that bastard Heydrich and those butchers in the SS. "But you must admit," Patterson said softly, "that while the Nazis did some horrible things, they were dreamers of a great dream."

Bickel wondered if he had heard correctly. Dreamers of a great dream? He looked over at Patterson and Patterson's eyes were closed. He held his snifter limply. His chest rose and fell rhythmically. The old man was sound asleep.

Bickel must have heard him wrong as he dozed off. Dreamers of a great dream? The thought was repulsive. All the more so because Bickel had often thought it himself.

Silently, Bickel walked out of the room and headed for the door. As he opened it, a beam of light from the hallway fell into the room and struck the row of pictures. In a split second, Bickel recognized the man whom Patterson stood next to on a balcony. My God, it was him, with Hitler. No mistake.

The shock passed as Bickel waited for the chauffeur to drive him home. Why should it have been a shock at all? Hadn't he already known that Patterson had been friendly with Hitler, for some purpose? And hadn't Patterson said that the killing of the Jews was unpardonable?

He looked out the windows of the Rolls-Royce as it glided silently over the streets of Northwest Washington toward his home. There were no other cars, and the houses were dark. It was dark all around, even inside the gleaming automobile.

"Dreamers of a great dream."

One thing was certain. Bickel was not going to let pique at an old man's choice of words ruin his elation at what Patterson had offered him. Everyone was eccentric. That was not what counted. What counted was what Patterson could do, and that was plenty. That was what won elections.

CHAPTER

11

At eight AM, the telephone next to Travis Bickel's bed rang. It was a Princess Trimline phone, the kind that easily slips out of wet hands, and, as Bickel ran out of the bathroom where he had been shaving to pick it up, it slipped out of his hands onto the floor. Bickel fumbled for it while he heard a voice coming weakly out of the receiver. Finally he got it, put it next to his ear. He habitually spoke softly, so that he would not wake up Lydia.

"Hello," Bickel said. He hoped that whoever was on the telephone had hung up. He disliked early-morning telephone calls.

"Hello, Senator Bickel?" said a male voice on the other end of the line.

"Yes," Bickel answered. The voice sounded familiar.

"This is Frank Roberts, Senator. We met last night at Mr. Patterson's house. I hope I'm not waking you."

"No, no. I was awake. I was shaving," Bickel said.

"Well, I'll be quick," Roberts said. His voice was well-modulated and polite, almost apologetic. "Mr. Patterson wants you to know how much he enjoyed last night's dinner."

Jesus, Bickel thought. Patterson is so rich that he has people make thank you calls for him.

Roberts continued. "Mr. Patterson called me early this morning to say that he wants to make available the facilities of the Institute for Contemporary Political Research to you for the important work you're doing on the Rearmament Treaty."

"That's kind of him. I hope you'll tell him how grateful I am," Bickel said.

"Of course, Senator," Roberts said. "You have only to tell me when it would be convenient to come over, and we'll lay everything out for you."

"I'm rather busy today," Bickel said, "but I'd certainly like for it to be soon."

"Whenever you want," Roberts said. "Mr. Patterson also told me that he was afraid that he might have fallen asleep last night, and he apologizes." Roberts paused for a moment. Bickel imagined him wetting his lips. "If I may say this, Senator, Mr. Patterson is completely alert, but he is not a young man. Sometimes, late at night, when he's had a little alcohol, he gets sleepy. I'm sure you understand."

Now it was Bickel's turn to say, "Of course."

"And also," Roberts said, "sometimes he talks in a kind of half-sleep. That sometimes happens before he falls asleep. He says things he hasn't thought about. Sometimes complete nonsense."

"I do understand," Bickel said. "I really do."

"Thank you again for coming to dinner," Roberts said, and then said good-bye.

In the shower, a moment later, Bickel marveled at how well Patterson covered all the bases. He looked at the rows of neat blue tiles and thought that for Elson Patterson, life must be like that—a series of neat squares, which he could arrange as he wished. Bickel glanced down at his waterproof Seiko wristwatch. He would be late for his appointment unless he hurried. He'd think about Patterson later in the day, when he talked to Kosters. But when he got out of the bathroom, he made a telephone call.

Less than a mile away, at the former Belgian ambassador's residence on Foxhall Road, Frank Roberts sat in a room paneled with oak. He was in a large chrome-and-fabric chair. He sat in front of a modern glass-and-chrome table. In front of the table was a stand with a television monitor and a videocassette player. On the monitor, the image of Senator Travis Bickel walking out of the den where Elson Patterson slept was flashing.

"You handled that extremely well, Frank," Elson Patterson said. He stood behind Roberts, wearing riding clothes—tailored breeches with black leather hunt boots and a beautifully cut old tweed racing jacket. Roberts wore a three-piece suit, gray on gray.

"Thank you, Mr. Patterson," Roberts said.

"Yes, indeed," Patterson said, "you handled that so well that he'll be wondering for a while just what the hell it was supposed to mean. That's what he's supposed to do. He's supposed to wonder."

"Thank you again, Mr. Patterson. Shall I go now, or can I help you here?" Roberts asked.

"No, you go over to the institute. I have a few things to do here, then I'm going out to the farm and ride a little. Call me around ten and let me know if you've heard from Bickel."

"Fine. I'll do that," Roberts said. He got up and walked noiselessly out of the room. It wasn't hard, since the floors were made of cork.

When he was alone, Patterson walked over to the Sony and punched the buttons. The tape of the evening started rolling again. Bickel was there, in living color, and Patterson watched him carefully. Even after he had watched snippets of the whole evening, Patterson could not be sure what to make of Bickel. There was more there than showed on the surface. That was for sure. But how much more? Was there enough to understand the whole thing and the part he could play in it.

Patterson pulled the curtains in the room and looked out a picture window at the park, where a light drizzle fell on the leafless trees. He would soon be late for his ride. That was all right. He had something weighty to think about. The grooms and the horses could wait. *Would* wait, in fact, all day if necessary.

Patterson could remember, as clearly as if it were yesterday, the walks with the *Führer* along wooded paths in Berchtesgaden. It was years before the war, and everywhere they turned, things were looking up. The Communists had been beaten in Spain. It looked as if Mussolini might be able to get the Italians to do something. The Russians were busily killing themselves. In Germany, there was order and growth. It was hard to believe that the *Führer* was not yet forty-eight, and yet his wisdom was saving one nation, out of all the world, from chaos and misery.

What was it the *Führer* had said about motivating people properly? Now Patterson remembered. It was, indeed, one of his most eminently memorable conversations with the *Führer*. It was at breakfast, in 1935, in the spring. Patterson was still a young man. He was in the enormous living room, with its magnificent view, of the mountains and the valleys with sun and shadow making beautiful contrasts, and the *Führer* was talking about the beginnings of the party. Only Patterson and Goebbels were in the room. God, how young they had looked then. Of course, Patterson remembered, he had looked younger too.

He even remembered the furniture in the room. It was heavy, overstuffed furniture, thoroughly modern— for the times—and yet extremely solid-looking. The *Führer* had been an artist, of course, and that showed. He had good taste in everything, but especially in furniture.

The *Führer* wore a double-breasted light brown suit with a light brown shirt. Patterson could not remember the color of Hitler's tie.

Patterson asked the *Führer* how he had managed to create a party out of what was basically nothing. How had he gotten the men to join and devote themselves to their task?

"It's a simple matter," the *Führer* said. "I learned from my own experience, which is always the best teacher." He had smiled and leaned forward in his chair, as he did when he was explaining something cheerful. "When I came to Munich, in 1913, I didn't know a soul. Not a soul. In Vienna, I had known hundreds of people. Still, I felt as if I belonged in Munich, because I could sense that it was a thoroughly German city, and I felt as if I belonged to the German race. So I felt at home immediately."

Patterson concentrated. What had the *Führer* said after that? It had something to do with belonging and joining.

"From that experience," the *Führer* had said, "I learned that if a man can feel that he belongs to some group that means something, he will do almost anything for it. You must make people know that they are part of something larger than themselves as individuals. Now the problem with the party was that it was so small that people were not yet willing to work for it and fight for it. It lacked grandeur.

"But that was only if it was considered separately from its mission. I had to explain to every new member that our mission was nothing less than the salvation of a race. That meant something. It meant that a new member was devoting himself not only to a small, struggling party, but to a race. Then," the *Führer* said with an air of triumph, "the new man felt he belonged to something great and he would dare great things."

The *Führer* leaned back in his chair and smiled, then frowned. It was a great moment.

In 1983, Patterson wondered if Bickel could be made to understand that he could belong to something great. Something with the almost facetious name of Croesus, but something that could restore that sense of purpose to the whole Western world.

He picked up the telephone.

At the time it had been finished in 1965, the Samuel Rayburn Office Building was the most expensive office building ever built. It had been constructed with a lavishness that only the federal government can bestow upon itself. In it, behind thick Italian marble, were gyms, swimming pools, saunas, steamrooms, theaters, restaurants, TV studios, handball courts, and even a few offices.

It squatted across Independence Avenue from the Capitol like a monstrously overgrown version of Lenin's tomb and a flattened pyramid combined. It was an architectural wonder—massive without being the slightest bit impressive, except for its ugliness. A visitor from a society still in prehistoric times would have had no trouble understanding that it served primarily a ritual function, which was to make the people who toiled within feel that they were massive and solid too.

But Travis Bickel, junior senator from California, did not feel impressive as he sat in room 3324, a special command center that the Democratic leadership had set up to guide the crucial fight on the Rearmament Treaty.

In fact, Travis Bickel felt positively confused after he finished smiling and joking with Senator Peyton Randolph, a crusty old gent from Wyoming, who was more than half crazy but whose vote counted for just as much as if he were sane. The white-haired senator had asked Bickel if he, Bickel, could guarantee that the Nazis would not somehow get the bomb.

"Of course I can, Senator," Bickel said. "Of course. It's easy to make that promise because there aren't any Nazis left except a few cranks in Arlington and a few more cranks in South America."

"How the hell do you know?" Randolph said, his face flushed. "How the hell do you know if I'm a Nazi? How do I know that you're not a Nazi?"

Bickel looked around the room. It had high ceilings, painted an eggshell white. The walls of the room were a light green. The room had no windows and was furnished like a lounge, which it was, with leather sofas and armchairs and only one small Colonial-style desk in the corner. Bickel sat in a brown armchair next to the brown couch where Senator Randolph sat. Above Randolph was one of the many photographs of distinguished former members of the House of Representatives. Was it Wayne Hays? It sure looked like him. What the hell kind of an answer could Bickel give Randolph? Was Randolph serious?

"Well, Senator," Bickel said, leaning forward earnestly in his chair, staring into the old man's wrinkled face, "I won't tell if you won't tell."

Randolph looked startled for a moment and then laughed uproariously. Then he sat bolt upright and said to Bickel in a sonorous voice, "You're a fine fellow, Travis. You've got my vote." Without another word, he walked out of the room.

Bickel breathed a sigh of relief when the old senator left. The public thought that it was well-nigh imperial to be a United States Senator, but the truth was that it was often like being a door-to-door salesman. You had a property to sell, and you were under the gun to sell it to the lunatics as well as the sane folk. There were some prospects who slammed the door in your face and others who invited you in for coffee.

But selling the treaty, like selling encyclopedias, was rewarding. Each time he changed someone's mind, Bickel got satisfaction. There was a psychic struggle involved in selling someone something, and Bickel was winning most of the battles. And when that treaty went over the top, Bickel was on his way to the nomination.

Satisfying as it was, though, Bickel needed a rest, and he was glad that Jeff Richards was coming to see him in a few minutes. There was a lot he wanted to talk about with Richards. Every so often, in what he himself recognized as his headlong dash to fame, Bickel paused to consider what was happening to him. And what he found at this morning's self-criticism session on the way to work was that too goddamned many unusual things had happened. Bad Kreuznach. The bomb that killed Kart. Kathy Dorn. Patterson. Damned small chance that it was just coincidence, but even if it were, it was good to look at coincidences carefully. That was where Richards came in.

Like most men who cannot share anything meaningful with their wives, Bickel had developed a circle of friends and acquaintances with whom he could share just about everything. Kart had been the innermost, but he was gone. Something was gnawing at Alexandra. She probably worried about Patterson. Bickel could tell from her unusually crisp manner. And Kosters was out of town again. That left Richards, who was probably the best choice anyway. He was, in Bickel's mind, the puzzle man.

Richards, at forty-seven, was probably the most highly regarded man in the CIA's Plans section—the section that did all the mischief, the undercover operations, the destabilizations, and so on. He had been a teacher at Yale Law School when Bickel was a student there. Already hunched over from his intense concentration, Richards had been considered the resident genius in a community of geniuses. He could always be caught in his office in the Sterling Law Building late at night, his huge head with its black curls poised over a book. Richards had specialized in only the most difficult kinds of problems, such as the relation of economic developments to particular legal developments.

It was that work that had brought him to the attention of Richard Helms. The former director had seen in Richards a man who could integrate a vast number of factors quite skillfully and quickly reach a successful conclusion. He was an ideal person to understand all the variables in a complex political situation and determine what event could tip the scales in the direction that the CIA wanted them tipped in.

With a combination of flattery and challenge, Helms lured Richards to Langley, Virginia, from New Haven. The challenge was to construct a computer model of every possible trouble spot on earth, with the appropriate data on every related individual and group. The idea was that when a coup threatened in Greece, for instance, the computer would be able to tell whom to reach to stop it and whom to reach to get the hooks into whoever had started it.

Even for Richards, it was a gigantic challenge indeed. Even though he lacked computer training he knew about the possible role of computers in his own work, so it was, in fact, too big a challenge to be turned down.

Over ten years, while his hair turned to a pepper-and-salt color and he watched his baby grow into a teenager, Richards constructed the computer model. Helms went, and Colby came and went, and Bush came and went, and Turner came and went, and the model kept growing. By the time Kosters became secretary of state in 1981, the operation was invaluable to United States policy-making. Many foreign affairs experts hypothesized the existence of such a model, but only a few people, including Bickel, knew it existed.

Bickel had kept in close touch with Richards ever since law school days, when Richards taught an abstruse seminar in legal process. Now he was about to ask Richards for the use of his enormous brains—the one in his head and the one in room 0101 in Langley, Virginia.

As Bickel thought about whether Richards would laugh at his question, as Richards sometimes laughed even at serious things, there was a rapping at the door of room 3324. Since Bickel did not like to shout, he got up and walked to the door to let Richards in.

"Hello, Jeff," Bickel said. "How are you?"

The stooped, middle-aged man looked as if he should have had chalk on his elbows. He wore a heavy wool overcoat, and, under that, a threadbare wool jacket that looked as if Western Costumes had sent it over to be worn by a professor in a 1930's movie. But the deep-set brown eyes were alive and sparkling. Richards met Bickel's blue-gray eyes and gripped his hand firmly.

"It's great to see you, Trav. I was awfully sorry to read about Si Kart. That was a blow," Richards said sincerely, still holding Bickel's hand.

"It was indeed, Jeff. It was indeed."

"But it doesn't seem to have slowed you down too much. I've been reading about how you not only negotiated the treaty but are leading the floor fight for ratification."

Travis smiled slightly. "When you grow up, no one gives you time to cry," he said.

"So true," Richards agreed. "How's Lydia?"

Bickel spread his arms, turning the palms upward.

"The same," he said. "Come sit down." He gestured to the couch where Randolph had been sitting. "Would you like a Coke?"

Richards was virtually addicted to Coca-Cola, and gratefully took a bottle, without a glass, from Bickel, who took it out of a small refrigerator, hidden in the wall and covered by thick paneling. That was the way Richards liked it—straight from the bottle.

"It was awfully good of you to come, especially on such short notice," Bickel said.

"Always a pleasure," Richards said with a smile. "You know us in the agency. We exist to serve." His tone was mocking but pleasant.

Bickel smiled wryly and sat in an armchair next to Richard's couch. "Remember back in New Haven when I asked you questions and you would say that the question made no sense?"

"I don't remember that," Richards said. "I remember that you used to ask very smart questions and sometimes I didn't know the answer. You never remember how smart you are."

Again a smile played across Bickel's features. "I do remember that you used to say how smart someone was before cutting him to pieces."

Both men chuckled and then Bickel reached over and put his hand on Richards's threadbare knee. The two men could hardly have been dressed more differently. Bickel's suits were custom made in Meledandri—a heritage from his grandfather, and his shirts were Brooks Brothers' top of the line. That morning he wore a gray plaid suit that looked as if it had cost an arm and a leg—which it had. But there was no mistaking the feeling in Bickel's voice when he touched the academic knee and said, "Jeff, if I'm going crazy, I'd like you to tell me."

"I'm sure you're not," Richards said, as if he meant it. His voice had a reassuring quality for Bickel. It always had.

"I'm going to tell you what's happened to me in the last ten days or so, and I'd like for you to make some sense out of it."

Richards looked sober. "I'll try," he said.

"And I'd like for you to keep it completely confidential, Jeff. I know you can do that," Bickel said, still touching Richards's knee.

"I can and will do that," Richards said. "You know I will."

"I know you will," Bickel said, and removed his hand from Richard's knee. He wiped his hand across his forehead and said, "I don't know where to begin. I guess it begins with Arthur Kosters's telling me that he wanted me to lead the delegation that was going to Bonn to negotiate the treaty. That was more than ten days ago. Maybe it begins with my driving down to Bad Kreuznach with Simon Kart."

For half an hour, Bickel described, in as much detail as he could, his trip to Bad Kreuznach, his escapade at the *Bibliothek,* his return to Bonn, the death of Simon Kart, his rendezvous with Katherine Dorn, his fights with Lydia, his meeting with Elson Patterson, and Alexandra's sudden change of heart about Patterson. Bickel tried to leave nothing out. He paused only occasionally to get Jeff Richards fresh Cokes. Richards loved them. While he listened to the narration, Richards thoughtfully drained one bottle after another, then lined up the empty bottles in a neat row at his feet.

When Bickel reached the part about his phone call from Patterson's aide, Frank Roberts, he said, "That was what made me decide to call you. Something's going on. Something strange. Something strange as hell. But I still don't know what the hell it is."

Bickel looked at Richards and then around the room. "Is all of this coincidence?" He paused and smiled. "Fat fucking chance."

Richards tilted his Coke bottle back and took a long swig. His Adam's apple bobbed in his thin neck. He took the empty bottle from his lips and neatly placed it on the floor, at the head of four others.

"What do you think is going on?" Richards asked. "I mean it. What occurs to you?"

Bickel stroked his chin. He stood up and walked over to the Colonial desk and then walked back to his chair.

"I hate to say this, Jeff, but I think the most suspicious thing is that business with Katherine Dorn. How come right out of the blue she comes up to me and tells me she loves me? That kind of thing just doesn't happen. All the rest can be explained. Kart was killed by terrorists trying to get me. Elson Patterson is anxious to feel like he's a mover and shaker, and he has some odd ideas about the Nazis. But where did Katherine Dorn come from?"

Richards asked for another Coke. Before he put it to his lips, he said, "I'll give you two answers. Off the top of my head, I'd say it's all coincidence. I just don't see the integration, the scheme, that makes it all fit together. I think you're wrong to wonder about the German girl. She didn't ask you for anything secret, and there hasn't been any percentage in sexual blackmail for espionage for a long time."

"What about him?" Bickel asked, pointing at the picture of Wayne Hays.

"Not the same thing at all," Richards said, after he swallowed several ounces of Coke. "Elizabeth Ray was not an enemy agent. No one would have been mad at Hays if she were. They would just have thought he was tricked by a worldly woman. The way it was, Hays came across as the heavy."

Inwardly, Bickel heaved a sigh of relief. It was possible, then, that Kathy Dorn loved him for himself, whatever that means. It was also possible that the affair might be continued at some later date.

Richards was still speaking. "The second answer is that I can crank all of this into the computer and see if it comes up with anything, any kind of pattern. I guess that's what we're looking for."

Bickel didn't say anything. He thought about his night with Kathy Dorn.

"Do you want me to put it into ONA?" Richards asked.

"Is that what you're calling the computer now? ONA?" Bickel asked.

"Right. One of the younger fellows thought it up. It has something to do with his knowing someone very insightful whose name is Ona," Richards said. "Do you want me to crank it into ONA?"

"That means some other people besides you will see it, right?" Bickel asked.

"Probably," Richards answered.

"And you're pretty sure that Katherine Dorn is not a factor in whatever's developing?"

"I can't guarantee it. But so far, she hasn't done anything that strikes me as suspicious. To be supercautious, we could put her into the computer, too."

Bickel got up and walked over to the refrigerator. "You want a Coke?" he asked Richards.

"Sure thing," Richards said.

"I think," Bickel said, "that I'd like for you to leave out the part about Kathy Dorn. I trust you with it, but you're about the only person I do trust about it. Does it make sense to do it without her?" He handed Richards a Coke, which he started to drink immediately.

"Sure," Richards said. "Sure thing. I'll start on it tomorrow. In fact," he said, as he drained the last of his Coke, "I'll do it this afternoon."

Bickel relaxed for a moment. "I still want it absolutely confidential. You know, a personal favor. Does that sound possible?"

"That's the only way I'd do it," Richards said. "It has to be confidential for it to have any value." He smiled. "Especially to a man who's running for president."

Bickel smiled. "Jeff," he said, "I have major plans for you if everything goes according to plan, my plan. I think you might be able to do a lot for this country in many ways, and I'd like to see it happen." Bickel felt uneasy saying it to Richards. It sounded so much like political eyewash, but it was, in fact, absolutely true.

"I'm hip," Richards said. "And, you don't need to promise me a thing. We're friends. But I appreciate it anyway."

After a few minutes of pleasantries about Mark, Jeff Richards's thirteen-year-old son, and the unseasonably wet weather, Jeff Richards stood up to go. As he walked to the door he burped several times, undoubtedly from the Coca-Cola. "One last thing, Trav," he said. "I can tell you this right now. You're not crazy. You're smart to try to find out what's going on. Very smart." Richards smiled and put his hand on Bickel's shoulder. "Keep on being smart. Don't go down any dark alleys."

CHAPTER

12

Lake Tahoe, which nestles in the Sierra Mountains on the border between Nevada and California, gave off an aura of danger and menace to the man with the ski cap. He sat in the living room of an isolated vacation house on Emerald Bay, one of the most secluded parts of the shoreline. Out the window in front of him he could see across the lake to the Nevada side. Enormous peaks dominated the view. The peaks were so enormous that they made the twenty-story resorts across the lake look like tiny matchboxes.

It was almost sunset, and shadows had formed across the valleys that led down from the peaks to the lake. Huge stands of pine trees became blackish-green spots on the mountainsides, adding to the unevenness of the color and light.

The waters of the lake, which were blue even at noon in most places, took on a purplish cast toward evening that made them look impenetrable. The man in the ski cap looked at them and thought that the Indians who had lived around the lake before white men drove them away must have had a lot of respect for that lake. The man in the ski cap could see his own reflection in the glass of the picture window of his cottage. He looked frightened. He realized that he had a lot of respect for the lake, too.

Gradually, over the course of no more than five minutes, the sun sank behind the mountains on the western rim of the lake. The man in the ski cap could still see the sun striking the eastern rim, but he knew that, soon, the mountains in the east would be utterly dark. Across the glassy expanse of the lake, he could already see the snow turning from white to gray, as less and less light fell on it. In another minute, there was absolutely no light except for a few dots coming from the casinos some fifteen miles away. Who was playing there these days? Mac Davis? Glen Campbell? He never could tell them apart.

Soon, the man in the ski cap should start to hear the boat's engine. He hoped it would be soon, because, frankly, he hated these goddamn winter evenings up at Lake Tahoe. You could keep the clean air and the beautiful views. They were fine in the daytime, but they were no consolation at night. It was dark as hell out there, and anything could happen. The man with the ski cap had worked all over the world, and there was no place where he felt quite as vulnerable as at Lake Tahoe. He didn't know why the hell they had chosen this place for these meetings anyway. It seemed too romantic, too exposed, for agents to meet in a place like this. He didn't see why he couldn't have done his job as well from somewhere else—maybe from a cottage in Las Vegas. That was what he really liked.

The faint sound of an inboard engine, a heavily muffled inboard engine, could be heard. Thank God. It was scary as hell waiting in these woods. He didn't care if the house was lavish and well stocked with food. It was definitely not a secure place.

He got up from the couch and walked to the bathroom. He wanted to look good. He knew that his visitor was an important woman from Washington, and he had heard hints that she was a knockout, too. He didn't want her to suspect that anything was even the slightest bit amiss. As he looked at himself in the mirror, he saw too many signs of age. His skin was starting to pucker around the eyes, in the cheeks, and, most of all, in his neck. He looked permanently tired. He was sick of looking at a face that looked tired.

Now, tonight, he was about to start on his way out of that tired state. With what he was getting paid just to turn over a few scraps of information to a man who was, after all, a distinguished American, he would soon be able to retire.

The sound of the boat was louder, and the man with the ski cap took a final look in the mirror at his bloodshot brown eyes and walked across the hall and out the door, down the front yard and out to the pier. He carried one small flashlight, which he definitely needed. When he reached the end of the pier, he held out the flashlight in front of him and waved horizontally three times.

In front of him, much nearer than he would have expected, a small light snapped on and moved vertically three times. In a moment, the twenty-five-foot Hatteras Lakecruiser pulled up to the pier. Its engines were throttled, and the craft made hardly any noise. As it drew alongside the pier, a man jumped out and said, "Hello." He was short, bearded man, who wore a baseball cap.

"Hello," the man in the ski cap said. "Where's your passenger?"

A tall, thin woman wearing a heavy mink coat appeared on the deck of the Lakecruiser. She shined a flashlight in the eyes of the man with the ski cap.

"Shut the hell up," she said crisply.

"What?" the man in the ski cap said angrily, whirling to face the woman.

"You heard me," the woman said. In the light from the flashlight, she appeared to be about thirty and extremely pretty, with dark auburn hair and fair skin. She had an air of command. "There is to be no talking outside," she said curtly to the man in the ski cap.

The short bearded man with the mooring rope reached into the boat to help her out. Without a word, she pointed her own flashlight, located the house, and walked toward the front door, as the man with the ski cap fell into step behind her.

Inside the house, she shined her flashlight around the living room, then spoke to the man in the ski cap. "You can turn on the lights after you pull the shades."

"What the hell is going on?" he said, after he had done what the woman said. "Is the Fatah on your trail? I mean what's left of them?"

"Just good discipline," the woman said as she took off her mink coat. Her long hair fell over a brown cashmere sweater which she wore over a pair of ordinary blue jeans.

"I want this to be very brief," the woman said.

"All right," he said. "Tell me about the senator."

"I'm extremely concerned about him," the woman said. "I think he wonders about Patterson, but he doesn't seem to realize how dangerous Patterson is. Since I've heard from Jerusalem, I've tried to hint it to him, but he just isn't buying it."

"Is he stupid or do you think he's playing an angle?" the man in the ski cap asked.

The woman looked perplexed for the first time in the meeting. "I'm not sure. That's why I said 'seems.' If I had to bet, I'd think that he knows that Patterson can do plenty for him, but he's a little worried about the price he's going to have to pay. I'd also say that he's leaning pretty heavily on the side of taking his chances with Patterson. I think even if he knew everything about Patterson, he'd still play along. Not that we know everything about Patterson ourselves. But I think even if Bickel knew as much as we know, he'd go with Patterson. Patterson can just do an awful lot for him."

"You think the Russians are active?"

"Of course they're active," the woman said, sharply.

The man in the ski cap didn't like the woman's brusqueness. He had a fleeting thought of killing her with just one blow to the neck. He had done it before. That was the way these bitches were. They thought they knew every goddamn thing. But he just played it very cool.

"I mean," he said patiently, "are they active in this deal?"

"I assume they are," the woman said. "But I haven't seen any evidence of it."

The man and the woman talked for a while longer, and then the woman got up to go. "Just one more question," the man with the ski cap said.

"Yes?"

"Why the hell do we meet here, out in the middle of nowhere?" he asked. "It just seems like begging to get caught."

The woman smiled. "I don't know. I really don't know. I suppose a wealthy American Jew donated the land or something."

The woman looked so pretty at that moment that he wished he had made a pass at her. Now she was halfway out the door. Damn! It would be another lonely night. He walked out the door and watched the boat pull away. Even though he was lonely, he figured that he would make a lot of money out of what he had heard that night, and that kept him company. Anyway, he would be at work with the radio for several hours, and then he would be sleepy. The next morning, he was going to have an important visitor.

Out on the lake, the Hatteras slipped almost silently back toward the Stateline. The woman in the mink coat huddled in the cabin, trying to ward off the ten-below-zero-degree cold on the water. The bearded man stood near her, at an inboard wheel.

He looked out carefully over the black water. "Why didn't we just kill the sonofabitch?" he asked the woman.

"You know I can't answer that," she said.

"It just seems damn strange," the short, bearded man said. "I don't know why we keep him there in that house, either."

"Well, that's not hard to figure out, Sol," the woman said. "Where he is, we can see every single thing he does. It's like he's in a glass case."

"It still seems too good for him," the bearded man said.

"It is," the woman said. "It is too good for him, but in a way, he's still serving his people."

"You just think that the people in Jerusalem always know what they're doing. I've seen different too many times."

"So have I," the woman said. "But this time, they're doing it right."

"I hope so," the short, bearded man said as the boat moved across the water. "I hope so."

The woman in the mink coat hoped so, too, as she watched the lights of Harrah's getting larger in the night. She had a plane to catch, and a long journey to be back in Washington by morning. But she could do it. She had done it before.

CHAPTER

13

Travis Bickel lay in bed and stared out the window. Not that there was much to see. There were few bright lights on Klingle Street, except for the occasional streetlights, and even those did not cast any light into the back yard where Bickel looked. Out there, somewhere, was a decayed birdbath, the legacy of an elderly woman who had sold the house to Bickel. Farther from the house was a pond, surrounded with fieldstone, in which a few hardy goldfish managed to survive in the summer until neighborhood kids killed them. At this time in early January, the pond would be frozen solid at night.

Bickel could see a light on in the garage of the house behind his. The light from a single bulb silhouetted the leafless branches of a large live oak tree in Bickel's back yard. It was the only tree that hadn't died from a tree disease that the Asplundh Nursery, at enormous expense, had been unable to diagnose or treat successfully. Now the bushes in the front were dying from it too. Bickel thought it was odd that his house was the only house in the neighborhood that harbored the disease. But whatever the cause, only one tree remained near Bickel's house, and Bickel could see the outline of its branches as he lay sleepless in bed.

Bickel wished he could sleep. He even wished he knew why he couldn't sleep. He walked across the hall to look at Lydia, who was sleeping soundly in her light brown night gown, her hair rolled in curlers. The room was painted a bright yellow—an unusual color for a bedroom, but Bickel liked bright things and had insisted. It was so dark in the room that the color could not be made out, though. Only the outlines of the Danish furniture and the Sony television set could be seen.

Why the hell can she sleep when I can't? he thought as he returned to his room.

After a few minutes more of looking out the window, Bickel turned on his right side and thought about the events of the day. Certainly, the meeting with Jeff Richards had gone well enough. There was nothing to worry about there. Then there was some routine palaver about the Rearmament Treaty, but no jokers like Senator Randolph's crazed questions had come up.

Bickel thought about his meeting with Kosters. The secretary of state had sent over a limousine to pick up Bickel at the Capitol steps. It was there at exactly one PM, just as it was supposed to be, gleaming and smooth in the winter sun. The driver, a slender young man with rust-colored hair and wire-rimmed glasses, jumped out of the front seat and ran around to open the door for Bickel.

"How are you today, Senator?" he asked.

"I'm fine, Hollis," Bickel said. He didn't know whether Hollis was the driver's first or last name, but it apparently didn't matter, since the driver responded with great cheerfulness that he was "doing great on this beautiful day."

The black Cadillac accelerated smoothly down Independence Avenue, heading away from Capitol Hill. In a minute, Bickel could see the Botanical Gardens on his right. The bizarre Victorian structure resembled an enormously overgrown gazebo, which was close to what it was. Basically, it was just a housing for a large garden that displayed some of America's more beautiful plants—healthy and growing, unlike those in Bickel's yard—and provided congressmen and senators with pleasant office plants.

A moment later, on the left, the limousine passed by the stolid headquarters of the Department of Health, Education, and Welfare. It looked as though it belonged inside the Kremlin, with its bast, blank exterior and its dull, clay-colored walls.

"Heard you had some excitement in Germany, Senator," the driver said cheerfully over his shoulder. The window separating the passenger and driving compartments was open.

"I did, Hollis. It was a great tragedy. I lost one of my closest friends."

"Yeah, I read that. I'm really sorry, Senator. Those Germans are dangerous," Hollis said. He looked chastised.

Bickel gazed out at the offices of the National Aeronautics and Space Administration, a quintessential 1960's building with wide expanses of glass and absolutely no character. Next to it on the right was the beginning of L'Enfant Plaza, a huge, modern sprawl of offices and hotels and shops, which had been intended to create a new multiracial center in a former black slum but had become nothing but an enclave that was white in the daytime and utterly deserted at night.

Occasionally, as the car passed by the old-fashioned complex of the Department of Agriculture, a car pulled up slowly to the side of the limousine and someone gaped into the back seat. But apparently no one recognized Bickel, or at least no one gave any sign of recognition. In a moment they were past the Bureau of Printing and Engraving, another old complex of mill-like buildings where the money came from.

The car wound through the parks around the Washington Monument, the Jefferson Memorial, and the Lincoln Memorial and emerged in front of the "new" entrance of the State Department on C Street. When it came to a halt in front of the glass doors of that entrance, Hollis again jumped out of the car and walked rapidly behind the car to open the door for Bickel. Bickel got out and straightened his tie while tourists looked at him and tried to figure out who he was. Hollis slammed the door behind him and walked briskly to the revolving door. As Bickel walked up to the door, Hollis gave it a slight shove and said, "Nice seeing you, Senator."

In an instant, Bickel was inside the lobby. It looked to him like the lobby of a high school in Lafayette, Indiana. It was far wider than it was deep, with windows on both long sides. A row of flags of the nations of the world greeted Bickel on the wide wall opposite the entrance. Across from them, one flight above ground level, was a balcony with stairs leading down to the lobby's entrance. Slightly to the right of the revolving doors and set out a few feet from the wall was a globe almost ten feet high. It was another relic of a recent architectural past, with its hollow interior open to the world through ribs that marked an occasional latitude or longitude.

Bickel's eye was caught for an instant by a girl in a denim jeans outfit who looked startlingly like Katherine Dorn. He started to walk toward her and then realized that it wasn't she at all. It had given him a start.

"Senator Bickel?" A young man with horn-rimmed glasses and a navy blue suit walked up to Bickel and stuck out his hand. He looked earnest.

Bickel looked at him, trying to remember his name. The young man was an aide to Kosters, and he had a fancy name, but Bickel was damned if he could remember what it was. "How are you?" Bickel said with a smile.

"I'm Terence Mandeville," the young man said. "I'd like to take you upstairs for your luncheon with the secretary, if you're ready."

"Certainly, Terry. How have you been?" Bickel asked, also with a smile, still holding Mandeville's hand.

Together, they rode up to the eighth floor in the secretary of state's private elevator, a small cubicle paneled with dark wood. It made no stops between the first and eighth floors. When Bickel and Mandeville reached the eighth floor, the door of the elevator slid open, and Bickel stepped out into Kosters's outer office with Mandeville close behind.

The room looked like the waiting room of an elegant law firm with modern furniture and Calder originals. Two secretaries sat at large desks with neat piles of paper in front of them. One of them was typing on a new red IBM Memory Selectric IV. It could remember an entire page of corrections and make them while the typist was otherwise occupied, filing her nails. *Fortune* had called it an "office machine breakthrough of historic magnitude."

Bickel and Mandeville passed silently between the two desks through double doors. The two secretaries did not even look up. On the other side of the doors was another secretary. Where the two outside secretaries had looked young, pretty, and efficient, the secretary inside the double doors looked middle-aged, pretty, and efficient. She looked up at Bickel and smiled.

"How are you today, Senator? May I get you coffee or a drink while you're waiting? The secretary will just be a minute."

Bickel smiled back. This was Liza, Kosters's secretary from his teaching days, who had been with him for almost twenty years. What she did not know about Kosters did not need to be known.

"No, thanks, Liza," Bickel said. "I'll just sit down and wait. Do you have today's New York *Times?*"

"Certainly, Senator," Liza said. She reached over to a table next to her desk and handed Bickel that morning's *Times*. "You're on the front page, as usual," she said.

Bickel took the paper and walked to a chocolate brown couch with chrome arms. As he sat down, Mandeville said to him, "Well, if you're comfortable, I'll go back to my office. If I can do anything at all for you, please let me know." He smiled and walked out through the double doors.

Liza went back to typing something and Bickel glanced at the front page of the newspaper. In the lower right-hand corner was a headline: "SENATE RATIFICA-

TION OF REARMAMENT PACT IS LIKELY." The story began,

Early and positive action on the U.S.–West German Pact to supply West Germany with strategic nuclear weapons appears likely, according to an extensive series of interviews by reporters for this newspaper on Capitol Hill. A massive, well-coordinated lobbying effort on behalf of the measure, guided by Secretary of State Arthur Kosters and Senator Travis Bickel (D-Calif.), is apparently swinging over to the ratification side all but the most determined opponents of the measure.

Bickel was about to read on when the doors to Kosters's office opened and a chubby African wearing a dashiki walked out with Kosters's arm around him. The secretary himself looked rumpled but cheerful. As always, his pin-stripe suit needed a pressing. His eyes were puffy but alert. Without taking his arm off the African's shoulder, Kosters winked at Bickel, then guided the man to where Bickel sat.

"Nathaniel, this is the young genius from the Senate that you've been hearing so much about," Kosters said cheerily as Bickel stood up and extended his hand.

The African took it without the slightest sign of recognition. "I am pleased to meet you," he said solemnly.

"This Nathaniel Mbazwe, the ambassador from Botswana, and a very close personal friend of mine, and this is Senator Travis Bickel," Kosters said, at last relinquishing Mbazwe's shoulder.

The African still showed no sign of recognition. Probably German rearmament was not a hot issue in Botswana.

"An honor to meet you, Mr. Ambassador," Bickel said as he pumped Mbazwe's hand.

The ambassador withdrew his hand and said farewell to Kosters.

"And you be sure to say hello to Ingrid," Kosters said, as the African passed through the double doors to where one of the secretaries waited with his coat.

When the doors closed, Bickel smiled at Kosters, then laughed. "What're you selling him?" he asked.

Kosters laughed so that his double chins jiggled. "More Swedish girls like his wife," he said and laughed some more. He put his arm around Bickel and guided him into his office.

Bickel had been a guest in Kosters's office many times, but each time was an experience. The room was enormous. Directly across from the doors was an immense desk of highly polished maple. It looked like what Louis B. Mayer's desk should have looked like. Behind it, and stretching across the entire west wall of the office, was one large window. It was faced on the outside by a balcony with a solid railing, which made Kosters's office utterly invisible from the street.

The windows looked out over the grounds surrounding the Lincoln Memorial, over the Reflecting Pool, out past the banks of the Potomac, across that brown and muddy river and over into Virginia. Even on a day when there were no leaves on the trees, it was a magnificent vista.

To the right of the desk was a conference table made of a highly polished maple, which went with the desk. There were eight chairs around it, and it did not look the slightest bit crowded. Between that table and the east wall of the office were two yellow sofas facing each other, with a large armchair between them, obviously for Kosters.

On the left side of the room there was a dining table with another eight chairs. Like the chairs around the conference table, they were cane-back antiques—the real McCoy. To the left of the dining table was a wall with a door. Bickel knew from experience that behind that door was the secretary's private kitchen.

Adjacent to that wall was another wall, in which there was another door. Behind that door was the secretary's private bathroom, with light brown tile. It included a toilet, a sink, a shower, and a small sauna.

"Sit down, Travis," Kosters said, gesturing expansively toward the yellow couches. "You've been doing great work. Tell me how things are going up on the Hill."

Bickel walked over to the couches and sat down on the one facing the desk. Sure enough, Kosters sat in the armchair.

"Well," Bickel said, "I think things are going along quite well on the ratification."

"How did your meeting with Randolph go?" Bickel asked. "You want some coffee? A drink? Lunch'll be ready in a minute."

"Nothing, thanks," Bickel said. "The meeting was strange."

As he recounted the meeting with Randolph, Bickel swept the room with his blue-gray eyes. There were the usual maps and watercolors of warships from Colonial days. But there was something new, right next to the double doors leading into the office. It was a large oil portrait of the President. It was obviously an original, since Bickel could see small globs of oil. The President was wearing a suit with a Western cut. He looked almost beatific, with his blue eyes and his brown hair. Behind the President was a large, heavily treed expanse, supposed to represent the Midwestern forests from which the President always said he drew his strength. Then why the cowboy outfit? Perhaps Kosters knew something about the President's fantasies that was not general knowledge. Maybe the President imagined himself a cowboy, riding over the prairies. At any event, it was obviously a damn smooth move having that picture there. Plenty of people visited both offices, and a few would surely tell the President that Kosters had a picture of him, an original oil picture that looked as if it cost plenty.

When Bickel had finished talking about his session with Randolph, Kosters laughed cheerily. "He's a fool, but he's a likeable old fool. He's got a good sense of humor."

Bickel leaned forward over a highly polished maple coffee table that sat between the two yellow couches. In the center of the table was a large crystal ashtray in the shape of a five-pointed star. At the center of the star was a blue circle, in which was the seal of the secretary of state. It was an eagle holding an olive branch in one claw and a quiver of arrows in the other claw, and looking as though it would greatly prefer to use the arrows. Behind the eagle was a bunch of spears, and around the outside of the circle was a band that read, "The Secretary of State of the United States of America."

"You think Randolph was just making a joke? I don't know. It shook me up a little," Bickel said. "It really did. You didn't hear him laugh. He sounded as if he knew something I didn't know. It made me uneasy."

Kosters looked more serious. "All Randolph knows is that when he was a little boy, people used to talk about how bad the Kaiser was, and when he was grown up, he fought against Hitler. To him, all Germans are frozen in the same mold. He'll never be able to viscerally"— Kosters's tongue lingered on every letter of the word, so that it sounded as if it had ten syllables—"think of the Germans as anything but Nazis. But you handled him just right. A bit of humor. That doesn't hurt a bit."

"I hope so," Bickel said. "I really hope so. I think the treaty is about a lead-pipe cinch right now. Just about a cinch."

Kosters reached over to the underside of one of the right-hand cushions on his chair. He fished out a buzzer and pressed it. It made no sound, but in a moment, a black woman wearing a black maid's dress with a white linen apron appeared and walked over to the secretary of state. She paused just to the left of his chair.

Kosters looked up at her and smiled. "I think we'd like to eat now, Thelma," he said with a slight edge in his voice that Bickel had not heard before.

"Yes, Mr. Secretary," the maid said, and withdrew.

"She doesn't understand anything, not anything," Kosters said irritably as Thelma left the room. "I try to get her to understand just a little bit about keeping the place neat, but I might as well be talking to a stone. I really mean it."

The secretary took a place at the dining table with his back to the expanse of glass. Bickel sat opposite him at the other end of the table. There were only two places set, each one with the china of the secretary of state of the United States of America, including his seal. The silver did not have the seal but had an eagle holding the arrows and the olive branch.

Thelma was nowhere to be seen. A black man in livery brought in two bowls of consommé, which he set down in front of Bickel and Kosters. Each bowl had the seal.

Bickel tasted his soup, took a few spoonfuls, then said, "I'm worried, Arthur. I'm more worried about this treaty than I'd tell anyone but you. I'm really worried."

Kosters looked sympathetic and set down his spoon. "What worries you, Travis? Perhaps I've missed something. I should have guessed that you were worried. When else do you come to see me?"

He sounded like a whining parent.

Bickel smiled at the thought. "I mean I'm worried about the treaty. I'm not worried about whether it'll pass. As long as I keep after everyone and kick a little ass, it'll pass. That's not it." Bickel paused and looked out the window. "What I mean is that maybe the whole goddamn treaty is a mistake. I mean, do we really need it? And, if we do need it, wouldn't it be better for us just to build more missiles? I hate to sound naive and outraged, but I'm beginning to wonder. The more I persuade the others, the more worried I am."

"The Germans," Kosters said with a severe look, "can be beasts. Absolutely. That's true without doubt. At least, I don't doubt it. I saw what they did to innocent people, Jews and Gentiles alike, under Hitler. I was lucky enough to get out, running like hell out of town before I could even finish school, but I know from history and from eyewitnesses, what they did. It was terrible. It was brutal. It was incredible."

"I couldn't agree more," Bickel said, finishing the last of his soup. "How come all of a sudden you trust them? People ask me that, and I wonder myself. They killed a lot of people, and you know it."

Kosters sighed and pressed a button next to his plate. Instantly, the waiter appeared and took away the soup bowls. "Did you enjoy your soup?" Kosters asked.

"Very much," Bickel said. "Was it beef with Burgundy?"

"Exactly," Kosters said, looking delighted. "Forgive me, Travis, but I have forgotten what kind of dressing you take with your salad. Is it Roquefort?"

"I think I'll pass on the salad today," Bickel said, "unless you've gone to a lot of trouble."

Kosters shook his head. "It's no trouble. I don't think I want any salad today either. Let's just go on to the main course. How does that sound?"

"Good," Bickel said.

"Thank you, Henry," Kosters said to the black man as he withdrew.

"It isn't all of a sudden, Travis. It's been building up for a long time. We could see, right after World War I, that the Germans were extremely unstable. The Nazis were just one example. The country was dangerous from the start.

"But things have just been completely different with the Federal Republic. Completely different. It's been stable from the very start. It is, I would have to say, more stable than this country. This is a great country, but, surely, it has shown some unstable behavior since the Second World War, while Germany has shown none. It has become the most stable democracy. We've had almost forty years of experience with the West Germans. They can be trusted."

The black waiter walked in, pushing a cart. From a copper flambé tray he served veal scallopini with a thin cream sauce. He also served each man a dollop of thinly sliced French-cut green beans and delicately sculpted pieces of eggplant. Before Bickel had a chance to taste the food, the black man took from a wine holder a bottle wrapped in a yellow cloth napkin and handed it to Kosters.

Silently Kosters examined it and then said softly, "That is all right for some of my guests, but not for Senator Bickel. I want a 1971 for him. There must be some left."

Bickel knew that the gesture was designed to impress him and had probably even been planned. Still, he ap-

preciated it. "Look," he said. "I'm taking the fucking
point on this—at your invitation. Now, you tell me: Am
I going to get my head handed to me?"

The waiter returned with another bottle. He showed
it to Kosters, who pronounced it satisfactory. Then the
waiter gave it to Kosters to taste, which he did deliber-
ately. He nodded, and the waiter poured a glass for
both men. The glasses did not have the secretarial seal.

"Not a chance," Kosters said. "Not a chance. You
should relax. Of course, now you're rattled. Of course. I
know I would be. I think the best thing is to work.
That's the best thing. Work cures everything. Work
makes you free." Kosters took a sip of wine and looked
satisfied.

That phrase sounded familiar to Bickel. Somewhere,
far back in his mind, a small bell rang, like a closing
bell in a library. Then it was silent.

The rest of the meal was uneventful. Bickel related
his meeting with Patterson, and Kosters laughed and
laughed. "He's a rich old bastard. He sounds a little
cracked, but people forgive it if you're rich. That's the
truth."

"Haven't you ever met him?" Bickel asked.

"Never," Kosters said. "I've been invited to speak to
his groups a number of times, but never to him."

"Do you think it's anti-Semitism?" Bickel asked.

"It might be. But I cannot think about that. If I
thought about that, it would drive me crazy. You understand."

"I'm hip," Bickel said, picking up Jeff Richards's locution. "That's a phrase I picked up from one of my
friends," Bickel apologized.

"Hip?" Kosters asked. "Is that like 'hep'?" He
sounded genuinely puzzled, as if some aspect of the
American culture had evaded him, an aspect of crucial
importance.

"About the same, I think," Bickel said. He drank a
small sip of wine. It was extraordinary. The best wine
he had ever tasted. "I'll tell you what I'm really worried
about is McMurray. You said in Bonn that you'd work
something out with him, and I haven't heard a word. In

addition, I need some help with the white ethnics. I'm
doing what I can, but you get a lot of chances to plug
me, and I'd like to hear a little more about it," Bickel
said.

"I know you're worried about that." Kosters smiled.
"I know that. But you can't get everything done at once.
However, I have spoken to McMurray. He knows you.
He knows a lot more about you than he did before.
That's fine. The things he knows are things I told him,
and he likes them."

This was more like it, Bickel thought. "When am I
going to meet him?" the senator asked.

"Very soon," Kosters said. "I'll fix it up." He picked
up the telephone next to him and pressed a button.
"Liza," he said into the receiver, "could you get me
McMurray on the phone? Right away, please. And after
him, Cardinal Arkajavec in Milwaukee." He turned to
Bickel. "Arkajavec is someone you simply must get to
know. Croatian. A very interesting man. Milwaukee.
Poles. Germans. You know."

Bickel was impressed. He wanted to meet Arkajavec.

Kosters set down the telephone receiver. "Now on
the white ethnics, here's what you do. I'm going to
speak to some Polish group in Chicago. I can't remember the name. I want you to come with me. Arkajavec
will be there, too. I want you to get up there on the
stand and say a few words about how much you love
Poland and all the captive nations. It'll get picked up in
the ethnic papers, and that's what counts."

"What are the polls showing?" Bickel asked. "I'd like
to see the raw data some time."

"On the raw data," Kosters said, "that's out. I can't
promise that there aren't any leaks here, and it would
make a hell of a stink if it got out. You know that," he
added, slightly reproachful, like a father to a son.

"Okay," Bickel said. "But what are the polls showing?"

"Still looking good for you," Kosters said. "Definitely
looking up. We put in a question about the negotiators,
not naming you personally, and we got extremely good
response. Leading the response on the treaty itself. You

come across as unselfish and hardworking, and that's very positive."

Bickel was happy. That was not bad at all. He still needed a lot of work with black voters, but he would work on that elsewhere.

There was a tinkling sound from the telephone, and Kosters picked it up. He held it for a moment without saying anything and then he said, in a cheerful voice, "Paul? How the hell are you?"

Bickel knew immediately that it was Paul McMurray, head of the AFL–CIO.

"Well, hell, Paul, you'll still be playing golf when you're in a wheelchair. I wouldn't worry about a little back trouble one bit." Kosters smiled to himself and to Bickel. The secretary of state was proud of his ability to make small talk with the high and the mighty.

After a moment's pause, Kosters said, in a serious tone, "Now, Paul, you remember young Senator Bickel. Well, I think the two of you should get together again. He has a lot to say about rebuilding the American merchant marine, and I think you need to talk to him. I really wish you would."

Another pause. "I know he'd like that, too. Fine, I'll have him call you."

Another pause. "And, of course, I'll see you at the dinner tonight. And no more whining about your back."

Bickel was impressed. He had to admit he was impressed. He was in the presence of power, and he liked it.

"Thank you, Arthur. That was great. That'll help a lot," Bickel said.

"I'm hip," Kosters said with a smile, and they both laughed.

As usual, there was a chocolate mousse for dessert. Bickel ate only a small amount. By that time, he was feeling so reassured in the presence of Kosters that he decided not to bore Kosters with the story of his domestic troubles. If he were a big enough man to spend this much time with Kosters, he was a big enough man to solve his own problems.

Later in the day, he went back to his office, but he

felt distracted, and he didn't know why. He looked out the window of his office in the Old Senate Office Building, alone with his huge government-issue desk and his government-issue portrait of the President. Why did he feel on edge? It might have had something to do with his meeting with Kosters, but that had ended extremely amiably.

Kosters even went down in the elevator with Bickel, something he rarely did. The two men, both without overcoats, walked over to the limousine, in front of which stood Hollis. His black jacket and slacks blended with the black finish of the car. When Hollis saw Kosters, he snapped to a rigid sort of attention, although he gave no salute.

While Hollis held the door open for Bickel, Kosters put his arm around the senator. While passersby gawked, Kosters said to Bickel, quite clearly, "You are a key man, Travis. A historic figure. You may not believe it, but it's true. A world-historic figure."

Again, that same alarm bell went off in Bickel's mind at the phrase.

Eight hours later, as the chiming clock above the fireplace downstairs marked three AM, Bickel still wondered what was going on. Why did he feel so jacked up? The more he thought about it, the surer he was that it had something to do with his talk with Kosters. But what was it? Kosters had said nothing unusual, and certainly nothing critical.

Slowly, Bickel started to drift into sleep. As he did, he thought about what excellent English Kosters spoke. You would hardly know he had been born in Germany and had spoken only German until he was a teenager. And Kosters had such good ideas about the world, such good ideas about how to lose yourself in your troubles.

Work, Kosters had said. Work was the answer. *Arbeit ist die Antwort.* Work makes you free. *Arbeit macht frei.*

Bickel sat up with a start. He was covered with sweat. That was it. He had seen that phrase before. It was in a picture of a gate. It was over the gate.

It was the gate to Dachau.

God. Poor, poor Kosters. That whole sick episode was so much in his brain that he said his persecutors' most horribly grotesque and ironic phrases as if they made sense. Poor Kosters.

Or maybe it was just a standard German phrase. Maybe it was like "haste makes waste" or something in American English.

Bickel got up and dried himself off. He changed into a fresh pair of pajamas and slept soundly.

CHAPTER

14

It was raining in Washington while Travis Bickel sat at his desk reading a news summary about the Rearmament Treaty. On a Sunday afternoon Bickel could get a lot done. There was no one else in his office except for the faithful Alexandra Denman, who was down the hall, working on a bill to curb the sales of enriched plutonium. For a few minutes, Bickel looked up from his reading and across the park to the Teamsters Union Building. Hoffa had built it but had never gotten to enjoy it. He was in jail by the time it was finished. It was a gaudy building that looked as if it had originally been intended as a Holiday Inn but at the last minute had been changed into an office building.

Bickel read again:

To those who say that rearming the Germans with nuclear weapons is a risk, there is one answer. What would the risk be of not rearming the West Germans? Given what we have seen of Soviet behavior under the "Strength through Socialism" program of current Russian leadership, is there any alternative to Soviet con-

tainment at the Oder by the West Germans themselves?
It is time to start dealing in 1983 realities. The Germans are no longer a threat to world peace and the
Russians are.

That was from the Baltimore *Sun*. It sounded as if it
had been written by Kosters himself and maybe it had.
Kosters was famous for the legions of friends he had in
journalism. A little talk with an editor in the secretary's
office, followed by cocktails with the secretary and a
tour d'horizon of the world's trouble spots, and the
views on the newspaper's editorial page changed noticeably.

It didn't always work.

We concede readily that the Soviets must be curbed and
that "Strength through Socialism" has as its ultimate
goal the communization of Western Europe. But we
wonder if rearming the West Germans is the way to go
about that task. There is the nagging feeling that it's a
cop-out of the real issue, which is the determination of
the United States to stand by its treaty and moral commitments.

That came from *The Wall Street Journal*.

There were about fifty pages of comments, editorial
and otherwise, typed neatly onto legal-size pages. It was
done by a small staff of the State Department. Bickel's
copy, of course, was a Xerox. About one hundred
other people also got copies, but only a few of them
were on Capitol Hill. Bickel's name was on the list because of "the very special service" he had rendered the
secretary through his work on the treaty.

There was a gentle tapping on Bickel's office door as
he started to read what the Miami *Herald* had to say
about the treaty. Bickel got up without bothering to put
on his shoes. In his stockinged feet—the stockings were
twenty dollars a pair at Bloomingdale's—Bickel walked
across the green wool carpet to the door, saying, "Just a
minute, Alex."

Bickel grasped the ornate doorknob and opened the

door. On the other side, Alex stood, smiling at him, wearing tan slacks and an orange sweater. Her long hair was loose around her neck.

"Got a minute, Travis? I'd like to talk to you about something," Alexandra said.

"Sure. Come in," Bickel said, making a sweeping motion into his office. He pointed at a brown leather couch in the office under the government-issue portrait of the President, and Alexandra sat down there. Bickel pulled an armchair of the same kind of leather up next to the corner of the couch where she sat.

"How come you're not watching television?" Bickel asked Alex, who was a football fan of great devotion. She often traveled around the country just to see the games.

"Well, I've got a lot of work to get done, and, anyway, there aren't really any good games left. It's all sewed up in the NFC," Alex said.

"You want a Coke?" Bickel asked.

"No thanks. I don't really need anything. I'm on a diet."

"You look thin enough to me," Bickel said. He looked down at the beige sweater over his own stomach. "I should be the one on a diet." He looked back up at Alex. "Whenever I see you on the society page of the *Post*, you look thin, too. Christ, I see you there more than I see the Iranian ambassador."

Alex laughed. "A girl's got to do something to keep busy."

Bickel felt a tug in his chest. In a soft voice, he said, "I wish you were still keeping busy with me."

"I am," Alex said.

"That's not what I mean," Bickel answered.

"I know," Alex answered. "We've been over that. I just know when to get in and when to stay out," Alex said. "That's all. I still feel for you, Travis. I still feel a lot."

Bickel laughed. He knew that he could not change Alex's mind. "Let's get back to business. I have got to come up with some kind of program for the blacks. I've just got to. You know that. That's the big hole in my plan."

"It's a problem area. I think we've got to think some more about that. I'm inclined to think that it shouldn't be a specific promise. More like general 'I love you and I would rather die than betray your trust.' It worked before." They both laughed. "That's just the opinion of a frivolous Okie girl," Alex said.

An image of the lovely girl lying on top of him kissing his neck came into his mind. Then he came back to reality. "If you're frivolous, I'd hate to see serious."

Bickel sighed. "Well, that can get ironed out. The main thing is that we've got to have the bill ready to go by the time the German thing gets to the floor. We've got to show people that I'm not shoving nuclear weapons all over the place."

"Of course, Travis, that's why we're doing this whole thing. We want you to look statesmanlike." Alexandra smiled when she said it, but Bickel still didn't like the tone in her voice.

Alexandra still stood in front of his desk. She fiddled with a diamond brooch on her suit jacket. "I just don't know, Travis," she said. "I don't know what the hell you have to be in bed with Patterson for." As soon as she said it, she regretted her choice of words.

Bickel stared at her. He could hear the rain falling behind him onto the window ledge. "I make those decisions, Alex. I did it for a lot of reasons, but I'm not going to have you second-guess me on something like this. I did it because it was the right thing to do." He sounded defensive and he knew it.

"You didn't need him, Travis. You didn't. You were doing fine without him," Alex said.

"You said I should do it," Bickel said sharply.

"I know," Alex answered. "It was a bad idea." She looked hurt. "You didn't need him, Trav. You know you didn't. You don't know all about him. I'm not saying I do, but there's a lot to know."

Damn her! She talked to me like I was a boy when I was fucking her and she still talks to me like I was a boy. Goddamn her.

"I'll find out about Patterson," he said.

"He's already found out about you," she said, a note of sadness in her voice.

The yellow telephone on Bickel's desk started to ring. Bickel looked down at it as if it were a snake. Only a few people knew the number, and one of them was Lydia D. Bickel. For a moment, Bickel did not pick up the receiver. The yellow phone sat on the desk next to a brown Call Director and Bickel wished that the yellow telephone would disappear.

"Hello," Bickel said as he picked up the phone. If he didn't answer, it would be even more suspicious.

"Hi, Travis. I hope you don't mind my calling you at the office," said a slow, deep voice. It was Jeff Richards, and it was also a great relief.

"Not at all, Jeff. I'm happy to hear from you. How are you?"

"Fine. How are you?"

"I'm fine. What's up?" Bickel asked, "You doing anything interesting on this rainy day?"

"As a matter of fact, I am," Richards said. "I'm over here at my office. Remember that research you asked me to do?"

"Of course. Have you been able to do anything?"

Richards' voice was slow and guarded. "This morning was the first time I was able to get any time on ONA when there was no other person from the planning division here. I got something kind of curious that I'd like to talk to you about. Could we get together?"

"Sure, Jeff. Is tomorrow at lunch all right with you?"

Richards coughed slightly. "Could we make it today? It really is quite interesting."

Bickel was starting to feel nervous. What the hell had Richards found out?

"Definitely. Why don't you come over here. Or I could meet you there?" Bickel said. Then he added, "Could you hold on a minute?" He cupped his hand over the mouthpiece and smiled at Alexandra. "Would you mind?"

She got up without a word and walked out of the room, closing the door as she left.

Bickel returned to the telephone. "I'm sorry, Jeff, but I thought that if it was as interesting as that, maybe no one at all should be in the room."

"You mean someone was in the room?" Richards's voice was raspy and excited.

"Just Alex Denman," Bickel said. What the hell was going on?

There was a sharp intake of breath on the other end of the line. "Listen, Travis. I guess I haven't gotten this across. This is extremely interesting. Extremely. I can't meet you at your office and you can't meet me at my office or at either of our homes. You can meet me between the Lincoln Memorial and the Reflecting Pool at three PM. That's two hours from now."

"Fine, I'll be there," Bickel said.

"And for Christ's sake, please don't tell Alex about it."

What the hell is going on? Bickel wondered. He had the same feeling he had felt at the Bad Kreuznach library. He wished he had a gun.

Across the Potomac and up the river a few miles, Jeff Richards ambled out of his office and down the hall to a Xerox room. He opened the door and there stood his son, Mark, making copies of his Jewish Youth Association newsletter. It gave Mark a sense of belonging to go into the office with his father on a weekend. There was nothing secret along these white-on-white corridors, except behind doors that were locked, so Mark did his copying and no one minded. No one minded especially today because no one else was there, except for a few guards and computer technicians making sure that ONA's circuits were always working perfectly.

Mark, at thirteen, was already five feet six and showed no sign of growing more slowly. He had a pale, freckled face and was almost painfully thin. His curly black hair was a clear sign of his parentage, in addition to all the other clear signs. "All set, Dad?" he asked as his father put his large hand on his son's head.

"Yep," Jeff Richards said. "We'd better get home now. You've got work to do."

"Is it still raining?" Mark asked. The hallway where he had been had no windows.

"I think so," Mark's father said, although ONA's room had no windows either.

"Can we stop by Great Falls and see if the river's gonna flood?" Mark asked eagerly. He loved, for whatever reason, to watch rising water.

"I don't know, Mark. You know your mother hates for us to get near those rocks."

"Oh, please, Dad. We're always careful You know we are. We'll stand far away from the edge. I just want to see it for a minute."

Richards stroked his chin. It might be a good idea. It would give him a few minutes to think about what ONA had kicked out a half hour before.

"Okay. But just for a few minutes. Then I have to run into town for a minute."

As Richards's battered Volvo pulled out of the CIA parking lot and onto the George Washington Memorial Parkway, the rain started to fall more rapidly on the roof of the car. The windshield wipers could not push it all away fast enough, so there was a slight blurring of the oncoming cars across the median strip. When Richards got to the belt highway, Route 495, the rain was heavier still, and the sky was growing darker. If he had promised anyone else, he would have turned left instead of right on Route 193 and headed for home. But he believed that a father should always keep his promises to his son, for many reasons, the best being that the son would then keep his promises. That was important to Jeff Richards.

Most people thought that Jeff Richards's main interest in life was his work, and in a way it was. But it was his work of love in bringing up his son to be a fine and self-reliant human being. He had studied it and he worked at it. He was himself the product of haphazard child rearing, and Mark's was going to be different.

The rain let up as Jeff Richards rolled down his window to pay his dollar parking fee. Amazingly, even in the downpour, there were many cars parked in the lot.

Mark must have something, Jeff Richards thought. A lot of people must like to see the river rising.

Then, as Jeff Richards got out of the car, he realized why there were so many cars parked there. To the left of the parking lot was a large utility-type building inside of which various wholesome things took place. On this particular rainy Sunday afternoon, there was a show of "The Fairfax Follies." Richards could see through a window that it was crowded with young mothers and their daughters and sons, watching a group of heavily made up people on the stage.

"That looks nice," Jeff Richards said to Mark. "Would you like to take a look in there?"

Mark squared his shoulders under his thin raincoat. "No, thanks, Dad. Let's go see the river."

That was good. Mark knew what he wanted. Father and son walked along a narrow pathway from the utility building to the rocky border of the Potomac River. From thirty yards away, they could see the river, grayish and ugly, pounding against the rocks of the falls. A heavy mist flew up as the rushing waters struck the jagged rocks.

"I think this is close enough, Mark," Richards said. "Let's just not get any closer."

"Okay, Dad," Mark said. "Could we walk up the river a little bit?"

"I think so," Richards said. "But let's stay well away from the river."

They walked along the edge of the rocks until they were a good distance away from the parking lot and the people watching "The Fairfax Follies." It was getting darker again, and the rain was coming down in large drops. Richards and his son walked into a small grove of trees that gave them almost no protection from the rain, since the branches had no leaves.

As he watched the water rush by, Richards thought to himself. It could all be a coincidence. It definitely could. And of course everyone knew, or at least suspected, about Patterson. But Jesus, that stuff about the Hitler Youth. That was the scary part. How the hell could he explain that? The translation of the German that was fed into the machine might not be right either. But if it was right, and if it wasn't just coincidence, then something awfully big was going on, and Bickel was definitely the right place to start in getting to the bottom of it.

How come no one had dug that stuff out of ONA before? Whoever put it into the computer must have known about it. Even the name alone should have raised some suspicion. Of course, the people who put the information in were just bureaucrats, and they weren't paid to think.

There was a rustling behind Richards. He turned around to see two men in heavy raincoats walking up behind them. Both men wore rain hats. One of them had a large mustache.

"How are you?" one of the men said.

"Fine," Richards said. "Some rain, huh?"

"Really amazing," the man with the mustache said. "Really amazing."

"I guess we better go back to the car, Mark," Richards said, loud enough for the two men to hear him.

The man with the mustache smiled at the boy. "I bet you'd like to stay here and watch the river," he said.

Mark looked at the stranger. "No, I think I'll go back to the car with my father."

The man with the mustache smiled at Mark as he and his father turned around. He made no move to hinder them until they were about ten paces away. Then he and his companion took lengths of pipe from their coats and walked rapidly up to Jeff Richards and Mark Richards. Mark took the first blow on the back of his head and did not feel anything after that. Jeff struggled until the third bash on his head made him unconscious and then dead.

"Let's get this thing over with," the man with the mustache said. "Let's take the kid first. I think he's still alive."

The other man bent over Mark and felt his throat. "No," he said, with a distinct Southern accent. "He ain't alive."

Bickel had left his office at 2:45 PM. The rain was now coming down in buckets and Bickel heard on the radio of his Oldsmobile Cutlass XJ that the water level at Great Falls was rising rapidly. Some flooding was expected in suburban Alexandria.

There was one large tourist bus parked next to the Lincoln Memorial, but aside from that there was almost no traffic. Bickel parked his car by the Memorial's back side and walked around to the front. It was almost three PM, but there was no sign of Jeff Richards. It was this goddamn rain. It made everyone screwed up—even someone as cool as Jeff Richards.

The busload of tourists was apparently from either Germany or Austria, because they were speaking German. January was an odd time to be visiting Washington, but maybe they got some kind of wonderful bargain rate. Jesus, though, it was desolate-looking. No life whatever hung on any of the trees. The streets were slick and ugly. It just didn't look nice, Bickel thought. It looked like Germany.

Bickel walked up the steps to the Memorial to avoid the rain. The tourists were mostly gone, and Bickel felt as if he had the huge statue of Lincoln to himself. But he didn't. An old woman with a plastic raincoat walked over to him, wobbling on her feet.

"Young man," she said. "I wonder if you could help me walk down those stairs."

It had been a while since anyone had called Bickel "young man," so he cheerfully took the woman's arm and led her down to the base.

"Thank you, sonny," she said, as she walked off.

Bickel walked back up the steps to the granite statue. It was almost 3:30. This was not like Richards. Christ Almighty, what was happening? What had Richards found out? Bickel wished he had made some other kind of arrangement. Anyone might come walking by the Lincoln Memorial. He should have met Richards somewhere private. He should have gotten some hint about what Richards had unearthed.

By 4 PM, it was time for Bickel to call his office and see if Richards had called him. There was no pay phone around, except one broken one, so Bickel got into his car. As he did, he heard a story about a man and his son who had fallen into the Great Falls of the Potomac and been dashed against the rocks. The man's name was Jeffrey Richards.

Bickel felt weak and dizzy.

CHAPTER

15

By the time Travis Bickel reached home, his wife had heard the news about Richards. She sat in the living room in a faded green armchair next to the fireplace and cried quietly. She was wearing a green robe, and all of her except her white face and her blue eyes blended into the chair. It gave her a sepulchral appearance.

She didn't even yell at Bickel for having left her alone on a Sunday. "I cannot believe it," she said as he walked in the door. "I absolutely cannot believe it. If ever there was a guy who deserved to live, it was Jeff Richards."

Bickel took off his raincoat and hung it in the hall closet, then walked over to Lydia and crouched down next to her. He took her hand—the first time he had done so in a long time. Her hand was cold and moist.

"I know, darling. And Mark, too," Bickel said.

"It just is not like him," Lydia said softly, pulling her robe tightly around her throat. "It just isn't like him. He's the most careful person in the world. How could he have fallen into Great Falls?"

The question was on Bickel's mind, too. First, Simon Kart and now Jeff Richards. Two highly talented men who had been helping him since he left Bad Kreuznach, two innocent, blameless men, were dead. Why? It simply could not be coincidence. That was too much. Did they know something? Or, more likely, did someone on some group think they knew something? Then why was Bickel still alive? And what the hell did they think Bickel knew? He couldn't think of anything he knew that a thousand other people didn't know. Were these killings meant to discourage him from working on the treaty? But he had received no threats, no warnings.

He looked over at Lydia. She was still crying. When she looked like that, vulnerable and soft, he could remember how he had felt about her when he married her. He did not feel that way often. He reached out and stroked her brown hair.

"He was an incredibly fine man," Bickel said. "I have never known a more concerned parent or a man who loved people more." He could feel tears coming. He fought to keep them down. If he started crying, too, there would be no stopping Lydia for the rest of the day.

"It had something to do with the CIA, didn't it?" Lydia asked. "It must have. What else could it have been? Careful people don't fall into the Great Falls."

"I suppose it did," Bickel replied quietly.

"What was he working on that people would kill him and Mark, too, Travis? You talked to him about that kind of stuff. What the hell could it have been? I thought spies didn't kill each other anymore."

"I wish I knew what it was, honey, I really wish I did. He worked on a lot of secret stuff. I can't tell you all of it. You don't want to know. But I don't know of anything new or superimportant," he lied.

"I hope somebody does something about it," Lydia said. "It just isn't right."

"Someone will," Bickel said. "I will."

The little brass clock on Arthur Kosters's desk was just chiming six PM when Travis Bickel walked in.

Bickel was still wearing the same sports clothes he had been wearing all day, except that he had changed his beige sweater for a tweed sports jacket. Bickel had called Kosters from home after he had given Lydia a Dalmane and put her in bed.

"I have to talk to you, Arthur. It's really urgent," Bickel said into the Trimline phone.

"Of course, Travis," Kosters said in a heavier German accent than usual. "I'll put my secretary on and she'll make an appointment for tomorrow, first thing in the morning."

"No," Bickel said. "It has to be right now. I told you, it's urgent."

"Vell then, come over right away. I'll have Liza clear you into the building. Why don't you park in the basement so that you don't get wet."

Now the clock chimed six times and Kosters rose from behind a stack of papers to greet Bickel. Even though it was a Sunday afternoon, Kosters wore a midnight-blue wool pin-stripe suit and a white shirt.

"What is it, Travis? You look terrible," Kosters said, motioning toward one of the yellow couches. "Do you want a drink? Do you want coffee?"

"No, nothing, thanks," Bickel said as he sat down.

"Well, for God's sake, tell me what's going on," Kosters said, as he settled down into his armchair next to the couch.

Bickel took in a deep breath of air. Then he looked over at Kosters's plump, kind face. "I'm worried," he said.

"I can see that, Travis. I can see that." The German accent was slightly heavy again, and "that" came out like "dot."

"It's more than the treaty. It's a lot more than that." Bickel paused and let out a heavy sigh. "Did you know that Jeff Richards and his son were found smashed to death in the Potomac near Great Falls this afternoon?"

Kosters looked profoundly sad. "Yes. I knew that. Naturally the director learned about it and told me. A terrible tragedy. He did great work. To be struck down like that. And his son, too."

"Why did he die? That's what I have to know," Bickel said firmly.

"You don't believe it was an accident?" Kosters asked, his eyebrows raised slightly.

"Do you?" Bickel asked.

Kosters looked even sadder. "Frankly, if it had been anyone other than Jeff Richards, I would have thought that maybe it was an accident. Maybe. But Richards was a careful man." Kosters stared up at the acoustically tiled ceiling. "No. I do not believe it was an accident. Neither does the director."

"Who does the director think did it?" Bickel asked urgently.

Kosters leveled his gaze down from the ceiling. "He doesn't have the slightest idea. At least, that's what he says."

Bickel glanced around the room that resonated with so much power and authority. "Arthur, who do you think did it?" he asked.

Kosters did not say anything for a full minute. Then he spoke in a low voice. "I do not know. But I am going to find out." His soft brown eyes seemed to bore into Bickel's harder, blue-gray eyes as he spoke.

"I have to tell you some things," Bickel said. "I want you to tell me what you make of them. They're important."

"Please. Go ahead," Kosters said.

"Let me start just before Christmas in Germany. You know that when I was in Bad Kreuznach, I searched for papers about the early Nazi period. It's sort of a hobby of mine. I was given some lists of members of the Hitler Youth and then they were taken away and the librarian said they didn't exist. That was before Kart was blown up. That was before the Mercedes mechanic that no one can find fixed the car and probably put a bomb in it."

Kosters furrowed his brow. "Why did you go to Bad Kreuznach, of all places?" he asked.

Bickel shrugged. "It was an easy drive and it was supposed to have good, undamaged architecture."

Kosters stroked his chin for a moment, then said, "Go on."

"A few days after I got back to Bonn, at a New Year's Eve party for the delegation, I was picked up by a girl, a beautiful girl, a reporter for *Der Spiegel*. Her name was Katherine Dorn. She took me back to her apartment and we spent the whole night making love. Now, I'm not a big one for false modesty, but that kind of thing doesn't happen to me too much."

"You think she's an agent?" Kosters asked.

"I don't know. Now here's more. I didn't tell you everything about my meeting with Patterson."

"Oh?" Kosters asked. He leaned forward in his chair and again furrowed his brow.

"The night I had dinner there, Roberts, his flunky, left us alone. Patterson said some damned weird things about the Nazis. I mean he condemned them for killing the Jews and everything, but as I left, he said the strangest damn thing."

Kosters leaned forward slightly more. Bickel could see the outline of the rolls of his stomach.

"He said that the Nazis were dreamers of a great dream. Now that is goddamn strange," Bickel said.

"It is indeed," Kosters said. "I'm not surprised he thinks it, but I'm very surprised that he said it."

"So, that takes us up to Richards. On Monday, the morning of the day I saw you, I asked Jeff to come over to the Hill. I told him what had happened and asked him if he could make anything of it. He said he couldn't, but that he would put it into ONA and see what he got." Bickel paused. "I asked him not to mention Katherine Dorn and he said she wasn't important. Well, around noon today, Jeff called me from Langley and said he had something very interesting that he wanted to tell me in person. He wouldn't say a word about it over the phone."

Kosters put his left palm to his forehead. "Oh, my God," he said with a sharp exhalation of breath. "Who else knows about this?"

Bickel was sweating slightly under his arms. "No one," he said. "Not a soul."

Kosters got up from his chair and walked over to the window. He looked out at the lights of the Memorial

Bridge going over to the Arlington National Cemetery.

He did not say anything. Bickel spoke. "Now I want to find out what the hell is going on. I cared about Jeff Richards and Si Kart, and they're dead. And more than that, I care about me. I have to believe that I'm next. Maybe I was supposed to be first."

Kosters turned around. His face was florid. "I will find out about it. And I'm not going through the director. That doesn't make sense considering that Richards was killed after he left Langley. It's something I'll handle with my own resources. I hope there's an explanation that's not going to make us cringe. I really hope so."

"I hope so, too," Bickel said.

"Do you want to get a bodyguard?" Kosters asked. "It seems like a good idea."

"Let me think about that overnight," Bickel said. "I'm not sure that a bodyguard would be adequate."

"Maybe not," Kosters said, as he walked back to Bickel. "But, I don't think you're next. If they wanted you to be dead, whoever they are, you'd be dead. And one other thing. You don't quite fit the pattern of the victims. You're well-known and a high official, for one thing."

"That's true," Bickel said. "For once, I'm glad."

"Travis," Kosters said, sitting down heavily in his chair and touching Bickel's knee, "this is a terrible blow. Terrible."

Bickel said nothing.

"But it cannot stop our work. It simply cannot be allowed to impede the progress of the treaty. Friends are important, and you and I are important, but the treaty is even more important.

Bickel said nothing.

"And your future is important. Do not think of yourself as an individual, although of course you are. Think of yourself as a historic figure, a man with a mission."

Bickel looked sideways at Kosters. "What the hell are you telling me?" he asked.

"It just would not make any sense for you to get sidetracked now," Kosters said. "We will run down the people who killed Richards. If the same people killed Kart, we'll get them too. I assure you of it."

"So?" Bickel said.

"So, you must continue in your work. I am trying to work out a trip to Warsaw for you after the treaty vote. By yourself, but as the head of a mission on normalizing relations. That's major stuff with the ethnics. We'll get other stuff done."

Bickel was almost speechless. Kosters was a veritable machine. Even in a moment of death and loss, he was planning for the future, planning for political stunts.

On the other hand, Bickel thought, why not? He couldn't bring back Richards or his son. The best thing was to forge ahead.

"While we're on the subject, Arthur," Bickel said, "I want to ask you a favor. The grape growers have a big meeting in Fresno next month. It would do me a lot of good if you put in an appearance."

"I'll check with Liza and the President. It might not be a bad idea. We'll try to work something out," Kosters said.

Neither man spoke for a minute, and then Kosters said, "There is a lot of violence and cruelty in the world. You should not become their prisoner."

"You're right," Bickel said.

"And, really, Travis, I don't think they meant to kill you," Kosters said slowly.

"Why not?" Bickel asked, seeking a ray of hope.

"You're not Jewish, and Richards and Kart were," Kosters said mournfully.

In that moment, in that office of muted paneling and oil portraits, of private kitchens and saunas and views out over the Virginia shore of the Potomac River, Travis Bickel realized that for the secretary of state of the United States of America, the image of childhood was not of baseball or sticks thrown into a pond or sitting in a classroom or going on his first date. It could not be. It had to be an image of a plump, bespectacled kid running in terror from other kids who called him a filthy Jew.

CHAPTER

16

The sun in Palm Springs, even in January, was clear and penetrating. Frank Roberts looked around at the desert as the limousine sped along Highway 111, past the town and farther out into the desert, and saw nothing but parched land, arid and harsh, broken occasionally by scrub brush and a billboard. The glare was powerful, even through heavily tinted windows. Roberts knew that Patterson had ordered this particular limousine specially built for desert driving. It had a double radiator and heavy-duty air conditioning, among other features, to make for more pleasant driving through these damned flats.

The telephone in the front seat of the car rang. Before the first ring had stopped, the driver picked it up and spoke into the receiver. Roberts could not hear, at first, because the window partition was closed. That also was custom made—doubly thick to prevent any possibility of hearing, and with additional tinting. Receivers were built into the right and left armrests in the back seat. Underneath each was a set of buttons. Almost immediately, one of the buttons blinked on and off. Roberts picked up the receiver on his left just as he saw a crushed snake in the highway.

"Frank Roberts speaking," he said. He knew who it would be.

"Hello, Frank," Elson Patterson said. "Having a nice time?"

"Fine, Mr. Patterson. I hope you're well."

"Yes, I'm fine. When are you going to get here?"

"It sould be very soon now, sir," Roberts said. "I would say no more than ten minutes."

"That's good. That's fine. I hope you had a nice flight. I think that it's time we got that Jetstar replaced by a newer model. It shakes too much. If I wanted to get shaken up when I fly, I'd take something else. I could take a regular airliner, just like everyone else," Patterson said.

"I'll make a note of it," Roberts said, fishing a pad out of his jacket pocket and jotting down a note—"New Jetstar." He replaced the pad in the inside breast pocket of his gray Southwick suit.

"It makes sense to me, doesn't it. Or am I wrong? Is there something wrong with that idea, Frank?" Patterson asked.

"No, Mr. Patterson. You're entirely right. I'll take care of it right away," Roberts said.

"I'll probably be taking a nap in a few minutes, Frank, so you just make yourself comfortable and have a swim or something. That's all right, isn't it?"

"Yes, that's very kind of you, Mr. Patterson," Roberts said.

Patterson hung up the telephone and Roberts put his receiver back in the armrest. Roberts looked up into the driver's seat and saw that the driver's receiver had been hung up, too. That was a relief. It was a sign that Mr. Patterson had confidence in him.

Five minutes later there was a turnoff in the highway marked by no sign whatever. The limousine turned carefully off the highway onto an unpaved lane leading away into the distance and over a ridge at least a mile away. The limousine hardly slowed down, throwing up swirls of dust as it raced along the dirt road. There was some swaying and bouncing, but not much. The road was exceptionally smooth, and the limousine had exceptionally good suspension.

In a moment the limousine came over the top of the hill and started down a long, gradual, smoothly paved asphalt road. About a mile ahead was an oasis of palm trees and hedges, surrounding a compound of one large, modern adobe-style house and several cabanas behind a large swimming pool. The house, at first glance, looked as if the Indians had built it. But a second look showed large expanses of glass and redwood beams across the flat roof. There was also a number of antennas on the roof of the house.

Before the limousine reached the oasis, it came to a stop at a guardhouse, where a barrier crossed the road. When the guard, in plain clothes, hefting a shotgun, saw the car and who was in it, he waved it on without a word. He went into the guardhouse and pressed a button, and the barrier lifted up.

When Frank Roberts stepped out of the limousine, he was dazzled by the sun. The air was not as hot as he had feared, but the sun was amazing—white and overpowering. Roberts walked across a constantly irrigated green lawn, which looked as if it might have been in Kent, and up to the front door of the house, a massive oak slab that swung open before Roberts knocked.

"How are you, Mr. Roberts?" an elderly Mexican asked.

"Fine, Carlos. How are you?" Roberts answered the man, who wore black trousers and a white shirt, like a waiter.

"Well, thank you. Mr. Patterson is in the study. He would like for you to come in there," Carlos said with a slight bow.

Roberts walked down a flagstone-floored hallway to the study. The walls were covered with photographs of Patterson with famous people, almost all of them Europeans. Roberts had memorized some of the larger ones, like the photos of Patterson with the Duke and Duchess of Windsor and the one of Patterson with Hermann

Goering. Both pictures were apparently taken in the same mountain setting. Probably Bavaria.

"How are you, Mr. Patterson?" Roberts asked as he walked into the study. The door was open. Patterson sat in a large chair facing a floor-to-ceiling window that looked out on a hundred miles of desert. His rugged face looked at home atop a western outfit of highly decorated shirt and plain denim trousers. The room was not lit except for the light that came in through the heavily tinted window. That was enough to make the room bright enough for reading, though, and that was obviously what Patterson used it for. Three walls of the room were lined with bookshelves. As was usual in Patterson's homes, the books were interspersed with photographs. The whole house was cool and dry, but Elson Patterson's study was noticeably colder. An air conditioner was running somewhere, but Frank Roberts had never been able to hear it.

Roberts walked into the room and shook hands with Patterson, who smiled a tight half-smile but did not rise. In his lap was an open and well-worn copy of *The Decline of the West,* with Patterson's right index finger inside as if to mark a page. There was a leather-covered couch about three feet out from the bookshelves on the left and Roberts sat down in it.

Patterson had not said a word. Beyond greetings, Patterson did not like to be spoken to while he was concentrating, as he obviously was. Roberts looked around the room at some of the other books in the room. Of course, there was the shelf of books about the *Führer,* featuring prominently John Toland's massive and highly favorable biography and Alan Bullock's much less complimentary study, as well as a number of German biographies, some from the prewar period.

Just below that in a place of honor were books about Charles Lindbergh. Patterson was one of the great admirers of the Lone Eagle, and he had virtually every book about him ever written, as well, of course, as every book written by Lindbergh.

Roberts hoped that Patterson was not going to launch into one of his lengthy discussions of Spengler's work.

Patterson liked to talk about Spengler a great deal, but he had not done so for several months, and Roberts was not as well briefed on the pessimistic German as he should have been. As it happened, Patterson did not say anything. He simply looked out the window, beyond the shimmering blue of the pool and out into the desert.

Above the bookshelves, Roberts noticed the same pictures that were always there. There was a portrait of Grandpa—Horace Patterson—standing in front of a gigantic structure, which was one of his steel mills. Then there was a portrait of Elson Patterson's grandmother, Alida Hooker, a famous society debutante and party-giver in the 1920's. She came from a wealthy family herself, one that had had money in it for far longer than the richer but upstart Pattersons. Roberts compared the two pictures. The difference was enormous and much in Alida Hooker Patterson's favor. Where Patterson's grandfather had heavy, bullying features and the look of a man who is not far removed from the stockyards, whence he had in fact come, Patterson's grandmother had a delicate and soft air about her. Her features were finely chiseled. No heaviness or bullying there. Where Horace Patterson showed a thick, heavily muscled neck, like a bull, Alida Patterson looked as if her head were held up by a slender ivory shaft, which Botticelli might have drawn.

There was no portrait of Patterson's father. Where it might have been, there was a bizarrely detailed oil painting of the suffering Christ. Unlike some other likenesses of the Savior in torment, this one was cruelly realistic. The centurions had apparently just speared Christ and the blood was pouring out. Beads of sweat stood out on the Nazarene's face, and his eyes were rolled heavenward in an attitude of excruciating pain. The portrait was at least two by three feet, far larger than either of the other oil paintings.

"I've been thinking, Frank. Thinking," Patterson suddenly said, breaking Robert's train of thought about the paintings.

"Yes, sir," Roberts said.

"I've been thinking about whether we're putting too

much on one man," Patterson said thoughtfully. "It could be the kind of mistake we made before. We don't want to do it again."

"No, Mr. Patterson," Roberts said.

"I wonder if everything got straightened out in Washington. Did it?" Patterson asked.

"Yes, Mr. Patterson. No problems," Roberts said. Even though the room was cool, Roberts started to sweat.

"I saw the item on the news. I didn't like them killing that kid. It's not good to kill small children, is it?" Patterson asked. He swiveled toward Roberts in his armchair as he asked the question. He looked extremely well-rested, Roberts thought.

"No, of course not, Mr. Patterson. Of course not. It was not good," Roberts said. Was Patterson asking him if he was going to blame himself for something two thugs, thugs controlled by an entirely different part of the organization, had done?

Apparently Patterson could read his mind because he quickly added, "Of course, I don't blame you, Frank. I know who chose those men. I know it wasn't you. Ours is a large operation, and you can't do everything. I know who chose them and he'll answer to me. Those men were wrong to do what they did, that's for sure. You agree?"

"Definitely, Mr. Patterson," Roberts said, relaxing. Those men were dead right now.

"Well, that's all I wanted to know. Of course, sometimes people get carried away. People get frightened that somehow they might be recognized. Then they do things that aren't good. But we can't be nitpicking all the time. But you don't agree?" he asked, raising his eyebrows slightly. The eyebrows were thin and white with strands of gray.

"No, I agree, Mr. Patterson. I fully agree. Sometimes people do things that are wrong, but that doesn't make them thoroughly bad people," Roberts said.

"I think that's right," Patterson said, swiveling his chair again so that it faced the window. "We can't be picking nits all the time. Not that a small child is a nit.

Far from it. But you know what I mean. But maybe you don't know what I mean?"

"I think I know what you mean, Mr. Patterson," Roberts said. "I think so." He said it without a hint of sarcasm.

"Let's get back to this other thing, this Bickel thing, Frank. What do we hear about him these days? Anything new?" Patterson asked.

"Well, of course, we have the report from our friend at the Lake who says that Bickel may know what's up but would still play along, maybe get totally involved. And, on the other hand, we know he's puzzled about what happened to Richards," Roberts said.

"We do know that?" Patterson asked. "How do we know that?" He seemed genuinely curious.

"We got a report about it this morning from our friend at the Lake. It wasn't from the girl. It was from someone sent by the girl," Roberts said. He glanced up at Horace Patterson. What the hell was going on in Patterson's mind? He must know about all this. Some of the grandfather's blood was running through Elson Patterson. He was on the trail of something.

"Do we trust that guy at the Lake? Do we?" Patterson asked. He stood up with a sudden heave and put his book back on the shelf. Then he walked over to an immense oak desk that abutted the couch where Roberts sat and seated himself behind it.

"I don't think we trust him as much as some other sources, but we don't think he's purposely feeding us trash, Mr. Patterson. Do you think that?" Roberts asked. "We can get rid of him right away if that's a problem."

"I know we can. I know we can, Frank. But, I just wonder if we could somehow use him a little more. Do you think we could?" Patterson asked as he picked up a crystal paperweight and dropped it from one hand to the other. Inside the paperweight was a dried scorpion.

"It's a fine idea, Mr. Patterson. The only problem is that I don't think he's set up to pitch. Only to catch. He's just a conduit," Roberts said.

"Of course he is," Patterson said. "Of course he is. I

know that. But if we really own him, why can't we ask him to slip in a few extra pieces of information that we'll give to him. Just to confuse the folks in Jerusalem a little. Does that make sense?"

"It's brilliant, Mr. Patterson," Roberts said. He meant it, too. "We assumed that the people in Jerusalem would naturally check with her about everything she sent. But why would they? If they think he's working for someone else, they wouldn't think he would do any more than sell what she gave him. We could give him something new."

"Exactly," Patterson said. "But you don't like that idea. I can tell." Patterson picked up a pen, an old Parker 51, from his desk and started to doodle. "Of course, we're all on the same side now, so maybe it's not a good idea. I just like to keep them guessing.

"No, Mr. Patterson. I think it's a wonderful idea."

Patterson swiveled his desk chair and reached over to the bookshelf. He ran his right hand along the shelves and started to pick out *Power! How to Get It; How to Use it*, then pushed it back into its spot. He turned to face Roberts.

"I wonder if we're making a mistake about Bickel. I keep wondering about him. Do you ever wonder about him?" Patterson asked.

"Yes sir, I do," Roberts said.

"I wonder if he can be counted on. We've bet heavily and had to close the game before, you know," Patterson said.

"I know it well," Roberts said.

"It was before your time, but believe me, we had very big problems with Nixon especially. Very big problems. I don't want that to happen again. Do you?"

"No, sir," Roberts said.

"Tell me, Frank. What did you think about the Jetstar? You can tell the truth. Do you think I should get rid of it? It's not the money, of course. That's not it. But maybe the new ones aren't as reliable as the old ones. That's a possibility, isn't it?" Patterson asked.

"I'll get you an option paper about it, Mr. Patterson. I'll find out about the reliability of the new small jets.

I'll give you all the data I can lay my hands on. After that, of course, it'll be up to you," Roberts said.

"Of course," Patterson said. He flicked an imaginary speck of dust off his cowboy shirt. "Well, all I can ask is that you get me the facts. Then I'll decide. Or is that wrong?"

"No, that's right," Roberts said. He looked out at the desert. Shadows were barely beginning to be visible in the distance. It was really true. The desert did turn purplish in the late afternoon during winter.

"You see," Patterson went on, cocking his gaunt head to the right, "the problem is the same with Bickel. We have to know all the facts about him. But it's not simply a matter of asking for his resume. Not at all. Because what we have to know is how he'll react to a new situation, one totally different from anything he's ever expected to happen. That's the problem. What do you think of that?"

"I agree, Mr. Patterson. That's a serious problem," Roberts said.

"That's all I have," Patterson said. He let out a long sigh. "All I have is problems, and I have to figure them all out myself, even down to what kind of a plane to buy." He looked around the study as if searching for some imaginary person to help him. "I don't mind, you understand. If someone has to do it and I'm the only one, then so be it. But I won't always be around, Frank, and then someone'll have to do it for himself." He stared forward into space.

Roberts looked down at the chocolate-brown rug. This was Patterson's way of complaining without asking for help. He did it more and more frequently these days. Perhaps his prostate was acting up again. Roberts tried to think of something to say.

"Could we give him some kind of test, Mr. Patterson? Something that would measure how likely he is to do what he's supposed to do?" Roberts asked.

"That would be awfully tricky, Frank, because we know that the situation we're talking about putting him in is unique. It could hardly be replicated before it happens," Patterson said.

"That's right, of course. But perhaps we could test him somewhat. We could test his ability to respond to crisis situations with more resilience than ever," Roberts said.

Patterson got up and walked back to his chair, the one that allowed him to look out the window without any obstruction. "It's definitely a thought, Frank. Of course, he's been tested by what's been happening to Kart and Richards. Frankly, he's been doing rather well."

"He certainly has, Mr. Patterson," Roberts said.

"But maybe he needs something else, something that'll really shock him so that we can measure something about how he snaps out of it," Patterson said.

"I'll try to make up some suggestions, Mr. Patterson," Roberts said.

"That would be helpful. Something genuinely effective as a test. Something shocking. Now tell me about the girl," Patterson said.

An hour later, Roberts was in one of the cabanas taking a nap, and Patterson watched the desert. Shadows were much longer than they had been just an hour before. The desert was a beautiful place, if a man took the time to appreciate it. But so few people did. So few people were concerned about the world around them or took the time to think about it.

He had taken the time. Patterson remembered talking to him about the mountains and sky of Germany. The *Führer* believed that they were an organic part of the Aryan character. Of course, he had carried that a little too far, with studies on whether Germans who ate potatoes from German soil were different from Germans who ate potatoes from French soil. But the principle was sound—a healthy interest in man's interaction with his world.

But the principle was far more important than that, and deeper. Man, the *Führer* believed, is part of the physical world, just as wolves or trees are. A certain kind of man is naturally in harmony with that world and a certain kind of *Untermensch* is not in harmony. It is not hard to see which is which, the *Führer* said one morning during a walk around his supreme OKW headquarters at the Wolf's Lair in Rastenburg.

"Look at German youth, marching through the mountains and valleys of our Reich. You've seen them," he said. "You've led them from time to time. You can see that they belong there, with nature. Anyone can see that."

The *Führer* still looked young. It was only six weeks after the beginning of Hitler's push into Russia, and things were still going well. Some German units had advanced so fast that they were daily outrunning their supplies. Already the entire Ukraine had been freed, and the Ukrainian people were rising to throw off Bolshevism and throw in their lot with their liberators. But that morning, walking around the gardens and woods surrounding the headquarters, there was no talk of the war. The *Führer*, as always, was thinking one or two moves ahead.

"Look at the Jew. He lives in cities. He knows nothing of the soil. He wants to know nothing of the soil. Put him out in the country and he doesn't know what to do. He has no relationship with nature. He knows only manipulation and scheming, nothing of appreciation of beauty or nature."

That made sense to Patterson. The Jews he had known in college were always making wisecracks and showing off their clothes and cars. They never participated in anything strenuous or physical. You could not find them enjoying the beautiful forests which surrounded Dartmouth. Instead they stayed inside and played cards or read. The *Führer* was clearly correct. There was a fundamental difference between Jew and Aryan.

An aide in a green orderly's uniform walked up to the *Führer* and his guest and offered them coffee or breakfast. The *Führer* had laughed and self-deprecatingly pushed the food away. Patterson followed his host's example.

"All men are mortal," the *Führer* said. "I, who served four years at the front, know that. I saw even the luckiest and healthiest of comrades blown to shreds. But in peacetime, we can do something to stave off mortality. We can eat less. Hardly anything is more important. Look at Goering. Always eating, always overweight, always pale and weak. A fine man, of course, but he should follow the example of the wolves. There is no such thing as a fat wolf, Elson," the *Führer* said.

Looking out at the desert, Patterson recalled that that was probably the first time the *Führer* had called him by his first name. In German it came out much as it did in English. The shadows out in the desert became even longer. Still, the sky was a brilliant blue, just as it had been on that August day in East Prussia forty-two years before.

Patterson remembered thinking even then that the *Führer* had the bluest eyes he had ever seen, as if in his very countenance there was a sign that he was in harmony with the most majestic elements of nature, like the sky and the seas. And the *Führer* called him "Elson."

Hitler had been wearing his military uniform minus the high peaked cap he usually wore in public. It was a simple gray double-breasted uniform, much less ostentatious than those worn by far less exalted figures. As the *Führer* and Patterson emerged from the woods, Patterson had wished the older man success in the Eastern campaign.

"That is assured, barring a natural catastrophe," the *Führer* said. "But I have a question for you." And here he had grasped Patterson's right forearm. "How will the American people react when America and Germany are the only two major powers left? Will they see that we have much in common, that our blood is their blood, or will they let the Jews make them fight?"

Those blue eyes burned into Patterson's own more watery blue eyes. "I do not know, my *Führer*. There is no underestimating the importance of the Jews. But the real problem is Roosevelt. Of course, I'll do my best."

Without removing his grasp from Patterson's forearm, Hitler continued to stare into Patterson's eyes. "I know you will, Elson. I know you will. You understand, just as I did when I was your age, the great things are accomplished only by the daring and will of individuals." The grip on his forearm tightened. "You understand that, and because you understand it, you will be able to do what is needed. I am confident of that."

There was more of that, of course. A great deal more of specifics of just what the *Führer* had in mind for Patterson. But what Patterson remembered as he stared at the sun beginning to sink behind the San Bernardino Mountains was the *Führer*'s grip on his forearm as he stared at him with those blue eyes and called him Elson.

It was sad that small children like Mark Richards sometimes had to die, but that was inevitable. And what was that compared to the vision of that man with the blue eyes?

As the desert turned black beyond the sweep of Patterson's searchlights, Patterson reflected on just how large a bet they had made on Bickel. Patterson knew he was not a young man. This might be his last chance. The key figures in Croesus were at the apex of their powers. If the thing could not be made to work now, then who could guide it after Patterson died? Roberts? That was a laugh. Roberts was a born flunky. Those lunatics in South America? They couldn't find their ass with both hands. And as for the other possibility, Patterson would never believe that he could handle it. He could never be trusted, no matter what anyone else thought. He had played along, but he could not be trusted. That was why the thing with Bickel had to work then and there. Now. While I am still alive, Patterson thought.

CHAPTER

17

A light snow fell on Capitol Hill as dusk settled over the nation's capital. Travis Bickel glanced at his wristwatch, a Cartier Tank model which Elson Patterson had sent over to replace his aging Seiko. The watch was small and rectangular, with a plain face and slightly ornate numerals. The hands were black and stubby. They told Bickel that it was not yet five o'clock. "For a great leader" was engraved on the back. Although he did not discuss the subject at all, even with Alexandra Denman, Bickel loved his new watch. He knew that watches like his, with real gold parts and a gold back, cost over eight hundred dollars. To Patterson, that was not a noticeable figure—although, like all rich people, he probably noticed every nickel—but it meant a lot to Bickel. He saw those watches on the rich men in Congress, and, even though by most people's standards Bickel was rich himself, he had never felt free to spend eight hundred dollars on a watch. Now he had it, and he had not spent a dime. He supposed that his liking a watch so much was a sign of a certain superficiality of character, but he thought he had few such signs.

In front of Bickel on his large desk were three folders, each with a neatly typed index tab. The one on top said "SENATORS—FOR." Under that was a folder tabbed "SENATORS—AGAINST." And on the bottom was "SENATORS—UNDECIDED."

The top folder grew steadily thicker. For each senator who had pledged to vote for the German Rearmament Treaty there was a single sheet of paper giving Bickel at a glance the date the senator had given his pledge and the reasons for each senator's support. There was also a note of what arguments Bickel had found particularly persuasive to that particular lawmaker.

A similar procedure was followed for the much smaller group who were in the "AGAINST" file. A single eggshell sheet of paper was allotted to each senator. On it was noted the most recent date he had personally or through a top aide told Bickel that he would not vote for ratification and would definitely vote against ratification. Also noted were the reasons given for opposing the treaty. Finally, there were extremely brief notes of which arguments had made any dent at all with the senator.

For the undecided group, the procedure was the same except that the date when last contacted was noted after the name. It was never more than four days before the date the senator was next called. The German Rearmament Treaty was far too important to die through inattention.

Not that it was even close to dying. Far from it, according to the papers in the three folders. But it was good to be careful. The negatives plus the undecided were still a formidable bloc. There was such a thing as shrinkage in the pro-Rearmament Treaty, if not now, then in the future. Good to be careful.

But today, January 25, was not helping much. Washington became paralyzed at any hint of snow, and the National Weather Service was predicting far more than a hint. Seven to nine inches were predicted by dawn of

January 26, and that would bring the city to its knees. The buses would stop running and traffic would consist of long lines of cars stopped dead, with engines on and lights blazing. Only the new subway, the Metro, would run smoothly on its underground tracks. Unfortunately, it did not yet run into the parts of the Washington metropolitan area where most U.S. senators and their aides lived—upper Northwest Washington, Alexandria, Chevy Chase, and Fairfax County. Perhaps it would never run to those places. Many of their residents preferred the inaccessibility that nonservice on the Metro conferred.

Still, the people who lived in those areas of large green lawns and three Volvos to a family had to get home somehow. When a snowstorm threatened, they chose a simple way: they left work early.

"How come you're still here?" Alex asked over the intercom. "Aren't you afraid of the snow?"

"Not at all," Bickel replied cheerfully. "Lydia is out of town, and if I can't get home, I'll just spend the night in my office. It's got a television and an electric blanket and it works just fine."

"What works just fine?" Alex asked.

"The whole thing—spending the night here," Bickel answered.

"I'd like to come in and talk to you for a minute, if you have time," Alex said.

"Sure. Come on in," Bickel said. "I have nothing else to do. We'll have a drink. And no more chewing me out about Patterson, okay?"

For some reason, Bickel had a cheerful, almost giddy feeling as he walked across the room to his miniature refrigerator disguised as a paneled box. He took out an ice tray and set it on the Formica top of the paneled box. From a cabinet above the refrigerator he took two glasses and a bottle of Amaretto.

Five minutes later, he raised his glass as Alex raised hers and said, "Here's to snowy evenings when you don't have to shovel the driveway."

Alex, who wore a green hopsack pantsuit and large emerald earrings to match, smiled and raised her glass.

"I love the snow here," Bickel said. "We never had it, of course, in L.A. I used to see it in movies and it always looked wonderful. Now we've got it and it's great. It feels cozy to be in it. It feels cozy to be out of it. It just plain feels cozy," he concluded with a smile. He put his feet up on the coffee table in front of the couch, knocking off a copy of *Washingtonian* magazine. The cover featured a picture of Secretary Kosters, looking worried but still smiling. He stood in front of the globe in the State Department lobby. The caption said, "ARTHUR KOSTERS—ATLAS WITH ANXIETY."

Bickel wore a brown herringbone suit with a yellow shirt and striped tie. His familiar Peal & Company loafers completed his outfit.

"We used to have amazing storms up in Poughkeepsie," Alex said. "Really amazing. But we didn't have to drive anywhere, and men would come and shovel away the snow from paths. So it wasn't bad."

Alex Denman noticed that Bickel was more relaxed than he had been since the murder of Jeff Richards. She wondered why. Maybe it was because Lydia was out of town. Maybe it was because events were moving smoothly on the rearmament bill. Maybe it was the snow. Frankly, she told herself, she didn't know what it was. But it was a pleasant change.

Alex and Travis sat there as the snow mounted in intensity outside the large sash windows, remnants of a time when there was no air conditioning in the Old Senate Office Building, a time when there was no New Senate Office Building. As he fondled his liqueur, Bickel thought of the last time he had seen snow—on some of the fields on the way to Bad Kreuznach. Then he thought about Simon Kart, and then about Jeff Richards.

Just the day before, Bickel had spoken to Kosters about Kosters's investigation of the murder. As usual, the conversation had taken place in Kosters's office.

"There's not a clue," the secretary of state said. "If Richards found anything, whoever got to him also got to ONA and cleaned out whatever was there. ONA doesn't even show any records of the last time that Richards asked the computer a question."

Bickel stared at Kosters's sad face. "That means we're talking about someone who's pretty well wired within the CIA, wouldn't you say?"

"I'll say," Kosters said. "I spoke to the director about it. He said almost exactly what you said. If Richards found out anything and if he was murdered, the murderer covered his tracks pretty well."

"What do you mean 'if'?" Bickel asked. "Don't you think he was murdered?"

"Of course I do," Kosters said. "But I was just being careful." He flushed slightly and looked embarrassed.

As he watched the snow fall, Bickel remembered that Kosters had promised that he would use other resources—resources ". . . that I'd rather not talk about"—to find out who had killed Richards. It did not seem like a firm guarantee of anything, but Kosters said it with such evident sincerity that Bickel sensed that something would come of all that genuineness and intelligence. In fact, as he thought about it, he felt as if, with Kosters clearly on his side, the bad things that had been happening would stop happening. Perhaps he had reached the nadir of his bad luck. Now, maybe things would start picking up. It was about time.

"You know," Alex said, snapping him back to the present, "somehow, and I really don't know how, word has gotten around about your meeting with Patterson."

"I'm not surprised," Bickel said, calling himself back from the reverie about changed luck. "I'm not sure it'll do me any good, but I'm not surprised. This is a very gossipy town." Bickel took a small sip of his drink and asked, "What are people saying?"

"I don't know what most people are saying," Alex said, running her left hand through her hair while her right hand held her drink. "But I know that Sabrina Schuller called me this afternoon and wants to talk to you about it."

Bickel sat up on the couch. He set his drink down on the coffee table. He was amazed. "Sabrina Schuller knows about it?" Alex nodded her head. "I can see someone here knowing about it, but an old biddy like that in Beverly Hills? How the hell did that happen?"

"I don't know," Alex said, shaking her head so that her dark auburn hair moved sinuously around her neck. "But I think you should talk to her. She did an awful lot of work on your last campaign."

"Oh, absolutely," Bickel said. "Absolutely. She was Southern California chairperson of Citizens for Bickel. She raised more money for me than anyone else in the state."

"And let's not forget, she got you an awful lot of the Jewish vote you wouldn't have had a prayer of getting without her," Alex said.

"I know it," Bickel said. "Christ, I remember her leading me around all those streets in Fairfax, introducing me to people and then telling them about me in Yiddish. By the time she got through, the old women wanted me to meet their daughters."

"Amazing," Alex said. "Really amazing."

"Absolutely," Bickel said. "Absolutely."

"So you'll see her? She's coming into town next week. Her husband has to see some people at the SEC," Alex said.

Bickel put his hands, palms out, in front of him and moved them from side to side. "I'll meet her, but I don't want to talk about the SEC. No way."

"I'll make sure she knows it," Alex said.

"Christ," Bickel said, "Sabrina Schuller. That *yenta*."

"Really," Alex said. "For sure."

Neither of them spoke for a minute. They simply looked out the window and let the beautiful snowflakes rebuild the good cheer they had both felt before Sabrina Schuller's name came up.

"Did she say she was upset about it?" Bickel asked, breaking the mood.

"She didn't say. But I don't suppose she called to congratulate you, do you?" Alex said.

"No, I don't suppose so. Jesus, how did she find out?" Bickel asked, putting his feet out on the table again.

"I don't know, Travis. I really don't know."

"God, Sabrina Schuller. What if she starts yelling and screaming to everyone in L.A. that I'm working with the Nazis?" Bickel asked, more jokingly than seriously.

"Yeah, really," Alex said, catching his mood.

"What's this 'Yeah, really' stuff?" Bickel asked with a smile. "I've never heard you talk that way before."

Alex laughed and picked up her glass, a small cylinder of transparent material without decoration. "I picked it up in California. It's funny, don't you think?"

"Hilarious," Bickel said.

"Yeah, really," Alex said and they both laughed and laughed.

Bickel got up and walked over to the paneled-box refrigerator and made new drinks for him and for Alex. Silently, he walked to Alex and handed her the brown liquid. He carried his glass to the window behind his desk and looked out at the snow. It was starting to accumulate quite a lot on the grassy slope outside the office. On Constitution Avenue, he could see snow swirling around the street lamps, brilliant pinkish blazes of sodium vapor, anticrime lights that kept everything brightly lit, except in a snowstorm, when the falling crystals blocked the light and created a cottony refuge of light in a world of blowing darkness.

"Jesus, Alex, I wish things could be the way they used to be," Bickel said, looking at her.

She stared at him warmly. "I know how you feel. I never stopped caring for you, Travis. I never did."

"Then why?" Bickel asked.

"Because I have to protect myself. No one else is going to protect me. I have to protect myself," Alex said softly.

"But, Jesus, Alex. I didn't hurt you. I never would hurt you," Bickel said. He meant it, too.

"Never on purpose," Alex said. "I know that. But when a man decides he has to be President, the people around him get hurt. That happens. I want to help you, but I don't want to get hurt. I don't want to be that close. Especially now that you've lined up with Patterson."

Neither of them said anything after that. Bickel

stared out the window. He was paying a lot for his ambition. That was the meaning of ambition. If it were free to gratify ambition, then a lot more people would be ambitious. He had lost someone who loved him, so that maybe he could get his picture on the cover of *Time* and then have Secret Service protection. And what then? What would it be like at the White House without anyone close to him? He couldn't be like JFK and just ball his brains out while Lydia dedicated parks. That wasn't his style. He would be alone.

Like his periodic assessments of what was happening to him, his fear of loneliness came and went. Now it was here.

In a moment, the feeling of euphoria that had guided Travis Bickel for the last few hours was transformed into a steep depression. He looked outside and instead of feeling warm and cozy, he felt a chill go through him. The cold spike was made up of shock and loss and loneliness and worry. What the hell had happened to Kart and Richards? Something was happening that he didn't know about. How had Sabrina Schuller heard about Patterson? What was to happen with him and Lydia? Why was he standing at that window, feeling so lonely, if he was such a big wheel?

As he thought, he realized that loneliness was what he felt most of all. The word came up in his mind over and over again. It was a curse that had slowly been settling over him for years, as he sacrificed more and more personal relationships to his career. He had gone much too far in the career direction. He was now thoroughly alone. Kosters was not interested in his personal feelings. Lydia had no sympathy for him, who, she believed, lived primarily to make her miserable. Even Alex, who seemed so happy and cheerful, was basically interested in work and socializing, and not in listening to his whining.

"Whining." He was in a bad way when he characterized his own complaints as whining. He had become so work-oriented, so geared to succeeding by running roughshod over his own needs, that a large part of him simply felt angry for feeling lonely. He was Travis

Bickel, the achiever, the succeeder, negotiator of the German Rearmament Treaty. He had gone on to finish his work when his best friend was blown to pieces. He stood manfully to his post when another friend and his son were murdered. But, Jesus, he was sick of it.

As Bickel turned around to face the back of Alex Denman, he noticed that a button on his Call Director was blinking on and off. He watched it from a psychological distance, as if it were something going on in a movie.

"Why doesn't Jenny pick up the telephone?" Bickel asked.

"I don't think anyone's here, 'cept us chickens," Alex said without turning around.

Bickel reached for the telephone. If it were a constituent calling from California, wouldn't he be thrilled and surprised to hear his senator answering the phone himself?

"Travis Bickel," the senator said, sounding like what he imagined a senator was supposed to sound like.

"May I speak to Senator Bickel?" asked a woman's voice. The voice was soft and girlish and had a German accent.

"My God, is this Kathy Dorn?" Bickel asked so sharply that Alex Denman jumped out of her seat and stared.

"Travis, do you answer your own phone?" Kathy asked, with a laughing ring in her voice.

"Where are you, Kathy? You sound as if you're right here in town." Bickel's heart was pounding. He felt dizzy. He felt the way he had felt that night in Kathy's apartment in Bonn.

"I am here," Kathy said. "I'm at Dulles Airport. When can we get together?"

"Christ. What are you doing here?" Bickel asked.

"I'll tell you all that soon. I'm going to be staying at the Watergate. Can we get together soon?" Kathy asked.

Bickel put his hand over the telephone. He said to Alex, who had taken her seat again, "Alex, could you excuse me for a minute? I have to talk to an old friend."

Without even looking at his face, Alex got out of her chair and walked out of the office, carefully closing the door so that it shut with a click.

"Kathy," Bickel said into the receiver, "I want you to take a cab to the address I'm about to give you. Tell the cabdriver that it's worth a lot of money. Offer him a hundred-dollar tip if he makes it without breaking down." He gave her his address on Klingle Street.

"Is that your home?" Kathy asked.

"Yes. There's no one there now but me." It seemed like a delicate way to put it.

"All right, Travis. I will pick up my luggage and see you soon." Kathy said. *"Wiedersehen."*

The trip home for Travis Bickel: his Cutlass grinding through the swirling snow, twisting and fishtailing on Pennsylvania Avenue. Sitting forever in stalled lines of cars with steam and smoke rising from the hoods, while headlights lit up the falling snow like anti-aircraft searchlights piercing the sky. Listening to horror stories on WTOP of cars stopped for hours on streets that lay in his path. Sliding uphill on Wisconsin Avenue because Rock Creek Parkway was closed, passing by shops that were filled with jolly shoppers unconcerned with the fact that traffic was not moving around them.

A Metrobus stopped across Thirty-seventh Street, completely blocking the street. Backing down, uncontrollably at times, to R Street to take a different route. The fairy tale beauty of the mansions and wooden fences on Foxhall Road. (Elson Patterson's house closed and dark.) The icicles hanging from fir trees as he neared Klingle Street. Smooth, white-covered lawns rushing by as his car skids to a stop when he sees a girl standing, stamping her feet, in his doorway.

A kiss in the snow, going into a warm inside. Throwing coats on the floor. Looking at a blond, flushed face with deep blue eyes matching his gray-blue eyes. Pale, uncovered arm and legs. A nude pallor stretched out on his bed, topped and bottomed with a straw fuzz.

Bright, blood-red lips and brown, smooth, and hard

aureoles. Forearm over neck, pulling it down to a warm and pulsing throat. A light sweat on two bellies, blending into itself. Thrashing and moaning and laughing.

An end to loneliness.

CHAPTER

18

Travis Bickel looked at the diminutive Sabrina Schuller, across the table from him at Sans Souci. She was talking nonstop, but he found it hard to concentrate. He thought, instead, of how happy he had been since Kathy Dorn arrived a week before.

"Listen, Senator, you should pardon the expression, but a fine young fellow like you needs Elson Patterson like you need cancer." Sabrina shrugged her thin, bony shoulders under her cream-colored I. Magnin suit and lifted her palms up about ten inches from either side of her frail, grandmotherly, wrinkled face. She shook her head so that her sparse, close-cropped gray hair moved slightly around her face. "What do you need him for?"

"Sabrina," Bickel said, trying to sound affable and interested, "I agree completely. I don't need him. I don't need him at all."

Sabrina put her hands down on the table in front of her and pushed slightly at the dish that had recently held an apricot tart. "So? So why are you hanging around with him already?"

Bickel laughed slightly. He smoothed an imaginary

wrinkle in his grayish glen plaid suit and looked around the room. It always amazed him that a restaurant as well-known as Sans Souci was as small as it was. Over in the corner near the door he saw Senator Percy with an Arab diplomat. Someone from the Kuwaiti embassy.

"I'm not hanging around with him," Bickel said quietly. "I'm not hanging around with him at all. He invited me over to his house for dinner one night and I went over there. That's all." Even as he said it, he glanced at his Cartier watch and realized that it wasn't quite all. Not by a long way. And he wouldn't give it up for Sabrina Schuller.

"But, Travis, listen to me. What're you doing with him at all? You weren't born yesterday. You know what kind of man he is. So what're you doing with him?"

A waiter fluttered into view and Bickel looked up. He glanced at the red wallpapered walls with their still lifes. It was really a most undistinguished room. There was also a set of fake gas lamps around the sides of the room. Bickel had eaten at some genuinely fine restaurants, and Sans Souci reminded him of an overpriced Emerson's.

"Would you care for more coffee? Espresso?" the waiter, a delicate-looking fellow, asked with arched eyebrows.

"Not for me," Sabrina said. "Do you have any Sanka?"

"Certainly, Madame," the waiter said. "One Sanka, and for M'sieur?" He smiled coyly at Bickel.

"Another coffee," Bickel said expressionlessly.

When the waiter was out of earshot, Bickel leaned forward. "You still haven't told me," he said in a conspiratorial tone, "how you knew that I saw Patterson. I haven't exactly taken out an ad."

Sabrina Schuller screwed up her mouth and made a pshaw gesture of pushing away some nonexistent thing with her right hand. "It's a good thing you didn't take out an ad, Travis. There are plenty of people who haven't forgotten about Elson Patterson. When they were burning down the synagogues on Crystal Night, he was breaking bread with Hitler."

"But, Sabrina," Bickel insisted, speaking even more quietly, as Sabrina gradually raised the level of her voice, "how did you find out?"

"Listen, Travis. If you felt so ashamed of it, why did you do it in the first place? Answer me that." Sabrina Schuller said, as her coffee arrived. Bickel had to admit that she was a fine evader of questions. She simply took her Jewish-mother tone with him and ignored them.

As he was thinking about yet another way to phrase the question, he felt a hand on his back. He turned around to see the small and crafty face of Bill Bray, the Washington representative of Thyssen Fabriken Gmbh., an immense German steelmaking firm. As usual, Bray was dressed just this side of foppishness, with a custom-made blue suit, peach-colored shirt, red knit tie, and large gold cufflinks. He smiled at Bickel and Sabrina.

"How are you, Senator?" he asked with a smile. "Don't get up," he added, placing his left hand firmly on Bickel's right shoulder.

"Bill, how are you? This is a very close friend of mine from Los Angeles, Sabrina Schuller. She's visiting town for a few days." He turned to Sabrina. "This is Bill Bray." No mention of Thyssen.

Bray smiled as broadly as his face would allow. He bowed slightly. "How are you, Mrs. Schuller?" he asked. "How on earth did you manage to pry this busy, busy man away from the Hill?"

Sabrina Schuller looked at him with as much interest as is generated by a crumb on a bread plate.

"Travis, you're a devil. You know how many times I've tried to get you over here. But I don't blame you. I'd rather eat with this lovely lady than with a boring old lobbyist any day." Bray's smile stayed plastered on his face.

"Call me sometime and we'll have lunch, okay?" Bickel asked Bray.

It was a kiss-off, and both men knew it. Nevertheless, Bray's smile grew larger, if anything. "Of course. I'll call this afternoon when you have your calendar in front of you." He patted Bickel on the back again and then turned to Sabrina. "And you, Mrs. Schuller, you have a lovely time in our city. Bring us some of that California sunshine." With a little wave, he was gone.

After he left, Sabrina Schuller cocked her head and squinted at Bickel. "Look, Travis. I want you to do something for me." She hesitated a moment and looked around, as if to make certain that no one could overhear. "Really," she said in a confidential tone, "it's more for you than for me."

Bickel smiled at her. What the hell was she getting at now? "Sabrina, I'm always interested in doing things for you and for me. What is it?"

"I want you to talk to someone who can tell you all about Patterson. You'll do that for an old woman, won't you?" Sabrina Schuller asked with a sad look.

"Sabrina, I already know that Patterson had some friends who were bad people. I know that," Bickel said, trying to be polite. His tone had a thin edge of annoyance.

Sabrina Schuller acted as if the annoyance wasn't there at all, even though she undoubtedly noticed it. She noticed everything. She put her hands on top of each other, palms down on the tablecloth, then looked up at Bickel with a small smile.

"Do you think I could get some more Sanka, Travis?" she asked.

"Of course, Sabrina," Bickel said and called over the waiter.

"Now, listen, Travis," Sabrina said when the waiter had taken the order, bowed, and walked toward the kitchen. "I want you to talk to a man who knows all about Patterson. I mean it when I say he knows all about him."

Bickel started to speak, but Sabrina shushed him by putting her right index finger in front of her pursed lips. "Listen, Travis," she said conspiratorially, "I don't think you know as much about Patterson as you should know. You may think you do, but you don't."

"If you know that," Bickel said evenly. "why don't you just tell me what I don't know?"

"Because, Senator, I don't know all of it. And I don't

have the equipment to tell you about it like Yichik does."

"Yichik?" Bickel asked. He had heard ugly names, but this one really broke the bank.

"Yes, Senator. Yichik Cohen. I'm telling you, it's important. He's in London, but it's worth going. I'll pay for it," Sabrina said.

"London? To hear something you already know most of?" Bickel asked.

"Yes, Travis. And when you go, you'll be glad I told you to go. You'll thank me for saving your job."

Six hours later, Bickel was still musing about Sabrina Schuller's offer to pay for his trip. He had turned it down, but he wondered what Yichik Cohen had to say. He drove across town while he wondered what he should do about Yichik Cohen. To see him seemed almost outlandish, and yet Sabrina Schuller was not a woman to offend. He would have to do some balancing.

Maybe Patterson had done some bad things. Obviously, he had had some disgusting friends. But he had some very good friends right now, and they were being pretty goddamned good to one Travis A. Bickel, United States senator from California.

Two days before, Bickel had had lunch at the Foxhall Road estate with Mason Reynolds, the legendary Jackson, Mississippi, civil rights leader, the man who had walked barefoot from the Gulf of Mexico to Chicago to dramatize the plight of sharecroppers. Reverend Reynolds was an old man now, but he was a black leader who could deliver votes in the deep south.

He was a special consultant to the Fund for Social Justice in America at $150,000 per anuum, plus nonaccountable expenses. The sole donor to the fund was Elson Patterson.

Dr. Reynolds had listened intently while Bickel told him that as a man who had studied the law and seen how the law had been used to hold back black people, he would, if he ever got the chance, see to it that the laws were made to put black people into their rightful place in America. "And Dr. Reynolds," Bickel had said, measuring his vocal rhythm carefully, "I would like to meet my maker tomorrow if I ever go back on that pledge."

Reynolds had taken the senator's hand in his and told him that Bickel must come down soon and preach a sermon at Dr. Reynold's African Methodist Episcopal Church. Bickel had said he would be honored.

On the other hand, the Reverend Special Consultant Reynolds could not do Bickel much good in Miami Beach. A balance had to be maintained. And, besides, Bickel wondered just what it was that Sabrina Schuller was peddling. It must be a hell of a story for Sabrina Schuller to take herself to Washington and then offer to take Bickel to London.

Bickel's car turned left from Constitution Avenue onto Virginia Avenue. It was after seven PM, and rush hour was well over. Lights still blazed in the Interior Department, a 1930's monolith on the right and in the Federal Reserve, a 1970's monolith on the left. As Bickel passed Twenty-second Street, he looked over at the State Department to see if he could glimpse any lights in Kosters's office. From that angle, though, he could see only the "Old" State Department facade, and not even a hint of Kosters's office was visible. Bickel realized that Kosters was not there anyway. A new international crisis had taken him to Uganda, where Idi Amin's successors were threatening to go to war with neighboring Kenya. The rotund dictator had died suddenly, apparently of food poisoning, but his followers had continued the same chaotic butchery that the fallen Amin had begun.

In a moment, Bickel passed by the Watergate development. He turned left across Virginia Avenue, made a U turn, and pulled into the garage of the Watergate Hotel. The Colombian parking lot attendants did not recognize him, which was just as well. Bickel walked swiftly across the blue-carpeted, kidney-shaped lobby and over to the elevator in the rectangular annex to the lobby.

He stepped in and pressed the button for the sixth floor. He glanced at his watch. It was 7:56 and 15 seconds. At exactly eight o'clock, he knocked on the door to Kathy Dorn's hotel room. Ten breathless minutes later, he was the happiest man in Washington. As he lay on the bed next to the pallid body of Kathy Dorn, she turned on her side and whispered, "I miss you every day, Travis. Every day."

He pulled her closer to him with his left arm and said, "Not like I missed you, Kathy."

She made a pouting face and brushed back her long, blond hair. She softly ran the fingers of her left hand across Bickel's chest. "This is a funny town, Travis," she said. "I really wonder if I will ever get my story done."

Bickel laughed. "Don't look at me. The longer you stay here, the happier I am."

She smiled. "The happier I am, too, Travis. You know that." She kissed his left shoulder. "But, I have to get some work done. Everywhere I go, though, no one will talk to me. Everyone is so—how shall I say it?—diplomatic. No one wishes to offend anyone."

"Well, Kathy, rearmament is a touchy subject. If it turns out it was a mistake, people aren't going to want to be on the record giving an unconditional guarantee that it's going to work."

"You still think it will pass, don't you?" Kathy asked him.

"Yes, I do. I definitely do. But no one's very excited about it. It's a little like going to the dentist. You know it's good for you, but you hate to go." Bickel never went into much detail with Kathy. No point in it. It would just complicate things.

Kathy sighed and did not say anything. Bickel looked around the room. It was a perfectly ordinary hotel room. He and Kathy lay on a large bed, probably what they called "Super Queen." The bed had floral-print sheets with a yellow background. There were also a yellow blanket, now at the foot of the bed, and a heavy, quilted bedspread of a light-brown material. Behind his head, Bickel could see the top of a dark wood headboard. Slightly above it were two cylindrical reading lamps. Each one threw a small circle of light in front of the reader's head.

Across the green-carpeted room was a low dresser of the kind of blond wood, probably ash, that was popular in the 1980's. The dresser had Plexiglas handles—another sign of the times. Kathy's makeup was on top of the dresser because on the wall above the dresser was a large mirror. To the right of the dresser was a small round table, about big enough for two to eat dinner at in comfort, which Bickel and Kathy had often done.

To the right of that table, with its two straightback chairs, was a color TV—a Zenith Ultracolor IV, with Magi-Brain, a new development which, Zenith advertisements claimed, allowed the set to replicate the color circuitry of the human brain.

To the right of that was a large floor-to-ceiling window, which slid back to allow a visitor to walk out to a small balcony—a recent addition to the hotel rooms, built when a D.C. District Court decision ruled that hotels were not responsible if guests jumped off the balcony after an especially severe disappointment. Although white curtains were pulled across the window now, Bickel knew that out it one could see the pool for Watergate East and the curvilinear facade of that apartment building, laced with sturdy concrete balconies.

Next to the bed on either side were rounded yellow armchairs covered with a heavy burlaplike fabric.

Bickel stopped his mental inventory of the room when Kathy nudged him slightly and asked him what he had done that day.

"Not much," he said. "I talked to a few people about the rearmament bill. I had lunch with an important constituent."

"Oh? A lobbyist?" Kathy asked.

"No," Bickel said. "A constituent isn't quite the same as a lobbyist." He explained the difference while thinking that this particular constituent was something of a lobbyist, too.

Kathy Dorn said nothing and Bickel thought about whether he should let Kathy in on his conversation with Sabrina Schuller. To do so in any meaningful way would have meant telling her about Elson Patterson. An image came into his mind of a book by John O'Hara called *BUtterfield 8*. In the part Bickel remembered, the call girl heroine debates whether to use the toothbrush of the man she has just slept with. She quickly decides that, considering that she has just had sex with him, using his toothbrush is a rather small thing. But the analogy was not quite apt. Political gossip was more significant than a toothbrush.

On the other hand, though, Lydia knew about it. Alex Denman knew about it. Frank Roberts knew about it. Of all those people, none was as important to him as Kathy. At the moment.

Bickel cleared his throat and asked Kathy a question as she stroked his chest. "Kathy," he said, "have you ever heard of Elson Patterson?"

She thought for a moment and then repeated the name. "Elson Patterson?" She was silent for a moment, then she asked, "Is he the rich old guy who was a friend of Hitler?"

Bickel laughed. "That's a good description. Actually, if you added that he was the crazy rich old guy who was a friend of Hitler, you would have it a little better." Kathy Dorn still did not seem to be very interested.

"Well, when I got back from Germany, he called me and invited me over for dinner. When I got there, he said a lot of strange things. He still likes the Nazis. At least some of them."

Kathy Dorn shrugged her shoulders. "So?" she asked. "A lot of people in Germany still like them, too."

"Well, it's a goddamn sight stranger here than in Germany. He was loved in Germany, after all. He was never loved here," he added, realizing as he said it that it was not entirely accurate.

"All right," Kathy Dorn said. "I guess you are right."

"So, Patterson really liked me and offered me all kinds of help from his library and everything. Now, a Jewish woman who helped me in my last campaign says that she wants me to learn more about Patterson from a man in London. Yichik something," Bickel said.

"Yichik?" Kathy asked, giggling slightly. "That's a funny name."

"Really," Bickel said. "It really is. Anyway, I don't know if I should do it. It's a lot of trouble."

"I don't know the first thing about it, Travis," Kathy said. "But Yichik is a funny name."

"Yeah," Bickel said. "Yichik Cohen."

"Well, you must live by the votes of the Yichik Cohens of this world, Travis. I must go to the bathroom. I also must find my cigarettes."

She leapt out of the bed and walked naked to the dresser. In dim silhouette, Bickel could see her lithe sleekness, her thin waist, her lean thighs. Even in darkness, she looked awfully good.

"Dammit," she said. "I can't find my cigarettes. I'm going to turn on the light for a second."

A small light flashed on and Bickel gasped quietly at how beautiful Kathy looked. He could see her both from behind and from in front because she stood in front of the mirror. Her pallor and beauty were overpowering.

Suddenly, there was a crackling sound, then the sound of breaking glass, ripping fabric, and bullets smashing into a mirror and a wall. The light went out but the crackling kept up, as a hail of slugs crashed into the room. Cold air, flying glass, and a girl's scream made Bickel shiver as he dived to the floor.

"Kathy! Get down," he cried.

He didn't hear any response. He got up and lunged toward where she lay. As soon as he got above the level of the bed, bullets started to fly. More broken glass, more crackling, more thuds of bullets smashing into the wall. No screams from Kathy. Outside the room, Bickel could hear running feet and screams.

The room was still dim. Bickel carefully pulled himself forward along the floor. He was still naked, and he wanted to avoid getting cut by the shards of glass. Just as he pulled himself to where Kathy's body was, there was another burst of gunfire. Through time, Bickel recalled the sound of the gun. He had heard it before in the jungles as men cursed and bled. It was an AK–47. Bickel threw himself on top of Kathy Dorn's body just in time to catch a painful splinter of glass in his right buttock.

Then the firing stopped and Bickel knelt next to Kathy. He pressed her throat. There was still a heartbeat. He turned to find the telephone, and as he did, he felt a puddle of something wet, warm, and sticky next to Kathy's head.

He crawled to the telephone and picked it up. It rang several times before an operator said, "Operator."

"There's an emergency in room 616. We need an ambulance up here right away," Bickel said hoarsely. Where the hell had all that blood come from?

"It'll take a minute," the operator said. "There's some kind of shooting going on here."

"Goddamn you, you idiot," Bickel said. "The shooting was here. A woman is dying. You get that ambulance in a hurry."

"All right," the operator said. "But you don't have to yell." Then she hung up.

Bickel crawled to the light switch for the overhead light. He flicked it on, then hit the deck. But there was no more shooting. In an instant, he was over by Kathy. There was a four-inch gash in her scalp, oozing blood and turning her thin, golden hair into a blackened and matted mess. She also had a number of other, smaller cuts. But as far as Bickel could tell, she had not been hit by any bullets. Was she in shock? Should he give her mouth-to-mouth? He bent over her mouth and listened to her breathing. It was regular if shallow. No mouth-to-mouth.

He turned around and saw the broken remains of a hotel room. Glass and bits of the mirror were everywhere. The curtain had come down and lay in a torn heap. Several bullets had smashed the television set. It looked like an immense, unfilled cavity. So that was what it looked like when you did it.

He heard a siren, and not far away. What the hell was he going to do? He was naked in a young girl's room at a hotel. She was naked, too. The girl was not his wife. What should he do? He wondered if he should get dressed and leave, before the ambulance got there.

It seemed like a cowardly thing to do. He should be with Kathy.

But no one had to know that he was there naked with her. Why couldn't he get dressed pronto and tell the police he had arrived at her door just as the shooting started and had burst in to try to save her? Why not, indeed?

He put a Kleenex into the wound on his ass and got dressed faster than he ever had before. Then he opened the door just a crack. Finally, he swept off the bedsheets with his hands. No sense leaving any hairs around. He did not like doing any of the evasion, but it didn't hurt anything important, he figured, and he would still be there with Kathy when she woke up.

There was a sound of panting in the hall, and an orderly appeared, in a white smock. Maybe he wasn't an orderly. That was the last thought Bickel had before a blur of activity that lasted for two hours. Bickel told the duty nurse at George Washington University Hospital what he had planned to say. The nurse, a pinch-faced young woman behind a Formica counter looked up at him with bloodshot eyes when he got to the part about not being in the room until after the shooting started. But she wrote down what he said.

An hour later, he told the story to a jowly young man from the District of Columbia police. Corporal Shea did not even take off his wire-rimmed glasses at the part about his being outside the room.

By midnight, a serious-faced hospital public relations man with a Fu Manchu mustache had appeared. Resplendent in a three-piece suit of dacron polyester double-knit material, the young man, Paul something, asked Bickel if he wanted to talk to newsmen.

Bickel looked at him and said nothing. Then he walked out, down back stairs and out to the street. He walked alone to the Watergate parking lot, three blocks away. He was able to think clearly for a few seconds every few minutes. And when he could think clearly, one question kept going through his mind. When will this nightmare end?

Lydia was still out of town, although she would

surely be home in a hurry when this news hit, as it surely had already. But she was not home yet, so Bickel sat alone in his living room until 2 A.M.

He tried to think. But all he thought of was the nightmare and when he would wake up.

At 2:30 AM, the telephone rang. Bickel decided to answer it. As he put the tan receiver to his ear in the darkness of his living room he said a faint hello.

There was a clicking sound and then the sound of long distance or a poor connection. "Hello?" Bickel said again. There was no answer. Bickel put down the telephone receiver. He got up to go to sleep, if he could.

He got up from his chair and walked across the living room and up the stairs. As he got to his bedroom, he switched on the light. There was a note on his pillow. Bickel threw down his suit jacket on the bed and picked up the note. In an elegant typeface, the note said simply, "Good-bye, Senator." If it was a threat, Bickel was simply too tired to care.

CHAPTER

19

Holmby Hills, even by comparison with adjacent Beverly Hills, was a neighborhood of elegant homes. Sweeping down from the hills to the border of the campus of UCLA in gentle rolls, Holmby Hills was home to doctors, lawyers, corporate types, and a host of entertainment-industry personalities. Large neo-Georgian, neo-Antebellum, neo-Spanish, and more contemporary homes with sweeping lawns, perpetually watered and perpetually cared for by Japanese gardeners, curving driveways with Mercedes sedans and Maserati coupes, and brick-and-iron fences and walls gave Holmby Hills a look of wealth that was not at all deceptive advertising.

In the middle of the section was the West Lake School for Girls. Among schools in Los Angeles, the West Lake School had no peer. Its girls were the most wealthy, horsey girls in Los Angeles. There was none of the trendy permissiveness of other schools at West Lake. The girls, in grades seven through twelve, still wore uniforms consisting of gray wool skirts just above knee length and white cotton oxford-cloth shirts.

Each day in the morning, a veritable cortege of limousines taking distinguished men to work took their lovely daughters to school at West Lake. A parade of sportier cars and station wagons driven by housewives or older sisters came by to pick up the girls at the end of the school day.

At the end of this particular school day in early February, though, the cars with the mothers or older sisters pulled down past the main administration building, Alznauer Hall, to a large parking lot. In the asphalt lot, in the looming shadow of the five-story, red-brick Alznauer Hall, were more Mercedes 450's than in the lots of the Beverly Hills Mercedes dealership.

A short jog to the right, past Alznauer Hall and down a slight decline, was the new glass-and-steel Burton Political Science Building.

That structure—named for the eccentric widow of an oil baron who had given money for a building to study "the influence of wealthy families and multinational corporations on American political and cultural life"— stood in the middle of a large, grassy area known as the Lower Lawn. In front of the building a stand had been erected on which there was a lectern draped with the school seal, a she-wolf standing astride a fallen stag with the motto, in English, "Always Victorious" in a ribbon above the fierce-looking wolf.

The headmaster of the school, Lawrence Wilson, sat directly behind the lectern on a folding chair. Next to him was Nancy Graham, the red-haired buxom senior who had been selected to give a speech on behalf of the students to commemorate the dedication of the Burton Poli Sci Building. To Nancy's right sat a grim-looking man with a crew cut and a large jacket. His eyes scanned the crowd continuously. His arms were folded across his chest. He had been introduced to Nancy Graham as Ray Abernathy, an assistant of Senator Travis Bickel, who sat on the edge of the stand wearing a worried look and a blue summer-weight suit. Nancy Graham was annoyed that Mr. Abernathy sat between her and Senator Bickel. Bickel was cute, even if his hair had sprinkles of gray.

On the other side of the dais were a group of proud faculty members, two elegantly dressed matrons who were the sisters of the benefactress, and two empty chairs. Two senior girls, one tall and thin with brown hair and a mournful face, the other short and chunky with an angry face, had risen from those chairs to deliver a short dialogue about the environment.

As the last of the parents filtered into the rows of chairs behind the first twelve rows, where the West Lake girls sat, composed in their uniforms, the two girls spoke from their hearts.

"Consider, Mr. Businessman, the muskrat," the thin girl said.

"What has the gentle muskrat ever done to you?" asked the chubby girl.

"Why do you drain his marshlands for your oil refineries and factories?" the thin girl asked.

"And make the poor muskrat have to live in cities?" the shorter girl asked.

Bickel stared out into the audience. He could hardly believe his ears. Still, Bickel thought, he was glad to be out of Washington. A speech at the dedication of the Burton Building had been on his schedule for a long time. Coming two days after the machine-gunning of Kathy Dorn's hotel room, it was a particularly welcome trip. There were a lot of reporters there. He was showing the flag in his home district—always a good move. And now he was protected.

Immediately after Bickel had picked up the note on his pillow, he put through a radiophone call to Secretary Kosters in Uganda. When Kosters learned what had happened, he rustled up a bodyguard for Bickel. Ray Abernathy didn't talk much, but he was obviously strong as a horse and did not ever need sleep, apparently.

By another one of Kosters's miracles, the news that Bickel had been at Kathy Dorn's hotel room had been kept out of the newspapers and radio and television. When Lydia called Bickel the next day, Bickel was delighted to learn that she knew nothing about the incident and was going to stay away for a few days longer.

"And, Mr. Businessman, what has the bluejay ever done to you?" the tall girl asked.

"Why do you torture and kill the dolphin?" the shorter girl wanted to know.

"Don't you know about love?" the tall girl asked.

"That we are all here together on one earth?" the shorter girl continued.

"Why do you kill the caribou and melt the permafrost with your pipeline?" asked the tall girl.

"Why is all that you care about money?" the shorter girl asked.

"Don't you know that trees have rights, too?"

"And what about the whalekillers?"

Bickel looked out at the audience again. In the third row was a blond who looked like the young Lauren Bacall, with long eyelashes and all. She looked up at the dais with green eyes that looked as though they had just been taken out of the U.S. Army cryogenics lab. She swept back and forth along the row and settled on Bickel. She looked him up and down and moved past, then moved back to him.

To Bickel, she looked awfully good. Not as ripe as Kathy Dorn, but still, awfully good. How could he make a pass at her? There was a lawn party afterward, and maybe he could start talking to her. It was not that far-fetched an idea. He was going to be in Los Angeles for two days. He still had his house in Benedict Canyon, which was practically next door. Yes, it could be done.

"And the virgin stands of redwoods along the misty coasts?" the taller girl asked.

"What will you tell your grandchildren when all that beauty is no more?" the shorter girl asked.

"Will you tell them that you did it all for money?" the shorter girl said, wrinkling up her nose and defiantly thrusting out her chin at the word "money."

"And the wolves in the trackless forest—where are they now, Mr. Lumberman?"

By this time tomorrow, Bickel thought, he would be able to talk to Kosters on the telephone about what had happened at the Watergate Hotel. That might clear the air. The D.C. police had acted as if it were the kind of thing that happened every day. Apparently a Cuban delegation to the Organization of American States was staying in the suite below Kathy Dorn and the gunners had mistakenly fired into the wrong suite. That was what the police believed. Bickel did not believe it for one second.

"Look," he had told the chief of police, "I really appreciate your keeping my name out of this. I really do. But, I'd also like to know who tried to kill me. I don't buy the idea that it's the anti-Castro Cubans. I mean, a person would have to be slightly batty to believe that."

The chief, a jowly black man named O'Malley, had not thought that was funny. "The way we see it, Senator Bickel, that's the only possible explanation. I don't mean to create a problem, but let's face facts, Senator. Why would anyone go to all that trouble to kill a woman reporter?"

In the chief's lime-green office—with pictures of him, glossies with all manner of visiting dignitaries surrounding the desk, and a large black plaque from the Afro-American Lawmen behind him—the question itself took on a bizarre air. Obviously, the chief had no idea that something extremely complicated and sinister was happening. O'Malley looked sour. Probably prostate problems. He would not be able to make anything out of a series of killings and attempted killings that had begun in Bonn. "Not my jurisdiction," he would say.

Bickel had shrugged his shoulders in the chief's office and walked out.

That girl in the third row was definitely giving him more than a once-over. How could he improve his speech so that she would definitely not be able to resist it, so that she would come up to him afterward and say, "Oh, wow, that was beautiful." His material was fairly cut-and-dried stuff, written for him by a talented Washington hand named Bakshian. Bickel quickly skimmed through the pages to see where he could fit in something moving.

Most of it was standard stuff about the young people's importance to America. Putting money into education was the best investment America could make. There was nothing so precious as young minds. Maybe Bickel could get a laugh if he added "and young bodies." Probably not a good idea, though.

The two girls on stage were finishing.

"And so, to you, the moon, and to you, the sun, we dedicate ourselves and our lives," the taller girl said.

"We know, that in defense of the forests and the animals and the fishes, we are invincible," the shorter girl said.

Parents in the audience clapped loudly while the students looked as if they had heard it before.

Lawrence Wilson, the headmaster, strode to the podium. His puppy face and long black beard flecked with white gave him the appearance of an absent-minded academic from Czarist Russia. He patted the two girls on the back and watched them fondly as they smiled and returned to their seats.

In a deep voice, Wilson said, "I think Lally and Petey have given us a great deal to think about. I don't know, when I hear about children who are growing up with the wrong values. I think that's not a problem here at West Lake."

There was more applause from the audience; again, most of it came from the parents. They were a rich-looking group, Bickel thought, with the wrinkle-free countenances that only rich people in certain areas of the world seem to have.

Many of the mothers were pretty. The husbands were a tanned, confident-looking lot. They wore summer sports jackets and shirts open at the collar, for the most part, although a couple of extremely young fathers sitting on the aisle, near the students, were wearing suits. Men that young could not have earned the kind of money necessary to send a daughter to West Lake. It must be inherited money, just as his was.

"Of course, everyone in California knows our next speaker," Wilson said. "We all have read about his heroism in working for the German Rearmament Treaty. Some may be for it and some against it, but I think that everyone admires, indeed must admire, the way that Senator Bickel has fought for the bill even when terrorists attempted to frighten him. We Californians are not easily scared."

The crowd clapped appreciatively, as if to show that they, too, were not scared, whatever they might have had to be scared of.

"Senator Bickel, whose mother went to the West Lake School—I won't tell which class—has done something remarkable. He has taken the time out of his incredibly busy Washington schedule to fly out here and say a few words at this dedication."

Another round of applause, in which the husbands, who knew what busy schedules were, showed their appreciation, well-earned indeed, for one of their own.

The headmaster did a half-turn toward Bickel and extended his right arm. Bickel stood up and walked to the lectern as Wilson sat down.

"Alumnae, parents, students, and friends. Dr. Wilson's introduction about how busy I am in Washington was flattering, but it missed an essential point. Being in the government in Washington is a lot like beating your head against a brick wall. It feels best when you stop."

Polite applause from the audience.

"But seriously, I think that if we start to think of donating a little of our time for our young people as a burden or a thing to be avoided, we haven't got it quite right.

"Let me tell you a little story about education," Bickel said. "If you took away the most valuable resource that America has, it would not be our fertile fields, or our steel, or even our great cities. It would be our young people's well-trained minds. By the same token, if I, or anyone, can do anything to help the process of education along, it is not only a duty, but a positive pleasure to do it."

More polite applause. The men in the suits were apparently reporters and not parents, or else they were very nervous, since they seemed to be fiddling with their briefcases and taking out some kind of mechanical equipment.

Bickel would have to be careful about what he said. Any general remark might be taken as a drawing back from his commitment to the treaty. That could be a serious problem. He stole a quick glance at the Bacall look-alike in the third row. She smiled broadly at him. These kids were fantastic.

"Lately, a lot of people have been asking if they should still pay the substantial sums which private education costs. After all, they say, we're paying a fortune for property taxes to support our public education. Why should we spend more for private schooling?"

Bickel looked out at the men in suits. Now they sat quietly with the tape recorders under folded hands. Bickel hoped that what he said would not come out the next day in the L.A. *Times* as "Bickel Takes Slap at Schools."

He took a sip of water from a glass and smiled at the girl in the third row. She smiled again at him.

"That's a question which only you can answer on an individual basis, for each child. But, speaking as a politician—yes, that's what I am—I can tell you that a diversity of educational forms is not just good, but crucial, for the American ideas of a pluralist society to flourish."

He had stolen that line from Carter, too.

Bickel glanced at the two men. Perhaps they had trouble with their tape recorders. They were doing something with them. The Bacall look-alike whispered something to the girl next to her and they both giggled. Maybe they were talking about how big he was.

He glanced back at the two men. They were obviously not getting the sound they needed, because they had stood up and were walking toward the stage, their tape recorders in their hands. Bickel hoped there would be a place where they could stand inconspicuously.

Behind them, he saw Abernathy rise quickly to his feet. Then he heard a roar, and Abernathy went flying backward off the podium with a huge red stain on his shirt. Bickel turned around to see that the two men were holding Uzis on him.

He dived to the floor of the podium just as the roar

started again. Bullets flew above him and he could see
the people on the dais blown out of their chairs, screaming and yelling as the bullets ripped into them. The two
girls who had lamented the trials of the muskrat were
being blasted into eternity by shells which practically
ripped them in two. Lawrence Wilson was hit but not
yet dead, since he was struggling to get off the platform.

In the audience, the girls were running everywhere,
screaming and crying. Occasionally a panic-stricken student ran into the line of fire and was knocked flat, like
a grotesque bleeding tenpin, by the bullets. The parents
were also running around screaming. And, in the middle of the crowd, stood the two men in suits, calmly
firing their submachine guns, taking new clips and firing again.

Bullets kicked up all around him as Bickel crawled to
the edge of the dais and rolled off onto the ground. He
quickly scrambled under the dais, behind the blue felt
bunting, and then, in the dark, clambered through the
steel supports to the back of the stand. He stood up and
could see, across the bodies on the stand, that the firing
was more sporadic now. Nevertheless, the two men continued to stand unmolested in the center of the seats.

Bickel glanced down beside him and saw the grisly
body of Abernathy. Blood was already starting to clot,
making the hole in his chest even more horrible, a red
and black swamp of death in the middle of a man's
chest. Panting and breathing rapidly, Bickel felt Abernathy's sports coat. The gun was still there. He reached
inside, shivering as he touched the oozing, clotting
blood, and pulled out the black S & W .38 police special. It felt heavy and deadly.

A rage seized Bickel. People had been killed around
him for the last month as if they were Barbie Dolls. It
was time to strike back. It was time to show whoever it
was that he could not simply kill people as if they were
not humans who could fight back.

The firing stopped for a second. Bickel poked his
head over the dais and saw the two men reloading their
Uzis. He aimed the revolver at the one on the right and
fired. The gun kicked in his hand and the man yelled

and fell backward. The second one looked behind him. Bickel fired at him. He missed, and the man turned around with his submachine gun blazing. Bickel ducked and moved to the side of the dais to get a better shot. He noticed that the firing had stopped again. He popped up and took aim. But the man was gone. Bickel caught a glimpse of him just passing the corner of Alznauer Hall.

Sirens were already starting to grow closer as Bickel walked over to the man he had shot. He was an ordinary-looking man with a square jaw, sort of like Abernathy's. He was like Abernathy in another way, too. He was dead. The area around the rostrum looked like a picture of the Gettysburg field after Pickett's charge. Everywhere were bodies and crying, retching men, women, and girls.

As the police arrived, Bickel wondered what had happened to the Lauren Bacall look-alike.

CHAPTER

20

Elson Patterson glanced at a copy of the New York *Times* as he sat in the gallery of Innisfree and watched the snow fall on the lake. The gallery ran along the top of the main hall of the residence. It was a rectangle, hollow in the center, and tiled with red, smooth brick. Its inner border was marked by a wooden railing anchored to the brick by fluted oak dowels. On the outside there was a row of leaded windows above a waist-high plaster-and-masonry wall. There were chairs and tables, such as might be found in a men's club, positioned so that a person sitting at a table would have an excellent view of either the main hall below or the graceful scenery outside.

Patterson sat on one of the chairs and read the first few paragraphs of the lead story:

GUNMEN KILL 7, WOUND 31 AT COAST SCHOOL MEET
Los Angeles, Feb. 3 (AP). Two unidentified gunmen opened fire on a ceremony at an exclusive private girls' school here today. Before the shooting had stopped, there were at least 7 dead and 31 wounded,

and, in addition, one of the gunmen was killed. The motive for the brutal assault is not known.

Travis A. Bickel, U.S. Senator from California, was giving a speech at the school, dedicating a new building, when the gunmen, who were dressed conservatively, according to survivors, strode to the front of the group and fired Uzi submachine guns. Bickel dodged the hail of gunfire and retreated behind the platform at which the gunmen were firing. Bickel retrieved the pistol of his slain bodyguard and killed one of the assailants. The other man then fled. Police do not know his whereabouts.

Outside Patterson's window was a lovely tableau of falling snowflakes and ivory-clothed trees and lawns. A squirrel occasionally darted across the lawn, paused to survey the situation, then returned to the margin of the woods. Once that morning a deer had cautiously appeared, its grayish-beige coat flecked with snow. The deer sidled up to the covered lawn furniture, where he found the food Patterson had left, then quickly ran away. Patterson felt he was making progress in getting the deer to trust him, and that was good.

There was a clattering sound along the gallery. Patterson did not look up. Instead, he stared at a smudge of newsprint on his brown trousers. He really should be more careful. It wasn't that he could not afford to have the trousers cleaned or replaced, of course. It was just that it was good to be clean and neat. It showed a certain respect for one's body and one's person.

The footsteps grew closer. Before looking up, Patterson looked at the sleeves of his white sweater. They also had a few smudges. He really must be more careful. It did not look good in front of Roberts, and that was that.

Patterson looked up just as Roberts reached the table. Without rising, Patterson smiled and said heartily, "Welcome to Innisfree, Frank. I hope you're having a good time in the snow."

"Thank you, Mr. Patterson," Roberts said. His pinstripe dark blue suit and white shirt made a striking contrast with Patterson's sportsman's attire.

"Well," Patterson said. "How have you been, Frank? How are you enjoying this weather? How are things in New York City?"

"I'm fine, Mr. Patterson. I like this weather very much. Things in New York City are dirty and falling apart, as usual," Roberts said. His face was pulled tight with concentration.

"Have a seat, Frank," Patterson said. "Things really that bad in New York City?" Patterson cleared his throat. "Why have the people in New York let things get so out of hand, Frank?"

This was one of Patterson's favorite conversational ploys—to ask Roberts to explain something that Patterson had explained to Roberts originally.

Roberts frowned. "I think it was trying to coddle people, Mr. Patterson. It was the government there trying to be all things to all people, taking care of them, babying them. I think that's the problem."

"You think so, Frank?" Patterson asked. "I think it's also because New York lost its ethnic identity. A city can be one thing or another. It can't be everything. Or am I wrong?"

"No, Mr. Patterson, I think you're absolutely right."

"Do you want something to eat, Frank? Some chocolate or something?" Patterson asked.

"No, thanks, Mr. Patterson. I had breakfast before I left New York City," Roberts said.

"I don't think that the people who run New York City ruined it on purpose, do you? I think they just tried too hard. Sometimes that can be just as bad, if you try too hard without thinking carefully about what you really want to accomplish. But you don't agree with me," he said, staring into Roberts's tight face and raising his eyebrows. "Why am I wrong?"

"You're not wrong, Mr. Patterson," Roberts said.

"You know, I'm glad you brought that up, that business about trying too hard," Patterson said. "That can be a problem for anyone, Frank. You know that?"

"Yes sir, I know it," Roberts said. This was it. Patterson was getting to it.

"Have you seen this morning's *Times*, Frank?" Pat-

terson asked. Without waiting for an answer, he picked
up the first section and put it on Roberts's lap.

"Read the lead story, Frank," Patterson said. He
looked out the window while Roberts read. A squirrel
ran out of the branches of a tree, shaking off snow as it
ran. It scampered down the trunk, then along the
ground toward the forest. For a moment it stopped,
raised itself on its hind legs, and looked around. Then it
resumed its all-fours position and ran into the snowy
woods. No whining about the cold from the squirrel. It
just did what it had to do to survive.

"You see, Frank," Patterson said while Roberts was
still reading, "now we have a problem. Yes, someone
can shoot into a girl's hotel room, and, especially if it's
above a Cuban delegation, people won't care that much.
That was a beautiful job, by the way. Which did you
move around, the Cubans or the girl?"

"The Cubans," Roberts said drily. "And thank you."

"But this business out at West Lake, Frank. That
could have been a nice touch. It could have been, if it
were handled with some subtlety. That's always the key,
Frank. Subtlety. But this business was awfully heavy-
handed. Now why was that, Frank?" Patterson asked.

Roberts hesitated a moment before answering. He
could not hear anyone else in the house. That was a
relief.

"Mr. Patterson, I regret, as much as anyone, what
happened to those girls. I am sorry about it. It should
not have happened. But, I think you have to agree that
we got some response out of Bickel that tells us a lot
more than we knew before."

Patterson waved his right hand airily. "Oh, of course,
I know that. I was happy about that. But just suppose
that Bickel had only wounded that fellow. Or, that
someone had caught the other man. And suppose either
of them had talked, and then the man above them had
talked, and so on. Well, it could never have gotten here,
but it could have been a bad thing. And, then, we have
those girls again. Yes, we had to do something with that
fellow whose father worked at the CIA. But, I didn't

even like that. Now, we have those girls to think about. That's just not good."

Roberts let out a long sigh. He knew that Patterson did not like whining, and he was not going to whine.

"Mr. Patterson, I agree entirely. I am sorry about those girls. I should have given strict instructions to fire only on the people in the stand. I should have done that."

"I guess so," Patterson interjected.

"But I think the operation worked all right. When the time comes, Bickel will know that he has to reckon with people who do not worry about blood when the cause is important. And, that's important. It must have some effect on him to see all those people killed. He has to wonder who could do that. When the time comes, he'll understand that it had to be done, and he'll respect us more for it," Roberts said quickly. He kept his eyes on Patterson's hands.

Patterson gave Roberts a sideways glance. "Are you explaining to me how I should be running this operation, Frank?" he asked slowly. His delicately manicured hands started to tremble, making a faint tattoo on the table top.

"No, Mr. Patterson. I am just trying to bring out some aspects of the situation that you may not be familiar with. Naturally, I mean no disrespect," Roberts said.

Suddenly Patterson stood up in his place, the veins in his temple throbbing and bulging. He stood over Roberts and slapped him hard on the right cheek with the back of his right hand. "You mean no goddamn disrespect," Patterson shouted. "You mean no goddamn disrespect. I can tell you a few things about people who mean no disrespect. When the New York *Times* has a front-page story about a mistake you made, then it's disrespect, and that's that." He glared at Roberts and then sat down. In a completely changed tone of voice, calm and almost friendly, Patterson added, "Or am I wrong?"

Roberts, his face ablaze where Patterson had struck him, never changed his position. "No," he said. "You're not wrong." This was where his actor's discipline paid off. Anyway, he would get back, and it would not be too long.

"All right," Patterson said. "You sure you don't want something to eat? Some chocolate cupcakes or something like that? Cocoa? Some of those new breakfast squares I keep reading about?"

"No, thank you," Roberts said. "I'll wait for lunch." He said it as if he had not just been struck in the face by the man who was now offering him cocoa.

"All right," Patterson said. "Suit yourself. What's next with Bickel?"

"It depends on who and what this Yichik Cohen is," Roberts said. "He comes right out of nowhere as far as we're concerned. We just can't pick up a thing on him."

"He's supposed to be in London, isn't he?" Patterson asked.

"Right, Mr. Patterson," Roberts said. "But, I really can't see a thing about him, not in any of our files. Not even in ONA."

"We could pick up Sabrina Schuller and get something out of her, I imagine," Patterson said. "Or is that wrong?"

"No, you're right," Roberts said. This time he would wait for Patterson to convince himself he was wrong. "It might be a good idea."

Patterson looked at him through lidded eyes. "I don't know, though. Maybe it isn't a good idea. Maybe we should try something else. Picking up an elderly lady like Sabrina Schuller could be a mistake. Sometimes they just suddenly die, and then where are you?"

"Good thought, Mr. Patterson," Roberts said.

"We'll just have to wait and see. We have some good people in London, don't we?" Patterson asked. "Maybe we don't, though. Am I wrong about that?"

"No," Roberts said. "You're not wrong about that at all."

"Good," Patterson said. "Now tell me honestly, Frank, you don't hold that little bit of discipline against me, do you?" Patterson sat forward in his chair. He smiled so broadly that the tight skin on his face looked like it was stretched to the breaking point. He took on the look of a face in rictus.

"No, Mr. Patterson. An organization needs discipline; I understand that," Roberts said.

"It's good that you understand that. A lot of men wouldn't. That's what makes you so valuable," Patterson said, still smiling. "Now, I think that the man that Bickel didn't get needs to be disciplined severely enough so that he won't make any more trouble for us. Not ever. You understand that?"

"Yes, I do," Roberts said. "That means exactly what I think needs to be done."

"But maybe I'm being too harsh. Do you think I'm being too harsh?" Patterson asked.

"Not at all," Roberts said. "Discipline is important."

"I agree," Patterson said. "That man acted like an asshole. Just like an asshole. We can't tolerate that, can we?"

"By no means," Roberts said.

"Now," Patterson said, "I want to hear what you've learned about helicopters. The new ones. You have found out about that, haven't you?"

"Yes, I have," Roberts said. "For your purposes, there are basically three choices, at least in my opinion."

"Your opinion," Patterson said, waving his hands slightly in front of him, "is almost always sound. Almost always. So please feel free to give me your opinion."

"Thank you, Mr. Patterson," Roberts said. "Thank you very much. Now, the Bell Aerocopter looks very good to me. Double ram-jet rotors . . ."

"Don't get me wrong, Frank," Patterson said. "I'm the one who has to decide. Always. That's only natural. The buck stops with me. I have to make the decisions." He waved his right hand in the air again. "Oh, not that I mind, you understand. Not that I mind. Someone has to do it, and it might as well be me. But let's make it clear that I understand I have to decide."

"It's clear, Mr. Patterson," Roberts said. "It's definitely clear."

Forty-five minutes later, Patterson said, with a glance

at his Timex watch, "I think it might be time for lunch. You hungry, Frank?"

"Yes, sir," Roberts said.

"You go down and wash up, Frank, and I'll be along in a minute," Patterson said. He smiled beatifically at Roberts.

Roberts got up and walked away from Patterson, along the gallery and down the stairs toward the dining room. When Patterson could not hear his footsteps any more, he put Roberts out of his mind and stared out at the snow-covered grounds once more.

This was how it had been, that last time in Rastenburg. It was December of 1943, and the *Führer*'s Russian campaign was falling apart. Some people claimed that the *Führer* did not know that his campaign was falling apart. Others said he knew all too well. The latter were right. When Patterson arrived in the Wolf's Lair, the *Führer* looked older than Patterson would have believed possible. His eyes still had a magnificent blue hue to them, but they were ringed with bloodshot speckles. His skin was mottled and bluish.

Still, when Hitler caught sight of Patterson, his spirits lifted. He turned away from his generals ("Most of them aren't fit to be dogcatchers," he said later) and took Patterson's right hand in both of his.

"How on earth did you get here?" the *Führer* asked excitedly. "We are quite hemmed in at this point."

"It was not hard, my *Führer*," Patterson said. "I flew from New York to the Azores, from there to Portugal, and from there by train."

"It's a trip that many people told us they would be making, but, now that we have had some reverses, all bets are off," the *Führer* said, looking off into space. He glanced around the crowded situation room, then at the huddled generals, and then over to Patterson. "It's stuffy in here. Let's go for a walk in the snow. Are you warm enough?"

"Of course, my *Führer*," said Patterson, deeply flattered that, at this crucial moment, the *Führer* would take time out to talk to him. The situation around Stalingrad was extremely fluid. The Eighth Army under Montgomery had routed the Afrika Korps. Slowly but surely, the Allies were moving up the boot of Italy. Still, the *Führer* made time for Patterson.

Dressed in a heavy tweed coat and boots, Patterson accompanied the *Führer* around the snow-covered compound. The latter wore a lined leather trenchcoat over his field marshal's uniform, which was still simple and unadorned compared to many Patterson had seen around the *Führer*.

They walked by a pair of SS guards who snapped rigidly to attention and presented their Schmeissers in front of them. Hitler lackadaisically raised his right arm, bent it back at the elbow, then bent back the hand farther still.

"Do you know what kind of fight we're putting up on the Eastern Front?" Hitler asked Patterson. Without waiting for a reply, the *Führer* continued. "We send out a new division of young men, some of them teenagers, and the Russians throw ten divisions of hardened soldiers, veterans, at them." The *Führer* looked down at the ground and shook his head. "Nevertheless, our men hold their ground. So the Bolsheviks send in ten more divisions. Still, our men fight and freeze until they run out of ammunition. Do you know what that is called?"

"No, although I would call it courage," Patterson said, as his breath came out frosted in the air.

"Exactly," the *Führer* said. "Exactly. It's courage. Raw courage."

Patterson said nothing, but watched the *Führer*'s face as it clouded over.

"If the Americans, or the British, or the Russians, were as brave as we have been, the whole world would be talking of it for centuries. But unless we win this war, the Jew press will make sure that no one ever hears of it. The finest moment of German manhood will mean nothing; the finest blood in the world being spilled on the snow. All for nothing."

Still, Patterson said nothing. The *Führer* continued. "Of course," he said, "we must win. There can be no doubt of that. But, when I think of the fine German women and children who are left without fathers and husbands, and the German mothers and fathers who are losing their sons, I could weep, if it were seemly. We Germans, who are carrying the banner for the entire Aryan people, must suffer for all of them while they put us on the cross with the Jews' nails. We are a bleeding people, Elson. Bleeding for salvation."

Impulsively, Patterson said, "My *Führer,* let me enlist. I speak German. I am a good shot. Let me raise a group of Americans who will fight against the Bolsheviks for you. Please, my *Führer.*" Tears started to come to Patterson's eyes.

The *Führer*'s eyes were damp, too, as he said to Patterson, "No, Elson. I am touched, of course. But we need you for more important things. You know that." Then the *Führer* put his gloved hand on Patterson's shoulder and said, "Nevertheless, I could not be more touched, Elson."

As the two men looked into each other's eyes, tears glistened in each set, the *Führer*'s blue eyes and Patterson's blue-gray eyes. A mystical embrace of souls took place, Patterson felt, which would never end, as far as he was concerned.

A tall, blond adjutant, Gunsche, if Patterson remembered right, walked briskly up to the *Führer*. He gave a smart *"Heil Hitler,"* which the *Führer* casually returned, and then smiled at Patterson. "Always a pleasure to see you here, Mr. Patterson," he said.

Before Patterson could reply, Gunsche turned to the *Führer*. "My *Führer*," he said, "Reichsführer Himmler is here. He is waiting to see you."

Hitler looked happy again. "I'll be there soon. Please make him comfortable."

Gunsche gave another *"Heil Hitler,"* bowed slightly, and withdrew.

"That's the only part of the war that's going on schedule," Hitler said as they turned back toward the low buildings of the Wolf's Lair. "The campaign to control the Jews. Himmler has done fantastic work on that. Really fantastic. I won't bore you with the details, but that's where the long-term victory will be—against the Jews."

At the time, Patterson did not know what the *Führer* meant and did not care very much either. If the *Führer* did not like Jews, well, a lot of people didn't like Jews. He didn't like them very much himself.

Before Patterson left two days later, there was still more bad news from Stalingrad. In addition, Allied convoys in the North Atlantic were turning that ocean into a trap for U-boats. Still, the *Führer* had offered a new U-boat to Patterson for his return trip. It could drop him in Buenos Aires.

Patterson declined. He could not, in good conscience, take a U-boat that was needed so desperately for the war effort, and use it for his personal convenience.

The *Führer* clapped him on the shoulder and said, "You are a man, a soldier, Elson."

Another deer walked carefully out of the woods. It looked back and forth, then came up to the lawn furniture, where the food was. With a quick, snapping motion, the deer picked up a few mouthfuls of food, then ran back to the woods with that bizarre stiff-legged gait of deer. When the deer left, the vision outside the house was perfectly still, except for a slight blowing of the breeze, which made the branches move and shake off snow.

That time in Rastenburg, in the snow, had been the last time Patterson saw the *Führer* in a mood of optimism. After that it had all been downhill. Still, Patterson remembered and would carry on. What kind of man could break faith with the *Führer?*

CHAPTER

21

Lydia Bickel was furious. What the hell had Travis been doing to get himself in the middle of so much trouble? To her it was simply impossible that a person could be utterly innocent and still be involved in so much death and destruction. She had thought about these things a lot. She had little else to do. Justice and right and decency were bright stars in her constellation. She tried to steer her life by them. Of course, she did not always succeed, but that was not from lack of trying. Her constant study was the way things would be if there were an order of justice, right, and decency.

For one thing, she would not be where she was. She was every bit as smart as her husband. In fact, when they had been in school together, she had been a better student. She had helped him with the brain-breaking course in Advanced Monetary Policy. She had helped him with Eastern Europe Since the War. Lydia could not remember any courses that Travis had helped her with.

There was also a lot of decency missing from the way Travis treated her. It really was not an extraordinary fact that she drank a lot when you considered the way Travis neglected her. People who drank a lot did not do so because they were thirsty. They did it because they wanted to escape from some kind of situation. In Lydia's case, it was many kinds of situations.

She was doing nothing with her life, for starters. She sat at home all day, or went shopping at Garfinckel's, or went to an inane meeting of the International Friends' Club (not that they were bad girls, quite the contrary). And she had the powerful and devastating feeling that life was passing her by. Occasionally she read about this or that friend from UCLA who was now writing a book or was an executive at an advertising agency, or any damn thing. And there she was, looking out the window at her back yard.

Of course, that was good, in a sense, because she was able to develop her thoughts without any interference from real world concerns. While people like Travis and his colleagues had to decide on this or that issue on the basis of compromise and meeting each other halfway, Lydia Bickel was able to inhabit a world of absolutes. She did not need to compromise. If someone had seriously transgressed against justice, right, and decency, Lydia had no qualms about sentencing that person to death in the always-sitting courtroom in her mind. The sentences were never carried out, of course, except in the courtyard in her mind.

Lydia enjoyed that freedom to make absolute judgments. It was one of the things that helped to ward off the devastating attacks of loneliness. They were the worst thing in her life. If she could somehow get over them, she would have made enormous progress. Without loneliness, she would not have to drink. The drinking, after all, was fundamentally a way of anesthetizing herself against loneliness. And, naturally, as with all anesthetics, more and more of the medicine was required to do the job.

The loneliness was Travis's fault. No doubt of that. He had started to leave her alone from the very first moments after they got married. He was out studying with his friends, or debating with his friends, or this, or that. And Lydia was at home, watching TV or cooking dinner, or something. That was how it had been for the last eighteen years. And it had gotten worse every year. At first, Travis might have had real things to do that kept him away from home. But now, she was sure, he stayed away from home as much as he could, expressly to be away from her.

So on this particular February morning, Lydia Bickel was seriously considering imposing the hypothetical death penalty on Travis. Part of her reasoning was that apparently some heavenly authority had already pronounced a rather stiff sentence against Travis. Why else would he keep getting shot at? Someone tried to blow him up and then someone tried to shoot him, and the FBI and the CIA did not seem to have a clue who was doing it.

When Travis returned from California, with reporters and cameramen all around, he was surrounded by five body guards. He rode in a bulletproof car. He looked weary and scared. Lydia had felt a pang of worry and sympathy for him. When they were alone that night in the kitchen Lydia touched his pajamaed arm and said, "Travis, why don't you and I go away somewhere? We could go somewhere far away, where no one could reach us. Wouldn't that be good?" She actually hoped that he might say yes.

Instead, he exhaled a long sigh. In a tired voice, he said, "I would love to do that. Lydia. I really would. But I can't go."

"Why not, Travis? It's your life we're talking about. It's not one of my crazy ideas that you're always making fun of. It's your life."

Bickel reached over and stroked her hair. "It wouldn't do any good. If the people we're talking about really want to kill me, they could find me in Afghanistan."

"What are you talking about, Travis? What do you mean 'If they want to kill you'?" Lydia asked.

Bickel closed the refrigerator door. He looked out the window at the light in the garage of the house behind his. As always, it silhouetted the branches of the huge tree in the back yard, making the already stark vista even more so. The view was particularly appropriate, Bickel thought, for the bedroom of Travis and Lydia Bickel. It reflected their situation magnificently.

"I mean," Bickel said, "that the people who have been shooting and blowing things up are not children. They aren't from the SLA. They're hired murderers. They're effective and they have no scruples. If they wanted to kill me, I would be dead by now."

"That's ridiculous," Lydia retorted. "They came damn close on two occasions. Do you think they could have planted a bomb to go off within a few seconds of when that bomb did go off, so that you wouldn't be in the car? Do you think they're such good shots that they could shoot the person next to you on either side in Los Angeles and be absolutely sure of not hitting you?" She was starting to get angry at what she took to be his air of resignation, of fatalism, of being serenely sure that he led a sacred life. Dammit! He was not so great that he led a charmed, preserved life, safe from murderers.

But Bickel had simply sighed again. "You may be right," he said, staring out the window, "but I just think that whoever is trying to do whatever it is is not trying to kill me." Somewhere out in the back yard were one, maybe two, bodyguards. Even in that garage there was someone.

Kosters had arranged it all. He had just arrived back in Washington when word reached there about the machine gunning at West Lake, and he immediately was on the telephone with the FBI director, who had Bickel placed under continuous protection immediately. After a day, the Secret Service took over, and now the protection was a mixture of Secret Service and plainclothes Executive Protective Service. It made Bickel a less tempting but by no means invincible target for determined killers.

Bickel reached over and touched Lydia's face lightly. "I know this must be driving you crazy, sweetheart," he said. "It's driving me crazy. When I get through with this rearmament thing, we'll go away somewhere."

Lydia fumed. "Don't do me any favors, Travis," she

hissed. "What I'm suggesting is to save your life, not mine. If you can't see enough to know that, you can't see much. Go ahead and do whatever you goddamn well please. I can't help you if you don't want to help yourself." She took his hand from her face, and walked out.

There must be some kind of curse working on Travis, she decided. Not a curse like from *The Exorcist,* but a wish for self-destruction, based on knowledge by him of his crimes, that was in play. He had transgressed against justice and decency, and now he was paying the price. His enemies were after him, and he, with full knowledge of their plans, would take no action to defend himself. Perhaps, very inwardly, he was paralyzed by his guilt.

The next morning, when Lydia awoke, Travis was already dressed and gone. It was not surprising. More and more, Travis rose early and stayed late at work. Who knew if he was really at work, as a matter of fact? Probably he was with Alexandra Denman, that bitch who tried to pretend she was a fashion model. All she was to Lydia was a cheap little government tart.

But as Lydia walked around in the cold back yard, wondering how Travis could be so stupid and feeling so much anger at him, she felt good about what she was doing for him. The woman from *Newsweek* had been so kind. She was clearly not a home-wrecking type, like Alex Denman. Maureen Worth was the woman's name. She was tall and thin, with fine cheekbones and modishly short hair. The gap between her two front teeth gave her a puckish quality.

Maureen had called up one day last week and confided to Lydia that *Newsweek* was doing a cover on Travis Bickel. Lydia was surprised, but Maureen had gushed, "Oh, please, darling. Your husband is a famous man. I mean, he's just totally happening. He's where it's at, these days."

Lydia had liked Maureen's breezy style from the very first time the reporter came to visit her. Of course, Lydia was no fool. She had called her friend, Moe Elflik, head of the Washington Bureau of *Newsweek*, and found out that Maureen was really a top-flight young reporter for *Newsweek*. It was a wise precaution. With the way people were taking shots at her husband, it was good to be as cautions as necessary. Not more cautious than that, but just that cautious.

As Lydia looked at the muddy fish pond in the back yard, she wondered whether it was time for Maureen to come interview her again. For the last three days, Maureen had come with her little Panasonic and asked questions about her and Travis. She was doing the "human interest" part of the story, she said each time, and needed a lot detail to get even a few pages of really good stuff.

"I can tell you," Lydia said at the very beginning, "that no one knows Travis the way I do. Not anyone." She smiled a patronizing smile at Maureen while they both sat on the couch drinking tea. "Oh, there'll be some who might tell you that they know him like I do, like maybe some of the people at the office, but they don't."

"But, darling, that's exactly what we need," Maureen said. "I talked to that little Alex thing, and I mean, she was no good at all. It's your stories that'll make this thing come alive." She smiled and patted Lydia on the back of her hand. Maureen was only in her early thirties, Lydia guessed, but she was easy to talk to.

At the end of the second session, Lydia had felt an odd sensation. She had spent so much time talking to Maureen, and Maureen had understood what was on Lydia's mind so well, that for the first time in absolutely months, Lydia did not feel lonely and defeated at the end of the day.

"You know," she said to Maureen, "I love helping you with this story. I'm going to be sorry when it's over. I'll miss talking to you."

Maureen, looking neat and trendy in her velvet slacks and white peasant shirt, smiled a small smile and hugged Lydia. "Darling," she said, "we can still talk. I live right near here, and I'll come over and chat with you whenever you have time."

So now Lydia had made friends with Maureen, and that would certainly help the story come out better, but

Travis did not know a thing about it. Maureen had asked her to keep it a secret for a while, and Lydia had. Utterly without any help or encouragement from Travis, Lydia was doing her damnedest to get him a good story.

Just as Lydia looked at the spot where her gladioli would be coming up next spring, she heard the familiar putt-putt of Maureen Worth's Volkswagen. Lydia looked around the side of the house, and there was Maureen, dressed in a shearling coat and jeans, with a man whom Lydia had not seen before. Heavyset and pale, he wore an immaculate vicuna coat and a blue suit. Short, straight hair and brown glasses gave him the look of an editor or a publisher.

Lydia went through the back door, through the kitchen, through the dining room, and then into the living room to the front door. Only as she opened it did she remember that she was still wearing her pajamas and her yellow housecoat. That might have been all for her tête-à-têtes with Maureen, but Lydia was embarrassed about appearing before the distinguished young man with her.

"Oh, Lydia, darling, how I envy you. You're still in bed. How lucky," Maureen exclaimed.

"I'm not really." Lydia blushed. "I'm just a little forgetful this morning. I've been in back, gardening a little."

Lydia held open the storm door and the front door as Maureen and her friend came in. "Lydia, darling, this is Freddie de Quiñones." The heavyset man extended his hand and smiled. He looked about thirty-five.

"I'm extremely happy to meet you, Mrs. Bickel," de Quiñones said. "Extremely."

"Freddie is our expert on male human interest," Maureen said, as Lydia took their coats. "He wants to ask you a few questions about Travis from the male point of view." Maureen sat down and giggled. "I mean, isn't it too funny? Sending a man to do a story about a man? They don't trust me altogether. How funny."

De Quiñones sat down next to Maureen on the couch. He carried a slender attaché case with the familiar Gucci stripe. Out of it he took a tape recorder with a microphone and a long length of wire.

"Please sit down, Mrs. Bickel, and let me hook you up with this contraption. It's a lot more sensitive than Maureen's little Panasonic," he said. His voice was deep and soothing.

"Shall I change into my regular clothes?" Lydia asked. "I feel foolish in this outfit," she said, gesturing at her housecoat with two hands.

"Not necessary for me, Mrs. Bickel," de Quiñones said. "But if you want, go right ahead."

Perhaps de Quiñones was excited by seeing her like this, Lydia thought. That would be all right. It had been a while since she had seen a man get excited by her. She would stay as she was.

"Oh, darling, not right now," Maureen said. "But let Freddie do you," she said, and giggled.

Freddie smiled and walked over to the green armchair next to the fireplace where Lydia sat. He held the tape recorder and the tape in his hands. Lydia noticed what rugged, strong hands they were as he approached.

When he was at the chair, he smiled at her, drew back his right hand, and punched her in the face so hard that she blacked out for a moment. A surge of pain clouded her entire face. She felt dizzy and confused.

Before she could react, de Quiñones threw the wire around her neck and started to pull on it. It was so tight that she could not speak, could not call out, could not do anything. She tugged desperately at the wire with her hands, but de Quiñones held it too tight. She could not budge it. It was cutting into her neck. The wire hurt. She tried to cry out to Maureen, who looked at her drily, as if nothing were happening. Lydia started to feel more dizzy. The last thing she thought, before she blacked out, was this: "What did I do?"

De Quiñones threw her on the floor. She was still breathing slightly. The wire was wrapped around her neck.

"Is she dead?" Maureen Worth asked.

"Not quite," he said. "Do you want to watch this?"

"Sure," Maureen said. "Why not?"

"Suit yourself," de Quiñones said.

Without another word, he ripped Lydia's housecoat and pajamas to shreds, took off his clothes, and raped her, while Maureen watched, also silent. Both acted as if it were something they did every day.

"I don't see any reason not to wrap this up," de Quiñones said, when he had finished and buttoned his trousers.

"I couldn't agree more," Maureen said.

De Quiñones took the wire that was still around Lydia's neck and pulled it for about two minutes, until Lydia's heart had stopped.

He left the wire around her neck. Maureen and Quiñones went to the closet and took out their coats, walked out the door, leaving it slightly ajar, and left in the Volkswagen.

As they pulled onto Foxhall Road, the woman who had called herself Maureen Worth said to the man who had called himself de Quiñones, "She went out like a light. That was easy."

He didn't say anything.

"I mean, darling, the people at *Newsweek* are the ones who are going to have trouble. Especially Maureen Worth."

They both laughed.

CHAPTER

22

The morning after Travis Bickel discovered his wife's body, Frank Roberts arrived in Washington via a new Jetstar Super III, which Elson Patterson had ordered. Patterson had shrieked at him on the telephone to get down to Washington from New York immediately. "I don't know what's going on anymore," Patterson said. "I can't have that. I absolutely can't." A pause. "Or am I wrong?"

A gray Cadillac limousine awaited Roberts at the airport, with a black chauffeur holding out an envelope. As the car sped over the highway along the Potomac, Roberts opened the envelope. On a sheet of cream-colored paper as thick as a piece of bread, in Elson Patterson's scratchy handwriting, the message read: "Please come here directly. Do not stop at Howard Johnson's for ice cream."

Roberts folded the paper neatly and put it into the inside breast pocket of his J. Press cavalry twill suit. This time would be difficult indeed, and, ironically, it would be the hardest to defend.

Patterson sat coiled in his chair glaring at Roberts.

Behind him, in the study, the woods were gray and dreary. Like a serpent, Patterson blended into the tan color of his chair. He was wearing a khaki outfit of shirt and trousers and light brown shoes. No necktie.

This time, Patterson did not even get up. A vein in his left temple stood out. "Sit down, Frank," Patterson said. "And close the door."

Roberts did as he was told.

"How are you, Frank?" Patterson said, baring his teeth.

"Fine, thank you, Mr. Patterson. How are you?" Roberts said. He locked his fingers together and pulled at them to release the tension. It did not work.

Patterson leaned forward in his chair. "Frank," he asked, "are you tired of living?"

"No, Mr. Patterson, I'm not," Roberts said. A slight note of fear crept into his voice. "Please let me explain. I—"

"You goddamned fool," Patterson spat out, "how can you explain something that may have blown this whole thing apart? It probably has. Do you know what you've done, you idiot?" Patterson reached under his right thigh and pulled out a short brown riding crop. He brandished it in front of Roberts. "This isn't for you, you fool. Do you know what's for you? Do you know how big something like this is? Do you know the risk you took with the most important plan in all history?"

"Please, Mr. Patterson. Let me tell you something . . ."

"I don't want any miserable mealy-mouthed excuses. I warned you that your people were getting out of hand after that fiasco in Los Angeles. I thought you got the message. I thought that because you usually do well, you would pick up what I was talking about without much trouble. I was wrong and that's for sure. Am I wrong about you?" Now the veins in Patterson's forehead stood out, too. "Don't you understand how important Croesus is? It's not a plan to break into a liquor store. Croesus is for the whole thing, Frank, or don't you know that?"

"Mr. Patterson, you are wrong about something," Roberts said quickly, fidgeting with the arm of his chair. While Patterson looked at him, momentarily speechless, Roberts raced forward. "We didn't do it, Mr. Patterson. It wasn't us."

"What?" Patterson gasped. "Are you trying to weasel out of this?" His whole face was suffused with a crimson color.

Roberts pursued his advantage. "I never gave any instructions about Mrs. Bickel. We weren't even following her movements. We didn't have anyone on her."

"It could have been someone else, someone you didn't order to do it. Maybe someone from a different part of the organization," Patterson said. His face was returning to a more nearly normal hue, but his hands were now trembling.

"It could have been, but I don't think so, "Roberts said. "After I heard about it on the radio, I turned the organization inside out. I even acted as if we wanted to reward whoever it was. I didn't come up with a thing. Not one thing." He paused for a moment to get a breath so that he could speak with emphasis. "Mr. Patterson," he said, "I think it was some other organization."

"Well, who the hell does that mean?" Patterson asked. "Wait a minute." He sat up as if he had an inspiration. "Could it be the people from Paraguay? They're crazy enough."

"I can't rule it out," Roberts said. "But why would they do it? They have a hard enough time just keeping themselves going. I can't see them butting in on this." For the first time, he looked slightly away from Patterson, to the rows of photographs on the shelf behind him. Patterson did not notice. He was too busy thinking.

"It could be those assholes in Paraguay," Patterson muttered, more to himself than to Roberts. "It definitely could be. They don't need a reason. They just have to do something every so often to show that they're around." He pounded his fist on a bony knee. "Goddammit, I bet it was them. They would do it just to show me that they're not kowtowing to me because I pay the bills."

"Mr. Patterson," Roberts said quietly, "I don't think

it was the people from Paraguay. I think it's people from somewhere a lot farther east."

Patterson looked up sharply. "The KGB? Why the hell would they do it?" he asked. The vein in his left temple was starting to throb again.

"I'm not sure, Mr. Patterson," Roberts said. "But I think it means they know all about our plans for Bickel."

"All about them?" Patterson asked. "How?"

"Maybe not all," Roberts said. "But enough."

Thirty minutes later, Patterson asked Roberts a question. "We can't scrub the whole thing, Frank. Would that be the right thing to do? Maybe we should do that." He wondered. Maybe it was hopeless after all. Then he thought of the *Führer*'s blue eyes. He would never give up.

"I don't think so, Mr. Patterson. Maybe we should do that later, but not now." He rested his chin on his fingertips and leaned forward. "I think we can still pull this out. But it'll require doing something with the girl."

"The girl?" Patterson asked. "Do we really want to bring her in?"

"I think we have to," Roberts said.

"Tell me about it, Frank," Patterson said, leaning back in his chair. "By the way, have you had lunch?"

"No, thank you, Mr. Patterson," Roberts said. He looked pleased and grateful. Inwardly he smiled too. Patterson would be an easy target. No sweat at all.

"I can't stand this, Arthur. I just can't stand it. It's a goddamn nightmare," Travis Bickel said, as he looked out over the Potomac at the lights twinkling in the Arlington National Cemetery.

Bickel wore a day's growth of beard. He had neither shaved nor slept since 7:14 PM the night before, when he had walked into his living room and seen Lydia next to the fireplace with wire around her neck and her clothes ripped to pieces. As he talked to Kosters, he wore the same suit he had put on the morning before. He had not showered or changed his clothes, either, since he had found Lydia's body.

"I know what loss is, Travis," Kosters said. He sat in his easy chair between the couches looking rumpled and puffy. His lower lip hung in a sort of sad, sulking, droopy pout. He looked more overweight than usual. "I know it's hard to take. I know that."

"You do?" Travis Bickel asked without turning around.

"Yes, I do," Kosters said, lifting his Scotch and water to his lips. "I definitely do. How many people in my family do you think survived Hitler? How many?"

"I don't know. How many?" Bickel asked, still without looking from the window.

"Not many," Kosters said sadly. "Not many, Travis, although it doesn't bring back Lydia."

"For God's sake, Arthur, why did they have to do what they did to her?" Bickel wheeled away from the window. His face was puffy and dirty. There were blotches of red on his face. His normally wolflike eyes were bloodshot and bleary.

"They are barbaric people, Travis, whoever they are," Kosters said wearily. "Perhaps the police will find them."

Bickel sat down heavily on the couch next to Kosters. He snickered. "If you think the police will find the people who killed Lydia, then you must think that the people who killed Simon Kart and the people who killed Jeff and Mark Richards, and the people who tried to kill Kathy Dorn, and the people who killed all those people at West Lake are in prison. Is that what you think?" He said it more with resignation than with sarcasm or anger.

Kosters sighed. "Something is going on. It obviously has to do with you and the treaty. That much I can figure out."

Bickel shook his head. "I can't believe it. What did Lydia have to do with the damn treaty?" As soon as he said it, he knew what Kosters would say.

"They want to show you their power," Kosters said. He looked around the room. It was dimly lit by rheostatted bulbs. "They want to show you that they can do anything to stop this treaty. We know that."

"How the hell do we know that?" Bickel asked wearily.

"We know that because there is no other possible explanation. When you have eliminated the impossible, the remainder, however improbable, is the explanation." Kosters smiled wryly. "A paraphrase from Arthur Conan Doyle."

"Well, what the hell is being done about it?" Bickel asked. "If we know who's doing it, why can't we just get to them and beat the hell out of them?" He rubbed his forehead with his left hand. "I mean, why can't we just beat them until they tell us who did it? If it's some kind of radicals, they must be known to other radicals somewhere." His eyes started to gleam with anger.

"Travis," Kosters andwered slowly, "the Federal Republic is turning the universities there upside down trying to find out who is involved. They've arrested more than three hundred people since Kart's death."

"It's not enough," Bickel said. He reached inside his pocket for a cigarette. He smoked only rarely, but now was a time perfectly suited to smoking. He pulled out a red-and-white package of Marlboros and extracted a cigarette. With trembling hands, he lit it with a match from a white book bearing the seal of the secretary of state.

"It isn't enough, goddammit," Bickel said. "If it were enough, they would have found the people who are doing it.

"In this country," Kosters continued, "the FBI has over two hundred and fifty special agents looking for the killers. The NSA is scanning all phone traffic with Germany. The Executive Protective Service is involved in doing some checking, too." Kosters spread his palms upright in a "What can I do about it?" gesture.

"It still isn't enough, goddammit," Bickel said. "I am a fucking U.S. senator. Someone has been killing the people around me in a very obvious way for about six weeks."

"I know," Kosters said, looking sad again.

"It's just ridiculous that whoever it is can't be found. I mean that's just ridiculous, that's all."

Kosters suddenly pulled himself upright in his seat. "It's worse than ridiculous, Travis. Something's going on. Something big."

Bickel tapped the ash off his cigarette into the ashtray that bore the seal of the secretary of state. "What are you talking about? I know that something is going on."

"No," Kosters said. "I did not want to tell you about this, but something quite unprecedented is happening, I think." Kosters looked ill at ease. "I think we are seeing a campaign of terror, which may be carried out by young German radicals, probably with the help of Americans. But I believe the strings are being pulled in Moscow."

"Are you kidding, Arthur?" Bickel shot back. "Would they dare to try to mount that kind of campaign and risk war?"

Bickel got up and tried vainly to smooth the wrinkles from his gray suit. He walked over to the window again. "It just sounds awfully goddamn farfetched," Bickel said.

"Try to think about it from their point of view," Kosters said, without moving. "Try to put yourself in the Russians' place. They're a fairly patient people. They seem to be doing just fine, trying to make the world safe for their brand of Communism. They see Europe, the second richest prize, falling into their hands like a ripe fruit."

"I know all that," Bickel said testily.

"Suddenly, the equation is changed fundamentally," Kosters continued, without taking any note of Bickel's tone. "Suddenly, the Russians are going to be the ones who live in fear. They fear and hate the Germans like no other people in the world. Now the West Germans are going to have the wherewithal to blow them to bits."

Bickel listened attentively as Kosters looked up at him. "They don't see the new, stable Federal Republic when they look at Germany. They see the Nazis shooting children. They're scared. They'll do anything."

"If they do too much, it's suicide in fear of death," Bickel said.

"All the more reason for them to do it very quietly," Kosters said.

"You call shooting people and blowing them up 'quietly'?" Bickel asked, almost breathlessly.

"It is if no one knows it's you who's doing it," Kosters said. "Besides, we've picked up some hints that something's going on at the KGB and that they're plenty worried."

"Anything firm?" Bickel asked.

"Not firm enough to go to war over, but firm enough for us to look awfully carefully. Firm enough for me to have talked to the President about it."

"Jesus," Bickel said. "Just Jesus H. Christ."

"Exactly," Kosters said. "A hell of a mess."

Bickel walked over and sat down next to Kosters. "So now," he asked, his hands on his knees, "what do I do to keep going?"

"That's what I want to talk to you about," Kosters said. "Tell me about Yichik Cohen again."

Bickel settled back into an armchair with a queasy feeling. When would he ever know the truth? Who the hell did know the truth? He was beginning to wonder if he wanted to hear it at all.

CHAPTER

23

Yichik Cohen looked just the way Bickel
had imagined he would. He was of medium height and
medium build, with gray and black hair curling back
from his temples. He looked about seventy years old. In
Bickel's suite at Claridge's, Cohen cut an unusual figure.
He was only slightly stooped over, and his clothes were
well-cut, but there was something in the eyes. They
blazed with a brown look of fear and anger, of having
seen far too much, of marveling that he was there at an
elegant hotel instead of in a mass grave. It was that look
of taking nothing for granted that distinguished him
from the people Bickel saw at Claridge's, or indeed, anywhere else. Bickel had seen a hint of that look before, in
an office of the Department of State.

Bickel and Cohen sat in a small sitting room adjoin-
ing the bedroom. At one end was a fireplace of brick
with a marble exterior, black, ribbed with white streaks,
in an old-fashioned rounded shape. In front of the
hearth were two wing chairs upholstered in white. In
front of each was a low hassock of the same material,
with lion's-paw feet.

Between the two chairs was a round, highly polished cherrywood table. On top of it was a lamp with a base made from an antique Chinese jar, with a swirling blue and yellow and white design. The shade was made of heavy linen material.

Next to the lamp was a folded copy of that day's London *Times*. The lead story was about a massive West German manhunt for the members of the radical gang believed to be responsible for various violent acts associated with Senator Travis A. Bickel. There was also a ceramic ashtray with an Oriental design similar to the one on the lamp.

Facing the chairs and the lamp at an angle were two sofas. Each was covered with a brocaded fabric of blue and white. The sofas had high arms and backs, in the style that had been considered stylish in the late nineteenth century and again in 1983. Between the two sofas was a low drop-leaf coffee table of the same highly polished cherrywood as the round table. On that table was a beat-up briefcase, snapped shut by a small combination lock. Bickel and Cohen faced each other on the sofas.

"I hardly even know Sabrina Schuller," Cohen said. "We have friends in common." He had a slight accent. Polish? Yiddish?

Bickel felt ill at ease. He had come to London only because Kosters had told him that it was crucial, that it might be the one way to stop the terror that had filled Bickel's life. It was also crucial, Kosters said, for the treaty, and that was more important than any one individual. So Kosters arranged for a small Air Force plane to take Bickel to London one day, give him one day there, and fly him back the next day.

If Lydia were still alive, he would have brought her a souvenir. Perhaps Irish linen. But Lydia was resting now, for the first time in many years. She needed no souvenirs.

"I don't know her terribly well myself," Bickel said, focusing on Sabrina Schuller. "She's a woman who knows what she wants, though," he added.

Yichik Cohen did not say anything for a few moments. That was how the conversation had gone since Cohen had appeared at the hotel room two hours before. Bickel would say something, Cohen would respond, and then Bickel would speak again, and Cohen would say nothing.

On the end table next to Bickel were the remains of lunch—sole Véronique. Claridge's did it well, with just the right kind of white grapes, perhaps from Greece. Cohen had declined to order lunch.

"So," Cohen said, "you want to know about Elson Patterson?" He said it with a kind of teasing, defiant air, as he had been saying it all afternoon. At first Bickel had said, "Yes, I want to know about Elson Patterson." Then he realized that Cohen would tell him only in his own good time.

"I would bet that you also want to know what is inside this briefcase. Don't you?" Cohen asked.

Bickel said nothing about the briefcase. "Would you like something from room service?" he asked.

Bickel wore an orange sweater and gray trousers, with black leather tassel loafers. It was a contrast to Cohen's far more formal gray suit, with slightly tan shirt and maroon tie, with black wing-tip shoes.

"Yes," Cohen said, ignoring the question about room service and scratching one of his thick black eyebrows, "I imagine you want to know about everything."

A thought suddenly hit Bickel. "Mr. Cohen," he said tentatively, "is it money you want?"

Cohen actually laughed out loud. "Money?" he said, when he stopped laughing. "You think I need money?"

"I'm not saying you need it," Bickel said. "I just thought that it might make you say something to me. I'm getting a little tired of waiting for you to talk."

"Money?" Cohen asked again. "That's funny. I mean, that's really funny." He pronounced "really" as if it were "rally." A tribute to his thorough Anglicization.

"All right," Bickel said disgustedly. "You don't want money. What the hell do you want?"

"Money?" Cohen said again. "Listen, Senator, let me tell you a few things about me. I don't need money. I have all the money I'll need for the rest of my life. I want to tell you a few things about me that you obviously don't know."

At last, Bickel thought. At last he's going to say something. "I'm seventy-three years old," Cohen said. "That's right. I'm seventy-three years old. And I never needed money. My father had a good trade. A fine trade. He could draw and he could engrave." Cohen chuckled. "He could engrave things in great detail." Another chuckle.

Bickel looked above Cohen's head at a portrait of a woman with blond hair piled high above her head and a gown with a tightly laced bodice. She wore a heavy cross on her chest. She did not look happy.

"You know what that meant?" Cohen asked. "It meant he could draw pictures of money, of stocks, of bonds, of notes. And they were good pictures. He could draw enough of them so that even if the police caught him, he could give them some of those pretty pictures, and they would leave him alone." Cohen chuckled again.

To the right of the woman's picture was a window looking out on a drizzly street. Bickel could not remember the street's name. He knew that it had a lot of elegant shops. He made a mental note to look for a suit if time permitted.

"We lived in Warsaw, Senator," Cohen continued. "When it became capital of an independent Poland, we did even better. There was no one we couldn't bribe. No one."

A wave of unhappiness began lapping against Travis Bickel's heart. Why was everything connected with this process so sordid? What had been happening since he left for the arms talks not more than two months ago? Even this man, whom Bickel had thought would be so touching, was turning out to be fairly repulsive. Would things stop being repulsive when he got inside the Oval Office? They had better be, Bickel thought. He was sick of the seamless web of violence in which he was traveling through time.

Bickel looked out at the street again. A man walked by wearing a bowler hat and carrying a tightly furled umbrella. It was good that some things did not change.

"I did not become a counterfeiter," Cohen said. "Why should I have? I had all the money I needed. I wanted to be an artist. And I was. I studied in Paris and in Leipzig. But I had the talent, you see?" He put his hands out on either side of his chest with the palms up. "Sometimes in Leipzig, just for the hell of it, I would draw an absolutely perfect mark from memory. Sometimes I would practice calligraphy and make up diplomas and certificates for my friends that were far more beautiful and elaborate than anything the institutes gave out."

Maybe, Bickel thought, maybe Cohen is just a braggart. That's not so terrible. I can live with that.

"I won't bore you with all the details about what happened with the Nazis. Of course, it was terrible." Cohen said it as if it had happened to someone else. "I was a young man, just starting a family. I dabbled in this and that, mainly doing things for my father. By then, he had bought so many real bonds with his counterfeit money that he hardly worked at all either." Cohen smiled a wistful smile. It was different from his laughter in that it had no content of cruelty or bitterness. It was pure nostalgia.

"The SS *Hauptsturmführer* who came to arrest me and my father had been a classmate of mine at the art institute in Leipzig. We used to go out to the same whorehouses together." Cohen looked down at his hands as if they did not belong to him. "That didn't even slow him down. Not a bit. But he was disappointed. My father had killed himself the night before."

Bickel had the sensation that he should not be there, that he was a weightless intrusion into a world of horror that had more claim to legitimacy than his world. He felt awkward. He wanted to tell Cohen that he must stop talking about his life, that he must only tell him about Patterson.

"They threw me into the cattle cars, just like everyone else. No difference. The man who had known me simply called me 'Jew.' No Yichik, no Cohen. Just 'Jew.' And there I was in the cattle car. On the outside of the car, someone had written, '*achtzig Juden.*' Eighty Jews. We were in that car for three days and nights."

He paused and looked around the room—at the marble fireplace, the gleaming tables, the fine upholstery. Then he looked down at his hands again and he laughed. It was not a pretty laugh.

"I wonder, Senator Bickel, if you can imagine what it is like to be in a cattle car for seventy-two hours—give or take a few—with eightly other human beings?" He looked straight at Bickel with raised eyebrows. He waited for an answer.

Bickel stammered. "I guess it would be pretty horrible."

Cohen smiled mockingly. "I guess so. There was no air conditioning. There were no toilets. You understand? No color TV."

Again, he looked at Bickel, obviously awaiting some kind of comment.

"It must have been horrible," Bickel said, looking at the woman above Cohen's head. What would she think of all of this? Could a seventeenth-century mind comprehend it?

"At Treblinka, it was actually better than it was in the railway car, Oh, the young ones and the old ones were killed. Certainly. But, you know, it's amazing how quickly you get used to that. Amazing. We who survived worked at loading shells with powder. Perfect work for us. If there was an accident, so much the better. If someone was injured, the treatment was simple. A bullet in the head. No need for medical treatment. I saw it, Senator. I saw it often,"

Again, Bickel had the sensation that he should not have been there—that he did not belong to the same world that Yichik Cohen belonged to.

"I saw many things that you would find hard to believe, Senator. I saw guards bludgeon teenage girls to death just for fun. Yes. I saw *Schäferhunde,* German shepherds, tear women to pieces. I saw it all. I won't even tell you all I saw. And food? You would not, in your country, allow pigs to eat the garbage we ate. Again, for the Germans, no problem. If we died, less work for them. Sound economics, huh?" Again, he looked at his hands. They were starting to tremble.

Bickel wanted to say something, but he did not know what to say. What can a person say? What can anyone say to someone who had been in hell? What can a person who makes a hobby of Nazi history say to someone who has been put in a cattle car marked *"achtzig Juden"* for seventy-two hours?

Cohen stared off to somewhere above Bickel's head. "I wish I could adequately describe to you what it was like in our bunks. I don't really think I can. Imagine a place where there are only latrines, where half the people have dysentery, where two men share a narrow cot, where the windows are locked at night, where there is no heat," and he paused to look straight at Bickel, "and also where you could be killed in any way at any time. Then you would not have even a small part of the horror of it."

Bickel began to feel dizzy. He did not know how long he could stand to hear this description. It was wearing him down.

Cohen somehow recognized the look on Bickel's face. Perhaps he had seen it before.

He smiled narrowly and said, "I won't bore you with this anymore. Please don't worry." He leaned back on the couch, spread his hands on either side of him, and crossed his left leg over his right leg. "Sometimes we had visitors at the camps. SS officials, Nazi Party officials. That kind of thing. They would tour the camp. They would look at us. The guards would lift up our heads with riding crops as if we were animals. I did not know who most of the visitors were."

He looked over at Bickel as if to excuse himself. "You understand. How could I, a Polish Jew, be expected to know anything about German officials?" He looked at Bickel for acknowledgement.

"Of course," Bickel said. "Of course."

Cohen nodded and smiled, then clasped his hands together over his left knee. "Of course," he repeated after Bickel, almost triumphantly. "But," he said, raising his right index finger, like a lawyer making a point, "I had not grown up in the *shtetl*. I knew some people in the world. I knew who Charles Lindberg was. I knew who Winston Churchill was. I knew all about the heroes of the world."

Bickel was still back at the cattle car marked *"acht-zig Juden."*

"One day, after I had been at the camp for perhaps six months, and was, of course, as thin as a rail, those of us in my section of the camp were called out for an inspection. Of course, the idea was to show whoever it was that we were completely docile and under control, ready to work or be killed as the occasion might demand. You understand?" He smiled a crazed smile at Bickel.

"No, I do not understand," Bickel said. "I don't understand how you're alive. I don't understand how any of us is alive. I just don't understand the whole thing." His voice was loud with anger.

"You don't understand?" Cohen asked softly. "Well, that is all to the good for you, of course."

Neither man said anything for a few moments. Bickel could see a young man and woman walking by outside, hugging each other. He wondered if he would ever get out of the room, out of the horrible, unspeakable past.

"Well, anyway," Cohen continued with a shrug of his shoulders, "one day we were called out for inspection, or did I already say that?"

Bickel did not answer.

Cohen stared at him. "I did say that already. You must stop me when I am becoming repetitive. Please."

In a flat voice Bickel said, "You're not being repetitive."

"Anyway, there we all were, lined up in our prison clothes—vile-smelling, lice-infested striped pajamas. We were told to keep our eyes downcast. There were several rows of us." He paused for a moment to look over his shoulder, out the window. There was nothing to see out there, as far as Bickel could tell. Cohen continued. "I would never have believed that I would forget how many rows there were, but a lot. Maybe twenty."

Bickel noticed suddenly that he was wearing an orange sweater and loafers to hear a man tell about life in a concentration camp. It did not seem like the right outfit. But then, what was the right outfit? Rags? Black tie and tails?

"Guards with whips and pistols stood around us. Suddenly the gates of the camp were thrown open, and a large car came roaring in, followed by several motorcyclists. The guards kept barking at us to keep our heads down. I kept mine down. I could hear the car door open and some conversation in German. Suddenly I heard a prisoner cry out."

Bickel had a feeling that he knew what was about to come out of Cohen's mouth. He started to feel queasy.

"I cannot remember exactly what the prisoner said. It was something like, 'For God's sake, tell people in America about us!' In an instant, the guards had brought him out of the ranks. There was so much shouting that I looked up for a moment to see who our visitor was." Cohen said it all in a monotone. "You know who it was, Senator Bickel. I hardly have to tell you. Do I?" He asked, in a slightly mocking voice, "How does Elson Patterson look today? He looked awfully good back in 1940."

With a great effort of will, Bickel asked Cohen, "You're sure, absolutely positive, that it was Elson Patterson?"

Cohen smirked an ugly smirk. "Am I sure? Are you kidding? Of course, I'm sure. I'm just as sure as I am that the guards took the prisoner and tied him to a post and then, with Patterson watching, whipped him to death." In a soft voice laced with irony, Cohen asked, "Senator, have you ever seen a man whipped to death? Have you ever heard the screams of a man flayed to death?"

"No," Bickel said in a breaking voice.

"I won't bore you with how it sounds," Cohen said, his monotone returning. "But we were ordered to watch. And since we had our heads up, we could see the people watching the whipping. Elson Patterson never took his eyes off the prisoner. When the man was dead,

Patterson laughed and then walked away, got into his car, and drove away."

Sweat broke out on Bickel's forehead. "Thank you for telling me this," Bickel said, as he wiped off his forehead with a monogrammed handkerchief. "It must have been hard for you. It must have been very hard." Bickel glanced at the watch Patterson had given him. It was going to be hard for him, Bickel, too.

Cohen leaned forward with a wolfish grin. "Oh, I am not finished, Senator. I am most decidedly not finished with your friend, Elson Patterson."

Bickel started to feel numb. He considered asking Cohen to stop for at least a while. The room was suffocating. He wanted to go outside, get a breath of air. The room was far smaller than it had been.

"Things got better for me right after that," Cohen said. "One morning I was dragged out of my row in the morning and told that a surprise was in store for me. It was going to be a big change." Cohen smiled an ingratiating smile at Bickel. "Naturally, I thought I was going to be killed. What other kind of change could there be?"

Bickel did not answer.

"But I was brought to my former schoolmate, the SS man, by now an *Obersturmbannführer*. He shook hands with me. He called me by my name. He said there were big plans for me. You can imagine, I thought I must be dreaming. But, no, they cleaned me up, put on civilian clothes, and drove me out of the camp. I never saw it again, of course."

The sweat suddenly stopped on Bickel's forehead. He felt as if he, too, had just gotten out of Treblinka.

"They took me somewhere in a suburb of Berlin. Perhaps, I thought, I am going to be released." He gave a short laugh. "Not likely, of course. No, they took me to a small prison for regular prisoners. I was given my own cell. And next to the cell was a small studio. What incredible luck!" Cohen smiled at the remembrance. "I was told that it was to be my job, for the rest of the war, to design posters and medals and certificates of all kinds for the *Führer*. My predecessor had died of wounds in France. No one could even dare to tell the *Führer* that his favorite calligrapher had been allowed to die in battle. So I was to take his place. Funny, huh?" Cohen smiled up at Bickel expectantly.

"Hilarious," Bickel said drily.

"Well," Cohen continued, "to me, it was funny. Mostly, I drew fairly simple posters, demanding total sacrifice for the fatherland and complete loyalty to the *Führer*. They were very popular. I did that for about two years. It was not so bad. The food was bearable. I was allowed a little exercise, even some sunlight. You can imagine, coming from Treblinka, what it felt like."

Bickel could not even start to imagine.

"Well," Cohen continued, "it was a great step upward for me. The only thing I really missed was women. None of them were allowed to me. A great pity," he said, looking morosely around the sitting room at the elegant furniture.

"One day, I think it was in 1942, near the end of the year, I was told that I had the most important project of my life. If I did it right, I would even be allowed to have women. Jewish ones, of course. Imagine my delight," Cohen said with an authentic grin.

Again, Bickel had the terrible sensation that he knew what was coming. He could not sit still any longer. He got up and walked over to the window, as Cohen followed him with his eyes. Down on the street, a Rolls-Royce lumbered slowly down the street. In the back seat, Bickel could see two elderly women. Bickel opened the window and a gust of cool air came in. It was refreshing to him. He did not feel as suffocated any longer.

"My big assignment was to design the official papers designating Elson Patterson as deputy *Führer* for North America, the same as Hess was in Germany. I still remember the exact title: Elson Patterson, *"Reichsleiter zu Befehlsführer in Amerika Nord."* You understand that? The *Führer* was so sure that he would have a Nazified America that he had already selected Patterson for *Unterführer*. It was to be a major document, signed personally by the *Führer*."

Bickel went back to his sofa and sat down heavily.

"That was not all, though," Cohen said. "I made three originals of the proclamation. One for the *Führer*, one for Patterson, and one for archives. The *Führer* liked them so much that he ordered a special medal struck commemorating the event. He wanted a likeness of Patterson on it. Well, how could I do that if Patterson was in America?" Cohen asked with a frown. "The solution was that Patterson was brought over to Germany and sat in my small studio while I drew him. Of course, there were guards there, and I was not allowed to talk to him. But I could see him, looking so healthy and tanned and fit, while I drew his profile, that strong profile with the angular nose and the hawklike eyes." Cohen said it with a bitter irony.

Bickel was starting to feel sick again.

"I won't bore you with the rest of my story," Cohen said with an airy wave. "Just suffice it to say that, here I am, alive and well, and I have a souvenir for you. Take it to any collector who knows about these things, any collector in the world, and find out if it's authentic."

He opened his briefcase and rummaged around inside it. He drew forth his right hand with a prize. It was a bronze medal with a man's face on it. Cohen dropped it on the coffee table with a clank. It rolled around, then fell flat. On it was Elson Patterson's profile, with the angular nose and the hawklike eyes. Around the top was the legend, in Old German lettering, *"Zu Befehl der Führer, Elson Patterson, Reichsleiter in Amerika Nord."*

"Take it with you," Cohen said. "Take it with you, and you don't even have to give me any money."

CHAPTER

24

$\mathbf{B}$ickel marveled at the scenery on the road to Innisfree. The slush of New York City had been left far behind for the tranquil beauty of the countryside. For mile after mile there were snow-covered forests stretching off as far as Bickel could see. Occasionally the Cadillac limousine passed by a tavern or gasoline station, but even they had a down home serenity about them. Pine and maple started at the roadside and ran up the mountains until they blended with the gray sky in the distance.

The car made no noise at all, except for a steady hum of tires on asphalt. It was still morning and the highway was virtually empty. On a map, Bickel located Innisfree and realized that he would be there in a few minutes.

He stole a sideways glance at McMurtry, the bodyguard whom Kosters had assigned to him after he returned from London.

"When you see Patterson, he won't want you to have an entire retinue. I'll give you one good man, one man who'll make him think twice," Kosters said.

Hence, McMurtry, who, with his curly blond hair and slack jaw, looked like the spawn of the West Virginia hills. Maybe he was, but he was as fast as a cat and could have his .38 out and ready to fire before a cat hit the ground. He only looked sleepy.

The call to visit Patterson had been waiting for Bickel when he got back to his office after his trip to London. Kosters had said to go. It was just as well, because Bickel had a lot that he wanted to talk to Patterson about. It would have been hard to know where to begin if Patterson had not called him first. It was also just as well that Patterson had summoned him to Innisfree. Just as well, because no one would see him there, and, considering what he knew, Bickel did not want people to know that he had ever been in the same room with Patterson.

But Bickel had to be careful. He must remember what Kosters had told him. He must not let his anger run away with him. Patterson was too important, his roots ran too deep, for him to be handled with anger. Besides, there were others involved. Many others.

The Cadillac sped through the morning air. The woods held a fascination for Bickel similar to the fascination of the snow. He had not seen woods like this when he was growing up, and now they were a special delight for him. Of course, there were woods in California, but they were not the same. Perhaps north of San Francisco they were the same, but down in the Southland, the woods always had a tentative look about them, as if a fire or a mudslide or a dry spell could erase them and bring on the eternal raw earth.

These New England woods were different. They would be around for a while. They were part of the earth here, not grafted on by landscape architects. There would be towns and suburbs and farms, but the woods would endure. There was a peace about them that could not be eliminated. It must be that peace from which Elson Patterson drew his strength to go on for as long as he did.

It was amazing, really, even for a man with the resources of an Elson Patterson. To continue with his life work—and what a life work—when, to every appearance, it was absolutely and completely hopeless. In a way, Bickel gave him credit. It took a kind of will to undertake what he had undertaken and to see it through to such length.

"It is so powerful that it cannot be attacked frontally. That much is certain. But we can use it and destroy it at the same time, if you play your part correctly," Kosters had said, looking mournfully at him. Kosters had looked unusually mournful since Bickel returned from London. The news from ONA had been waiting, and the pieces that Bickel had added from his meeting with Yichik Cohen simply put the finishing touches on the completed jigsaw puzzle.

God, Kosters thought things through. His plan was brilliant. The only problem was that it relied for its success on two highly imperfect vessels—Patterson and Bickel.

"Even if I do it just right, how can we tell how Patterson will react?" Bickel said. Everything happened so fast. Lydia's murder. The funeral. The trip to London. Everything was loading up in a major way. Patterson might still be three moves ahead of them.

"We cannot say for sure what Patterson will do," Kosters said. "That is true. But we can say that he has reacted in a certain way for a long time, and it makes sense to assume that he will continue to act that way." He paused and ground out his cigar in the ashtray. It was the first time Bickel had seen him smoke. "But we do know that he has certain plans for you, at least as of very recently, and he cannot change them unless he plans to come back from the dead and try it a second time."

"What if I fuck up?" Bickel said. "What if I just can't control myself?"

"You will be able to control yourself," Kosters said. "You have to. It's urgent. Not just for you. Not just for the treaty. But to kill this snake that has infested the whole government. It's just too big for you to not do right," Kosters added solemnly.

More woods slipped by. The gray buff seats of the

limousine were also blending with the sky. Somehow the whole scene did not feel right. It would have felt right if Bickel were going to nearby Poughkeepsie to give a speech. But for a meeting with Elson Patterson on something this big, all that snowy peace did not seem right.

To confront a tenacious evil in a beautiful place stretched Bickel's ready imagination. He had to summon an extra measure of creativity to convince himself that it was really happening, that he was going to confront Elson Patterson himself in his lair and, what's more, to do him in.

"I think you have to do it," Kathy Dorn had said. "Your responsibility is to do it. Do it, and finish him," she had said emphatically, as they lay in bed the night before.

Bickel had told her about Patterson and Croesus. She had come close to dying for him, so it was only fair and proper that she be admitted to the secrets of his life.

She had been so strong after Lydia's death. She was at the Washington Hilton in a guarded suite, courtesy of Kosters. Her scalp still had stitches, but otherwise, she looked well. She cried when he walked in the door after Lydia's funeral.

"In a way," Bickel said, "I'm glad she's dead."

"What?" Kathy gasped.

"She couldn't handle living very well," Bickel said. "It's just as well she's in a place where she does not have to think about the things that aggravated her. It sounds harsh, but there it is."

After that first gasp, Kathy did not judge him harshly. They did not make love the day of the funeral, but soon afterward they spent every night together. The bodyguards stayed in the next room. He thought of her face now as the Cadillac slowed down for the gate to the long driveway that led to Innisfree.

Somehow, since his return from London, she had been more passionate, more responsive, than before. A sort of abandon had carried her away repeatedly through the nights of lovemaking. Her slim, blond body had a lithe tightness, like a high carbon steel spring, waiting to be unleashed by his touch. In a world full of deceit and falseness, her physical responses to him were a point of truth, of genuine feeling.

"I still don't understand the whole thing, to tell you the truth," Bickel said to Kosters before he set out. "I don't understand what the treaty has to do with Patterson, for one thing." They had been riding in the limousine that took Bickel to Andrews Air Force Base in Suitland, Maryland, that morning.

"No one understands it all, Travis," Kosters said. "But I think Patterson had nothing to do with the treaty, except that it brought you to his attention, which is good." Both of them looked out the window at the dismal Prince Georges County countryside. Row after row of slum apartments lined the route.

A slush similar to the slush of all woebegone areas in the winter ran in a continuous flow miles long by the side of the highway. Battered old cars were stuck in the driveways of dilapidated single-family houses, which had probably looked good to people fleeing the black tide in Washington forty years before but which had long since become black themselves, and then replicas of the downtown slums.

"The treaty has not got anything to do with Patterson that we know about," Kosters repeated. "That's where, I think, the KGB comes in. I think they're trying to get you to think that Croesus is even bigger than it is. I'm not saying it isn't awfully big. It's just not that big."

"The treaty's coming up for a vote within a week," Bickel said. "We could stall it, but it might look as if we're worried about the votes."

Kosters looked firm. "No. No stalling. It's too important to be wrecked by either Patterson or the KGB. No way. We've got the votes. We'll bring it to the floor and pass it. The thing for you to do is get Patterson taken care of, and then we'll handle the rest with you as President."

The Cadillac now was bouncing in and out of ruts in Elson Patterson's long driveway. Bickel was surprised that someone as neat and orderly as Patterson would allow so many potholes. The roadway turned around a boulder, and there, a few hundred yards away, was Innisfree. It looked like a fairy-tale manor, boarded and thatched in English countryhouse fashion, covered with snow, not a hint of dirt or disharmony anywhere.

How could such a thing happen here?

"The most important thing," Kosters had said, "is to be strong. Patterson can offer a lot. He can rationalize everything. But you have to be strong. Remember who he is. Remember what he did." Kosters had looked at the runway tarmac where Bickel was about to board his airplane. "Think of what he's done and who he is, and be strong."

The Cadillac stopped in front of an enormous oak door, set in a gray stone doorway. Before the driver was on the ground, the front door opened and Frank Roberts walked out. He looked businesslike in a blue pinstripe suit, white long-collar shirt, and blue, red, and orange rep tie. He extended his hand to Bickel with a cheery smile as Bickel stepped out of the car.

"How are you, Senator?" Roberts asked. "It was good of you to come on such short notice."

"Thank you, Frank," Bickel said, keeping one hand in his camel's hair coat. "I hope Mr. Patterson is here." Bickel looked around Innisfree. It was amazing that one man owned all of it. Innisfree was something out of the Middle Ages, when men held absolute power over other men. The manor house dominating the huge forests and the lake symbolized Patterson's power even in 1983, a hold less nakedly visible, but definitely there nevertheless.

Roberts led Bickel and McMurtry into a flagstone-covered foyer, where a black butler wordlessly took their coats. They stepped into a large hallway which was lined with photographs of Patterson scaling various peaks. The floors were hardwood with a red runner carpet along the center part of the floor. Bickel looked up and saw that the ceiling was covered with beams, like those of English taverns.

"How was your trip?" Roberts asked with a smile. "I hope that the roads up from the city were safe."

"It was beautiful," Bickel answered honestly. He

wondered where Patterson was. Then he remembered that he had forgotten to introduce his companion. "Frank, this is my friend and assistant, Fred McMurtry. Fred, this is Frank Roberts."

The two men shook hands. Roberts might have winced slightly at the power of McMurtry's grip. Roberts glanced over to Bickel. "Will you need Mr. McMurtry for your talk with Mr. Patterson?"

"I don't think so," Bickel said. "Will Mr. Patterson need you for my talk with him?"

"Not if you don't need Mr. McMurtry," Roberts said. He did not stop smiling.

To the right was a large living room, or whatever the equivalent was in a place like Innisfree. It had large oak ribs ostensibly holding up a vaulted ceiling, which sloped down on the opposite wall to large, oblong, leaded windows. The furniture was quite different from the room, though. It was modern furniture of heavy cloth and metal. Someone with extremely elegant taste had obviously figured the whole thing out, because the furniture made a perfect combination with the room. Portraits of people whom Bickel did not recognize hung on the walls. The people looked stern and unworried. They too, in some way Bickel could not understand, went well with the modern furniture. The room projected peace and taste. It occurred to Bickel that the room would probably not look as good if Yichik Cohen were in it.

From the far end of the room, apparently appearing out of thin air, came Elson Patterson. He looked rosy-cheeked and healthy. His chiseled features and blue eyes were those of an alert and healthy man. He wore a checked wool sports jacket, a blue button-down shirt, and gray trousers. At his neck was a scarlet ascot. He walked rapidly toward Bickel and extended his hand. Bickel decided that it would be a foolish and useless gesture not to shake it.

"How are you, Travis?" Patterson said warmly. He turned to McMurtry. "And who is your friend?"

"This is Fred McMurtry, Elson," Bickel said. "He's an important friend and assistant of mine."

Patterson pumped his hand warmly. "If you're a friend of the senator, then you must be a fine man," Patterson said.

"Thank you," McMurtry replied. "It's a pleasure to meet you." His voice was deep and soothing.

Patterson coughed slightly. "Travis," he said, "what I wanted to talk to you about shouldn't take Mr. McMurtry's time. If you don't mind, Travis, maybe Frank and Mr. McMurtry could take a little tour of the house or of the grounds or something and then eat together while you and I talk. Maybe some chocolate for Frank. Would that be all right?" He asked it with great uncertainty, as if it might not be all right.

"Yes," Bickel said. "That would be all right." Kosters had told him that as long as Patterson was alone, it was all right for Bickel to be alone.

A few minutes later, Patterson led Bickel into a long corridor lined with paintings and photographs and through a heavy door into a room with one wall made entirely of glass. Through that window, sun reflected off snow and poured into the room with a dazzling whiteness. In a corner of the room that was not struck by the dazzling light, a table was set for two. It was a round table, covered with a white tablecloth and elegant china and crystal.

Bickel noticed that in this room, too, there were paintings. He knew little about paintings, but these looked familiar. There was one of a pond of waterlilies. Another was of a blue-black sky filled with yellowish-white stars, with the silhouette of a city in the background. Still another was of two Polynesian-looking bare-breasted women holding a tray of fruit. It amazed Bickel that he could not remember the names of the artworks.

"Sit down, Travis," Patterson said. "You must be hungry after that long trip."

"I am hungry, but I have to talk to you. At this point, I think it's more important that we talk than that we eat," Bickel said.

"Well," Patterson said with a smile, "there's no reason we can't do both. I'm not going to feed you so much that you can't talk."

"Fine," Bickel said. He thought of this courtly man watching a prisoner flayed to death at Treblinka. It took his appetite away.

As Bickel sat down, he noticed the heavy silver, with a crest he did not recognize. He sat facing the window and Patterson. "Elson," he said, staring straight at Patterson, "I know about Croesus. I know all about it."

Patterson looked at him and smiled slightly. "I know you do, Travis. I know all about Yichik Cohen."

Bickel was floored for a moment. Where was the leak? Was it Kathy Dorn? It wasn't important, Bickel thought.

"It doesn't matter that you know about Yichik Cohen," Bickel said. "Yichik Cohen hasn't done anything wrong. It's you who have more to answer for than you can possibly answer for. It makes me queasy that I'm even here with you now."

"Queasy, Travis?" Patterson asked mockingly. "What, in the real world of grown men, does that mean?"

"It means," Bickel said, "that you watched a man being tortured to death by the Nazis simply because he was a Jew and then you eagerly joined the Nazi cause. That makes me sick. I shouldn't have said queasy. I should have said 'sick.'"

"Before I answer that, Travis," Patterson said, "is cream of asparagus soup all right with you?"

This, Bickel thought, is a surrealistic vision come to life. "Yes," he said, "cream of asparagus is fine."

Patterson pressed a small buzzer next to his plate, and in a moment, a black woman in a maid's uniform appeared with a tray containing two bowls of soup. She placed one in front of Bickel and then served Patterson. The bowls had the same crest as the silver.

"We're going to have London broil," Patterson said. "It's a simple dish, yes, but I like it a lot. Shall we have a red wine?"

Stranger and stranger, Bickel thought. "A red wine will be fine," he said.

Patterson pressed the button again, and the maid

reappeared. "Hilda, you may bring out the wine now," Patterson said kindly.

After Hilda had brought out the wine, which Patterson served himself, Patterson looked at Bickel calmly and said, "Travis, I swear to you on everything that is significant to me, I never saw a man tortured to death at Treblinka. I never saw Treblinka. I never knew about Treblinka. I never knew what was going on at those camps." He paused and sipped the wine. Bickel could see only a small part of the label. It looked like Château Margot. "I should have known. I should have asked Himmler to tell me. Yes, I know that you know that I knew all those people. I know that. I don't deny it. But I did not know they were killing Jews in those camps. I absolutely did not know."

For some reason which Bickel could not define, he had the overpowering impression that Patterson was telling him the truth. Still, he knew that Patterson must be a smooth liar.

"Elson, if you know that I talked to Yichik Cohen, you must know that I heard from his own lips that he saw you there," Bickel said. He took a sip of his cream of asparagus soup. Delicious.

"Travis, I know everything that Yichik Cohen told you. I had a transcript before the day was over. Never mind how I got it. He is mistaken, that's all. I never was in Germany at that time. Yes, I traveled to Germany during the war. Yes, absolutely. But I was never in Treblinka. Never, no matter what Cohen says."

Bickel looked at Patterson and still believed that he was telling the truth. An amazing liar, to be sure, Bickel thought. "I hope you won't be offended if I point out that I have not heard you denying that part about Operation Croesus," Bickel said.

Patterson spooned up the last bit of his soup. "No," he said, "I won't deny it. It's true. That's all. It's true. But before you go charging off on a morality horse, I want you to hear about Operation Croesus. You must hear about it, really, because it concerns you vitally."

"I thought it did," Bickel said.

"Well, you were right," Patterson said. "By the way, are you ready for the salad?"

"Certainly," Bickel said. "The soup was excellent."

Patterson smiled a genuine smile. "Thank you, Travis. I believe that when important things are being discussed, it's vital to have good, solid food. Poor food can distract you. Or am I wrong?"

"No," Bickel said. "You're not wrong."

After Hilda served the salad, Patterson resumed his speech. "Now, Travis, I'd like for you to think about what I'm going to say on a very serious level. Also, I'm going to tell you about things that will surprise you. And I'm going to speak plainly. So, please try to bear all that in mind." He paused with a fork of lettuce. "Or would you like me to not tell the truth?"

"Of course I want to hear the truth," Bickel said. He wondered what was going on in Patterson's head. Perhaps he had overestimated Patterson.

"It's hard to figure out exactly where to begin," Patterson said. "I imagine it would have to be in the Depression." He waved his right hand in the air, as if waving away a fly. "Of course, you don't remember it. Not at all. But it was a mess. Terrible. Men had no dignity. Men left home because they were ashamed to be poor. I wasn't poor, of course, but lots of people were. I used to see it. It was terrible. A whole generation was being robbed of self-respect and dignity."

Bickel looked at him sharply. "It's going to take a lot of imagination to get from the breadlines to Treblinka," he said.

"I told you, I was never at Treblinka," Patterson said calmly. "So, to continue, I went mountainclimbing in Germany. I knew nothing about politics. Nothing. I did pretty well, climbing. The *Führer* asked to see me. He talked to me like no one else. It was astonishing. Have you ever talked to someone who simply amazed you? Anyone at all?"

"In a positive way?" Bickel asked.

"Of course," Patterson said.

"I don't think so," Bickel said.

"Well, neither had I," Patterson said, "until I talked

to the *Führer*. He had a vision. And he saw how to get from here"—Patterson made a mark on the tablecloth to the right of his salad plate—"to there." Patterson made another mark to the left of his salad plate. "No vague generalities. He had a plan. And the first step was to rekindle the pride of the German people." Patterson put down his fork and pointed at Bickel with his right index finger. "And it was working. The German people seemed to have all the self-respect that had vanished from the rest of the Western world. People seemed to be happy, to be going places, to be full of life."

"For Christ's sake, Elson," Bickel said, "what about all the people he killed? What about what he was doing to the Jews?"

Patterson swallowed a piece of tomato and then set down his fork again. "Get your facts straight, Senator. I'm talking about the early thirties. Hitler had not killed anyone. The laws about the Jews were just starting. There were plenty of Jews in Germany who didn't think Hitler was doing anything but rabblerousing. Have you looked into that period? I think you have and you know that I'm right."

Bickel said nothing. As a matter of fact, he had looked into the period, and Patterson had a point.

"I became interested in National Socialism, and the *Führer* became interested in me. He was extremely keen on physical fitness, as you might say, and he admired my mountainclimbing. And, let's face the facts, he was impressed by my being a Patterson."

Bickel felt a wave of revulsion and anger welling up in him. A man sat in front of him justifying his admiration for the most wicked man of all time. This was talk for a psychiatrist, not for Travis Bickel.

"I don't want to hear about how you fell in love with the *Führer* and he fell in love with you," Bickel said loudly, hitting his right fist against the table. "Nothing you could possibly say would make me like the *Führer* or think well of you for being his friend or serving him. There's something wrong with the soul of a man who admires a mass killer. That's all." Bickel flushed with anger.

Patterson looked at him wide-eyed, then looked calm and even smiled. "You're quite right," he said. "I can't persuade you to see the *Führer* as I saw him. I never can. I shouldn't have even tried. You're quite right." Patterson paused and looked down at his salad. "Are you ready for the London broil?" he asked.

"Yes," Bickel said. "But I want to hear more."

"Of course," Patterson said. He pressed the button. "I love this room," Patterson said. "Of course, I have many rooms, but I like this one about the best at this house. I can see out the windows and feel as if I'm in the outdoors, and still be warm inside. That may be lazy of me though. Is that lazy?"

"I don't know," Bickel said.

"It may be lazy. I don't know either," Patterson said.

Hilda appeared with a serving tray. She gave a heave of her shoulders and put the entire London broil on the table.

She looked at Bickel with a plaintive face and asked, "Do you like it rare or well done?"

"Rare, please," Bickel said. He had the feeling, as Hilda carved, that he was involved in something so monstrous that it took on a fantasy quality. A maid asked him how he liked his London broil while he was told about why a madman loved the *Führer*.

Hilda carved some well-done London broil for Patterson, served them both French-cut string beans and potatoes, and then withdrew. She left two bottles of wine on the table as well.

Before starting to eat, Patterson said, "Let me get to the part that concerns you. I think that's the only thing you're interested in."

"I think so," Bickel said.

"But maybe you're interested in some of the history of this house," Patterson said. "Are you?"

"Not now," Bickel said. "I want to know why you killed Simon Kart."

Patterson sighed. "It was a mistake, Travis. And, I'm really sorry for it. I really am. I don't know if you can accept my apologies, but I'm awfully sorry," Patterson said. "I'd like to make it up to the family somehow."

"How might you do that?" Bickel asked.

"Well, with money, of course," Patterson answered. "How else? I must make sure that you understand that I didn't ask anyone to kill him. It was a mistake, but it was done by people who work for me, in a sense, so I have to be responsible." A pause while he chewed a piece of London broil. "But, maybe I'm not responsible. What do you think?" Patterson asked.

"I think you are," Bickel said. He wondered if Kosters could have been wrong. How could this man, this lunatic, be in charge of the largest conspiracy of all time?

"What about Jeff Richards, and his son?" Bickel asked. "Was that a mistake, too?"

"The son part was a mistake," Patterson said. "We make all too many mistakes. I've reprimanded people about that. I really did. In fact, I had the men responsible terminated." He chewed another bite of London broil. "With extreme prejudice," he added with a smile.

"What about West Lake?" Bickel asked with a note of near hysteria in his voice. "Those were innocent people. Some of them were children."

"You know, Travis, I could answer you by simply saying that people get killed every day. Because they do get killed every day. And if those girls hadn't gotten killed that way, they might have died of cancer. I could answer that way, but I'm not going to."

Patterson seemed to be wrestling with a difficult problem. "I could answer it that way. It would be the easy way and I could do it that way, that's for sure." He looked earnestly at Bickel. "I could answer it that way," he said for the third time, "but it would be wrong."

Oh, Jesus, Bickel thought.

"The basic problem is that I have to be responsible for everything. That's the problem. Oh, it's fine if there's not that much to do. Roberts can do a few things, a few other people can do a few things. But when something really big comes along, like you, then I have to take charge of everything. You understand? It was fine when there wasn't much to do, but now that things are busy, I have to take care of everything. And frankly," he said in a petulant tone, "I just can't do everything."

Bickel stared at Patterson. It was incredible what a person who, by sheer chance, had a great deal of money and, also by sheer chance, happened to be a maniac could get done.

"How did the whole thing start?" Bickel asked.

Patterson snapped out of his self-pitying mood. "I can tell you exactly," he said. "It started the day that the French sued for peace. I can't remember it exactly, but it was in the summer of 1940. I was visiting the *Führer*, and he told me that world victory was inevitable, and that one of his biggest problems was going to be the administration of North America."

Patterson paused to lift the stem of his glass of wine and drink a little of it. "I think you'll have to agree that this is excellent wine," Patterson said. "But you don't agree." He stared at Bickel. "Why am I wrong?"

"You're wrong because I don't give a damn about the wine," Bickel said. "I want to hear about Croesus."

"Of course," Patterson said. "Although you should try the wine."

"All right," Bickel said. "I'll try it." He took a sip. It was excellent. He said nothing.

"The *Führer* told me that he hoped for a National Socialist United States without a fight. I won't bore you with all of his reasoning, but I do want to assure you that he never mentioned a word to me about killing American Jews. Not a word," Patterson said.

"I don't believe you," Bickel said.

"It doesn't matter," Patterson said. "I was there and you weren't." He looked serenely at Bickel. "Now, the *Führer* wanted me to lead the country to National Socialism. But I'm no politician. So, others were designated for that job. You can understand that. It takes a certain flair to be a politician, and I don't have it. The idea was that I would be a pro-consul for the *Führer* himself, above politics, carrying on a grand scheme."

Patterson looked over his shoulder, through the clear glass, toward the snow. A wind was picking up, and the sky was clouding over. Both Bickel and Patterson sensed that more snow was coming. Patterson looked back at Bickel. His face looked old.

"Of course, the *Führer* recognized by 1942 that his plan was going to be chancy, at best. He had risked everything on daring strokes. It worked for a while, but once the United States and Russia were against him, he knew he could not win except by a miracle," Patterson said. "He was far more realistic than many people thought."

"I don't want to hear about your love affair with Hitler," Bickel said. "I want to hear about what concerns me."

Patterson squinted at him. "Yes. Well, that part begins in 1944. It was my last visit with the *Führer*. I had to go from Spain across the middle of France, one step ahead of the Allies. Of course, I arrived in Berlin just after the *Führer* had been injured in a bomb explosion. Count Stauffenberg and those traitors. You know, it was July 20 . . ."

"I don't want to hear about how you told him how wonderful he was. Tell me about the part that has to do with me," Bickel said.

Patterson looked miffed. "Some day you will beg me to tell you these stories," Patterson said. "But, for now, we'll talk about something else."

"Not 'something else,' " Bickel said. "The part of Operation Croesus that touches me."

"Right," Patterson said. "The *Führer* told me on that visit that everything was finished. The only hope was to fight on so that a great legend of the German fighting man would be born. He said that the struggle of the Aryan people, of the West against the East, was far from over, though. And he entrusted that struggle to me, after he was gone. I was to work with other people, but I was to be the backbone of the effort."

"What was the goal of the effort?" Bickel asked. "A new Nazi Germany?"

Patterson laughed. "Oh, no Travis. Not at all. It was to raise Germany to the first rank of nations again. The *Führer* believed that if that happened, simply by natural processes, Germany would look out for the Aryans of the world. But Germany had to be raised from the vanquished.

Bickel had a terrible, sinking feeling.

"By that time, I had a fairly sizable network of people in the government and in key places in industry working with me. They did not know exactly what they were working for, but they knew that they liked getting a few thousand extra each month, so when I wanted a favor, they were ready to oblige. The first thing I worked for, after the war, was the Marshall Plan. It was perfect for everyone. It strengthened Europe against the Russians, and it laid the foundations for rebuilding German industry," Patterson said.

"Just tell me something," Bickel said. "Who were the other men you were to work with?"

Patterson waved his right hand in an airy motion. "Oh, one of them was a Nazi bigwig in Germany who is almost dead now in Paraguay. The other one is dead."

"Okay," Bickel said. "Please continue." He felt as if he were being taken on a tour.

"My biggest opportunity came when the OSS was made into the CIA. Many of my kind of people were brought on board. They were solid men, from good families, and I had no trouble convincing them that a strong Germany was in the best interests of America. By then, Croesus had gotten to include so many people that to become involved was to help one's career. Sometimes by quite a lot. It was like a brother-hood at the CIA," Patterson said with pride.

"Is this still going on?" Bickel asked.

"Of course," Patterson said. "Of course. Why not?"

"Why indeed?" Bickel asked, with quiet amazement.

"Like all bureaucracies, the organization grew," Patterson continued. "The CIA was then reading everyone's mail and listening to everyone's telephone, so I got the chance to learn about a lot of people. I was able to persuade some of them to join me. It didn't matter whether they were Republicans or Democrats or anything like that. All that mattered was that they wanted a strong Germany."

Bickel had long since finished eating. Now he listened in silence.

"By the end of the 1950's, the economic miracle was well underway," Patterson continued. "The natural drive of the German people, plus a few key decisions by American institutions, had made Germany into Europe's foremost economic power. And this was a divided Germany," he added. "Wait a minute," Bickel said. "Are you going to tell me that your Croesus organization was responsible for the German economic miracle?"

"Not at all," Patterson said smoothly. "By the way, would you like some dessert? A hot fudge sundae perhaps? That's what Frank would eat, if I'd let him."

"Not now," Bickel said. "What about the economic miracle?"

"Well," Patterson said. "Banks here in the U.S. have many places they can invest. If I can tell a man I went to school with that I would consider it a particular favor that he look kindly on a loan to a German concern, well, it helps. And if I can tell a Congressman that it would mean a lot to me personally if his committee lowered the tariff on a certain kind of dye made in West Germany, that helps, too. Bits and pieces," Patterson smiled, "but they add up."

"Go on," Bickel said. This was getting better and better.

"By the time Kennedy came into office, we were ready for a really major move. It was time to reunite the two Germanys," Patterson said.

"My God," Bickel exclaimed. "Are you kidding? The Russians would go berserk."

"Exactly the problem, Travis," Patterson said with a long sigh. "Are you sure you wouldn't like some strudel, perhaps?"

"Yes, I'm sure," Bickel said. "What did you do about your plan?"

"Well, through friends. I approached Kennedy with the idea. He seemed like the natural choice after he said he was a Berliner." Patterson paused. "Or is that wrong?"

"Look, I'm not Roberts; I'm not going to play those games with you," Bickel said.

Without missing a beat, Patterson said, "Then you think I'm not wrong?"

"All right," Bickel said. "You're not wrong."

"But," Patterson said. "I don't want you to say I'm right if you think I'm wrong. Am I right or wrong?" He looked earnestly at Bickel, and started to stroke the tablecloth with his knife.

"No," Bickel said. "You are not wrong."

"Fine," Patterson said with a grin, and he sat back in his chair. He held on to the knife though. "Well, if you can believe this, Kennedy thought the idea was crazy. I said we should tell the Russians that it was war unless they allowed free elections in all of Germany. He thought that was ridiculous."

Bickel had a terrible premonition.

"Not only that," Patterson said bitterly, "but he wanted to know more about my organization. He started his goddamn brother investigating everything I was doing."

"Oh, my God," Bickel said, clapping his right hand to his forehead.

"What are you doing?" Patterson asked. "You think I had Kennedy killed?" He laughed. "Not a chance. Not one chance. But I will say this. We did pick up some rumblings that the Cubans were awfully mad at him and were planning something bad for him." He leaned forward and looked at Bickel closely. "Now, if Jack Kennedy had been willing to be a better friend to me, I would have been a better friend to him, and told him about those plans." He spread his palms apart and tilted them upward in a "so what?" gesture.

"Oh, for Christ's sake, Elson. You might as well have killed him," Bickel said with disgust.

"Not at all," Patterson said. "Not at all. Just think for a minute. At that time, we had no independent intelligence capacity. Everything we got we stole from the CIA. So they had the information first. They could have warned Kennedy."

Bickel looked up at the ceiling. It was white, with

brown oak beams forming hexagons on the ceiling. Bickel wondered how many cameras and microphones must be up there. "Don't you realize," Bickel asked, "that maybe the reason people at the CIA didn't pass on anything was that they knew you had an out with Kennedy and they were trying to anticipate your wishes?"

"A possibility," Patterson said. "That's all. Just a possibility. No more than that." He started stroking the tablecloth with his knife again.

Kosters had not adequately prepared Bickel for an organization of this magnitude. Perhaps Patterson was exaggerating. Even rich people occasionally exaggerated, just like everyone else. That was a more appealing explanation of what Bickel was hearing than that it was the truth.

Patterson cocked his head to the right side and asked, "Would you like some fruit? I grow it all myself, y'know. Frank doesn't like it, of course. Not sweet enough. But I think it's pretty good. Oranges? Pears? I gave you some pears before. How were they? All right?"

"They were fine," Bickel said.

"Of course, you could have something else altogether," Patterson said. "A piece of cheesecake? We have everything here."

"Nothing, right now," Bickel said. "Please go on with your story."

"Of course," Patterson said. "Well, we couldn't do a thing with Johnson. I mean, he wouldn't even listen to us. I couldn't blame him, like I blamed Kennedy, because he was involved in that Vietnam thing. Of course, we tried to show him what we could do to him, with Walter Jenkins," Patterson continued lackadaisically.

"What the hell did you have to do with Walter Jenkins?" Bickel asked in a state of amazement.

"Well, someone had to supply the other fellow in the toilet booth and tell the police when Jenkins would be there," Patterson said, as if it were the most obvious thing in the world. "As a matter of fact, that was Frank's first big project. He did pretty well, I must say." Patterson smiled and looked over to Bickel for approbation. None was forthcoming, so Patterson continued. "And then, we wanted to show him what we could do for him, so we sent a lot of advertising to his station in Austin. He liked that," Patterson said with a chuckle.

"So?" Bickel asked. He noticed that Patterson's knife was starting to cut a hole in the tablecloth. It was a small incision, but it was there nevertheless.

"Well, I talked to LBJ once. Just once. He told me that what I suggested was absolutely out of the question. No showdown with the Russians about Berlin or free elections in Germany. He said that if he weren't tied down in Vietnam, he would consider it, but as it was, there was no way," Patterson said. "Now, we're not maniacs," he laughed to himself, "although some may think we are, and we don't ask the impossible. So when LBJ said that, we believed him. We could have gotten rid of him. It would have been child's play. But, there was no point. We recognize reality." Patterson looked over at Bickel. "Are you following this?" he asked pleasantly.

"Every word," Bickel said. And it was true. By following every word, by following every nuance of Patterson's conversation, it was possible to lose the thread of a man following the wishes of Adolf Hitler almost forty years after his death. More, it was possible to think of each operation separately and not of the total craziness of Croesus.

"Well, we had been in touch with Nixon for a long time. He was our great hope. Anti-Communist, tough as hell, always ready to make a deal. Our great hope. We stayed in touch with him all through the sixties. He was a frequent guest here. A fascinating man. Really, a piece of work," Patterson said, looking nostalgically out into some space above and to the right of Bickel's head.

Bickel was so absorbed in what Patterson was saying that he had not noticed that snow had started to fall. Large, heavy flakes fell in profusion onto the lake and the lawn behind the window. As far as Bickel could tell, several inches had already accumulated. What would the roads be like? Best not think of that, Bickel knew.

Think only of the story you hear and of the beautiful tableau behind Patterson's head, a tableau of peace and serenity, of resting and ceasing to struggle and to deceive.

"When Dick got into office, we thought things were pretty much set to roll. Now, understand, we didn't make any deal with Dick. He wasn't that kind of man. Nothing explicit. But he knew that we would do what we could for him if he put it to the Russians." Patterson laid down the knife.

"But, we were disappointed again. He made that arrangement with the Chinese, and we thought that he was about to try a squeeze on the Russians from both sides." Patterson shook his head and picked up the knife and started carving on the tablecloth again, in a new place. "I went to Dick and asked him when he was going to put the heat on the Russians. You know what he said?" Patterson looked at Bickel as if he really and truly expected an answer. "You know what he said?" Patterson shook his head. "Now, this is really amazing. He said that I had better leave the country. That he was going to use his own White House aides to fold up my organization. Haldeman was there with him. He was going to fold it up." Again, Patterson shook his head in wonderment.

"Now, I have to make it clear that I never knew whether that was a bargaining ploy so that Dick could take over Croesus himself, or just what it was. Dick was a clever fellow, right?"

"I didn't know him," Bickel said. "Never met him. Never laid eyes on him, except on television," he added drily.

"Really?" Patterson said. "He's a character. A real character. People may think I'm eccentric, but Jesus, you should talk to Dick Nixon."

"So I've heard," Bickel said.

"Well, we couldn't have Dick doublecrossing us that way. So it wasn't that hard for some people we knew at the CIA who never liked him anyway, and some people we knew in the media, whom we never have had any trouble with, to get together on Dick Nixon. He never knew what hit him." Patterson resumed serious slicing of the tablecloth. "Oh, I think he does now; but what can he do?" Patterson asked. He looked over his shoulder briefly and then added, "Now, I think you should have some coffee. It's from my own place in Brazil. I think you'll like it." He pressed the button.

As Hilda came in, Bickel noticed that the skin around Patterson's eyes was starting to droop. His jaw was hanging down slightly. His speech, while just as rapid, had a tinge of slur.

Obviously, Bickel thought as he contemplated his coffee, Patterson is tired. Telling this story takes something out of him. He's no longer a tireless mountain climber. And even if he's crazy, crazy people get tired too.

The cup in which the coffee was served was the thinnest cup Bickel had ever seen. Beyond translucent, the cup and saucer were almost transparent. They were slightly yellow, as was the other china. Around the border of each piece was a laurel crescent, which separated and then joined together at a crest consisting of a mailed fist clutching a lightning rod, above which was a chalice with the initial "P" and the legend "*Non Olet*."

As Patterson had predicted, the coffee was excellent. It was not just good. It was superb, the best coffee he had ever tasted.

Patterson sipped his coffee, then put it down. With great seriousness, he said, "Now, Travis, just because we're having coffee now, that doesn't mean that you can't have dessert, too. I don't stand on ceremony on things of that kind."

"No, thanks, Elson," Bickel said. "Maybe later."

"Well, suit yourself," Patterson said with a smile. "Now, our story comes to you, Travis. And, I'm sure that's the part you've been waiting for."

"Frankly, it's all been interesting," Bickel said.

"Of course it is," Patterson said. "But, I think you'll like this part the best."

He smiled like a salesman about to tell a customer that the price is lower than the prospect had anticipated. "After our bad experience with Nixon, we decided that we couldn't try to persuade a President already in office that he should be attached to Croesus. It just didn't work. We had to get someone up and coming, someone who understood and had a vision, and make him one of us."

"That, I suppose, is what you think I am," Bickel said.

"Well," Patterson said with a still larger smile, "we certainly hope so. Is that wrong of us? To hope for someone young and brave, someone with vision, to pick up the reins of Croesus, to follow through on my dreams and ambitions? You know," he said with a fatherly tone, "I won't be around forever. Someone's got to take over." He said it as if he were talking about a small-town grocery store. "Travis," he said, laying down his knife, "I'd like for that someone to be you."

Bickel looked at Patterson calmly. "You mean to take over killing millions of innocent people, including my wife?"

"Travis," Patterson said, "people get killed every day. If a few people have to get killed to bring about the salvation of the Aryan race, that is a small price to pay. And really, Travis, we don't want to kill the Jews. I think you know that about your wife."

Bickel wondered how the hell Patterson knew that.

"If you didn't kill my wife, who did?" Bickel asked, lowering his head.

"The KGB did it, to make you think I had done it," Patterson said.

"What about Kart?"

"That was a mistake by some local ex-Nazis who thought you were prying into Croesus. They were trying to kill you, as a matter of fact, not Kart." He actually giggled. "But that wasn't me. They didn't even consult me. When I heard about it, I ordered the men responsible to be severely reprimanded."

"What about Richards and his son?"

"That was me, I must tell you. It just so happened that a million-to-one shot came through. Richards was so goddamn smart that he put the right things into ONA so that he got a complete breakout on Croesus. There were enough bits and pieces lying around so that he could put together the dinosaur from one bone, if you know what I mean. It was just no good. My people at the CIA told me what was happening, and I told them that Richards had to be terminated." He sighed. "Of course, I hated like hell that the kid got it. I told you before that I had those men wiped away."

Bickel's head was whirling. He was sitting talking calmly about cold-blooded murder with a cold-blooded murderer. And he found that he could take it—with ease.

"What about those people in Los Angeles? What about shooting up Kathy Dorn's hotel room?" Bickel asked.

"Let's take these things as they happened," Patterson said. "Now, about the room at the Watergate. Yes, that was us. Definitely. We did it for a good reason. To test you," Patterson said earnestly.

"You shot someone to test me?" Bickel shouted.

"We didn't shoot anyone," Patterson said in a loud voice. "If we had been trying to kill you or her, do you think you'd be alive?"

"How the hell were you trying to test me?" Bickel asked in a quiet fury.

"Just by seeing how you reacted under fire, that's all. I think it makes sense. After all, we're not trying you out for office boy," Patterson said with a touch of sarcasm.

"And you killed all those people at West Lake for the same reason?" Bickel asked. "To test me, you killed innocent children?"

"Travis," Patterson shouted, the veins standing out on his forehead, "innocent people get killed every day. Few of them are lucky enough to die for something worthwhile. These people were. We wanted to see again how you reacted in a panic situation. You did very well indeed. Think of it like a fraternity initiation." He stopped shouting and started to move his knife back and forth on the tablecloth again. Bickel noticed that he had made another incision in the tablecloth.

In a quiet, firm voice, Bickel said, "You are crazy. Your whole idea is crazy. You belong in a hospital for the criminally insane, and I'm going to do my best to put you there. I'm leaving," Bickel said, and pushed back his chair to get up.

"Just one minute, please," Patterson said angrily. He pushed back his chair and got up, still holding his knife. "You think you can just come in here, learn all about Croesus, be flattered and offered everything under the sun, then call me crazy and walk out of here?" Something in his voice held Bickel captive.

He watched as Patterson walked toward him, still clutching the knife. "You see those paintings behind you, Senator? Those aren't reproductions. Those are originals. Never mind where I got them. They're originals." He pointed at the canvas of the waterlilies. "That's an original Monet." He pointed at the two bare-breasted women. "A Gauguin." He pointed at the blue sky with the bright stars. "That's Van Gogh's *Starry Night*."

Bickel turned to look at the pictures. Patterson now stood next to *Starry Night*.

"Look at it, Senator. It's beautiful. It's priceless. It took me a long time and a lot of trouble to get it. Tell me, isn't it beautiful?"

"Yes, it is," Bickel said. It must have been stolen, Bickel thought. But it was magnificent.

"But, it's like you. It's not irreplaceable," Patterson said, and took his knife and plunged it into the panting over and over again, slashing it back and forth.

Bickel could hardly believe his eyes. Patterson dropped the knife on the floor and walked back to his seat. Bickel no longer felt like leaving.

"We can put you in the White House, Travis," Patterson said in a calm voice. "The election funding laws can be circumvented. I can make it happen. I have a lot of friends. I like you. Even the way you called me crazy impressed me. You've got balls, Travis, and that's what counts."

Bickel stared at Patterson. He was an amazing man.

Behind him, the outside was so white that it framed Patterson in a blinding white mantle.

"We don't ask for you to kill the Jews or to kill anyone. Not at all. Nothing like that. We just want you to go to the mat to get Germany reunited. It can be done now. The Rearmament Treaty is a big first step. If you are President, you can get it done."

"I don't know," Bickel said. "How do I know you won't blackmail me once I'm President?"

"How do I know that you won't use my own organization against me?" Patterson asked with a good-natured smile. "Because you're going to inherit the organization, if you'll join. All the networks, all the foundations, everything. It's all yours. I never married. I have no heirs. You'll be my heir. Of course, Roberts will get something—he's Jewish, you know; that should tell you something—but you'll get almost all of it."

"Do I get it before or after the free elections?" Bickel asked.

"As soon as I know that you've made a good-faith effort to get Germany reunited," Patterson said, with a smile, "I'll start transferring parts of the organization to your control. Naturally, you won't get the money until you leave office. It wouldn't be seemly."

"But, what would I need the organization for, once I've made the pitch to the Russians about Germany?" Bickel asked.

"Well, that's a good question," Patterson said. Behind him, the snow was falling harder. Patterson was almost whited out by the brightness of the snow. "I think you know the answer, though, don't you?"

"No, I don't," Bickel said. "Why would I ask you, if I knew?"

"There are two reasons you want that organization, Travis, although I'm sure you know them. First, it gives you a control over the intelligence bureaucracy that no President has ever had. That's almost always the weak spot in a foreign-policy apparatus. I know it was with the *Führer*. He could never trust the *Abwehr*. That bastard Canaris was conspiring against him from the first to the last."

"I want to know about me, not about Canaris," Bickel said. He was getting restless.

"The second reason is that reuniting Germany is the biggest step, but it's not the final step," Patterson said.

Bickel felt nervous. Was Patterson about to say that the next step was the racial purification of America?

Patterson apparently could read the look on Bickel's face because he said, with a smile, "Don't worry, Travis. I told you that I didn't want to kill the Jews, and I don't. By the way, are you part Jewish? You seem so nervous about it. You might be Jewish. You see, I haven't even had that part of your background looked into," he lied.

"I'm not Jewish, Elson," he said firmly. "You don't have to be Jewish to feel enraged that Hitler killed all those innocent Jews."

"Of course, I can see that. Of course. People get killed every day, but somehow, when it's Jews, the media raises hell. A million people can starve to death in Bangladesh, and no one gives a damn. But if a Jew gets hurt, everyone is whining about it," Patterson said petulantly.

"Goddammit, Elson, I don't like that kind of talk," Bickel said. "You're not going to make an anti-Semite out of me, no matter what else you may do."

"All right, Travis. You've made your point," Patterson said. "The other reason that you'll need Croesus working for you is that a reunited Europe is your fundamental goal, after German reunification. I think that's essential. A greater Europe, at least a greater Central and Western Europe, is absolutely essential to the future of the world. Now, that's not something that anyone's going to go to war over, but it takes steady persuasive work, and I think you're the man to do it."

"That doesn't seem unreasonable," Bickel had to admit. "Or am I wrong?"

Patterson apparently did not get the joke. "No," he said, "you're not wrong."

"If I agree even to think about this," Bickel said cautiously, "that has to be the end of the killings. I mean, the end. You understand?"

"Yes, I understand what you're saying," Patterson said. "I can't guarantee that, but at least they won't have anything to do with you. We have other interests, and we have to look after them, too." He made the sound of a weary sigh. "I think that's exactly the reason we have to get new blood into the top of the organization. Now, I have to figure out everything myself. I don't mind, of course, someone has to do it. But I need someone to help and eventually take over. I can't always do it all myself."

The snow was letting up. Patterson's face appeared in a sharper focus. He looked tired. He probably wasn't lying about wanting someone to help him out.

"Elson, I wonder, if you're doing things that give the Communists heart palpitations, just why they've let you live as long as they have. The KGB could get to you," Bickel said. He was starting to feel tired, too.

"It's fairly simple," Patterson said. "I could be killed, yes, certainly. But, Croesus would just kill every Soviet diplomat in ten countries. They know that. I think that deters them. Or is that wrong? You think I'm wrong, don't you? Why am I wrong?"

"I don't think you're wrong," Bickel said.

"Well, what do you think?" Patterson asked cheerily.

"It's worth careful thought," Bickel said. "But the killing has to stop. It absolutely has to."

"I told you it would," Patterson said.

"Then I'll think about it as a serious proposal, and I think I'll come out with you. But, I'm not sure," Bickel said. "It's an incredible concept."

Bickel got up and walked to the window and looked out. Patterson did, too. He put his thin, bony arm around Bickel's shoulder.

"Travis," he said affectionately. "What we're talking about here is power, raw power. Think about all the times people have been cruel to you. Think about all the times people have belittled you and blocked and obstructed you. Just think about that. Think about how often you've said to yourself that you'd do something differently if you were in charge." He paused and patted Bickel on the back. "Well, Travis, I'm going to put you in charge. You're going to be the one calling the shots."

"It's worth thinking about," Bickel said.

"It's power, Travis. Raw power. Power for you," Patterson said.

Outside, the snow had stopped falling altogether. Bickel could see things more clearly than he could all afternoon. The lake was covered with ice. It looked thick enough to walk across. All around the lake, everything was white, as far as he could see. Only the sky was a bright blue.

The dead were dead. There was nothing Bickel could do about them. Nothing. His obligations were to the living, and to himself. Patterson might or might not have been at Treblinka. Bickel was not sure. Even Kosters thought the KGB had killed Lydia. Everything could be rationalized, and everything could be replaced. And, again, there was that bright blue sky.

CHAPTER

25

Two days after Senator Travis A. Bickel returned from Innisfree, one day after Bickel spent the morning with the Secretary of State, the following things happened:

A well-dressed woman wearing a ranch mink coat stepped off a Douglas Turbojet executive airplane into the evening air of the South Lake Tahoe airport. A short, bearded man wearing a peajacket and a pair of heavy boots shook her thin, delicate hand inside the terminal and asked her about her flight.

"It was too long," she said, taking off her mink hat and running her hand through her dark auburn hair. "I wish there were direct flights from Washington. I'm sick of going through that damned airport in L.A."

"Will you be staying overnight?" the man asked.

"No," the woman said. "Definitely not. The pilot is going to go over to Stateline, have dinner, and then be waiting for me back here. We're cleared to take off again at nine PM."

"We've been getting some good stuff from Emerald

277

Bay," the man with the beard said, as they hopped into a 1979 Ford Torino. Snow lay more than a foot deep along most of the route from the airport to the boat slip.

"What kinds of things?" the auburn-haired woman asked.

"Oh, stories that Patterson isn't interested in Bickel anymore, that Bickel's a free agent at this point. The usual crap," the man said, keeping his eyes on the road in the dusk.

"Oh, for Christ's sake," the woman said. "Is Patterson really that stupid?"

"Apparently," the short man said.

"I can't believe he is," the woman said. "Still, there's never any point in making people smarter than they are. He's old, and he could just think we're buying it."

"It could be," the man said.

Across the lake, one half hour later, a man stood in a freezing wind on the end of a pier. He wore a ski cap, which, even with his heavy parka, skiing pants, and boots, was not enough to keep out the cold. Tahoe had been unusually cold this February, and there were small chunks of ice in front of his pier at Emerald Bay. The man with the ski cap hoped that if the boat hit one of the pieces of ice, the fiberglass hull would be strong enough to withstand the blow.

Actually, the man in the ski cap would just as soon have the boat sink like a stone along with the people in it. But then he wouldn't have anything to report to the people who were going to make his retirement years so much more pleasant.

In a minute, the man could hear the sound of a powerful inboard engine. The Lakecruiser was still around the wall of rock that formed one side of the cove, so that the man in the ski cap could not see it. But he turned on the pier lights anyway. Who else could it be?

Another minute, and the man in the ski cap could see the running lights of the boat. He felt a surge of apprehension. Surely they must know what he had been doing. Maybe not, though. He had to get out of the habit of thinking that because someone was his superior, he or she knew everything. It just wasn't true. His transmissions were routine and there was no necessary way that Mosa'ad would know about them. Still, if they did know, there was nothing they would not do.

The boat's engine was throttled, and it pulled alongside the dock. As always, the short, strong man with a beard threw a line to the man with the ski cap. When the boat was secured, the man in the ski cap helped the woman in the mink coat up the step to the dock.

"Welcome," he said, "or should I say 'shalom'?"

"I don't give a damn what you say," she said crisply. "Let's get inside. It's too cold out here."

Inside the cabin, heated almost to seventy-five degrees, the woman clapped her hands together to get warm.

"Picking up anything interesting these days in the Lake?" the woman asked, looking at him sideways.

"Not much. It's too cold to sit outside and fish these days," the man said.

"Well, I have an important transmission for you," the woman said. "I think this had better be sent in the ultra code. Do you need refreshing, or can I just give it to you to encipher it?" She looked at him quizzically and struck her arms against her sides to get circulation going.

"I think I know it," the man said. "What's the message?" He tried to look nonchalant and gazed at the pictures of wild mountain flowers that dotted the otherwise plain walls of the cabin.

"He's going to run, and he says he has major support," the woman said. "I think he means very major support. I think he means the most major kind of support he could have. I want you to send it like that."

"Any doubt about it?" the man asked. "This is a serious message."

"Of course, it's serious," the woman said. "I'm not telling you about it as a joke. He's been converted. Something's happened to him. You can send that, too."

The man in the ski cap did not know exactly what all of this meant. "We're definitely talking about Bickel," he said, in a tentative tone, "you're sure about that?"

"Of course, I'm sure," the woman said. "Jesus Christ,

do you think I'd come way the hell out here if I weren't sure?"

The man in the ski cap did not know for sure, but he thought that the people who paid him his monthly bonuses would be happy to hear it.

On the way back, the short man with the beard asked the woman with the mink coat a question. "Why are we letting that bastard think about living it up with Patterson's money? Why don't we just get rid of him?"

"It's not up to us, remember?" the woman said. "They'll get rid of him when the time is right. They don't like wasted motion."

As the Lakecruiser cut through the frigid lake, the woman with the dark auburn hair looked at the lights of the casinos. She herself had hardly understood the significance of the message she had delivered tonight. But it meant a lot, that much she knew. Her boss was running for president, and that meant something big, because her other boss had told her that it was the most important message of her life.

Of course Alex had suspected for years that Bickel would run for president. She had put the idea in his head at least three years before. That was part of her work, too. Everything was part of her work. Someday she would quit and just grow roses. And she might play a lot of bridge, too. She would have to do many fairly routine things for many days to get her system back to normal.

Her life was so confused. First coming from Oklahoma to Washington. Then working for Bickel. Then Mosa'ad, and then, with Mosa'ad's blessings, for the man with the money. It would take a long time for her to see only surfaces again.

But she would. She could concentrate and succeed.

She looked out at the lights of the casinos again. They were reflected off the lake. The scene made her think of all the girls as Vassar dreaming of the Great Gatsby gazing at the lights on Daisy's dock. But Alex had seen the lights up close. They were not good for much, except as toys. There was not much illumination in a light on a dock. Maybe there was for college girls, but not for Alex. Not anymore.

The telephone rang in the second-floor bedroom of the house at No. 19 Baradero, next to the bed where the wizened man lay with tubes coming out into various bottles and machines. Outside the house, on the embarcadero, couples strolled in one of the balmy February evenings that were the best of Asunción's climate. None of the strollers could hear the telephone, though, because the windows of the room where the telephone rang were two inches thick, and no noise passed through them.

Next to the door, the two blond men who held automatic rifles looked at the young man next to the telephone, who let it ring. He looked unusually serious. In his lap he held a copy of the international edition of the *Herald Tribune*, in which he was reading a story about the likely passage, the next day, of the German Rearmament Treaty, which had already passed in the Bundestag by a wide bipartisan margin.

Finally, the man put down the newspaper and picked up the telephone. "Hello," he said. As he listened to the voice speaking rapidly on the other end of the telephone, he watched a line on a screen which monitored the old man's bodily functions. The line, which had been rather wavy only a few days before, was close to being flat. The man listening on the telephone thought that the machine was an electroencephalograph. Something like that. Some kind of Jew machine for interfering with normal bodily processes.

"Can this be?" the young man said in surprise at something that was said on the other end of the line. There was more rapid talk in the receiver. "Of the *greatest* significance, I would say," the young man said. "Well worth waking up Herr Bauer for. Please hold the line."

The young man held the receiver in his hand as he noticed that the old man, who had gradually curled into a fetal position, was no longer making any motion whatsoever. The line on the machine was flat. A nurse looked rapidly from the old man to the machine, and then back to the old man. Another nurse, who looked like she might have been part Indian, looked at the dead old man and crossed herself.

Tears came into the young man's eyes as he held the telephone to his chest. With great effort, he fought back sobs. After a minute or two, when he had calmed himself, he said into the telephone, "Herr Bauer sends you his most sincere congratulations and sends also a most hearty 'Heil Hitler.'"

The young man put the telephone receiver into its cradle. He looked from the old man, from whom the nurses were already starting to remove the tubes, to the portrait of the Führer, looking defiant and proud. Of all times, the young man said to himself. Now, when the Reichsleiter is dead, the dream is about to live again.

How the old man would have loved to see the day! Still, he, the old man's son and heir, would be there. He would, in fact, go to Washington, D.C., on the date. It was a great prospect.

But the prospect of future glory could not overcome the sadness Martin Bormann's son felt at his father's death. He began to sob, as he watched the nurses put away their medical paraphernalia, their Jew medical paraphernalia that just tricks people and doesn't keep them alive any longer. The scar on his cheek began to throb.

The Cosmos Club occupies a mansion at the corner of Massachusetts Avenue and Florida Avenue. Northwest Washington, D.C. It is not a mini-mansion or a mansionette or some other variant of a mansion. It is an authentic mansion, with a massive stone face, a long curving driveway, imposing wrought iron fences, a look of impregnability, and huge, languid rooms. It was built in the early part of this century and served for a time as a residence for Sumner Welles, scion of a wealthy manufacturing family, who was a division chief in the State Department in Woodrow Wilson's administration.

Shortly after World War II, it became a club for Washingtonians and visitors with some pretense to intel-

lectual distinction. Its membership was different from
that of other clubs in Washington because the members
were chosen not for wealth, as at the Metropolitan
Club, nor for social position, as at the Chevy Chase
Club or the Sulgrave Club, but for some kind of accomplishment that requires thought.

Journalists, social scientists, natural scientists, and
even a few lawyers sat in the huge sitting rooms, reading the newspapers of the world by dim light and reflecting on problems that might not have been accessi-
ble under bright light. Occasionally they looked up as
someone passed by, to or from the large and sunny
dining room, which had once been the greenhouse of
Sumner Welles.

Since the membership was generally advanced in
years and had seen a great many of life's heroes and
villains, their heads did not stay up for long while people passed by, unless something unusual or someone especially noteworthy passed by.

On the second day after Travis Bickel returned from
Innisfree, someone noteworthy passed by. Leonard
Lawrence Crest, syndicated columnist in over three
hundred newspapers, and far and away the most well-
known member of the Cosmos Club, walked into the
entry of the club and picked up the London *Times* from
the newspaper table. He lowered his white-maned head
and took off his glasses to see how the staid British
newspaper was responding to the impending German
Rearmament Treaty. Even amid a company of distinguished elderly men, Crest stood out. He was tall and
thin, and despite his sixty-seven years, his posture was
absolutely straight, a relic of his days as a major in the
Second World War, one of the most rapidly rising stars
in the American imtelligence apparatus. He dressed
more like a banker than a writer, typically in a dark
blue suit with a white shirt and a maroon tie with repli-
cations of his dog, a champion Weimaraner.

It was no surprise that people looked up when he
passed by. When a President or a secretary of state or a
particularly powerful senator wanted to explain something to the press so that his position would be dis-

cussed at the highest levels of journalism, it was Crest whom they called.

It was said in Washington that LBJ knew that the establishment would no longer support the Vietnam war when, in 1967, Crest ran a column questioning the continued U.S. involvement there. Richard Nixon simply refused to allow his family to read Crest's columns after the "Saturday night massacre." A nightly TV news show in 1974 had featured a clipped copy of the L.A. *Times* op-ed page, with Crest's column cut out. Supposedly, that was the way the page had circulated at the White House.

Today, Crest idly glanced at the inside pages of the London *Times* as he waited for his guest. He especially liked the advertisements for British products. Both the products and the advertisements had a rich quality that life in America sorely lacked.

As Crest looked up from an advertisement for the 1983 Bentley Saloon, he saw his guest stride through the door. Travis Bickel did not look as tired as a man should who had been shot at and had been working tirelessly for the passage of the German Rearmament Treaty. That, Crest thought, was a good sign. A politician on the way up should have enormous reserves of energy. He should be able to look healthy and alert after a day's campaigning or a day's heroics or a day's logrolling. That was damned important. And that was the way Bickel looked. His blue-gray eyes scanned the room and immediately recognized Crest.

"I'm happy to see you here, Mr. Crest," Bickel said. "How are you, sir?"

"It's Larry, Senator," Crest said with a fatherly smile. "It was kind of you to meet me here in the midst of all of your work. And every writer in Washington must want to talk to you. You're bigger than Elvis Presley when he died. They're going to have to make you President and give you an Oscar."

They headed in through several hallways and anterooms into the dining room. The headwaitress always reserved the best table, the one against the windows facing out over the garden, for Mr. Crest, and he was shown there immediately. Heads all over the room looked up to see the extremely obvious match of the superstar young senator and the king-making columnist. A few people called out greetings to Crest, which he answered in a friendly, although offhand, fashion. They stared respectfully at Bickel, "a living legend of courage and patriotism," as Walter Cronkite called him.

The tables were quite ordinary wooden affairs with white tablecloths, much like those the members had known at Dartmouth or Princeton, or wherever they had studied. On each table was a thin glass vase with a single flower in it. The Cosmos was definitely not a club for rowdies.

"Travis, if I may call you that," Crest said, "you are a man near the top, and that is for sure." His voice still held a trace of the accent acquired in his childhood in Savannah.

"Thank you, Larry," Bickel said. "If I am on the move, it's only because I have so many things I want to get done."

"Of course," Crest said. "Of course. That's what makes you a fine public servant."

A waitress walked up and handed the two men menus. "I think you'll find that the snapper or the whitefish is a damn fine dish, Travis." He looked up at the waitress. "Shirley, you just tell Leroy out there in the kitchen that I want what I always get."

"Sure thing, Mr. Crest," the waitress said.

"I'll have the whitefish if you recommend it," Bickel said.

"Son," Crest said, "I know you'll like it. My stomach hasn't been too good for a long time now, so my usual is an omelet. That's a poor thing for a man to have for lunch, but that's what it is."

Bickel smiled without saying anything.

"Travis," Crest said in a greatly lowered voice, "I know that we're going to hear big things from you. Very big things. I just know that. And son," he said, "when you decide you want people to know about them, I'm your man."

"Well, to tell you the truth, Larry," Bickel said, leaning forward earnestly, "I think that public service is as high a calling as any man could aspire to. I really do believe that." He was starting to fall into country locutions himself. "I'm confident that this treaty will pass, and that the President will sign it."

Crest chortled. "You're goddamn right, boy. There's no way on earth that treaty isn't going to pass. You and Arthur just about have those votes locked up in Fort Knox."

Bickel tried to look humble. "Well, we've worked hard on it, and that's the whole ball game, I guess."

"Now, I want you to tell me, Travis," Crest said in a conspiratorial tone, "when you go over to that White House to brief the President on things, can't you just see yourself there a little bit? I mean as a domiciliary," he added, pronouncing each syllable. The waitress brought each of them a glass of water and a napkin.

"Well, as I was saying, Larry, I'm pretty sure the treaty will pass, and I believe that's just the beginning of a whole new era of movement and change in our foreign policy. I'm just like any other citizen," he said, looking down at the table. "I want to do my part."

"Sure you do, Travis," Crest said with a grin, still in a low voice, "but what's that part going to be? You're sure as hell not going to be a stagehand." He took out a pen and started sketching on the paper napkin.

"I'll tell you the truth," Bickel said. "I'm very proud to be in the United States Senate. I'm not looking for any call to the White House."

"I know all that crap," Crest said, still smiling. "And you know you're the next President. You have it locked up." He did not look at Bickel, but instead at the napkin on which he was absent-mindedly drawing.

Bickel's face changed to a frown. "I think that for any man to think of political advancement while so many deaths have occurred around him so recently would be almost macabre."

"Look, Travis," Crest said. "Let's cut out all this shit. I know you're running, and I want to know what you want to do as President." He took a roll from a wicker basket covered with a red napkin and broke it in half. He started to chew on the roll without buttering it. No doubt that also was part of his "usual," Bickel thought, just as browbeating presidential hopefuls was part of his "usual." Crest still looked down at his napkin.

Bickel smiled. "Of course if you're asking what I think needs to be done by whoever is the next President, I have ideas about that," he said. It was amazing how easy it was to play games, even with a powerhouse like Crest, when you had something he wanted. "And, I'd like to share them with you, Larry. Not to get exposure, but to get your ideas, too. You've been around, and you know what's going to work and what can't work, and I'd like to have help in telling the difference."

Bickel laughed to himself again. He knew that he sounded like a parody of a politician, but he also knew that that was the way politicians sounded. And Crest did not mind. He looked up from his doodling on the napkin long enough to say, "Go ahead, Travis. Shoot."

"Well, Larry," Bickel said. "I think that the big movement in this country has to be in foreign affairs in the next decade. We've seen that the problems of the cities are pretty much intractable and that the economy largely takes care of itself, without too much government interference."

"Uh-huh," Crest nodded.

"But the American people are discouraged about the future of democracy. They see it shrinking all over the world. And you know," he added, jabbing his index finger on the table for emphasis, "it's a trend that can't continue forever. We both know that." Bickel looked over and saw an old clubman breaking into an omelet with the delicacy that a safecracker might use at Van Cleef & Arpels.

"What can we do about it?" Crest asked. "Are you talking about rollback?"

"You know," Bickel said, "that's an obsolete term for it. But I am talking about getting to the largest group of pro-American people outside America, the Eastern Europeans, and letting them know that we're concerned."

"What are you talking about, specifically?" Crest asked. He looked up and around the room for a minute, then returned to the napkin.

"Well, of course I'm not the President or the secretary of state," Bickel said, trying to look modest, "but I think that someone ought to campaign for office on the broad philosophical ground that we are not going to abandon to Soviet domination forever whatever countries in Eastern Europe are really eager to get out from under."

The waitress appeared with two cups of Boston clam chowder. The cups were an ordinary white china, with a tiny package of saltines in the saucer.

"Good soup," Crest said, after his first spoonful.

"Very good soup," Bickel said. "Isn't the Cosmos Club famous for its soup?"

"Could be," Crest answered. "I didn't know it was famous for anything." He abandoned his doodling long enough to spoon more soup into his mouth. Bickel wondered if the writing on the napkin revealed something about Crest's personality. Psychologists were supposed to know about those things, but Bickel felt fairly certain that they did not know anything. He vividly remembered that the stupidest and most deranged fellow he knew in college had somehow metamorphosed into a highly paid psychologist in New York City.

"I think," Bickel said, "that the American people could be rallied by a call—not to roll back Communism, that's got a bad ring to it—but to expand freedom. Let's tell people that we're on the winning side. Let's tell people that for the first time in a long time, we've got the momentum. How does that strike you?"

"As daring, very dangerous, and just right," Crest said as he swallowed the soup that the Cosmos Club might be famous for. "How would you do it?"

"We've got to explain to the Russians in a most convincing way that we're very serious about it. That may mean more arms spending, but we could do that without even raising taxes. And the votes are in the states that have the arms industry."

Crest finished his soup and resumed his doodling. "It

sounds good to me. Tell the American people that it's time for the momentum to shift to our side." He doodled more intensely.

"I'm not saying we should go to war over it, but I think we might let the Russians think that we're almost crazy on the subject."

"It could win for you," Crest said. "If you have the right people helping you."

"Well, if I ran at all, mine would be a people's campaign," Bickel said, laying down his soup spoon. "I wouldn't want to be dependent on special interests."

"Of course, you wouldn't, Travis. You wouldn't seek out powerful people, but they might seek you out and support you. Powerful people have interests, too," Crest said with a grin. He looked down at his napkin and drew several slashing diagonal lines across his sketch. "I think you can count on a lot of support. Your ideas even sound good to me," Crest said. "I think you can tell that from now on, we'll be doing all we can to help. You're important to us. Damned important."

The waitress came and removed the soup bowls. As she did, Crest moved his hand, and Bickel could see his sketch. Considering that it was done on a napkin, with a ballpoint pen, it was a remarkably good likeness of Van Gogh's *Starry Night,* with slash marks through it.

CHAPTER

26

John Chancellor looked out earnestly from behind a large, curving table that said NBC ELECTION HEADQUARTERS in red, white, and blue. In his hand he held a sheaf of papers. Behind him was a map of the forty-eight contiguous states of the union with a number corresponding to the state's electoral votes inside the outline of each state. Some states were red and some were blue. Most of them were blue. To the left of the map was a portrait of Travis Bickel, next to which was a large light in the form of a check mark. The check mark was blinking on and off.

"With the NBC News Election Center's projection of Travis Bickel's home state of California for Bickel, he is now decisively over the 270 electoral voites needed to make him the next President of the United States," Chancellor said in sonorous tones.

The camera moved to pick up Tom Brokaw, who sat farther to the right on the curved desk, pressing an earpiece to his ear. "And, I might add, John, that Senator Bickel's margin in both the electoral college and the popular vote is going to be comfortable indeed. Our computers now show that Senator Bickel will pick up Ohio and Pennsylvania too, which had been teetering all evening, and probably Texas also, which would give Senator Bickel close to 400 votes in the electoral college."

Chancellor, dressed almost identically with Brokaw in a gray suit with a peach-colored shirt and a striped tie, chimed in: "And as you said, the popular vote is going to Bickel by a very healthy 55-percent-to-43-percent margin, which is about the largest since Richard Nixon's landslide win over George McGovern in 1972." Chancellor shuffled his papers in his hands and looked out at the camera. "All in all, a most impressive evening for the junior senator from California, who, a few years ago, was a relative unknown."

"John," Catherine Mackin said, breaking in from Chancellor's left, "I think that Senator Bickel surprised all of us this election year with his emphasis on foreign-policy issues, almost exclusively ideological issues, when most so-called 'experts' thought that elections are won on the pocketbook issues. His campaign theme of turning the tide for democracy, which he repeatedly stressed, went over very well in almost all sections of the country."

Elson Patterson sat in his cavernous study at Innisfree, watching the television. To the right of the set, a Toshiba Ultra-Hyperion Mark VI, a log fire burned in the stone fireplace. The fire and the television set were the only illumination in the room. Patterson reclined in a large red armchair and smoked a pipe, a rare indulgence. Next to him, seated on a smaller director's chair, sat Frank Roberts.

Patterson's casual dress made a sharp contrast with Roberts's neat blue suit. Christ, Patterson thought, contemplating his own handmade Dunhill smoking jacket, Roberts will always look like a clerk. Nothing I can do about it.

"Congratulations, Mr. Patterson," Roberts said. "I think this is it. Shall I get out the Champagne?"

"Good idea, Frank," Patterson said, without stirring. "Of course, the staff is in bed now, so you'll have to get it yourself, if you don't mind. Would that be a problem?"

"No problem, Mr. Patterson. I'm glad to do it."

Roberts disappeared from the room for a moment and reappeared with a tray carrying an unmarked bottle and two glasses. Although the Champagne bore no label, it was Elson Patterson's own brand, from his own vineyards in the Champagne district of France. It was considered so superb that to receive a bottle of it from Patterson was, to a wine fancier, about the same as receiving a Ferrari would be to a car buff.

The glasses were frosted. Roberts had had the foresight to put them in the refrigerator before the election coverage even started. He poured each full of Champagne, then handed one to Patterson and kept one himself.

"I think you should propose the toast, Mr. Patterson," Roberts said.

"Frank, before I propose this toast, I want you to reflect on what we've gone through to get where we are. It hasn't been easy, has it?" Patterson asked.

"Not at all," Roberts said.

"Some people might have thought it would be easy because I was born with so much money. But you and I know that isn't true. Or am I wrong?" Patterson asked, as the TV screen showed a commercial of a cat doing handsprings for some kind of catfood.

"No, you're quite right, Mr. Patterson," Roberts said.

"Who would have thought we could carry it off? I mean, almost forty years after the end, who would guess that we could have gotten the whole thing rolling again?" Patterson said. His right hand grasped the stem of the Champagne glass.

"An impressive accomplishment, Mr. Patterson," Roberts said.

Patterson wondered if he should allow Roberts to call him Elson. Perhaps the day deserved that kind of special recognition. No, better not. One thing could lead to another. Best to know who was boss.

Patterson's thoughts went blurry and then back to almost forty years ago, when he had last seen the *Führer*.

It was in January of 1945, and everyone knew that all was lost.

Patterson's visit had been circuitous. A flight to Lisbon, then by train through Spain and France, then to England by ship, and from there by air to Sweden, and by boat, through waters full of Russian submarines, to Hamburg, which had been rendered utterly unrecognizable by the bombing. The *Führer* had a car pick up Patterson in Hamburg and drive him by roundabout routes to Berlin. There were almost no passenger trains left, and main automobile routes were subject to constant bombardment by the Allied fighters and fighter bombers that roamed at will over the German countryside.

The whole landscape appalled Patterson. The picturesque and reassuring beauty of Westphalia was a mass of bombed-out villages and towns. The sandy farms of Pomeranian Prussia on the approaches to Berlin were littered with burned vehicles of every description. People in the fields and in towns stared sullenly at the car bearing Patterson toward the *Führer*.

Berlin itself was incredible. There was no other word for it. It's broad boulevards and parks were masses of tangled wreckage. A permanent smell of smoke and burning hung over the city. Shards of broken glass lay like rhinestones over the streets and sidewalks. A house or shop with its windows intact was a rarity. The people looked like moles—pallid and grim-faced, walking hunched over, and shivering in the January cold.

On walls, posters appeared by the thousands with an animalistic, fierce-looking Russian soldier seizing a beautiful and frail-looking German woman, whose dress was already ripped. Although no message was necessary, the poster said, "KAMPFEN BIS ENTGULTIGEN SIEG." Fight on Until Final Victory. Other posters showed a strong-looking Hitler with the legend "VERTRAUE DEM FUHRER." Trust the *Führer*.

Patterson was heartsick by the time he arrived at the Reich Chancellery. He heard the sirens start to wail just as he stepped out of the car and headed for the shelter. He went down a circular stairway for what seemed like forever, then emerged into a concrete-lined hallway. A large portrait of the *Führer* greeted him. An orderly appeared and told him that this was now the *Führer*'s headquarters, "for the duration of the emergency." Even Patterson could sense the irony in that locution. "The emergency" would obviously end with the Russians planting the hammer and sickle over the ruins of the Chancellery.

When Hitler appeared, he shook hands with Patterson with a limp grasp. "I am not yet quite dead," he told Patterson with a frown. "But things are not good. I am surrounded by traitors and incompetents. Every single thing that gets done is only accomplished because I take the time to do it. Can you imagine it? Now, when my time is more important than ever, I have to straighten out fights between Goering and Himmler, between Speer and Bormann. Really, it is incredible."

The spoke in the living room of Hitler's apartment in the bunker. It had a homey, Bavarian look. Although the *Führer* appreciated good modern design, he preferred the more traiditional, heavier furniture for his own personal use. The *Führer* was in a state of permanent rage at his generals and never ate with them. Instead, he ate alone, with his Alsatian, Blondi, by his feet. On that day, however, he ate with Patterson.

"No one understands discipline anymore," Hitler said, picking listlessly at his lentil soup. "The entire German Reich was to be built on discipline. An entire world Reich could be built on discipline. But," he added morosely, "not in my lifetime."

"My *Führer*," Patterson protested, "you must have thought everything was lost in 1923, after Munich, and you emerged victorious. It can happen again."

"No," Hitler said curtly. "Then, I was surrounded by a few brave men. Now I am surrounded by many cowards and traitors. I have always believed in fate, and this is my fate."

They talked for a short time, and then the *Führer* told Patterson why he had asked him to make such a dangerous journey. "Operation Croesus must continue. You must make it succeed, although you too must understand that your way will be difficult as well. Most people in this world are cowards and traitors."

Patterson struggled for the words to explain to his *Führer* that he, Patterson, was not a coward or a traitor, that he would be with the *Führer* when the end came.

Hitler waved his protestations away with a trembling and scarred hand. "What Germany needs is not pointless sacrifice. Germany needs your skills. Germany needs your resources." Hitler leaned forward and stared with his deep blue eyes into Patterson's eyes. "Above all, Germany needs your perseverance."

It was after that that Patterson could not contain his tears any longer. The *Führer* said nothing to him while tears flowed down Patterson's cheeks, then Patterson said, "Those tears are a mark of your devotion. I will cherish them in the days ahead. But there are difficult days ahead for you too. Days of sacrifice. Days of restraint and of taking new courses. Above all, you must do for Germany what I have tried to do. You must make yourself and your own needs subservient to the needs of the Aryan people."

As Patterson watched a black newscaster appear in the ballroom of the Century Plaza Hotel in Los Angeles, where Senator Travis A. Bickel, President-elect, was about to appear, he remembered that it was then that the *Führer* had told him about the Phoenix process. At first, Patterson was taken aback, but then he realized that it was a daring stroke from a man whose specialty was daring strokes. It was true that Patterson would have to swallow some pride, but it was *zu befehl der Führer*—at the *Führer*'s command.

And that had been the last Patterson had seen of the *Führer*. Another car took Patterson back to Hamburg, and from there by ship to Sweden, and then retracing his route to New York. At the end of April, when Hitler's death was announced in the United States, Patterson was at Innisfree. As the news flashed on the Mutual Broadcasting System, Patterson sat in the same room where he now watched the election returns. He had not been surprised. He thought of the *Führer*'s face and of his parting words to Patterson.

"Individual men, even exceptional men, come and go. What counts is the future of the race."

The present snapped back into focus for Patterson. A pretty girl with red hair, wearing a powder blue jumpsuit, stood next to a white Pinto station wagon, on a cliff with San Francisco in the background. "Why is Pinto the number-one-selling small wagon?" she asked with a smile. "It's easy to look at. And consider the new options this year."

Patterson still held his Champagne glass, but Roberts was now standing off to his left, next to one of his shelves of mementos. After a slight shuffling noise, Roberts reappeared.

"Mr. Patterson," Roberts asked with a smile, "have you thought of a toast?"

"I think," Patterson said, pulling himself up in his chair, "that the only appropriate toast would be *'Heil Hitler.'* "

And with that, Patterson lifted his glass and drank it all in one gulp. Roberts, too, drank, although only a small sip.

"Mr. Patterson," Roberts said, "may I ask you a question?"

Patterson wondered what this whining halfbreed wanted now. "Of course. I think I've always encouraged you to ask important questions," Patterson said. "Or am I wrong?"

"No, you're not wrong," Roberts said. "Mr. Patterson, is following orders important?"

Patterson smiled. The little sonofabitch was going to ask for a raise. It was all right. He deserved it. "Yes, that's the most important thing, Frank," Patterson said. He wouldn't anticipate the request. He would wait and make Roberts ask him.

"Thank you, Mr. Patterson. I hope I've always been satisfactory at following orders."

"Yes, in general, you have been," Patterson said. He liked toying with Roberts.

"Then you will understand that you are not my only superior. Mr. Patterson, and you will understand this," Roberts said softly.

Patterson looked up sharply and saw the muzzle of a Luger pistol, in Roberts's hand, pointed at his forehead.

"What the hell does this mean?" Patterson shouted.

"I chose this particular pistol with care," Roberts said, "I know that it was a gift from the *Führer* himself." He turned the Luger slightly to the side so that Patterson could see the inscription "A.H." just above the trigger.

"I think you will also agree that, all things considered," Roberts said, "I chose a particularly good time, a time when you could see the fruition of a large part of your life's work."

"You are a goddamn lunatic, Frank. Put down that gun. It isn't even loaded, you fool," Patterson screamed.

"Oh, I think it's loaded," he said. He squeezed the trigger, there was a crash, and Elson Patterson's face caved in just between the eyes. Without a sound, he fell back against the seat. The report of the Luger was absorbed in the rich upholstery of the room. "Or am I wrong?" Roberts asked the corpse.

On the screen, Travis Bickel walked along a hallway with camera crews and lights following him.

"That's Travis Bickel, three years ago a minor figure in the United States Senate, now a major force in world history, on his way to make his acceptance speech. For Senator Bickel, it must be a very big night indeed," John Chancellor said.

"A very big night, John," Tom Brokaw said.

CHAPTER

27

Travis Bickel looked out his window at the swarms of neighbors on Klingle Street who were crowded around his house. Secret Service men, dressed in warm fleece-lined coats, kept the curious off his lawn, but not much farther away than that. It was an unusually cold January 20, 1985, and Bickel was impressed that people would stand so patiently in the wind to catch a glimpse of him.

And, of course, it would be only a glimpse. He would rush out of the house in his business suit and homburg—a throwback to the Eisenhower Inauguration—and the limousine would take him downtown to the White House, where he would pick up his friend, the President, before the final pre-presidential leg of the trip, the jaunt down Pennsylvania Avenue to the Capitol.

Bickel was upstairs in what had been his and Lydia's bedroom long ago. It was still furnished sparsely, as it had been when Lydia was alive. Of course, Kathy Dorn was not in it, as she had been before the campaign began, but he was the first bachelor President-elect since

Grover Cleveland, and he would make Kathy Dorn a major celebrity by marrying her while he was President. That would be compensation to her for all the skulking around they had had to do. "It doesn't matter," she always said. "You don't believe me, but it is true. It really does not matter. What matters is that we get to see each other at least sometimes. That, and for you to become President," she said.

But on this morning, in the bedroom, instead of the lithe and beautiful form of Kathy Dorn, there was the pudgy and pouting secretary of state of the United States, Arthur Kosters. He looked severely ill at ease in the small yellow rocking chair that had been Lydia's favorite piece of furniture.

His tailored gray, vested suit looked ill at ease, too, as if it had been fitted some time before Kosters ate several good meals. The white shirt clutched at Kosters's neck, as if it had a mind of its own and was trying to strangle him. Arthur Kosters did not look as happy as a man who was about to witness the Inaguration as President of his best friend and protégé should look.

"I have been wanting to talk to you now for days," Kosters said hoarsely. He had a cold, which added to his look of general unhappiness.

"Well, I've been busy," Bickel said. "I've read all those briefing papers you sent over. And, I've seen all those men you wanted me to see, so what's the problem?" He looked out his window again at the people in the back yard. Even when he announced for President, a crowd had gathered to welcome him back from California. Wesley Heights was a friendly neighborhood.

"But I wanted to talk to you in person," Kosters said. "There's a lot you don't know yet."

"Well, I know that," Bickel said. He sat down on a corner of his bed next to where Kosters sat. He reached over and patted the older man on the knee. "What's the problem, Arthur? You look as if you were afraid that Patterson would come back and get you."

"It has something to do with that," Kosters said, looking down at the floor.

"What do you mean?" Bickel asked, jerking his hand

away from Kosters's knee. "Is Patterson still alive?"

"No, of course not," Kosters said. "But there's a lot you don't know about Croesus that you have to know."

"Well, can't it wait?" Bickel asked. "I have to leave in fifteen minutes. And it's not one of those things that people like to be late for. I don't need a history lesson right at the moment."

"I think you'd better hear it now," Kosters said. "I'll tell you quickly."

He exhaled a heavy sigh and looked down at the floor. The room became quiet enough that Bickel could hear the people outside chanting his name—"We Want Travis"—in a slow and good-natured way.

"Do you know where I was born, Travis?" Kosters asked.

"Of course, I do. In the Eastern Zone. Everyone knows that," Bickel said impatiently. A fugitive worry entered Bickel's mind. Where was Kosters from? His mind was working furiously.

"Not quite," Kosters said. "I think you should spend a few days sometime thinking about things that everyone knows and which are nevertheless not true."

Bickel said nothing. He could hear the chanting outside dissipating amid a lot of giggling.

"Sometimes," Kosters said in a heavy voice, "people get caught up in things, are moved by currents that they understand only dimly. Years later, they're washed up by the currents on a shore far from where they thought they started. But then there are new currents, and they move, too, and suddenly, a man who started off in a valley is on top of a mountain."

"Arthur," Bickel said. "I really love the imagery, and it sounds a lot like what happened to me in the last few years, but what does it have to do with Croesus?" He could hear the crackle of the radios of the police and Secret Service cars outside. He could not hear what the radios were saying.

"Travis," Kosters said, "of course, I'm talking about you. You have been grasped, picked up, carried aloft by an eagle of power. Do you know how rare that is? Do you?" His face started to turn pink. "It wasn't that easy for me, in Germany. It was a struggle. A real struggle."

"It must have been terrible," Bickel said. "But that was surely a long time ago. Look where you are now."

"I'm not talking about that," Kosters replied sharply. "You have no idea of how I got where I am, do you? You don't even know how you got where you are."

"I have an idea," Bickel said. "I know you worked out something with someone about Patterson. But that's behind us now, isn't it? I mean, Patterson's gone, isn't he?"

"In a way, yes," Kosters said slowly. He glanced at his watch. "It's time for you to go. Let me ride with you to the White House. I'll have my car follow. No one will mind, if you don't mind."

"Fine, Arthur," Bickel said. "We'll ride together."

Both men got up and walked down the narrow stairs of the house. To Bickel, it was not so much impressive as it was funny that he would soon be walking along enormous marble staircases instead of these rickety and dark steps. The feet would be the same. Only the steps would be different.

The living room looked completely different from what it had looked like the morning that Lydia was murdered in it. There was almost no furniture except for Army Signal Corps consoles at which impassive and pale men sat, speaking into telephones in hushed voices. Secret Service men spoke into small walkie-talkies as Bickel and Kosters put on their dark gray overcoats.

Another Secret Service man opened the door for Bickel and he walked out onto the front lawn. The crowd of friendly faces started to chant, as if they were a high school football crowd, "We Want Travis—We Want Travis." Bickel could recognize the neighborhood children pressed up against a Secret Service cordon. A lot of the parents were there, too. It was a prosperous-looking group. Many of the women wore mink. Bickel walked over to the rope and shook hands with a number of the children and their parents. Most of the faces were smiling broadly. It buoyed up Bickel. He obviously had the people with him, no matter what Kosters was about to tell him.

"God bless you, Mr. President," an elderly woman who lived across the street called out to Bickel.

"Come back and see us," a freckle-faced teenaged boy said to Bickel as Bickel squeezed his hand.

"Let me kiss you, Travis," said the woman who lived across the hedge and whose daughters cut Bickel's lawn. Bickel leaned forward, and the woman, a tall brunette named Mary Dellabatta, kissed him on his cheek.

A thin blond man whom Bickel did not recognize stood next to Mary. As Bickel's face came near his face, the man whispered in his ear, "*Gutes Glück, mein Führer.*"

Bickel snapped his head back and looked at the man sharply. He was in his twenties and pale, but with an overlay of suntan that was almost gone, as if he had been in a southern latitude and had recently come north. He had an unearthly smile and a scar on his cheek. What did the guy say? Bickel wondered. Did he call me *"Mein Führer"*? It would be impossible to stop and find out, especially since the man smiled, then turned around in the crowd. His place was taken by a large black woman, whom Bickel recognized as the wife of the doctor who had recently moved in at the corner of Forty-fifth and Klingle.

What in hell had that man said?

Bickel waved a few more times to the crowd of well-wishers, then noticed that Kosters was already in the car and was beckoning to him, pointing at his watch.

As Bickel settled himself in the limousine and smiled out the window, he asked through clenched teeth, "Arthur, someone in that crowd just told me I was his *Führer* and wished me good luck. What the hell is going on?"

The limousine started down Klingle Street. Now Bickel could see that there were crowds of well-wishers all the way down the two blocks of the street. A small girl held up a hand-lettered sign that read, "WE LOVE YOU TRAVIS, OH YES WE DO."

Kosters spoke quickly. "Do you imagine that an or-

ganization the size of Croesus could exist and flourish
without making a large mark on the foreign-policy establishment of this country?"

"But the policy is decided on by the President,"
Bickel said.

"Of course. But the President chooses among options
that the foreign-policy professionals give him." Kosters
looked disgusted, then looked over to Bickel. "Look,
Travis, we won't approach it that way. Try another
way. Think of all the things that have happened around
you. Think of them. And you're not only still alive, but
my best friend. Does that mean anything?"

"Patterson was testing me. He told me that. He
wasn't trying to kill me. That's why I'm alive," Bickel
said. The limousine made a right turn onto the far
larger New Mexico Avenue and headed south. There,
too, on both sides of the street, were well-wishers. On
the west side of the street, an elderly couple stood atop
a recreational vehicle and waved at Bickel as if they
were trying to fly.

"But why was it you, Travis? Did you ever think
about why it was you that Patterson chose?" Kosters
asked.

Neurons in Bickel's mind were firing like the cylin-
ders of a race car. Lights lit up and wheels rotated and
made connections. In the computer of his mind, something was starting to come out. The typing element
whirled and bobbed furiously, as if about to commence
typing. But no ink hit the paper.

"Or we could approach it from another direction,
Travis," Kosters said. "Where the hell did Kathy Dorn
come from? Did you ever think of that? And where did
Alexandra Denman go on all of those trips? And where
did Sabrina Schuller come from? And was Yichik
Cohen lying about seeing Patterson at Treblinka or was
Patterson lying?"

Out the window, the clouds were receding. It was
going to be a bright and sunny Inauguration Day. The
water from the night's drizzle would dry and the
weather would be crisp, cold, and dazzling. Bickel's
mind raced, and the circuits heated up so that the infor-

mation could flow along more rapidly, so that the com-
parisons and connections could be made, so that things
could fit into a pattern where they could be said to be
governed by logic and order, so that they could be explained.

"Or go back to the beginning, Travis. Go back to
Bad Kreuznach. Think what you were doing there when
everything started. You weren't going to come across
anything about Patterson. You were looking at records
from 1932. He had never even been to Germany in
1932," Kosters said. "Who in hell was from Bad Kreuznach, Travis?"

The ink started to spray out over the paper. It was
writing someone's name. The package was coming out,
neat and clean. But something was wrong.

"But, Jesus, Arthur. How could it have been your
name on that list? You're Jewish," Bickel said. "Was it
your name?"

But Kosters did not answer directly. "Think of what
you have done, Travis. You went to Bad Kreuznach
and your closest associate was killed. You could have
stopped then and there and said you didn't want anything more to do with politics. Then, you met a beautiful girl who threw herself into your bed. You said it
yourself. It doesn't happen every day. How did it happen that time?" Kosters sounded impatient. "Then Richards. Then those girls in Los Angeles. Still, you plow
ahead with your ambition. Then you wife is killed and
you only slow down for a moment. Finally, you allow a
man to make you President, knowing that you are going
to help kill that man."

Out the window, an elementary school class from the
Horace Mann School, four blocks from Bickel's house,
lined up neatly on New Mexico Avenue. They held a
droopy banner that read, "COME BACK AND SEE US,
PRESIDENT BICKEL."

Bickel said nothing. His mind was no longer racing.
He began to feel numb. He wondered if he would be
able to read his Inauguration speech. He wondered if he
would be able to do anything.

"For Christ's sake, Travis. Do you think you are the

first person who has wanted power the way other men want a drug? Do you think that a Jewish boy from Bad Kreuznach—hear that? Bad Kreuznach—could not want to be with the powerful so badly that he would find a way to get himself into the Hitler Youth, find a way to make himself more valuable to the Nazis because he *was* Jewish? The National Socialist regime was not an entire monolith. There were people who thought that if a boy was really bright, they could find a use for him. Even if he was a Jew. And if he did well, then they might think that if they wanted to build for a world *Reich*, the agent that no one would suspect would be a Jew who had come as a refugee when he was still a teenager," Kosters said. He was talking unusually quickly.

The limousine had crossed Wisconsin Avenue at Calvert Street and was heading for Massachusetts Avenue. On the right, Bickel saw the sprawling grounds of the Naval Observatory. They rose to a modest hill, on top of which was an almost comical Victorian mansion, which was the official home of the Vice President of the United States.

At the corner of Calvert and Massachusetts, a small guard of sailors stood at attention and snapped off a smart salute as Bickel's car moved by. Bickel waved mechanically.

"So there I was, a refugee with no money, and friends, and along comes a whole parade of prestigious and important people who want to help me, who push me along. After school, they find me the most powerful university and research posts. And the war is over, but not for me, because the same people are still pushing me along, and I like it. I see my colleagues stagnating, and I, like you, have been picked up by an eagle of power and borne aloft," Kosters said. "And I did not even know who Patterson was until 1953. That's how well Croesus was organized."

By now the limousine was past the Georgian palace that housed the British ambassador's residence and the blunt, enormous statue of Winston Churchill, striding purposefully forward with an immense cigar clutched in his hand. Next to Churchill was the ultramodern Brazilian embassy. Dark men and women leaned out from the upper floors and waved at Bickel's car.

"I gradually did more and more work for Patterson. Of course it was completely confidential. Completely. But I got into the guts of Croesus the way Patterson never did from above. And eventually I began to think, why shouldn't I be running this organization?" Kosters said. "And that was where you came in."

Bickel looked at the bridge over Rock Creek Park and the people who lined its sidewalks to see Bickel pass by. There were a lot of young people, rosy-cheeked from the cold, who waved to Bickel and shouted things. The windows were rolled up, so Bickel could not hear what the well-wishers shouted, but they looked friendly.

"Croesus was leading up to having a President to call its very own. I guess Patterson told you about that, didn't he?" Kosters asked.

"I'm sure you have a transcript of the conversation, Arthur, so why bother to ask?" Bickel said. On the street two young men, perhaps college students, stood in front of the mosque on Massachusetts Avenue with a sign that read, "WE'LL GROW QUICKER WITH BICKEL." It had been one of Bickel's campaign slogans.

"Right," Kosters said. "I do have that transcript. But I read so many things like that these days that I can't remember all of them, and it was almost two years ago, to be fair."

On the right, the car was slowing down for Ward Circle. By now, the crowds were sometimes two deep on the sidewalks. Bickel saw the first protest sign— "PRESIDENT BICKEL—FREE IRANIAN POLITICAL PRISONERS." It was held by three young men wearing masks.

"We had friends all over the world, in very high places. I don't think Patterson told you about that. How do you think I was able to get the goddamned Arabs to agree to so many things? They thought they were helping to trick the Jews and build a Fourth Reich." Kosters chuckled to himself. "But we didn't have a President. And Patterson was absolutely determined to have a President."

"Why was I chosen?" Bickel asked.

"We actually had several men picked out, but Patterson liked you. I don't really know why." He hesitated a moment. "Well, maybe I do. You were the perfect young American. Clean-cut looking, with absolutely no moral center whatsoever. That was what we wanted. I'm not saying that there weren't others, but you were good-looking, well-to-do. I don't know, Patterson just picked you out," Kosters said.

The limousine was pulling around DuPont Circle. The crowds were denser still, and now there were D.C. policemen stationed every few yards to keep the crowds well back from the street. Bickel had a burning desire to throw himself from the car, to run into the crowd and disappear. He also had a sense of hopelessness. "Be naive and outraged," Kosters had said. Bickel had had no idea just how naive he had been. But what the hell did they want him to do?

"The idea was that you would become the head of Croesus when Patterson died. He had no idea that I was going to become the head myself. By that time, being Jewish was no problem. The movement had no ideology at all. That's the way it is in the world today," Kosters sighed. "There's really no ideology anymore." He laughed out loud. "Did you know that Kathy Dorn first started in with you because the KGB told her to?"

Bickel was too numb to respond. At that point, nothing would have surprised him.

"That's right, Travis. A KGB agent. That's exactly right. But we got to her and offered her a lot of money. That's what we do with everyone. And usually it isn't even that much money. That's just the way it is these days. We could buy Brezhnev if we had enough money," Kosters said. "But Kathy Dorn is pulling only for you now, Travis. Only for you. Don't you worry about that. She'll be a great wife."

The car was starting to slow down again, this time to make the jog around Farragut Square to Connecticut Avenue. The sidewalks now were five deep with people waving and calling out for Bickel. He could see the first TV cameras, following him along the route.

"My problem was how to make sure that you would give me the okay to get rid of Patterson and get it on tape. Of course, you know that's on tape, don't you?" Kosters asked. He didn't wait for a reply. "I had to have it on tape so that I could play it for the people in Croesus, so that they would know we were acting together in getting rid of Patterson. You understand that, don't you?" Kosters asked.

The driver pressed his earpiece against his ear, then stopped the car at Lafayette Square in front of the Army-Navy Club, and rolled down the dividing window. "Are you ready, Senator Bickel? The White House is asking us if we're ready."

"Ask them for just two minutes, Charles," Kosters said. The driver nodded and rolled up the window.

While motorcycle police formed a ring around the car and the Secret Service men in front and behind the car looked anxiously into the crowd, Kosters continued. "That's why I had to get Sabrina Schuller and give her that bullshit story about Patterson and Treblinka and Yichik Cohen. Patterson never even knew about the concentration camps. He was hardly anti-Semitic at all. But it worked. It made you willing to have him killed. And, then, to make sure that Patterson would still want to work for you, we sent that girl, Alex, from your office to give him hot tips about you." He laughed again. "It was all so complicated, but that was how Patterson liked it. He never believed anything straightforward. That was how he was. So damned complicated. Paying off the Israelis, too. Getting those fools at Lake Tahoe to feed false information everywhere just for the hell of it. It led absolutely nowhere, but they don't care. They love the Federal Republic."

The two minutes passed quickly, and the car started up again. It passed down Connecticut Avenue and by Lafayette Square. People were wall to wall, but there were no more banners. Perhaps the police would not let them be shown there. It would disturb the solemnity of the event.

Bickel started to speak but could not find his voice. Kosters continued. "Of course, the damned thing had gotten to be enormous by the time you were involved, so that we could really do almost anything. My end of it, Phoenix, had blended with Croesus, and we could pull in half of the national news staff of the three networks if we wanted to."

Again, Bickel started to speak, but Kosters silenced him.

"We never would have touched Lydia, though. Patterson was clumsy, but not like that. You have to believe me. We just didn't do it. It was probably the KGB. Some day we'll get them back. Don't worry."

"I'm worried because a man like you is sitting in the car next to me. That's why I'm worried," Bickel said fiercely. "A man who would trade on the martyrdom of his people to get ahead."

Kosters sighed. "Travis," he said, "you talk like a child. I couldn't do anything for those people. I could do something to make sure that it didn't happen again, or that if something like it did happen, that it wouldn't happen to the Jews."

"I'm going to see you in hell before you get away with this," Bickel said.

"You think so, Travis?" Kosters asked lightly. "You think you're going to throw everything away? I have tapes of everything. No one's going to believe you if you said you were innocent, and, of course, we come to the most interesting part: You're not innocent. There's plenty of blood to go around. Kart; Richards and his son; those girls in California, Lydia—well, no, not Lydia. But Patterson.

"Just how stupid could you have been, Travis? Did you think everything would be done for you, that you would have the services of Croesus and Phoenix and then that you would just stand up there like Abe Lincoln?" Kosters's voice was raging with irony now. "The golden bashful boy from California? Is that what you thought you were? You jerk. We bought you. We own you. For some people it's a summer home or a car or college for the kiddies. We paid a lot more for you, and you know it."

"So?" Bickel said evenly. "What now?"

"You had the election sewed up before you ever met Patterson," Kosters said. "But you had to nail everything down, get every vote, even if it meant getting into bed with Patterson. And now, because you made yourself a prisoner by being a glutton, now you're whining about it?" Kosters shook his head. "You didn't need Patterson to win. You wanted everything, and so you have to pay."

The computer started making connections in Bickel's mind again. How old was Kosters? Pretty old. And far from invulnerable.

Meanwhile the look on Kosters's face changed. "It started in Bad Kreuznach, when you showed that you wouldn't flinch at a close friend's death. You handled it very well. You showed Patterson you were his boy, and you showed me you were the one to help me get rid of Patterson."

And that's not all, Bickel thought.

"And of course, here you are," Kosters said in a friendly voice. "You don't really have to do anything but look pretty. We'll handle everything substantive. I want you and Kathy to have a nice life in the White House. You've been through a lot." He smiled in an avuncular way. "And Kathy really loves you. It was a job, at first, but now she really loves you." Kosters patted him on the back.

"I suppose you're eventually going to kill me, too?"

"Travis," Kosters said soothingly, "don't talk about killing. There's been too much killing. But if I were you, I'd think pretty carefully about going public with the idea that you were made President by a group of people founded by Adolf Hitler, and now you want out, after you ordered the man who helped you killed. I think Frank Roberts would tell a pretty good story. Anyway, don't play noble. You wouldn't change a damned thing if it kept you out of here."

The car paused in front of the White House gate. The heavy black iron gate swung back on its hinges as three White House policemen saluted stiffly. Then the car heaved itself up into the driveway and swung around toward the front door.

"Why?" Bickel asked. "Why are you doing this? Is it to reunite Germany? Are you going to drop the bomb on Moscow? Just what the hell do you want?"

"No," Kosters said. "I told you before, we have no ideology." He smiled.

A White House usher, an elderly black man in breeches and a frock coat, throwback to some other era, with graying hair, reached out to open the door.

"Then why, for Christ's sake?" Bickel pleaded.

"Travis," Kosters said, staring at him. "The devil came and got Doctor Faustus in Bad Kreuznach. Then he came and got you. He made you President of the United States. And now you're asking why? We all did it for the same reason. We made you President for the same reason, you let us do it. It's power, Travis. Power, power, power—just like Patterson said. It's fame. It's everything you wanted. And Travis," Kosters said with another smile, "I won't live forever. We can work on you. Smarten you up. There's no reason you can't run things some day. And then you'll be the power."

The usher opened the door of the Cadillac. Bickel stepped out, followed by Kosters. A whir of cameras thirty feet away was clearly audible.

In front of the White House, Kosters smiled and shook hands with Bickel. "Good luck, Senator," Kosters said, and bowed slightly.

Bickel wondered how Kosters had gotten to Frank Roberts. If Frank Roberts could be reached, the people around Kosters could be reached.

Bickel smiled broadly then waved his hands energetically at the crowd in Lafayette Square. As the incumbent walked out the door, Bickel smiled, then shook his hand. He greeted him, then put his arm around Kosters. "Mr. President," Bickel said. "I want to promise you that I'm going to keep this man over at State. He's much too valuable to lose."

"Smart move," the President said. "Very smart."

"I am honored, Senator Bickel," Kosters said, and

bowed, this time even more slightly. "It is always an honor to serve one's country."

"I couldn't agree more. Always an honor to serve," Bickel said. "Or am I wrong?"

EPILOGUE

In a spare, utterly unfurnished room in the Lubyanka prison, a man in a well-tailored Italian-made suit faced a corpse lying on the floor. The room reeked of urine and the peculiar odor of old, dead men. The man on the floor had skin pulled tightly across his face, showing teeth that even in rictus looked sick and brown. The dead man's eyebrows were noticeably thinner and lighter than those of the Russian people who had captured him in a shattered Berlin almost forty years before.

A fat man in a coarse double-breasted suit walked in. "How long has he been dead?" Adjutant Okhmansky asked.

"He died while he was reading the teletype report of President Bickel's speech," Comrade General Codlitsk answered without taking his eyes from the dead man.

"I wonder if he thought he had the last laugh," Okhmansky asked.

"It only means that we have to work on the men around Bickel, that's all," Codlitsk said.

Neither man took his eyes off the corpse. "So

Mueller could not help us," Okhmansky said. "Or maybe he did not try to help."

"It's irrelevant now. The whole thing is irrelevant. I hope that the chairman is not having a sinus attack when we tell him about Bickel and Croesus," Codlitsk said.

"You mean no one has told him yet?" Okhmansky gasped, shocked. He could feel the cold in the room pressing on him. Outside it was minus twelve Celsius and a strong northeast wind had been blowing across Moscow for days.

"No one," Codlitsk said. "Would you like to be the one?"

Okhmansky only shuddered.

"What will he do?" he finally asked.

"I do not know," Codlitsk answered. "He will become unhappy. Neither of us will remain for long. That bastard Patterson and that Jew Kosters háve turned everything against us. Everything. China on one side and Croesus on the other."

"Even Hitler would not have dreamed of it," Okhmansky said.

On the stone floor, the light from a single bare electric bulb on the ceiling shone in Mueller's eyes, even in death a pale and vivid blue.